THE TALE OF THE HEIKE

Volume II, Books 7–12 and Epilogue

THE TALE
OF
THE HEIKE

Heike Monogatari

Volume II
Books 7–12 and Epilogue

translated by
HIROSHI KITAGAWA
BRUCE T. TSUCHIDA

UNIVERSITY OF TOKYO PRESS

Translated from the Japanese original
HEIKE MONOGATARI
English translation © 1975 University of Tokyo Press
UTP Number 1093-87242-5149
ISBN 0-86008-189-3
Printed in Japan
First paperback printing, 1977

The character used for the title page of each book represents the italicized word in the quote taken from the *Heike* and printed on the page following. The characters are reproductions of those in the original text of one version of the *Heike*, the Kakuichi bon (Kakuichi text). The Kakuichi bon is owned by the Department of Japanese Linguistics, Faculty of Literature, University of Tokyo.

For
Kitagawa Torajiro
who through his poetry inspired
this translation of the Heike Monogatari
and
whose last wish in this world
was for the completion
of this valuable work

CONTENTS

VOLUME I

THE TALE OF THE HEIKE

Volume II, Books 7-12 and Epilogue

BOOK SEVEN

"When the Heike *fled* . . . [Kyoto], they set fire to more than twenty mansions . . . ."
—Book 7, Chapter VIV, page 435

CHAPTER I

YOSHISHIGE, THE SON OF YOSHINAKA

In the beginning of the third month of the second year of the Juei era [1183], hostility arose within the Genji family between Yoritomo and Yoshinaka. Yoritomo gathered more than a hundred thousand mounted soldiers and set out for the province of Shinano. At the time Yoshinaka was at the castle of Yoda. Upon hearing of Yoritomo's expedition, he left the castle and encamped on Mount Kumasaka, at the border of Shinano and Echigo provinces.

No sooner had Yoritomo arrived at Zenkō-ji in Shinano Province than Yoshinaka sent his foster brother, Kanehira, to him with this message: "I cannot understand why you intend to destroy me. Now that you have conquered the eight eastern provinces, I believe that you are going up to the capital on the Tōkai-dō highway to overthrow the Heike. For my part, I have no other wish but to subjugate all the provinces along the Tōsan and Hokuroku highways and fall upon the Heike. I will not allow even a single day of delay in this plan. Why must we divide our efforts? If we alienate each other, we will be mocked by the Heike. I must, however, apologize to you. My uncle Yukiie felt some enmity toward you and sought refuge at my place.[1] I thought that it would be too cruel for one of his kin such as I to rebuff him, and so I allowed him to stay with me. That is all. I have no enmity toward you."

To this message, Yoritomo replied: "Now you wear an air of innocence, but I have it from a trustworthy source that you have woven a plot to raise a rebellion and destroy me."

Ignoring Yoshinaka's excuses, Yoritomo ordered his retainers Sanehira and Kagetoki to set out to attack him.

Upon hearing of this order, Yoshinaka, to prove his innocence, sent his eldest son, Yoshishige, a boy of eleven, to Yoritomo as a hostage. Yoshishige was escorted by the renowned warriors Unno, Mochizuki, Suwa, and Fujisawa.

"Inasmuch as he has sent his own son as a hostage, Yoshinaka must be loyal to me. Since I have no grown son of my own,[2] I will adopt him." So saying, Yoritomo took Yoshishige with him and returned to Kamakura.

[1] Defeated by the Heike at Sunomata, Yukiie fled to Kamakura and became Yoritomo's retainer. But dissatisfied with only a small reward, he left Kamakura to seek support from Yoshinaka.

[2] Since Yoshishige's coming of age had been celebrated, he was considered "grown."

CHAPTER II

THE MARCH TO THE NORTH

Ｉt was rumored that Yoshinaka had conquered all the provinces along the Tōsan and Hokuroku highways and had set out for the capital with a force of some fifty thousand soldiers. The Heike had had premonitions of this event in the previous year, saying: "Next year, at the time that horses eat young grass, a war will break out."

Acting upon these premonitions, the warriors on the side of the Heike from the San-in,[1] Sanyō,[2] Nankai,[3] and Saikai[4] districts came rolling into the capital like a thick fog. From the districts along the Tōsan Highway came the men of Ōmi, Mino, and Hida provinces; but from the districts that lay to the east of Ōmi along the Tōkai-dō none came up to the capital. All the western districts sent warriors to the capital; but those that lay to the north of Wakasa along the Hokuroku Highway dispatched not a single man.

The Heike decided to crush Yoshinaka and then attack Yoritomo, so they sent their army to the north on the Hokuroku Highway. The command was assumed by Lieutenant General Koremori; the lord of the third court rank Michimori; the governor of Tajima Province, Tsunemasa; the governor of Satsuma Province, Tadanori; the governor of Mikawa Province, Tomonori; and the governor of Awaji Province, Kiyofusa. To aid these commanders, some three hundred and forty warriors, renowned for their bravery, were selected. Among them were Moritoshi, Tadatsuna, Kagetaka, Nagatsuna, Hidekuni, Arikuni, Moritsugi, Tadamitsu, and Kagekiyo. At the hour of the dragon [8: 00 A.M.] on the seventeenth day of the fourth month of the second year of the Juei era [1183], they led a force of more than a hundred thousand horsemen toward the northern provinces.

The Heike warriors had been permitted to search for provisions among the villagers, and they confiscated even the rice meant to pay for the land tax stocked at the estates that lay along their line of march. As the Heike marched, plundering in this manner, from the Osaka Checkpoint through Shiga, Karasaki, Mitsukawajiri, Mano, Takashima, Shiotsu, and Kaizu, the villagers found no way to resist them and fled to the mountains.

[1] The San-in District consists of the eight provinces of Tamba, Tango, Tajima, Inaba, Hōki, Izumo, Iwami, and Oki.

[2] The Sanyō District consists of the eight provinces of Harima, Mimasaka, Bizen, Bitchū, Bingo, Aki, Suhō and Nagato.

[3] The Nankai District consists of the six provinces of Kii, Awaji, Awa, Sanuki, Iyo, and Tosa.

[4] The Saikai District consists of nine provinces and two islands—Chikuzen, Chikugo, Buzen, Bungo, Hizen, Higo, Hiuga, Ōsumi, Satsuma, Iki, and Tsushima.

CHAPTER III

THE TRIP TO CHIKUBU-SHIMA[1]

Two of the Heike commanders, Koremori and Michimori, pressed on their way, but three others, Tsunemasa, Tomonori, and Kiyofusa, were detained at Shiotsu and Kaizu in Ōmi Province. One of these generals, Tsunemasa, was greatly talented in poetry and music. Even in the midst of turmoil, he found solace in these arts. Tsunemasa went out to the shore of Lake Biwa and looked across the lake. Seeing an island far off the beach, he summoned his retainer Arinori and asked: "What do they call that island?"

"That is a famous island, Chikubu-shima," replied Arimori.

"Oh, so that is Chikubu-shima. Let us go over there."

Tsunemasa, escorted by Arinori, Morinori, and several retainers, boarded a small boat, which was rowed toward Chikubu-shima.

It was the eighteenth day of the fourth month, and twigs still bore the bright young leaves of early spring. The song of a nightingale in the valley was already past its prime while cuckoos here and there sang mellowly of the dawn of their season. The scene was so beautiful that Tsunemasa hurried to leave his boat and climbed up the steep banks toward the island's summit. He was enthralled by the magnificent sight.

Of old Emperor Shi-huang of the Ch'in dynasty and Emperor Wu of the Han sent young men, women, and magicians as emissaries in search of a paradise island called Hōrai,[2] hoping to discover the elixir of immortality. "We will never return home till we find it," they said. But they grew old in their unending search, unable to find the island that had so enchanted their dreams. Tsunemasa and his retainers, filled with wonder at the beauty of the scene, felt as though they had arrived at Hōrai.

In a sutra it is written: "In the Djambu-dvipa there is a certain lake, in the middle of which is an island of pure crystal where angels dwell. It rises from the center of the earth." Chikubu-shima must be that island!

Tsunemasa stood before the main image of the island's shrine and prayed: "O thou, Goddess Benzaiten, who art known from old in the name of Nyorai and deigns to manifest thyself here in an image of a bodhisattva! Though we invoke thee by these two names, Benzaiten and Bodhisattva, thou art one and the same in saving all sentient beings. I hear that a visitor to this place of worship is granted fulfillment of his ambitions, and so let me beseech thee that the wishes and petitions I offer before thee will be accepted."

He knelt before the shrine and chanted the sutra as the veil of night fell over the lake, and the moon of the eighteenth day of the fourth month rose over the waters. Now the lake and the shrine were bathed in the moon's white beams. So beautiful was the scene that the priest who lived there brought out a biwa for Tsunemasa and offered it to him, saying: "We have often heard of your fame as a skillful player of the biwa."

When Tsunemasa played the biwa and sang the melody of *Shōgen-Sekishō*,[3] serenity pervaded the shrine. Charmed by the liquid sounds, the goddess appeared in the form of a white dragon hovering at Tsunemasa's side. Awestruck and in tears, Tsunemasa composed a poem:

> My humble petition
> Must have been well accepted
> By the divine one,
> For a manifest sign came
> From the depths of the water.

Now encouraged by this sign from the goddess, Tsunemasa started back to the mainland with the firm belief that the rebels would soon be crushed.

---

[1] A small steep island in the northern part of Lake Biwa.

[2] Early Chinese believed that somewhere to the east lay a paradise island, Hōrai. Some scholars have suggested that it might have been Japan.

[3] Literally "Heaven and Earth," one of the three secret melodies. These melodies are traditionally accepted as being the most beautiful ever written for the biwa.

CHAPTER IV

THE BATTLE AT HIUCHI

Yoshinaka had remained in the province of Shinano. Now he ordered that a stronghold be built at Hiuchi[1] in the province of Echizen. Within this fort were stationed some six thousand soldiers commanded by two priests, Saimei from Heisen-ji and Bussei from Togashi, and nine warriors, Shinsuke, Saitōda, Mitsuakira, Tsuchida, Takebe, Miyazaki, Ishiguro, Nyūzen, and Sami. The fort was strategically located, surrounded on all sides by towering crags and peaks. The Nōmi and Shindō rivers flowed in front of the fort. Where the two rivers ran together, scores of great trees were piled up to hold back the water, creating a lake.

There is a Chinese poem:

> Deep and vast upon Lake K'un-ming[2]
> Lie the shadows of Mount Chung-nan.
> The setting sun melts into the waves.
> They glitter like a piece of brocade.
> At the bottom of this lake are sands
> Of gold and silver;
> On the surface float the boats
> Of the virtuous emperor Wu.

Unlike the beautiful vision of the Chinese poem, the murky waters of the lake at Hiuchi were not soothing but frustrating. As the Heike could not cross over, their great army encamped on the mountains and could only idle away the days.

One night the priest Saimei, a man who had received many favors from the Heike, left the fort secretly and went around the lake to the foot of the mountains. He wrote a letter, put it into the head of an arrow, and shot it into the Heike camp. The letter read thus: "This is not a natural lake. If you send foot soldiers under the veil of night to chop away the timbers that support the dam, the waters will soon run out. Then it will be simple for your horses to ford the stream. Cross over quickly. Let me shoot arrows at the rear guard of the Genji. This is truly a letter written by Priest Saimei from Heisen-ji."

The commander of the Heike read it with satisfaction and lost no time in sending foot soldiers to cut away the timbers. The vast lake formed by the two blockaded rivers drained quickly. Without difficulty, the great force of the Heike crossed over. The soldiers within the fort resisted stubbornly but were soon overcome, for they were greatly outnumbered by their enemy. By thus showing his loyalty to the Heike, Saimei helped win the battle at Hiuchi.

Shinsuke, Saitōda, Mitsuakira, and the priest Bussei fled from the fort to the province of Kaga. In order to fight the Heike once more, they formed a new line of defense at Shirayama and Kawachi.

The Heike immediately pursued them into the province of Kaga, burning the castles of Hayashi and Togashi. It seemed that no force could oppose them. From several nearby post stations[3] they sent messengers to convey word of their victory to the capital. The state minister and all the men of the Heike who had remained in the capital were overjoyed and encouraged.

On the eighth day of the fifth month, the Heike gathered all their soldiers at Shinohara in the province of Kaga. There they divided their army. The main force, which numbered some seventy thousand, was led by Koremori, Michimori, and Moritoshi. They marched toward Mount Tonami on the border of Kaga and Etchū provinces. The smaller force, which numbered some thirty thousand, was led by Tadanori, Tomonori, and Saburō-Saemon from Musashi. They marched toward Shiho on the border of Noto and Etchū. At the time Yoshinaka was at the provincial capital[4] of Echigo. When he received news of the Heike's march toward Tonami and Shiho, he galloped toward Mount Tonami with fifty thousand men. Following the example he set when he defeated the Heike at Yokota-gawara, he divided his force into seven parts. First, he ordered his uncle Yukiie to lead ten thousand horsemen toward Mount Shiho. Nishina, Takanashi, and Yamada no Jirō were ordered to lead seven thousand horsemen toward North Kurosaka to attack the enemy from the rear. Kanemitsu and Kaneyuki were sent to South Kuro-

saka with seven thousand horsemen. More than ten thousand horsemen were sent to the foot of Kurosaka, to Matsunaga-no-Yanagihara, and to Guminoki-bayashi. At all these places they were
ordered to find good hiding spots in which to wait for the enemy.
Kanehira, leading some six thousand horsemen, forded the Washi
Rapids and encamped at Hinomiya-bayashi. Yoshinaka forded the
Oyabe River with ten thousand horsemen and occupied positions
at Hanyū to the north of Mount Tonami.

[1] Located to the southeast of present-day Imashō, Nanjō-gun, Fukui Prefecture.

[2] Located to the west of Ch'ang-an, K'un-ming was a great dam built by Emperor
Wu.

[3] Along the important trade and military routes, there were inns that served as hotels
and a variety of other functions, including primitive post offices.

[4] Present-day Naoetsu City in Niigata Prefecture.

CHAPTER V

YOSHINAKA'S PRAYER

Inasmuch as the Heike have a greater army than ours, they will surely come across Mount Tonami to the plain below, where they can best use their superior numbers and hope to win a decisive battle," said Yoshinaka. "The victory that arises from such an open battle depends on the number of soldiers. If the greater force of the Heike falls upon us, we will be in danger. However, if our men carry more white banners and spread them thinly in our ranks, they will say: 'The Genji are moving forward. Their force is larger than ours. They are well acquainted with this area, while we are strangers here. If we commit a rash act and expose ourselves on the open plain, we will be surrounded. This mountain is rocky on all sides. They will never be able to attack us from the rear. Let us dismount and give rest to our horses for a while.' With these words, the Heike will stay upon the mountain. Then we will only pretend to fight in order to draw their attention. But let the day pass into the night and we will drive the entire army of the Heike down into the Kurikara Valley."

Yoshinaka ordered his men to move forward with thirty white banners and set them up at Kurikara.

As he had expected, the Heike were deceived. "That must be the vanguard of the Genji!" they cried. Concluding that the Genji army was larger than their own, they resolved not to risk a battle in the open plain. Unaware of the Genji force concealed behind them in the woods, the Heike believed they were safe from attack from the rear because of the steep rocky mountains. "Here is plenty grass and water for our horses. Let us dismount and rest them," they said. The spot where the Heike rested was Saru-no-baba among the mountains of Tonami.

Now as Yoshinaka in Hanyū was carefully studying the terrain, he saw, far off amidst the green trees of the mountain, a red shrine fence with the crossed roof beams of the shrine above and a gate standing before it. Yoshinaka summoned a guide from the province and asked him: "What shrine is that? Which god is worshiped there?"

"It is the shrine of Hachiman," replied the guide. "He is the god of this area."[1]

Delighted with this reply, Yoshinaka summoned his secretary, the priest Kakumei, and said: "How fortunate I am to find myself now before a branch shrine of Hachiman. I am about to fight and will surely win! What would you think of my offering a prayer in writing to the great bodhisattva Hachiman for the good fortune of my descendants as well as my victory?"

"I think that is a very good idea, my lord," replied Kakumei, riding forward immediately. He dismounted to write the prayer. Kakumei wore a dark blue battle robe and armor laced with black cords. His sword was in a black lacquered sheath, and his twenty-four arrows were fletched with black feathers plucked from the underside of a bird's wing. He carried a bow bound with lacquered rattan. After slinging his bow by the string across his shoulder and hanging his helmet at his back, he took out an ink stone and some paper from the bottom of his quiver. He sat down respectfully before Yoshinaka and began to write. Indeed, he looked like a great master in the arts of the pen and the sword.

Kakumei was born of a family of Confucian scholars and was known as Michihiro when he worked as an archivist in an office of the Government University. Later he became a monk with the name of Saijō-bō Shingyū, and he often visited Nara. When Prince Mochihito entered Mii-dera for refuge and the priests of Mii-dera sent letters of appeal to Mount Hiei and Kōfuku-ji, it was Shingyū who composed the reply from Kōfuku-ji to Mii-dera. In his reply he had called Kiyomori the "chaff and sediment" of the Heike and a "dust speck of the military clans."

When Kiyomori heard this, he was incensed: "Damnable Shingyū! He speaks of me, Jōkai, as the 'chaff and sediment' of the Heike and a 'dust speck of the military clans.' Such insolence! Arrest him! Put him to death!"

Shingyū learned of Kiyomori's wrath and fled from Nara to the northern provinces, where he became a secretary to Yoshinaka and changed his name to Kakumei.

Now the prayer Kakumei had written was this: "I obey thy commands with my head bowing down to thy feet, O great bodhisattva Hachiman! Thou art the lord who guardeth our sun-descended realm and the mighty ancestor of our heaven-blessed imperial line. Reveal thyself in thy three golden buddha persons to protect the throne and help the people. Open thy mighty gates to reveal the three golden bodies.[2] For some years the world has been ruled by Kiyomori, the Priest-Premier. In his arrogance he has been holding heaven and earth in his sway and has brought confusion to the people. He has broken the Buddha's Law and is an enemy of the throne.

"I, Yoshinaka, born of a military family, have inherited my father's skills in war. When I think of Kiyomori's evil doings, I can no longer remain patient. Let me trust my fate to heaven. Let me offer my body to my country. I have raised a loyal army. I am about to crush the rebels. Now as the two military families of the Genji and the Heike stand face to face in battle, I know that the spirits of my soldiers have not yet been tried in combat. At such a moment when I fear for the hearts of my soldiers and yet must unfurl my banners before the foe, I suddenly find myself before the altar of thy threefold manifestation. I believe my prayer will be accepted, and the rebels will be put to the sword. Tears of joy rush down my body. Moreover, since my great-grandfather, Yoshiie, the former governor of Mutsu Province, dedicated himself to thee and took the name of Hachiman Tarō, his family have all worshiped and served thee. I, Yoshinaka, a scion of this family, have for many years bowed my head before thee. The task that I am about to undertake is great, as great as that of a child who measures the water of the ocean and that of a mantis that raises its claws against a chariot. This undertaking is not intended to benefit my kin and myself but is for the sake of my country and the throne.

"I believe that the gods are favorable to me. This is encouraging. May the gods and the Buddhas join their powers to enable me to crush the enemy with a single blow and make them flee. If this prayer is heard and I am granted thy mighty protection, I beseech thee to show me a special sign!

"The eleventh day of the fifth month of the second year of Juei. Offered reverently by Minamoto no Yoshinaka."

Yoshinaka and thirteen of his retainers near at hand took turnip-headed arrows and placed them with the written prayer before the sanctuary of Hachiman. Perhaps their earnest prayer moved the heart of the merciful bodhisattva, for three wild doves came flying down from a cloud and circled, fluttering round the white banners of the Genji.

When the Empress Jingū went forth to attack Shiragi,[3] her army was weak and the foreign foe strong. Although almost certain of defeat, Jingū lifted her voice to heaven in prayer. Suddenly three doves came down from a cloud and fluttered over the shields of her soldiers. In the fight that ensued the empress drove her enemy to defeat.

Again, when Yoshinaka's own ancestor, Yoriyoshi, fought against Sadatō and Munetō, his army was weak and the barbarous enemy was strong. Yoriyoshi set fires in the face of the enemy and cried: "These are not my fires, but the divine fires from heaven!"

Then the wind began to blow in the direction of the enemy, and Sadatō's stronghold at Kuriyagawa was burned down. Sadatō and Munetō were defeated.

Now Yoshinaka, remembering these examples, alighted from his horse, took off his helmet, washed his hands, rinsed his mouth, and made obeisance to the holy doves with his heart full of faith in the god. How purified his heart was!

[1] Each area had local shrines to gods considered special protectors of the area.

[2] In Mahayana tradition the Buddha's three "bodies" are his Law Body, Bliss Body, and Transformation Body. This threefold form of the Buddha has often been compared to the Christian Trinity.

[3] One of the ancient kingdoms (57 B.C.—A.D. 934) of Korea.

CHAPTER VI

DOWNFALL AT KURIKARA

Now as the tale tells us, the armies of the Genji and the Heike faced each other ready for battle at a distance of only three chō. But neither of them moved forward. Then the Genji selected fifteen of their strongest bowmen to take up a position between the two forces and let loose turnip-headed arrows at the Heike. In reply, the Heike, not knowing the real intentions of the Genji, sent fifteen of their strongest bowmen to shoot arrows at the Genji. When the Genji sent thirty horsemen, the Heike sent the same number. When fifty rode forth from the Genji, fifty of the Heike appeared to meet them. When a hundred horsemen were sent from the Genji, another hundred came from the Heike. These men from the Heike and the Genji advanced to the front lines. They were anxious to plunge into battle, but the Genji had been ordered to restrain their troops to avoid premature combat. The Heike, for their part, never dreamed that such strategy would allow the Genji to hold them in check until sunset and drive the entire Heike army down into the valley of Kurikara. It was a woeful day for the Heike that they let the light pass into evening darkness without knowing the Genji strategy.

It was twilight when the rear forces of the Genji on the north and south sides of the valley, numbering some ten thousand, assembled around the Fudō-myō-ō Shrine on the peak of Kurikara. Then they suddenly began to beat on their quivers and sent up a great war cry. The Heike, turning toward the sound, saw a cloud of white banners fluttering high above, and they cried: "This mountain is rocky on all sides. We never thought that they would attack us from the rear. What is the meaning of this?"

Then Yoshinaka ordered his main force to join in the war cry of the soldiers on the peak of Kurikara. It was intensified in turn by the shouts of his ten thousand soldiers lying in hiding at Matsunaga-no-Yanagihara and Guminoki-bayashi and by those of the six thousand horsemen under the command of Kanehira at Hino-miya-bayashi. The mighty roar of forty thousand voices seemed great enough to bring the mountains to the point of crumbling and to push the waters of the rivers over their banks.

The Heike were hopelessly trapped, for they were attacked from front and rear in the growing darkness. Some began to flee. There were many who shouted: "Disgrace! Go back to fight! Go back to fight!" But inasmuch as the majority of the Heike had begun to withdraw, it was impossible for them to try to retake their positions. Thus every one strove to be first to flee on horseback down the valley of Kurikara. Soldiers behind were unable to see those in front; they believed that there was a road at the bottom of the valley. Now the entire army went down one after another, son after father, brother after brother, and retainer after master. Horses and men fell one on top of another, piling up in heaps. The valley was filled with some seventy thousand horsemen of the Heike. Blood seemed to spurt out of rocks, and the piles of corpses were as large as hills. It is said that in this valley the marks of arrows and swords can be seen even today.

The outstanding commanders of the Heike—Tadatsuna, Kage-taka, and Hidekuni—perished with their men at the bottom of the valley. A man of great strength, Kaneyasu of Bitchū Province, was taken alive by Narizumi of Kaga Province. The priest Saimei of Heisen-ji, who had betrayed the Genji at the fortress of Hiuchi, was also taken alive. When Yoshinaka was informed of his capture, he exclaimed: "Damnable priest! Put him to death immediately." At this command, the act was committed.

The commanders of the Heike, Koremori and Michimori, managed to flee to Kaga Province. Out of the entire army of seventy thousand men, barely two thousand survived.

The next day, the twelfth of the fifth month, Yoshinaka received a present of two swift horses from Hidehira of Mutsu Province. He had beautiful saddles made for them out of gold and silver and dedicated the horses to the shrine of Shirayama. Yoshinaka said: "I have won. My position in the war is now secure, but I am worried about my uncle Yukiie in battle at Shiho. Let us go help him if he needs us."

Yoshinaka rode off with some twenty thousand brave men and

fast horses chosen from his army of forty thousand. When they came to the inlet of Himi, which had to be crossed, the tide was high. As they were unable to determine if the water was shallow enough to ford, Yoshinaka drove ten saddled horses into the waves. They reached the far bank, wetting no more than the lower part of their saddles.

"The water is shallow! Let us ford!" they cried, and the entire army of twenty thousand horsemen forded the inlet. When they reached the other side, they found that Yukiie's army had been soundly defeated by the enemy. Yukiie, in retreat, was resting his men and horses when Yoshinaka appeared.

"This is what I feared," said Yoshinaka.

Taking command, he rode forward, uttering a thunderous battle cry, with the twenty thousand fresh men and horses into the thirty thousand Heike. The Heike defended their position for a while, but soon they were obliged to withdraw. Tomonori, the youngest son of Kiyomori, was killed. Yoshinaka then crossed Mount Shiho and encamped before the tomb of the prince of the blood Ōirikine at Odanaka in the province of Noto.

CHAPTER VII

THE BATTLE AT SHINOHARA

To commemorate his victory, Yoshinaka presented various of his land holdings to many shrines—Yokoe and Miyamaru to Shirayama, the manor of Nomi to Sugau, the manor of Chōya to Tada-no-Hachiman, the manor of Hanbara to Kehi, and seven villages of Fujishima to Heisen-ji.

The warriors who had fought against Yoritomo at the battle of Ishibashi in the previous year had fled to the capital and joined the Heike. Chief among them were Kagehisa, Sanemori, Sukeuji, Shigechika, and Shigenao. As these men rested, in wait for another fight, they amused themselves by playing host in turn every day at a drinking bout. When Sanemori held the banquet at his house, he said: "So far as I can judge the present trend, the Genji are winning over the Heike. What do you think about going over to Yoshinaka?"

The rest of the warriors seemed to show no objection to this proposition. The next day, however, when they gathered at Shigechika's quarters, Sanemori asked: "Did you think about the suggestion that I made yesterday? Let me hear an opinion from each one of you."

At his request, Kagehisa came forward and said: "We are all renowned warriors in the eastern provinces. It would be a disgrace for a warrior to change from one side to the other simply for his better fortune. I do not care what most of you want to do, but I, Kagehisa, have already made up my mind to die on the side of the Heike."

"To tell you the truth," Sanemori replied with great laughter, "what I suggested yesterday was only to test you. I also am determined to die in the coming battle. I have already declared it to Lord Munemori and others as well."

Upon learning of Sanemori's resolution, the rest of the warriors agreed to follow suit. Pitiful it was that, faithful to their promise, all these warriors, without exception, died afterward in the northern provinces.

The Heike, who had retreated to Shinohara in the province of Kaga, remained there for a while to rest their men and horses. At the first hour of the dragon [8: 00 A.M.] on the twenty-first day of the fifth month, Yoshinaka appeared with his army at Shinohara and made a thunderous war cry.

Among the soldiers of the Heike were two brothers, Shigeyoshi and Arishige, who had been specially selected for these battles in the northern provinces. Since the Jishō era their duty had been to guard the capital. Now they received the following order: "You are veteran warriors. Go and show our men how to fight a war."

The brothers moved forward with some three hundred horsemen to confront the Genji. From the side of the Genji, Kanehira rode forward with some three hundred horsemen. In the beginning the Heike and the Genji dispatched five men each, and then ten, to see which side would prove the better. After these preliminary contests the two forces attacked each other in a wild melee. It was high noon on the twenty-first day of the fifth month. The sun blazed upon the heads of the fighting warriors. The sweat poured over their bodies as if they had just bathed. Many men under Kanehira were killed, while a greater number of the Heike were slain; and so the two brothers were compelled to withdraw.

Now, from the Heike side, Takahashi no Hangen Nagatsuna rode forward with five hundred horsemen. Out of Yoshinaka's force rode three hundred horsemen led by Kanemitsu and Kaneyuki. For some time each side struggled to master the other. Nagatsuna's men, however, had been recruited from outlying provinces. Unable to withstand the onslaught, they were the first to flee the battle. Though Nagatsuna himself was a valiant warrior, he was obliged to retreat. He was galloping away alone when he was found by Yukishige. Thinking that he must be a renowned warrior of the Heike, Yukishige whipped and spurred his horse toward him. Coming up alongside, he grappled with Nagatsuna. Nagatsuna, however, grasped Yukishige and pressed him hard against the pommel of his saddle, saying: "Who are you? Let me hear your name and title."

"I am Yukishige," he replied, "a native of Etchū Province— eighteen years of age."

"What a pity!" exclaimed Nagatsuna. "If my son, whom I out-lived last year, were still alive, he would also be eighteen. I could twist your neck and cut off your head, but I will let you go."

Nagatsuna alighted from his horse to recover his breath, saying: "I will wait for a while and see if some of my soldiers come."

Yukishige also dismounted, apparently resigned to defeat, but he thought to himself: "Though he spared my life, he is, after all, a famous leader of my enemy. I must, at all costs, cut off his head."

Nagatsuna, never dreaming of such treachery, talked amiably with Yukishige. Suddenly Yukishige, who was renowned for feats of agility, pulled out his sword and drove two lightning-quick thrusts under Nagatsuna's helmet. As Nagatsuna staggered back from the blows, three men of Yukishige's troop appeared. Valiant warrior though he was, Nagatsuna met his fate. He had been seri-ously wounded and there was no chance for him against such heavy odds.

Now Arikuni of the Heike collected some three hundred horse-men and galloped against his foes. They were met by five hundred horsemen of the Genji led by Nishina, Takashina, and Yamada no Jirō. In a short desperate fight many men of Arikuni's platoon were killed. Arikuni, having penetrated deep into the ranks of the enemy, found that he had used all of his arrows and that his horse had been wounded. Dismounting, he drew his sword and wielded it with all his might. He killed many of the enemy, but, finally, pierced by the shafts of seven or eight arrows, he died. Even after his last breath, he remained on his feet, his eyes open wide as if glaring at his enemies. Seeing how their master met his end, Ari-kuni's retainers gave up the fight and fled.

CHAPTER VIII

SANEMORI

Among the warriors of the re-
treating Heike was Sanemori, a native of Musashi Province. Though
he admitted defeat and saw all of his companions trying to flee,
he turned his horse back to the battlefield again and again to look
after the rear guard of his troops. Sanemori wore a red brocade
battle robe over armor laced with green silk cords and a helmet
decorated with a pair of metal sickle-shaped horns. He carried a
sword in a sheath studded with gold and a quiver of arrows feathered
black and white. His bow was bound with lacquered rattan. He
rode a dapple gray with a gold-studded saddle.

One of Yoshinaka's men, Mitsumori, saw him and, because of
his gorgeous battle garb, thought that he might be a warrior of
great fame. Riding forward, Mitsumori exclaimed: "A brave man!
Your men are all running away, but you have remained here. How
gallant you are! Let me ask your name and title."

"Who is he that asks me who I am?" replied Sanemori.

"I am Mitsumori, a native of Shinano Province."

"If that is who you are," said Sanemori, "your sword deserves a
fight with mine. I do not mean to offend you, but I have good
reason for not declaring my name. Come now, Mitsumori. On your
guard!"

As he urged his horse alongside Mitsumori's, one of Mitsumori's
retainers, fearing that his master might be killed, rushed up and
thrust himself between them. Now he grappled with Sanemori.

"Splendid! You want to fight with the greatest warrior in
Japan," cried Sanemori, as he caught the retainer in his arm, pressed
him hard against the pommel of his saddle, and cut off his head.
Mitsumori, seeing his retainer fall, slipped around to the left side
of his opponent, and lifting the skirts of Sanemori's armor, stabbed
him twice. Sanemori weakened. As they jumped from their horses,

[414]

Mitsumori fell upon him. Tough and valiant though he was, Sanemori was pressed down and beheaded, for he had already been exhausted by the long battle, too severe for a man well advanced in years.

Mitsumori, having given Sanemori's head to one of his retainers to carry, galloped back to Yoshinaka's camp and said: "I have brought you, my lord, the head of a strange fellow whom I fought and killed. Though he wore a red brocade battle robe and he looked like a great leader, he had no retainer in attendance. When I asked his name, he demanded mine but would not give his own. He spoke in Kantō dialect."

"Splendid!" exclaimed Yoshinaka. "This must be Sanemori. I saw him once when I went to Kōzuke Province. At that time I was only a little boy, but I remember that he already had grizzled hair. Now it must be white all over. But, strangely, this hair and this beard are black. Kanemitsu has been a friend of Sanemori for a long time, and so he must know him well. Summon Kanemitsu."

Kanemitsu answered the summons, and, after a glance at the head, he burst into tears, saying: "What a pity! It is the head of Sanemori."

"He must have been more than seventy," said Yoshinaka. "Why is his hair still so black?"

Kanemitsu, now repressing his tears, replied: "When I think of why it is, I am moved to tears. A man of the bow and the sword must leave some memorable words to the world. Sanemori used to tell me: 'If I go to fight after I am past sixty years of age, I will dye my hair and beard black so that I may still look young. I would be considered impetuous if I had white hair flowing in disorder as I competed with younger men. Surely I would be scorned as an old fool.' It is true that Sanemori dyed his hair and beard. My words will be proven if you have them washed."

When Yoshinaka had the head washed, indeed the hair and beard turned white.

The reason Sanemori had worn a red brocade robe is as follows. When he took leave of Munemori, the state minister, he said: "Last year when I went down with our men to the eastern provinces, I was startled by the noise of the waterfowl and fled in panic from Kambara in Suruga without shooting a single arrow against the enemy. There were of course many others who fled also, but the fact that I did is a disgrace for me. Now I am an old man. I am going to the northern provinces, where I am determined to die. Echizen is the province where I was born. It is only in later years that I have lived in Nagai in Musashi Province, the domain that my lord has bestowed upon me. The proverb says, 'Wear a brocade robe when you return to your homeland.' Now I beg you to grant me the right to wear brocade battle garb."

It is said that Munemori was moved by Sanemori's bravery and thus allowed him to wear a brocade battle robe into his last battle.

Long ago in China, Chu Mai-chen[1] flaunted brocade sleeves on Mount Hui-chi. In the same manner Sanemori raised his name in the northern provinces. He left to this world an illustrious name, though his soul had departed from his body. How sad it is that his corpse mingled with the dust of that northern province!

When a hundred thousand horsemen of the Heike set out from the capital on the seventeenth day of the fourth month it seemed that none would be able to match their strength. Now at the end of the fifth month, barely twenty thousand of them were able to return to the capital. Some men of learning said: "If you fish out all the rivers, you will get a lot of fish, but next year you will find none to catch. If you burn a forest for hunting, you will catch a lot of beasts, but next year you will find none to hunt. The Heike should have kept some troops behind the lines in reserve for the future."

[1] (d. 109 B.C.). As a young man he was very poor and so immersed in learning that his wife was dissatisfied and deserted him. Later, going to the capital, he became a retainer of Emperor Wu and was appointed governor of his home province, Hui-chi.

CHAPTER IX

GENBŌ

Tadakiyo and Kageie lamented over the deaths of their sons in the battle in the northern province. All the land, far and near, was in mourning, for parents had outlived their sons and wives had lost their husbands. People in the capital closed their doors and chanted Buddhist prayers, weeping and screaming relentlessly.

On the first day of the sixth month, the archivist Sadanaga summoned the aide to the ritualist Chikatoshi to the parlor of the Seiryō-den and told him of the emperor's[1] wish to pay a visit to the Ise Shrine after a truce had been reached.

The deity of the Ise Shrine is the Sun Goddess, Amaterasu, who descended from heaven to the earth. In the third month of the twenty-fifth year during the reign of Emperor Sujin,[2] the shrine was moved from Kasanui in Yamato Province to a point upstream from Isuzu in the county of Watarai in Ise Province. There the great pillars of the shrine were set down firmly, and the people began to worship the Sun Goddess. Since then it has been incomparably holy among the three thousand seven hundred and fifty shrines, large and small, throughout the more than sixty provinces of Japan. Despite its importance, no emperor had visited the shrine before the reign of Emperor Shōmu. At that time there was a man named Hirotsugi, a son of the lord chamberlain, Ugō, and a grandson of the minister of the Left, Kamatari. In the tenth month of the fifteenth year of the Tempyō era [743], Hirotsugi gathered several thousand soldiers at the county of Matsuura in the province of Hizen and endangered the throne. Emperor Shōmu ordered General Ono no Azumaudo to destroy Hirotsugi, and thus it was in celebration of this victory that Shōmu paid the first imperial visit to Ise Shrine. It was said that the emperor wished to follow the example set by Emperor Shōmu.

Hirotsugi had a swift horse that was able to run from Matsuura in Hizen to the capital in a day. When Hirotsugi fought the imperial army and all of his soldiers were destroyed, he rode this horse deep into the sea. Thereafter, because of his evil spirit, many dreadful things occurred. On the eighteenth day of the sixth month of the sixteenth year of Tempyō [744], Bishop Genbō was requested to appease the evil spirit at the Kanzeon-ji temple in the county of Mikasa in the province of Chikuzen. Genbō climbed the high platform and rang the bell. The sky was suddenly covered with clouds and thunder roared. A bolt of lightning struck him, tore off his head, and carried it into the clouds. This is how the evil spirit of Hirotsugi was appeased.

The bishop had once accompanied Kibi[3] to China and had taken the teachings of the Hossō sect back to Japan. At that time a Chinese warned Genbō: "Genbō means 'return and die.' You will meet a tragic event after you go back to your country."

On the eighteenth day of the sixth month of the nineteenth year of Tempyō [747], a skull inscribed with Genbō's name fell from heaven to the yard of the Kōfuku-ji temple; it roared with laughter as great as that of a thousand people. Now Kōfuku-ji was a temple of the Hossō sect. Genbō's disciples made a mound for the skull and called it the Tomb of the Head. Even now the mound stands there. The spirit of Hirotsugi, too, was preserved at Matsuura. The shrine is now called the Mirror Shrine.[4]

During the reign of Emperor Saga, the abdicated emperor, Heizei, raised a revolt at the instigation of Fujiwara Kusuko.[5] To pray for peace on the land, Emperor Saga sent his third daughter, Princess Yūchi, to the Kamo Shrine. This act originated the custom of sending imperial princesses to pray at the Kamo Shrine in difficult times. During the reign of Emperor Shujaku, a special prayer was performed at the Yahata Shrine to calm the revolts raised by Masakado and Sumitomo. These examples were now remembered as various kinds of prayers were performed.

---

[1] Antoku.

[2] The correct name of this emperor must be Suinin, who reigned from 29 B.C. to A.D. 70.

[3] A descendant of Prince Kibitsuhiko, he lived in Kibi and hence was called Kibi no Makibi. In 716 he went to China to study and returned to Japan in 735. He brought

back the art of embroidery, the game of *go*, and the biwa. In 752 he went again to China, and upon his return in 754, he was appointed governor of Dazai.

⁴ Present-day Kagami-mura, Matsuura-gun, Saga Prefecture.

⁵ A daughter of Vice-Councilor Fujiwara Tanetsuna, she first married Fujiwara Tada-nushi and afterward Emperor Heizei. After Heizei's abdication in favor of his brother Saga, Kusuko, with her brother Nakanari, tried to relocate the capital at Nara and induce Heizei to reascend the throne. The plot was discovered. Nakanari was put to death; Heizei was forced to become a monk; and Kusuko took poison.

CHAPTER X

YOSHINAKA'S APPEAL TO MOUNT HIEI

Y oshinaka arrived at the provincial capital[1] of Echizen, where he summoned all of his hereditary retainers and held a council. "When I go up to the capital," said Yoshinaka, "I am afraid that the monks of Mount Hiei might stand in my way. It will be a simple task for us to destroy them and march to Kyoto. But I must remember that the Heike have violated the Buddha's Law by burning down temples and killing priests. I am heading for the capital to prevent them from committing more evil deeds. If I fight with the monks of Mount Hiei simply because they side with the Heike, I may have to repeat the very same deeds. A very simple task as I said, but also a very difficult one. What do you think?"

Now Kakumei, who served as a secretary to Yoshinaka, replied: "There are three thousand monks on Mount Hiei. Many of them, however, will not side with the Heike, for they all have different opinions. Some will side with the Genji, and some with the Heike. I advise you to send a letter to them. A reply will enable you to find out which side they support."

"What you say is most reasonable," replied Yoshinaka. "Write a letter."

Kakumei wrote: "When I, Yoshinaka, examine the evil deeds of the Heike, I see that they have been disloyal to the imperial family since the Hōgen and Heiji eras. The people, rich and poor, priests and laymen, are helpless, serving at the feet of the Heike. The Heike appoint and dismiss emperors at their will, steal provincial wealth, ignore reason, arrest members of influential families, and kill or banish the ministers and retainers of the emperors. They distribute these stolen honors and wealth to their own clansmen and descendants. Above all, in the eleventh month of the third year of Jishō [1179], the Heike confined the cloistered emperor at the North Palace of Toba and exiled the kampaku, Motofusa, to an out-of-the-way place near the western sea. People kept quiet, but when passing on the road, they made signs of grief and wrath over the violent acts of the Heike.

"Furthermore, in the fifth month of the fourth year of Jishō [1180], the Heike frightened the court when they besieged the palace of Prince Mochihito. I had received a letter from the prince, requesting my aid. So when the prince secretly sought refuge at Mii-dera to avoid the Heike's unreasonable persecution, I intended to whip my horse to be at his side. There were, however, too many enemies standing in my way. Even the men of the Genji near the capital could not rally. How much more difficult it was for me, far away! The allied forces of Mii-dera and Genji were not powerful enough to keep the prince safe from the Heike's attack. So that he would be free from danger, they tried to escort the prince to the south capital. When a battle broke out on the Uji Bridge, their leaders, Yorimasa and his son, fought desperately, holding their sense of loyalty above their lives. Overcome by the greater numbers of the enemy, the Genji warriors perished. Some of the bodies were left on the moss of the riverbank, and some were left to drift in the waters of the great river, Uji.

"The contents of the letter from the prince remained as a lasting impression; the death of Yorimasa, who was one of my kin, stirred my blood. Indeed, his death inspired all the kinsmen of the Genji in the northern and eastern provinces to go up to the capital and destroy the Heike.

"Last autumn I raised my banners and took up my sword to honor a long-cherished hope. I set out from my province and met Nagashige, a native of Echigo Province, leading several thousand soldiers to fight against us on the banks of the Yokota River. I stamped out the enemy with my force of only three thousand men. When the news of my victory spread throughout the country, the generals of the Heike collected a hundred thousand soldiers and set out for the north. I fought against them several times at the forts of Etchū, Kaga, Tonami, Kurosaka, Shiosaka, and Shinohara. My strategies surpassed those of my enemy, and victory was always on my side. At every fight the enemy was defeated. Whenever I made an attack, I won. It was just like the winds of autumn sweeping the banana tree clean of its leaves and the frost of winter cracking the earth. Truly the gods and the Buddha brought these victories to me.

"Now that the Heike's force has been defeated in the northern provinces, I intend to go up to the capital. I am about to pass by the foot of Mount Hiei before going into Kyoto. At this moment I am not certain of one thing—that is, are the monks of Mount Hiei on the side of the Heike or the Genji? If you support that band of devils, I shall be obliged to fight you. If this happens, the destruction of your temples will be unavoidable. What grief that should bring! I have risen against the Heike who tormented the emperor and destroyed the Buddha's Law. What a pity if I were to fight three thousand priests against my will. To shoot an arrow toward Yakushi Nyorai of the holy mountain on my way to the capital will cause the people to criticize my honor as a warrior in the days to come. I am indeed at a loss as to what I must do, and so I simply ask you to clarify your stand. Let me pray of you three thousand priests, to side with the Genji and destroy the Heike for the sake of the gods and the Buddha and the country and the emperor. The great blessing of the imperial family be with you. I have written this to you with the utmost sincerity and reverence. On the tenth day of the sixth month of the second year of the Juei era. To the Chief Priest of the Tendai sect. From Minamoto no Yoshinaka."

[1] Present-day Takefu City, Fukui Prefecture.

CHAPTER XI

THE REPLY

As expected, when the monks of the mountain read Yoshinaka's letter, their opinions varied. Some wished to side with the Genji and some with the Heike. They discussed the matter for many hours. The old priests held a council and concluded: "We are here to offer prayers to the Buddha for the long life of the sacred emperor. The Heike are related by blood to the reigning emperor, Antoku, and worship our holy mountain. Therefore up to now, we have prayed for their prosperity. But they have grown more and more eccentric. They do evil deeds contrary to the Buddha's Law and have invited the hatred of people throughout the land. Though the Heike sent their armies to many provinces to calm revolts, they were defeated by the rebels. In recent years the Genji have won several fights against the Heike. Good fortune is about to return to the Genji. Why do we alone side with the Heike, who are now approaching their doom, and stand against the Genji, who are at the beginning of their prosperity? Let us forget the favor that we have received from the Heike and declare our alliance with the Genji."

They wrote a letter of reply to Yoshinaka. Yoshinaka gathered his hereditary retainers and clansmen, and ordered Kakumei to open it. It read: "Your letter dated the tenth of the sixth month arrived here on the sixteenth day of the month. When we read it, the dark mood of the recent days was dispelled in an instant. Year after year the evil deeds of the Heike have continued and the court has been kept in turmoil. This is well known to the land, so we need not dwell upon it here. We maintain the excellent temples to the northeast of the capital and pray for the peace of the country. The country, however, suffers hardships caused by the evil deeds of the Heike. Achieving peace on land and sea seems hopeless. It seems that the doctrines of esoteric Buddhism have fallen into decay and their guardian gods have become powerless.

"You were born of a military family, outstanding in the arts of the bow and the sword. Your effort against the Heike has been carried out most gallantly, for you raised an army in the cause of justice and established your fame at the risk of your life. Now only two years after beginning your campaign, your name is already known the world over. We, the priests on the mountain, are most impressed by your military achievement and wisdom, which have benefited the nation and the people. We are pleased to know of the success of our prayers. We desire the protection of the gods and the Buddhas on land and sea. The Buddha, who is worshiped at the main shrine of Hiyoshi may be delighted to know of the revival of the shrine's laws and the renewal of the people's respect and worship. Be aware of our true feeling. In the world beyond the Twelve Divine Commanders will join the brave warriors for the righteous cause as the servants of the Buddha. In this world we, the three thousand priests on the mountain, will lay aside our studies and prayers for a while and aid you and your righteous army in destroying the enemies of the emperor.

"The winds of the Buddha who teaches ten doctrines[1] on the mountain will blow away the wicked retainers of the emperor from our land, and, in reply to our mystic prayers, the rain of the Law will moisten the dry land so that it will return to the righteous days of Yao. We have thus concluded our council. Be aware of our true intention. On the second day of the seventh month of the second year of Juei. The Monks of Mount Hiei."

---

[1] Ten doctrines that tell how to give up illusions and attain enlightenment are taught by the Tendai sect.

CHAPTER XII

THE HEIKE'S JOINT APPEAL TO MOUNT HIEI

The Heike were not aware of the decision made on Mount Hiei, and so ten courtiers of their kin who were above the third court rank assembled for a council and wrote their appeal to Mount Hiei in the form of a prayer. It read: "We revere Enryaku-ji as one of our house temples, and Hiyoshi as our tutelary shrine. Thus we unswervingly respect the Buddha's Law of the Tendai sect.

"Here is a special prayer that all kinsmen of our house join in their hearts to offer thee: Ever since Dengyō Daishi established the Buddha's Law of the Tendai sect and the great teachings of Dainichi Nyorai on the mountain upon his return from China during the reign of Emperor Kammu, Mount Hiei has enjoyed nothing but prosperity as the holy place that protects the nation through Buddhism.

"Now Yoritomo, the exile in Izu Province, does not regret his offenses but mocks the Imperial Law. To support his vicious plans a number of the Genji, including Yoshinaka and Yukiie, have stood against us. They have confiscated several provinces and have stolen all the products and tributes to the court. We had an imperial edict issued that ordered the immediate destruction of the rebels. Following the honorable examples set by our ancestors, we have fought to the best of our ability with the bow and the sword. Up to this point, however, our forces have not prevailed. This is largely because our enemy has employed a fan-shaped battle formation. With banners flung like the stars and with spears shining like lightning, we have marched, but the rebels have won successive victories. Without the aid of the gods and the Buddha, how can we hope to destroy the traitors?

"Now when we look back upon our ancestors, we see that our house first founded your venerable temple. We have respected and worshiped it from age to age. Now and henceforth we shall be your partners in both joy and sorrow. Our descendants shall never forget this bond.

"Since the Fujiwara worshiped the god of Kasuga and the Buddha of Kōfuku-ji, they have long revered the Mahayana doctrine of the Hossō sect. The Heike are similarly bound to the god of Hiyoshi and the Buddha of Enryaku-ji. We have revered the perfect teachings of the holy law of the Tendai sect. Kōfuku-ji is now behind the times. It is concerned only with the glory of the Fujiwara family. Your temple remains righteous. Our prayer is offered to you for the sake of the imperial house. We pray that our efforts to punish the rebels will be successful.

"We beseech you, O Gods of the Seven Shrines and you bodhisattvas who protect the east and west of the holy mountain. O Yakushi Nyorai and Twelve Generals! Behold our true wishes and come to meet us with your gracious aid. May the hands of the emperor's enemies be bound at the gate of our camp! May we bring their heads in triumph to the capital! All lords of our house are hereby united in this prayer to you. On the fifth day of the seventh month of the second year of Juei.

"Taira no Michimori, junior grade of the third court rank and governor of Echizen Province; Taira no Sukemori, junior grade of the third court rank and lieutenant general of the Imperial Guard of the Right; Taira no Koremori, senior grade of the third court rank, lieutenant general of the Imperial Guard of the Left, and governor of Iyo Province; Taira no Shigehira, senior grade of the third court rank, lieutenant general of the Imperial Guard of the Left, and governor of Harima Province; Taira no Kiyomune, senior grade of the third court rank, chief of the Imperial Guard of the Right Gate, and governor of Ōmi and Tōtōmi provinces; Taira no Tsunemori, senior grade of the third court rank, lord chamberlain for the empress dowager, chief of the Palace Repairs Division, and governor of Kaga and Etchū provinces; Taira no Tomomori, junior grade of the second court rank, vice-councilor and commander-in-chief against the barbarians; Taira no Norimori, junior grade of the second court rank, vice-councilor, and governor of Hizen Province; Taira no Yorimori, senior grade of the second court rank, overseer of Dewa and Michinoku provinces; Taira no Munemori, junior grade of the first court rank."

The chief priest of the Tendai sect was deeply moved by this prayerful appeal, but did not show it to the other priests at once. He kept the appeal at the shrine of Jūzen-ji, and, after offering a prayer to the god there for three days, he showed it to them. When it was unrolled, a verse that had not been noticed before was seen on the top of the scroll:

> Peaceful is the house,
> Now when the flowers are gay,
> Hushed before the storm.
> It is like the moon waning,
> Only to sink in the west.

The Heike had prayed to the gods of the mountain for sympathy, and had begged the three thousand monks of Mount Hiei to lend their aid. However, they had previously offended the will of the gods and ignored the concerns of the people for many years, so their prayers were no longer accepted. Seeing the events that had come to pass, the monks of Mount Hiei, though they felt sorry for the Heike, would not acquiesce to the Heike's appeal: "We have already sent a reply promising our aid to the Genji. How can we take that decision lightly and change our minds now?"

CHAPTER XIII

THE EMPEROR'S DEPARTURE FROM
THE CAPITAL

On the fourteenth day of the seventh month of the second year of Juei [1183], the governor of Higo Province, Sadayoshi, returned to the capital after having put an end to the rebellion in Kyushu. He was accompanied by three thousand mounted soldiers under the command of Kikuchi, Harada, and Matsuura. However, even though the revolt in Kyushu had been put down, there was no hope of bringing peace to the northern provinces.

At midnight of the twenty-second day of the month, there arose great confusion at Rokuhara. Horses were saddled; girths tightened. People scurried in all directions, carrying their personal belongings to hiding places. It seemed that attackers would fall upon them at any moment. The morning after, the reason for this confusion was made clear.

There was a certain warrior of the Genji from Mino Province named Shigesada, a man who had turned traitor and arrested Tametomo[1] during his flight subsequent to the Genji's defeat at the time of the Hōgen Insurrection. As a reward, he had been raised from the position of lieutenant to that of captain of the Imperial Guard of the Right. Since he had sided with the Heike, he had been regarded as an enemy by his family. Now he galloped by night to Rokuhara with this message: "Yoshinaka is making his way up to the capital at the head of fifty thousand mounted soldiers. They are occupying East Sakamoto. Six thousand of them, including Yoshinaka's secretary, Kakumei, under the command of Chikatada, one of Yoshinaka's hereditary retainers, ran up Mount Hiei. United with the three thousand monks, they are now falling upon the capital."

Upon hearing of this attack, the men of the Heike were upset and sent soldiers in every direction to engage the enemy. Three

thousand horsemen under the command of Tomomori and Shigehira set out from the capital, taking up positions at Yamashina.
Michimori and Noritsune at the head of two thousand men rode
out to hold the bridge at Uji. Yukimori and Tadanori led one
thousand men to guard the highway along the Yodo River. Meanwhile, it was reported that several thousand men of the Genji under
the command of Yukiie had already crossed the bridge at Uji and
had entered the capital. Another battalion of the Genji under the
command of Yoshikiyo, the son of Captain Yoshiyasu, had crossed Mount Ōe. Yet another band of the Genji, coming from the
direction of Kawachi in Settsu Province, had gathered like a cloud
in the capital. Now, to provide a better defense, the Heike were
obliged to recall to the capital all the soldiers who had been
dispatched to the provinces.

A Chinese poet said: "The imperial capital is a busy place where
people seek for fame and gain. After cockcrow it has no rest."
The capital is a restless place even when it is peacefully governed.
How much more frantic it must be during a time of confusion.
The Heike would have liked to flee deep into the heart of Mount
Yoshino. However, now that all the surrounding provinces were
hostile to them, they could no longer find refuge. None of them
could deny the truth of these golden words in the *Lotus Sutra*:
"In the Three Worlds there is no rest; it seems as if we are in a
burning house."

On the twenty-fourth day of the seventh month, late at night,
the former minister of the Right, Munemori, went to visit Kenreimon-In at Rokuhara: "I have clung to a faint hope of an im-
provement in our situation, though the country has turned against
us. This may be our last chance to regain our glory. Many of our
men want to stay here and show their courage. But it would be
unfortunate if you came to any harm now. Thus I think it advisable
for you to retire for a while to the western provinces with Emperor
Antoku and the cloistered emperor, Go-Shirakawa."

"If the situation is as serious as you say," replied Kenreimon-
In, "then I will agree to whatever you advise."

As she spoke, tears rushed down her face and wet the sleeves
of her imperial robe. Munemori too moistened the sleeves of his
robe.

Perhaps the cloistered emperor had secretly heard of the Heike's intention to take him away to the western provinces, for he slipped out of the Cloistered Palace by night, and hid himself at Kurama. He was accompanied by only the captain of the Imperial Stables of the Right, Suketoki, the son of Councilor Sukekata. No one was aware of the departure of the cloistered emperor.

Among the warriors of the Heike was a certain fellow of quick mind named Sueyasu. He was often summoned to the Cloistered Palace to stand guard. The night of Go-Shirakawa's departure, he was on duty there. Although he was some distance from the private apartments, he had a notion, from the noise here and there and the sound of the suppressed weeping of the ladies-in-waiting, that a catastrophe had occurred. Upon his inquiry, they replied: "The cloistered emperor has suddenly disappeared. We have no way of knowing his whereabouts."

Sueyasu was frightened, but hurried straight to Rokuhara and reported the cloistered emperor's disappearance to Munemori.

Munemori galloped to Hōjū-ji to make sure of the truth of the report. There he himself found that the cloistered emperor had fled. The ladies-in-waiting constantly in attendance upon the cloistered emperor—Tango-dono and all the others—were no longer there. When questioned by Munemori, not one of those who remained knew where the cloistered emperor had gone. They were completely mystified.

No sooner was it known that the cloistered emperor had left the capital than all the people of Kyoto were upset. The confusion of the Heike was so great that it seemed as if the enemy were actually pouring into the capital. The Heike had made preparations to send the reigning emperor and the cloistered emperor to the western provinces, but now they had been forsaken by the cloistered emperor. The Heike felt like one who takes shelter under a tree that does not keep off the rain.

"Even without the cloistered emperor we must carry out our original plan of sending the emperor to the western provinces." So saying, at the hour of the hare [6: 00 A.M.], they made the imperial palanquin ready for the august departure. The emperor was only six years of age, and so, without knowing anything of what lay before him, he was seated in the palanquin. His mother, Ken-reimon-In, rode with him. The three imperial treasures were carried out of the palace to go in the imperial procession. It had been ordered by Councilor Tokitada that the imperial seal and key, the imperial waterclock, and the imperial biwa and koto should also be taken with them. However, the confusion was so great and sudden that many objects were left behind. The emperor's sword was among the forgotten items. Tokitada, Nobumoto,[2] and Tokizane[3] in ceremonial court robes accompanied the procession. They were escorted by the imperial guards in armor, carrying their bows and quivers. They proceeded along Shichijō to the west and Shujaku to the south.

The day that followed was the twenty-fifth of the seventh month. Dawn began to break as the Milky Way faded out in the sky; the clouds hovered over the mountain range of Higashi-yama; the moon grew whiter and whiter while the cocks crowed. The Heike had never dreamed of such a hasty departure from the capital. It reminded them of the abrupt relocation of the capital that had taken place the year before, and they thought of it as an evil omen.

The sesshō, Motomichi, also joined the procession. When it came to Shichijō Ōmiya, a young boy with his hair bound up was suddenly seen, as if coming from nowhere, running by his carriage. On the left sleeve of the boy's kimono, Motomichi saw the characters *haru-no-hi*, or "spring day," which could be also read "Kasuga." Kasuga was the guardian god of the Hossō sect and the tutelary god of the Fujiwara family. Motomichi was greatly encouraged by the association of the characters *haru-no-hi* with his first ancestor, Fujiwara Kamatari, who had founded the Kasuga Shrine and now seemed to be protecting his descendant. While he was meditating upon this, he heard a voice issuing eerily from the youth:

> No one can prevent
> The tips of wisteria leaves
> From fading away.[4]
> Why do you not leave your fate
> To your god, Haru-no-Hi?

Sesshō Motomichi then summoned his retainer Takanao and said quietly: "When I ponder the state of the world, I find that this emperor's trip is being made without the accompaniment of the cloistered emperor. I do not think that good fortune awaits us at the end of the trip. What do you think?"

In reply, Takanao winked at the ox tenders of the carriage and said nothing. They immediately caught the signal and, turning the carriage, whipped the oxen along Ōmiya to the north. They went at a great speed, as though flying, and entered the Chisoku-in temple at the foot of Mount Funaoka.

[1] (1139–70). The eighth son of Minamoto Tameyoshi, he joined his father during the Hōgen Insurrection. Defeated, he was exiled to Ōshima. Tametomo is the hero of *The Tale of Hōgen*, a war chronicle similar to the *Heike*.

[2] A cousin of Tokitada, he was head of the Imperial Storehouses.

[3] A son of Tokitada, he was governor of Sanuki Province and vice-councilor.

[4] The Japanese for "fading away" also means "getting away"; thus it suggests that Motomichi had better get away from the procession.

CHAPTER XIV

KOREMORI'S DEPARTURE FROM THE CAPITAL

Ône of the Heike warriors, a man named Moritsugi, saw the sesshō running away. Seizing his sword, he hurried to overtake him but was held back by others, and could do nothing.

Lieutenant General Koremori had long dreaded the thought of parting with his wife and children to do battle in distant provinces. Now when that day came his grief was boundless. His wife, the daughter of the late Councilor Narichika, was a lady of peerless beauty. Her complexion was like a peach blossom wet with dew; her large eyes were wondrously dark and brilliant; and her long raven locks streamed about her shoulders like willow shoots in the wind. She had two children, a son of ten named Rokudai and a daughter of eight. They all clung to Koremori and begged him tearfully to take them with him to the western provinces.

But Koremori explained: "As I have told you, I must go with the men of the Heike to the western provinces. I wish I could take you with me. But the enemy is lying in wait for us along the way, and I do not think we will be able to get through without danger. Even if you hear that I have been killed, you must never become a nun. Never! Rather you should look for another husband to help you bring up the little children. I am sure there are still kind men in the world who would take care of you."

Though he sought all the words that might comfort her, she was choked with tears. She fell prostrate, her head covered with her sleeves. When Koremori was just about to leave, she clung to his sleeve, crying: "In the capital I have neither father nor mother. If I am deserted, who else can I marry? It makes me sad to hear you say 'look for another husband.' Because we were promised in marriage in a former life, I have received only your affection. Who else can love me? We swore to each other that we would never part,

[433]

but that we should both melt into the dew of the same plain, or sink to the bottom of the same stream. Ah, these were all lies, nothing but the sweet evening whispers of lovers. If I were alone, I would forget my sorrow. I would resign myself to my sad fate and stay in the capital. But these little children—who do you imagine would take care of them? Tell me what to do with them. You are going to leave us—it is more than I can bear."

"Truly," replied Koremori, "you were thirteen and I was fifteen when we first met and loved each other. I remember we swore we would be together till the ends of our lives, till the same fire or water would enfold our bodies. Now listen to me—today I must wear armor and leave the capital under the enemy's threat. You would be wretched if I were to take you along unknown paths where you would face nothing but hardships. Worse yet, there is no place for you in this maneuver. When I have found a spot to settle down, be it only a hut on the beach, I will surely send for you."

He walked with firm steps out to the middle gate, where he put on his armor and called for his horse. He was about to mount when his son and daughter ran out and caught hold of one of his sleeves and the skirt of his armor, crying: "Father! Where are you going? Please take us too! Let us go with you!"

Koremori was helpless for a moment, feeling the inseparable ties of a father to his children in this fleeting world. Then his five younger brothers, Sukemori, Kiyotsune, Arimori, Tadafusa, and Moromori, rode through the gate into the courtyard and called out loudly: "The imperial procession has gone far ahead. Why are you so late in leaving?"

Without speaking, Koremori sprang onto his horse. Before whipping his mount, however, he turned around to the edge of the veranda, and, raising the bamboo curtain with the tip of his bow, said: "Look here! Everybody! These little ones have twined themselves around me. That is why I am still here."

As he spoke, tears streamed down his cheeks. His brothers were moved to weep in sympathy; the sleeves of their armor were wet with their tears.

There were two warrior brothers, Saitō-go and Saitō-roku, who always waited upon Koremori. The elder one was nineteen years of age and the younger one seventeen. They took hold of his horse's bridle on each side, and said. "Wherever you may go, we will follow you."

"When your father, Sanemori, went forth to do battle in the northern provinces," replied Koremori, "you were eager to follow him. But he left you, saying, 'I have a plan,' and he died alone in battle. Veteran warrior that he was, he knew that the Heike would end tragically. Now I must leave my son, Rokudai, behind, but I have no one but you two with whom I can entrust him. I ask you to yield and stay behind."

They could do nothing but comply with their master's commands, and, suppressing their tears, they stayed behind.

As Koremori rode off, his lady cried out: "Never had I thought that he would be a man of such cold heart!"

She buried her face in her sleeves and fell prostrate on the floor. The children and the ladies in the household stumbled out from behind the curtain and wept loudly. Perhaps the sound of their cries echoed in the ears of Koremori until he reached the western sea, where it echoed again in the wind and waves.

When the Heike fled from the capital, they set fire to more than twenty mansions, including Rokuhara, Ike-dono, Komatsu-dono, Hachijō, and West Hachijō. These mansions had all been residences of kinsmen of the Heike who had enjoyed positions as nobles and courtiers. The houses of their retainers and some forty thousand private homes in Shirakawa also went up in flames.

CHAPTER XV

THE RUINS OF ROKUHARA

The Heike's mansions had been visited even by emperors. Where once they had alighted from their carriages, nothing now stood but the foundation stones. In the gardens where empresses and princesses had enjoyed dances and banquets, the wind alone now howled and dew fell like mournful tears. All the magnificent apartments—the chambers with ornate doors and curtains, the pavilions in the woods for hunting or on the shores of ponds for fishing, and the residences of the nobles and courtiers and ministers— were reduced to ashes in half an hour, leaving no hope for future glory. Far worse was the loss of the lodges of their retainers! The flames devoured all the houses in the area for several chō.

In China, when the power of Wu was suddenly destroyed, the remains of the Ku-su Tower[1] were overgrown with dew-laden thistles. When Ch'in lost its violent power, the smoke of the Hsien-yang Palace obscured the battlements. Though two mountains, along the Han Ku checkpoint stood in protection of Ch'in, the northern barbarians broke in. Though the great river lay as deep as the Ching and the Wei,[2] the eastern barbarians took possession of the palace.

Who could have imagined this sad turn of events? The Heike were suddenly driven from their homes and obliged to flee to unfamiliar places. Yesterday they were dragon gods riding in triumph upon the clouds and commanding the rain. Today they lay like dried fish exposed for sale in the market. People had vaguely apprehended such an outcome, but they could not have expected the tide of the Heike to run out so precipitously—flood yesterday and ebb today. During the days of Hōgen, the Heike flourished like flowers in spring; now in the days of Juei, they fell like scarlet-tinged leaves in autumn.

Warriors who had served to guard the palace since the seventh month of the fourth year of Jishō [1180]—Shigeyoshi, Arishige and Tomotsuna—were to be killed at the time of the Heike's departure from the capital since they were not family members and could not be trusted. Lord Tomomori, however, expressed doubts about their execution, saying: "Our fortunes have begun to decline. If a hundred, or even a thousand heads, were cut off, we could still not bring any change to the world. It would only bring sorrow to the wives and children who are waiting for the return of their loved ones. If our position should ever be restored, they may come again to the capital to serve us. To release them now would be a virtuous act! Let us unbend and send them home."

"That is quite reasonable," replied Munemori, as he set them free.

On hands and knees the three warriors bowed their heads to the ground. Tears of gratitude ran down their faces as they pleaded: "Since the days of Jishō our lives have been saved by your affection and benevolence. Let us accompany you to the end of your journey."

But Munemori replied: "Your hearts must be in the eastern provinces with your families. We cannot take you, mere shadows of your former selves, down to the western provinces. Return to your homes."

They finally gave in to Munemori's words and left the capital in tears. They found it hard to restrain their grief when they thought of those whom they had served for twenty long years.

---

[1] Part of Wu's palace.

[2] The Ching is a river in Kansuh Province that flows into the Wei, a tributary of the Yellow River, in Shensi.

CHAPTER XVI

TADANORI'S DEPARTURE FROM
THE CAPITAL

The governor of Satsuma Province, Tadanori, who had already left the capital, rode back with a small train of five retainers and a servant to see Lord Shunzei. But when he came to the gate of Shunzei's mansion, he found it tightly closed. Even when he gave his name, it was not opened. The people within were running about, crying out that one of the fugitives had returned. Tadanori then dismounted from his horse and called out in a loud voice: "It is I, Tadanori. My visit should be no cause for alarm. I have come back only to say something to Lord Shunzei. If you will not open the gate, please come near it so that I may speak to you."

"If it is truly Tadanori," Shunzei said to his retainers, "he must have come for some important reason. There is nothing to fear. Show him in."

The gate was opened, and Tadanori was ushered in. Their meeting, at a time of adversity, was indeed a sad one.

"Ever since I became your student in the art of poetry years ago," said Tadanori, "I have neither neglected studies nor forgotten you. But for the last few years the disorder in the capital and the rebellions in the far provinces, all directly concerning our house, have prevented me from coming to see you. The emperor has already departed from the capital. Our days of glory have come to an end.

"Sometime ago I heard that an anthology of poems would be compiled by imperial command. Then I thought it would be a great credit to my life for even a single poem of mine to appear in the anthology. When the anthology was postponed due to the unsettled state of the country, I felt great regret. Someday in the future, when peace is restored, another imperial command will certainly be issued for an anthology to be made. In this scroll are some of my works. If you would be so kind as to grant me the favor of having one of them listed in the anthology, I would be grateful to you, even when my spirit rests under the shade of grass. My soul will come to you for protection, even to the world beyond."

With these words, Tadanori drew from beneath the sleeve of his armor a scroll containing a hundred verses that he considered his best.

"Inasmuch as I have this memento of yours," said Shunzei as he opened the scroll, "I will never forget your request. Your coming now is deeply moving. I cannot restrain my tears."

"If I sink to the bottom of the western sea, or if my body is exposed on a mountain or plain, there is nothing else that I wish to leave in this fleeting world—farewell."

So saying, Tadanori sprang onto his horse, tightened the straps of his helmet, and rode away toward the west. As Shunzei stood a long while, looking until Tadanori could be seen no more, he heard a Chinese poem being recited in a voice that sounded like Tadanori's:

> Far is the road I must travel;
> And so I send my thoughts
> To the evening clouds over Mount Yen.[1]

Overcome by awaré, Shunzei regretted his parting from Tadanori. Tears rushed down his face, as he slowly turned back to his mansion.

Sometime afterward, when peace was restored to the country, Shunzei received an imperial command to compile an anthology called *Senzai-shū*. He remembered his last meeting with Tadanori with deep sorrow. He found many excellent pieces in Tadanori's scroll; but as Tadanori had been punished by imperial law, only one of them was allowed to appear, without the name of the poet, in the anthology. The title was "Flowers of my Native Land."

> The sight of Shiga,
> The capital on the lake,
> Is now desolate.
> Only cherry blossoms are
> As beautiful as before.

[439]

Since Tadanori had been condemned as an enemy of the imperial house, Shunzei could do no more for him than this small favor. It was indeed sad.

[1] Located in Shansi Province in China.

CHAPTER XVII

TSUNEMASA'S DEPARTURE FROM THE CAPITAL

The eldest son of the chief of the Palace Repairs Division, a man named Tsunemasa, was an aide to the chief of the Board of the Empress's Affairs. As a child, he had served the imperial abbot of Ninna-ji at Omuro. Now, although he was urged to set off on a retreat to the west, it flashed through his mind that he should pay a farewell visit to the abbot. He took a few retainers and galloped to Ninna-ji. Alighting from his horse, he knocked at the gate and cried out: "The men of our family have already departed in despair from the capital for distant places, where their fate awaits them. All I regret in this fleeting world is that I must part from my lord. From the time I first came to this temple at the age of eight until the ceremony for my coming of age at thirteen, except for a single interval of sickness, never did I leave my lord's side. It is a pity for me that from this day on I shall be obliged to wander along the shores of the western sea, not knowing when, if ever, I shall return. I wish I could see my lord but once more. However, I hestitate to ask for a private audience, for I am wearing armor and carrying a bow. I am afraid it would be very offensive to my lord."

The abbot felt pity for Tsunemasa and replied: "Let him in as he is, without changing his dress."

That day Tsunemasa wore a purple battle robe and armor laced with green silk cords, shaded from light to dark green. A gold-studded sword hung at his side, and a quiver of twenty-four arrows with black and white feathers was strapped to his back. Under his arm he carried a bow bound in black and red lacquered rattan. Taking off his helmet and hanging it from his shoulder, he entered the main garden in front of the abbot's chamber. His Reverence immediately appeared, and ordering his retainers to raise the hanging on the veranda, invited Tsunemasa in. When Tsunemasa had seated himself, he ordered his retainer Arimori to bring a red brocade bag containing his master's biwa. Tsunemasa laid the instrument before the abbot and said in tears: "I have brought this famous biwa, Seizan, which Your Reverence presented to me last year. I am sad to part with it. But I would be sadder still if I took such a marvelous instrument into the dust of the country. If a better lot should ever befall our house and I should return to the capital, may I receive this once again from your hand?"

The abbot was greatly moved and replied with this poem:

> So I will keep this
> Unopened—your fond instrument—
> As your memento,
> For I see your great regret
> To part with my old treasure.

Then Tsunemasa borrowed his master's ink stone and wrote:

> The world has been changed
> Just like the running water
> In your bamboo spout.
> Never will I cease to desire
> To remain here by your side.

When Tsunemasa took his leave, all who were living in the temple—servants, acolytes, monks, and priests of all ranks—clung to his sleeves and pulled them, and wept, regretting to part from him. Among them was a young priest named Gyōkei, a son of the councilor Kōrai. He had been barely more than a servant when Tsunemasa was there to wait upon the abbot. Gyōkei was so reluctant to let Tsunemasa leave that he went with him as far as the banks of the Katsura.[1] At last, when farewells were exchanged, Gyōkei wept and composed this poem:

> A wild cherry tree,
> Be it old and gnarled or young,
> Blossoms out briefly.
> All fare alike—fade and pass,
> Leaving no flower behind.

Tsunemasa replied:

> Each night from this day
> On my journey to the west

I shall lie alone.
I shall slumber and then go
Farther and farther away.

Then he unrolled his red banner and raised it high. His waiting soldiers rushed into formation—a band one hundred strong. They whipped their horses and galloped to overtake the imperial procession.

¹ A river flowing through the western part of Kyoto.

CHAPTER XVIII

THE BIWA SEIZAN

When Tsunemasa was seventeen years of age, he was sent as an imperial envoy to the shrine of Hachiman at Usa to present an on-pei-shi. At that time he took with him the biwa Seizan. When he arrived at the shrine, he played one of the three secret melodies before the abode of the god Hachiman. The assembled priests, who had never heard such a masterful performance, were so deeply impressed that they wet the sleeves of their green robes with tears. Even for those who had no hearts, the melody was as moving as a shower of heavenly grace.

The story of this incomparable instrument is as follows. During the reign of Emperor Nimmyō, in the third spring of the Kashō era [850], when the chief of the Headdress Office, Sadatoshi, went to China, he met a famous master of the biwa named Lien Ch'ieh-fu. From this master, Sadatoshi learned three styles of playing. Before returning to Japan, he was presented with three biwas called Genjō,[1] Shishimaru,[2] and Seizan. But during his return voyage, the Dragon God, who must have envied him, raised a great storm. To calm the Dragon God, Sadatoshi cast Shishimaru into the waves. Thus it was that he brought back only two biwas to our country. These instruments were presented to the emperor, who designated them imperial treasures.

Long afterward, one autumn night during the Ōwa era [961–963], Emperor Murakami sat in the Seiryō-den hall, playing the biwa Genjō as the white moon shone and the cool wind blew. Then a shadowy apparition rose before His Majesty and began to sing gracefully. The emperor ceased to play the biwa and inquired: "Who are you? Where did you come from?"

"I am Lien Ch'ieh-fu," replied the shadow, "a Chinese player of the biwa who taught Sadatoshi the three styles of playing many years ago. Of these three there is one for which I did not give the entire secret. For this fault I have been thrown into the land of devils, where I am still waiting. Tonight I heard the wondrous sound of the biwa streaming from this place. This is why I have come. Now let me give this melody to Your Majesty so that I may attain Buddhahood."

The shadow took Seizan from the emperor's side and tuning the strings, taught the emperor the melody *Shōgen-Sekishō*. Thereafter the emperor and his retainers were all afraid of playing this biwa, and so Seizan was transferred to the Ninna-ji temple at Omuro. It is said that when Tsunemasa was still a child, he was favored by the abbot above all others, and therefore the biwa was presented to him. It had been made of rare wood; the back was covered with purple rattan and on the front was a picture of the dawn moon peeping through the green trees of summer mountains. Hence the biwa came to be called Seizan, that is, "Green Mountain." It was an excellent instrument, in no way inferior to Genjō.

---

[1] Literally "Black Elephant." This biwa had a picture of a black elephant on the front.

[2] Literally "Young Lion." This biwa had a picture of a young lion on the front.

CHAPTER XIX

THE HEIKE ABANDON THE CAPITAL

Councilor Yorimori set fire to his palace, Ike-dono, and set out from the capital. But when he came to the gate of the North Palace of Toba, he stopped to rest with the three hundred horsemen under his command. Suddenly he had them tear the red badges from their armor. With his men, Yorimori then started back to the capital on the pretext that he had forgotten something. A warrior of the Heike named Moritsugi saw them and galloped to his master, Munemori, to report: "Look, my lord! Councilor Yorimori and his retainers have turned around. They are all heading for the capital. This is strange. My hands hesitate to release an arrow against the councilor, but at least allow me to loose an arrow at his retainers."

"They have forgotten the great favors that they received from our house for many years," replied Munemori, "but they do not want to see how we meet our end. Let those heartless fellows do as they wish. Now what about the sons of Lord Shigemori?"

"So far," replied one of Munemori's retainers, "we have not seen them coming, my lord."

Vice-Councilor Tomomori then said in tears: "It is still no more than a day since we left the capital. What a pity it is that many of our men have already had a change of heart! I had a premonition that more and more would turn traitor once we were out of the capital. That is why I suggested we stay there. Did I not tell you so?" With these words, he cast a sorrowful but bitter glance at Munemori.

The reason Yorimori started back to the capital, abandoning the rest of the Heike, was that he had been on friendly terms with Yoritomo. Yoritomo had already sent to him many letters and pledges of support, saying: "I always wish well for you, for I have a special feeling of gratitude to your late mother, Ike-no-Zenni.

I swear by the great bodhisattva Hachiman that you are welcome at my house anytime."

Furthermore, whenever he sent soldiers to attack the Heike, Yoritomo had given special instructions to them, saying: "Be careful! Do not loose an arrow at Yorimori's men."

Thus it was that Yorimori returned alone to the capital, trusting the favorable words of Yoritomo, even though the entire Heike clan was fleeing in despair from the capital.

Yorimori's wife, Saishō-dono, was the foster mother of Princess Hachijō. Because she was living at the Tokiwa mansion of the Ninna-ji temple, Yorimori took refuge there.

Saishō-dono asked Princess Hachijō: "If the worst should happen, I beg you to be kind enough to do a favor for my husband, Yorimori, so that his life might be saved."

But Princess Hachijō could not give any assurance to Saishō-dono: "I am not certain if I can. In a world like this, no one knows what might happen."

Princess Hachijō knew that Yorimori had been favored by Yoritomo, but wondered if this alone could be any guarantee that Yorimori would be safe. What would other Genji do to him?

Yorimori had already parted from the Heike. Uncertainty began to tug at his heart.

Meanwhile, the six sons of Lord Shigemori, led by Koremori, at the head of a thousand mounted soldiers, caught up with the emperor's procession at the beach of Mutsuda on the Yodo River.

Munemori, delighted to see them, inquired: "Why are you so late in coming?"

"I am late," replied Koremori, "because I was obliged to take time in parting from my little ones. They all begged to come with me."

"Then, why have you not brought Rokudai with you?" said Munemori. "You are a hard-hearted father! You have left him behind!"

"Well, I thought of our uncertain future . . .," said Koremori, but he was unable to continue. Tears rushed down his face.

The men of the Heike who fled from the capital numbered some seven thousand. There were the former state minister, Munemori, Councilor Tokitada, Vice-Councilor Norimori, the new vice-councilor, Tomomori, the chief of the Repairs Division, Tsunemori, the captain of the Imperial Guard of the Right Gate, Kiyomune, Lieutenant General Shigehira, Lieutenant General Koremori, Lieutenant General Sukemori, and the governor of Echizen Province, Michimori. There were courtiers who were listed in the scroll of visitors at court—Nobumoto, Tokizane, Kiyotsune, Arimori, Tadafusa, Tsunemasa, Yukimori, Tadanori, Noritsune, Tomoakira, Moromori, Kiyofusa, Kiyosada, Tsunetoshi, Narimori, and Atsumori. There were also priests of high rank—Senshin, Nōen, Chūkai, and Yūen. Among the warriors were a hundred and sixty who held responsible posts in provincial offices, Police Commissioners Division, and the six divisions of the imperial guards. All of them had survived several battles in the last few years in various provinces of the north and east.

Councilor Tokitada stopped the imperial palanquin at the ruin of the detached palace of Sekido at Yamazaki and knelt on the ground. Bowing toward the Yahata Shrine, he offered a most pathetic prayer: "I humbly adore thee, great bodhisattva Hachiman! We beseech thee to grant that the emperor and all men of our family may again return to the capital."

It was from the ruin at Sekido that they all looked back toward the capital and saw nothing but smoke rising from the places where they had lived.

Vice-Councilor Norimori composed a poem:

> How melancholy!
> Householders wander away
> From their fire-parched homes.
> As flames stretch up to lick clouds,
> Homeless like smoke will they roam.

Lord Tsunemori, the chief of the Repairs Division, sighed as he recited this poem:

> When we look homeward,
> We see only a fire-swept plain.
> Yet again we look
> In regret of departure,
> Riding on the waves of smoke.

How sad it was when they found themselves separated from

their homeland by a smoky cloud. They brooded over the long journey before them.

Before the Heike departed from the capital, it had been rumored that some of the Genji were lying in wait for them at the mouth of the Yodo River. In order to eliminate this threat, the governor of Higo Province, Sadayoshi, had set off from the capital at the head of five hundred mounted soldiers. However, finding that the rumor had been groundless, he turned back to the capital. Near Udono[1] he encountered the imperial procession. Hurriedly alighting from his horse and still carrying a bow under his arm, he sought his master, Munemori. Sadayoshi said: "Could I ask you, my lord, why you abandoned the capital? Where do you intend to go? If we were to go down to the western provinces, we would be considered fugitives. We might risk attack everywhere we go, which could lead to nothing but destruction. This would be a great shame for our house. I beg you to turn back to the capital and make a last stand."

But Munemori replied: "Sadayoshi, you do not know yet that Yoshinaka is now marching to the capital with fifty thousand mounted soldiers from the northern provinces. The areas around Mount Hiei and East Sakamoto have already been covered by the vast throngs of his soldiers. Last night the cloistered emperor disappeared. Our men are not afraid of a fight, but I could not bear to endanger the imperial ladies—Kenreimon-In and Nii-dono. The best we can do now is to escort the emperor and the nobles and ladies of high rank to some safer place in the western provinces."

"Now I can better understand your position," replied Sadayoshi, "but as for me, I will ask your leave to return to the capital and see what I can do there."

Sadayoshi ordered almost all of his five hundred men to join the retainers of Koremori, and then he rode back to the capital with only a small band of thirty mounted soldiers.

When it was rumored in the capital that Sadayoshi was coming back to attack the traitors of the Heike who had stayed behind, Yorimori was terrified, saying: "He is coming back only for me!"

As soon as Sadayoshi arrived at the capital, he had a tent stretched to enclose the ruin of West Hachijō and spent a night there. Though he had expected that some of the Heike might return and join him there, he soon realized that none of them would return. He could see little hope for the Heike's success in the future, and so he felt forlorn. In gloom, he went to the grave of his master, Shigemori, and had Shigemori's bones dug up so that they might not be trampled by the hooves of the Genji horses. Kneeling before the bones, in tears, he spoke: "How terrible this is! Behold the fate of your glorious house! This reminds me of the time-honored saying, 'All who flourish are destined to decay. Pain comes when pleasure is at its height.' But now I cannot bear to see the truth of these words with my own eyes. Long ago, knowing what would take place, you prayed to the gods and the Buddhas to shorten your life. How wise and virtuous you were! At that time I, Sadayoshi, should have accompanied you to the world beyond. I have lived in vain this long only to meet an ignominious end. I pray you, when I die, come to meet me and guide me to the same Buddhahood as yours."

After speaking thus to Shigemori in the other world, he sent the bones of his master to Mount Kōya and had the earth of the tomb thrown into the Kamo River. He then made his way in the opposite direction—toward the eastern provinces. Since Sadayoshi had once taken care of Tomotsuna, from Shimotsuke Province he imagined he might be able to depend upon his former friend in the eastern provinces. It is said that Tomotsuna showed a great deal of kindness to Sadayoshi in return for his favor done in former years.

¹ Present-day Takatsuki City, Osaka.

CHAPTER XX

THE HEIKE ABANDON FUKUHARA

Munemori and the rest of the Heike of high rank, except Koremori, had taken flight to the western provinces with their wives and children. However, the situation had prevented courtiers of low rank from bringing their families. They had, therefore, left them behind without knowing when they would see one another again. When a man leaves his family—even when the date and hour of his return are fixed—the parting is truly a wrench. They struggle impatiently through the slow passage of time, longing for reunion. How much more anguishing it is when people part perhaps not to meet again! The sleeves both of those who went and of those who stayed were wet with tears. All, young and old, set out, looking back again and again, recalling many a favor received.

Some made their way by sea, drifting farther and farther away on the waves, and others went by land, riding on horseback, only to suffer from the toilsome journey. Their hearts were in torment as they sculled their boats and whipped their horses.

When he arrived at the former capital, Fukuhara, Munemori summoned several hundred of his most trustworthy retainers and addressed them: "Ancestors who do many good deeds bequeath a source of good fortune to posterity. Evil deeds, however, are always followed by unhappiness. Now we have exhausted the good deeds of our house and have been overcome by its accumulation of evil deeds. Thus it is that we have been abandoned by the gods and deserted by the cloistered emperor. We left the capital to wander like homeless vagabonds. Upon whom can we now rely? Remember this—a sense of close companionship can grow out of simple encounters, brief interludes. Two strangers may stand close together under a tree to take shelter from a summer shower, or they may share a drink at the same spring. This is because they have already become acquainted with each other in former lives, or because they have been bound by karma in a world gone by or in a world to come. You are not my casual retainers for a day or two, but my hereditary retainers. Some of you are related to me by blood. Some of you are bound to me by love, the love aroused by your sense of gratitude for a great many favors received from our house from generation to generation. It is true that you hoped to enjoy your own prosperity when our house flourished. Consider how many benefits you received from us in the days gone by. Is it not time that every one of you should repay these favors? Inasmuch as we are escorting the sovereign who has mastered the Buddha's Ten Precepts and who has risen to the supreme place of honor as the emperor, and inasmuch as we are carrying with him the Three Sacred Treasures, why do we not devote ourselves to His Majesty to the last, even to the end of the world?"

To this address, all men of the Heike, young and old, replied as if with one voice, weeping: "Even lowly creatures like birds and beasts know how to repay kindness. How can we, men with hearts, forget? It has been nothing but your kindness that has enabled us to feed our wives and children and take care of our retainers for more than twenty years. Above all it is a great shame for a man of the bow and the sword to be treacherous. We will follow you and His Majesty even beyond the boundaries of Japan, even to Shiragi, Kudara, Kōrai, and Keitan,[1] or even to the end of the sea and sky."

These words brought a feeling of some confidence back to Munemori and other nobles of the Heike.

That night they stayed at Fukuhara. There the bow-shaped new moon of autumn was shining bright in the sky. The air was clear and calm. They took for beds mats of grass. Dew and tears raced each other to wet their pillows. Everything they beheld was a source of sorrow. Since they were not certain of returning to this place, they wished to take a last look at the buildings that their lord, Kiyomori, had built—the pavilion on the hill for flower-viewing in spring, the palace on the beach for moon-viewing in autumn, the Spring Palace, the Pine Shade Palace, the resort for horse racing, the Two-Story Palace, the Snow-Viewing Palace, the mansions of the nobles, and the Inner Palace, roofed with jewels. The construction of this palace had been overseen by Councilor Kunitsuna. Now all these buildings had fallen into disrepair in the short space of three years. The roads were thickly mossed; the gates were closed by autumn grasses. On the tiles ferns sprouted, and on the walls ivy clustered. Over the mossy terraces, only the breeze came blowing from a clump of pines. The curtains were gone; the bedchambers lay open to the eyes of the sky. The only visitors to this old palace were moonbeams.

When morning came, the Heike set fire to the Inner Palace of Fukuhara. They then escorted the emperor to his boat, and all set sail. Though not so painful as their departure from the capital, this parting also wrung their hearts with grief. The evening smoke of torches burned by fishermen; the voices of the deer at dawn on the mountain; the sound of the waves lapping the beach; the moonbeams shining over sleeves wet with tears; the chirping crickets among the grass—every sound and sight made them feel melancholy and deepened their sorrow.

Only recently, when the Heike had ridden side by side to crush the rebels in the eastern provinces, they numbered one hundred thousand. This day, when they weighed anchor on the western sea, they numbered only seven thousand. The clouds hung low over the calm waters, and the blue sky began to darken. A solitary island in the offing was covered by the evening mist, and the moon rose over the waves. The boats made their way over the boundless sea as if rising into the low-floating clouds. As the days went by, the capital receded farther and farther beyond the mountains and rivers, even beyond the clouds. The thought of being far away from home overwhelmed them with endless tears. When they saw a flock of white sea birds flying over the waves, they remembered the beloved *miyako-dori*, or "birds of the capital," that appeared in the poem by Arihara no Narihira composed by the Sumida River as he longed for his family and friends in the capital.

Thus it was on the twenty-fifth day of the seventh month of the second year of Juei [1183] that the Heike completed their departure from the capital.

[1] Shiragi, Kudara (15 B.C.—A.D. 663), Kōrai (37 B.C.—A.D. 668), and Keitan (713–926) were ancient kingdoms of Korea. Although Kōrai was conquered by Shiragi in 668, its name was used for the whole of Korea until the country took the name Chōsen in 1392.

BOOK EIGHT

"... the Genji were advancing ..., so they boarded small fishing boats and wandered over the *waves*."
—Book 8, Chapter IV, page 473

CHAPTER I

THE CLOISTERED EMPEROR VISITS MOUNT HIEI

On the twenty-fourth day of the seventh month of the second year of the Juei era [1183], the cloistered emperor slipped out of his palace by night and fled to Kurama. He was accompanied only by Suketoki, son of Councilor Suke-kata. The priests of Kurama Temple, however, considered their temple still too near the capital to keep him safe from the Heike. Thus they took him deep into the forests of Mount Hiei through the steep hills of Yakuōzaka and Sasa-no-mine and transferred him to the small temple of Jakujō-bō at Gedatsu-dani in the precinct of Yokawa. Then, when Jakujō-bō was outfitted to serve as a temporary palace, the monks of the East Precinct on Mount Hiei became angry with the decision, saying: "Our East Precinct is the place where the cloistered emperor should establish his palace."

Therefore the cloistered emperor was again obliged to move his palace, this time to Enyū-bō at Minami-dani in the East Precinct. There he was strictly guarded by the monks and warriors.

The cloistered emperor, Go-Shirakawa, had escaped from the capital to high on Mount Hiei; the young emperor, Antoku, had left his palace for the western sea; the sesshō, Motomichi, had taken refuge deep in Mount Yoshino; and the imperial ladies and princes had hidden themselves at Yahata, Kamo, Saga, and Uzumasa, and other remote places in the hills that lay to the east and west of Kyoto. All the Heike had left the capital. Despite the Heike's departure, none of the Genji had yet appeared to take their places. For a while the capital remained unoccupied by lords and ministers. Since the beginning of Japanese history, there had been no precedent for this. Yet, had not Prince Shōtoku prophesied these events?[1]

No sooner was it known that the cloistered emperor had established his administrative offices on Mount Hiei than all courtiers and officials rallied again to his support. They were the former kampaku, Motofusa, the sesshō, Motomichi, the premier, Moronaga, the ministers of the Left and the Right, the state minister, the councilors and their deputies, the state councilors, and all courtiers of the third, fourth, and fifth court ranks. Those who had attained some position in the world and those who were desirous of obtaining office and promotion came to present themselves. None of them wished to miss this rare opportunity. So great was the number of people gathered round Enyū-bō that the chambers up and down the temple and the places within and without the gates were filled with them. It seemed that the present prosperity of this temple, where the founder's law had long been maintained, now gave great dignity and credit to Mount Hiei.

On the twenty-eighth day of the month, the cloistered emperor returned to the capital. He was escorted by Yoshinaka and more than fifty thousand of his horsemen. At the head of the procession rode Yoshitaka of the Genji from Ōmi Province, bearing the Genji's white banner. The white banner had not waved in the streets of the capital for more than twenty years. What an impressive sight!

Yukiie and his retainers crossed the Uji Bridge and entered the capital. Yoshikiyo, the son of Yoshiyasu, came into the capital over Mount Ōe. The Genji of Settsu and Kawachi came rolling into the capital like a thick fog. The city was now filled with the warriors of the Genji.

At the command of the cloistered emperor, Vice-Councilor Tsunefusa and Superintendent of the Police Commissioners Division Saneie summoned Yoshinaka and Yukiie to the veranda of the Cloistered Palace. That day Yoshinaka wore armor laced with twilled silk cords over a red brocade battle robe and carried a sword studded with gold and silver. His quiver held twenty-four arrows feathered black and white, and he carried a black lacquered bow bound with red rattan. He removed his helmet and hung it from his shoulder cord. Yukiie wore armor laced with scarlet silk cords over a dark blue battle robe. His sword was studded with gold, and his quiver held twenty-four white-feathered arrows. Each feather was marked in the center with one black bar. His bow was bound with rattan and lacquered black. He also took off his helmet and hung it from his shoulder cord. Now Yoshinaka and Yukiie knelt down and made obeisance.

Then the cloistered emperor ordered them to destroy Mune-mori and the rest of the Heike. They solemnly received this order in the courtyard. After a while, they explained that they had no proper place to lodge in the capital. In response to this appeal, Yoshinaka was given the mansion of Naritada, the chief of the Imperial Household Division, at Rokujō Nishi-no-Tōin, and Yukiie, the Reed Palace, the so-called Minami-den, which was in the compound of the Cloistered Palace.

The cloistered emperor regretted that Emperor Antoku had been carried away by his maternal relations, the Heike, to be set adrift on the waves of the western sea. Now he sent an imperial edict to the Heike demanding that they immediately return Antoku and the Three Sacred Treasures to the capital. But the Heike ignored the edict.

In addition to Antoku, the late Emperor Takakura had three more sons. Of them, the prince second in succession to the throne had also been taken away by the Heike in the hope of making him crown prince. The other two princes, third and fourth in succession to the throne, had remained in the capital.

On the fifth day of the eighth month of the year, the cloistered emperor summoned these princes. When they were brought into his august presence, the cloistered emperor turned first to the five-year-old prince, third in succession to the throne, and spoke to him: "Come here! Come close to me!" The prince, however, shrinking at the sight of his grandfather, began to cry loudly. The cloistered emperor granted his leave, saying: "Take him away! Let him go home quickly!"

He then turned to the four-year-old prince, fourth in succession to the throne, and said: "Come here! Come close to me!" The prince did not hesitate to step forward and get onto his grandfather's knees, nestling there affectionately. He looked as though he wished to be held in the arms of his grandfather for a long time. The cloistered emperor cried with joy and said: "If we are not related by blood, how can he be expected to come and nestle by the side of an old priest like me? See how sweet he is to me! Oh, he is my grandson! He is the perfect image of his father, the late emperor,

[459]

in his childhood. Ah, I must blame myself for not having noticed this charming likeness of my son until now !"

Nii-dono of Jōdo-ji, who was still only a lady-in-waiting at the time, was in attendance upon the cloistered emperor. Now she asked him: "Have you decided that this prince shall succeed to the throne?" "Certainly," replied the cloistered emperor.

In the meantime, a secret divination was performed. It was found that should the fourth prince become emperor, his descendants would rule Japan for a hundred generations.

The mother of this prince was the daughter of the chief of the Palace Repairs Division. When Kenreimon-In was still only a consort, this girl had waited upon her at the palace. As the girl was often summoned to the side of the late emperor, she was soon much favored by him. She bore him many children. Since her father, Nobutaka, had many daughters, he fervently wished that one of them would become imperial consort or empress. Once he was told that if he kept a thousand white fowls, one of his daughters would become an imperial consort. Perhaps because he did so, this daughter became an imperial consort and bore many princes. Nobutaka was extremely pleased, but fearing that he and his daughter would become the objects of envy to the Heike and the empress, he did not show his love as a granfather to the princes. Taking note of this, Kiyomori's wife, Nii-dono, sympathized with Nobutaka and assured him of the safety of his grandsons, saying: "There is nothing to fear. Let me see to bringing up your grandsons and making one of them an heir to the throne."

Nii-dono then provided the princes with many wet nurses and kept the children under her care. Later the fourth prince was accepted by the superintendent of the Hosshō-ji temple, Nōen, who was the elder brother of Nii-dono. Nōen had set out from the capital with the Heike for the western provinces in so much of a hurry that he left his wife and foster son behind. He sent a messenger to his wife, saying: "Bring the little prince and his mother with you and come down to the west at once."

Nōen's wife was overjoyed to receive this message and set off with the prince. She had gone as far as West Hachijō, when her elder brother, Norimitsu, stopped her: "You are doing such a foolish thing ! What evil spirit has possessed you to take the little prince from the capital? Can you not see that fortune is about to smile on him?" The next day the cloistered emperor dispatched a carriage to bring the prince to the palace.

Thus it was that fortune came to the young prince, Takanari, and so he was indebted to Norimitsu for this change in his circumstances. Later, when he succeeded to the throne, calling himself Emperor Go-Toba, he let many days and months pass before bringing this matter to mind. Forgotten by the emperor, Norimitsu still clung to a faint hope that he might be able to receive some imperial reward. Almost desperate, however, he penned the following two poems and sent them to the court to convey his discouragement:

> Sing at least one note
> If you can still remember
> Your old woods—Cuckoo!
> —Away from your forest home
> Where you spent many a night.

> Pity the tomtit!
> Although he conceals himself
> In a humble home,
> Taking for friends moonflowers,
> What he longs for is a cage.

When the emperor deigned to read the poems, he sighed: "What a pity it is! He has lived on in this world unnoticed. How stupid I have been to give him no consideration!"

The emperor immediately rewarded him by promoting him to the senior grade of the third court rank.

---

[1] It was believed in the middle ages (late 12th–early 13th century) that Prince Shōtoku had been an incarnation of Kannon the Savior and had predicted later political turmoil in Japan. A book on this subject entitled *The Future* is said to have been excavated near his tomb in 1054, but no one can give evidence for its existence.

CHAPTER II

CONTEST FOR THE THRONE

On the tenth day of the eighth month of the year, Yoshinaka was appointed chief of the Imperial Stables of the Left and governor of Echigo Province. In addition, he received an edict naming him Rising-Sun General.[1] Since he was not eager to receive the stewardship of Echizen Province, he was given that of Iyo instead. The province of Bingo was to be presented to Yukiie; but as he disliked it, he was given the richer province of Bizen in its place. Ten or more of the Genji were appointed provincial governors, captains of the Police Commissioners Division, or members of the Imperial Guard.

On the sixteenth day of the eighth month, about a hundred and sixty men of the Heike were dismissed from their offices and their names were struck out from the scroll of visitors at court. Tokitada, Nobumoto, and Tokizane, however, remained on the list.[2] This was because the cloistered emperor was still negotiating with Tokitada for the return of Emperor Antoku and the Three Sacred Treasures to the capital.

On the seventeenth day of the month, the Heike arrived at Dazaifu in the county of Mikasa in the province of Chikuzen. Takanao, who had accompanied the Heike from the capital, suggested that he go over to Ōtsu-yama to have the checkpoint opened. But he went back to his own province of Higo, where he shut himself up in his castle and gave no heed to the Heike's summons for him to return. The warriors of Kyushu, Iki, and Tsushima[3] who had pledged their allegiance to the Heike did not appear at Dazaifu. Only Tanenao[4] now served them.

The Heike went to Anraku-ji where they chanted poems to please the god. At that time Shigehira composed this poem:

Great is our longing

[462]

For the dear old capital
Where we used to live.
The deity of this temple
Might remember his own days.

All of those with him who read the poem wept.

On the twentieth day of the eighth month, the fourth prince of the late Emperor Takakura was raised to the throne. The coronation was held at the Leisure Palace. Lord Konoe resumed the title of sesshō. After all chiefs and archivists had been appointed, the ceremonies were over. The wet nurse of the third prince regretted with tears the ill fate of her master, but she could do nothing.

There is a saying: "Heaven permits no double days, nor double kings upon the land." Now, due to the evil deeds of the Heike, there appeared to be two emperors—one in a faraway place and the other in the capital.

Long ago, when Emperor Montoku passed away, on the twenty-third day of the eighth month of the second year of Ten-an [858], there were many princes. They all prayed secretly to the gods for their own rise to the throne. The emperor's first son was Prince Koretaka, who was also called Kobara. He always disciplined himself to be a ruler of high caliber. So powerful was he that he held the safety and peril of both heaven and earth in his palm; so wise was he that he was the only one who could master the laws and examples set by a hundred wise rulers. The emperor's second son was Prince Korehito, who was born to Some-dono, the daughter of the sesshō-kampaku Fujiwara Yoshifusa. Since this prince was attended by many kinsmen of the powerful Fujiwara family, he was also well qualified to succeed to the throne. According to the natural order of primogeniture, the first prince stood nearest to the throne. The second prince, however, had the advantage of a greater number of wise retainers, competent enough to conduct all affairs of state. Both princes were so well qualified that there was difficulty in choosing one for the throne.

The prayers for the first prince, Koretaka, were entrusted to his maternal grandfather, Bishop Shinzei, who was one of Kōbō Dai-shi's disciples and the superintendent of the Tōji temple. The prayers for the second prince, Korehito, were entrusted to Bishop Eryō of Mount Hiei, who was the chaplain for his maternal grandfather,

Fujiwara Yoshifusa. People whispered to each other: "They are saintly priests. No quick decision will be made between the two."

In the meantime, upon the death of the emperor, the nobles and courtiers held a council and concluded: "If an emperor were chosen by his own retainers, there would be the danger of a biased decision. The people would certainly criticize us. Let us try our luck with a horse race and a sumo match. The throne shall go to the victor's side."

On the second day of the ninth month of the year, the two princes presented themselves at the race course at Ukon-no-Baba. At this place the dukes, nobles, and courtiers wearing colorful costumes gathered like clouds. The bits of their caparisoned horses shone like stars. They presented a scene most rare and spectacular to the eyes of the people. The nobles and courtiers divided themselves into two groups, according to which prince they supported. With their hearts beating and their hands clasped tightly, they watched this unparalleled contest. The priests who had been requested to offer prayers—how could they deliver them to the gods and the Buddha lightly? Shinzei set up his altar at the temple of Tōji, and Eryō, at the temple of Shingon-in within the Inner Palace. During the prayers Eryō spread a rumor that he had died while offering his prayer, so that Shinzei might slacken. In reality, however, Eryō prayed fervently, calling forth all his powers.

The horse race began. Out of ten races, the first four were won by the party of the first prince, Koretaka, and the next six by the party of the second prince, Korehito. Then the wrestling match began. From the side of the first prince stood forth the captain of the Imperial Guard of the Right, Natora, a giant who had the strength of sixty men. From the side of the second prince appeared the major general Yoshio, a small and delicate man who looked as if he could be thrown by his opponent with one hand. Yoshio volunteered for the contest because he had had a dream in which he had been bidden to undertake this bout. Natora and Yoshio faced one another, and, after feinting and thrusting to test each other's weak points, they stood apart some distance in preparation for the main fight. At their first encounter Natora gripped Yoshio, lifted him off his feet, and threw him two jō. But Yoshio landed on his feet and recovered for another attack. This time he sprang at Natora and with a grunt tried to tumble him to the ground. In response, Natora counterattacked. They seemed to be equal in their strength. But Natora was a man of enormous size, so he now tried to take advantage of his physical supremacy over the smaller Yoshio. Since Yoshio was in danger of being pushed down, Some-dono, the mother of the second prince, sent many urgent messengers— as many as the teeth on a comb—to Bishop Eryō at the Inner Palace.

"Our side is likely to lose," cried the messengers. "What shall we do?"

Eryō, who was offering his prayer to Dai-itoku-myō-ō,[5] groaned: "What a shame!"

Eryō then took an iron pestle, cracked his head against it, took out some of his brains, pounded them and mixed them with milk, and put them in the sacred sesame fire. A thick black smoke arose. With this mystical performance, Eryō offered his plea to heaven until, at last, Yoshio won the contest.

This was how the second prince, Korehito, rose to the throne. He was called Emperor Seiwa and was afterward known as Emperor Mizuo.

Thus it was that thereafter, whenever something similar occurred, the priests of Mount Hiei said: "Eryō cracked his head and the second prince was made emperor. Son-i[6] wielded the sword of wisdom and the angry spirit of Michizane was calmed."

These had been events that were settled by the power of the Buddha's Law. It is said, however, that all other such superhuman events were concluded by the will of the Sun Goddess, Amaterasu.

When the Heike in the western provinces heard that the fourth prince had been made emperor, they were pierced with regret, saying: "This is intolerable! We should have brought the third and fourth princes with us too!"

"Even if we had done so," said Tokitada, "there is yet another of Prince Takakura's sons whom Yoshinaka intends to raise to the throne. The guardian of this prince is Shigehide, the governor of Sanuki Province, who advised the prince to enter the priesthood and flee to the northern provinces. I am sure Yoshinaka will try to raise him to the throne."

But someone said: "How is it possible for a prince who has returned to lay life from the priesthood to succeed to the throne?"

"What absurdities you speak!" replied Tokitada. "It is possible

[465]

because there are some precedents set by tonsured princes in other countries. In our land too, when Emperor Temmu was crown prince, he was attacked by Prince Ōtomo, and so he entered the priesthood and fled to Mount Yoshino. After Prince Ōtomo had been destroyed, he came back again to the capital and succeeded to the throne. Empress Kōken too was once so deeply impressed by the teachings of the Buddha that she laid aside her sovereignty and took the tonsure. She thenceforth called herself by the Buddhist name of Hōkini. But some time afterward she resumed the throne and changed her name to Shōtoku. There is no reason why Yoshinaka should not make this former priest emperor."

On the second day of the ninth month of the year, the cloistered emperor sent an envoy to the Ise Shrine. The envoy was State Councilor Naganori. For an abdicated emperor's dispatch of an envoy to the Ise Shrine there were three examples set by Shujaku, Shirakawa, and Toba. But all of these missions had been sent before the emperors had entered the priesthood. This was therefore the first time that an abdicated emperor had sent an envoy to the Ise Shrine after he had entered the priesthood.

---

[1] At some point Yoshinaka gave himself this title, which has never been considered official.

[2] Tokitada's sister was the wife of Go-Shirakawa, so his entire family enjoyed greater privilege than the rest of the Heike; Tokizane was his son and Nobumoto a cousin.

[3] Iki and Tsushima are small islands off the coast of Kyushu.

[4] A native of Chikuzen Province in Kyushu, he was deputy-director of Dazai.

[5] One of the five great fierce forms of the Buddha that destroy all evil spirits.

[6] A disciple of Enchin of Mount Hiei, he mastered esoteric Buddhism. When Emperor Seiwa was tormented by the angry spirit of Michizane, Son-i was requested to dispel it.

CHAPTER III

BALL OF THREAD

In Kyushu the nobles and courtiers of the Heike held a council to discuss plans for establishing the court, but they found it difficult even to decide the site of a new capital. Thus it was that Emperor Antoku was obliged to live at Iwado[1] in the house of Ōkura no Tanenao, a petty official, and his retainers were left in the fields and farms without roofs over their heads. Save for the sound of a mallet beating hemp, this out-of-the-way place was just like the hamlet of Tōchi.[2] The Heike nobles recalled the temporary country palace[3] of Empress Saimei that had been built of logs. They soon began to enjoy the rustic beauty of their new place.

At this time Emperor Antoku took a trip to the shrine at Usa. There the house of the chief priest was rearranged to serve as his palace. The nobles and courtiers of the Heike made their abode in the main building of the shrine. The courtyard was filled with the warriors of Shikoku and Kyushu in full armor with bows and swords in their hands. It seemed that the faded vermillion of the shrine fence now resumed its ancient brilliance. There the Heike spent seven days and nights to offer their prayers. Toward dawn on the last night of the seven days, Munemori had a dream in which he received a sign from the god of the shrine. He saw the door of the inner shrine open from the inside and heard a solemn and noble voice recite the following poem:

> The god pays no heed
> To your earthly petition
> To dispel your gloom.[4]
> Now can you tell me for what
> You tax your ingenuity?[5]

Upon awaking from the dream, Munemori found his heart beating fast. He mumbled this old poem:

My remaining hope
And the chirping of insects
This autumn evening
Have become weak and wretched—
Whatever will be will be.

It was the end of the first third of the ninth month. Slender reeds bowed down in the evening gusts of wind. Lying alone on a hard bed, every man thought of his wife at home and wet his sleeves with tears. Pathos in waning autumn makes anyone, at any place, feel melancholy—how much more so when one is on a journey! The moon of the thirteenth day of the ninth month was bright, but it was only a blur to the tearful eyes of the Heike. They remembered the moon when it had shone upon the palace in Kyoto in the days of their grandeur. Tadanori lamented his fate:

Those with whom I saw
The moon of the selfsame night
In Kyoto last year
Must be thinking of me now
As long as they are still there.

Tsunemori too penned a verse:

This moon reminds me
Of a woman whom I left
In the capital.
It was this night of last year
That she lay awake all night.

Tsunemasa's poem was:

I have come thus far
Through the thickets of wild grass
From the capital,
Sustaining a dewlike life,
Only to see this sad moon!

At that time the province of Bungo was the fief of Lord High Marshal Yorisuke. Having remained in the capital, he had sent his son, Yoritsune, to be his subordinate in that province. Now Yoritsune received a letter from his father in the capital. It read: "The Heike have been forsaken by heaven and the imperial family. Driven out of the capital, they are now fugitives, or no more than exiles, adrift here and there on the waves. It is therefore absurd that the people of Kyushu should treat them warmly. Let them do as they please, but not in my province. Unite your warriors to stand with the Genji against the Heike and expel them from my territory."

Upon reading this letter, Yoritsune summoned Ogata no Saburō Koreyoshi, a native of Bungo Province, and ordered him to dispel the Heike. Now Koreyoshi was a descendant of a terrible man. Here is a story about him. In a mountain village of Bungo Province there lived a young girl. She was the only daughter of a prominent family. Though she was not married, she was visited by a certain man every night. She kept it secret even from her mother. After some months, however, she came to be with child. Thinking this very strange, her mother asked her: "The man who visits you—what kind of man is he?"

"I only see him come," replied the girl, "but I never see him go."

"Well, then, my dear," said the mother, "fasten something to him and tie a thread to it so that you can trace him."

So the girl, heeding her mother's advice, stuck a needle into the collar of her lover's light blue hunting suit, to which she affixed the end of a ball of thread. Before dawn he left silently. She followed the thread as it led her. She walked on and on until she came to the border of Bungo and Hyūga provinces. There she saw the thread leading into the mouth of a great cave at the foot of a peak called Uba-ga-Take. When she stood at the mouth of the cave, she heard someone groaning within. She cried out into the cave: "It is I. I have come this far to have a look at you."

At her words, a response came from the cave: "I am not in the shape of a man. If you see me, your soul will depart from your body from the shock. Now go back to your home! The child you bear will be a boy. He will grow up to be a fine warrior. In the two islands of Kyushu there will be none to equal him in the arts of bow and sword."

These words did not satisfy the girl, and so she pleaded again: "I do not care what form you wear. How can you forget our binding ties? I want to see you, and I want you to see me."

In answer to her request, from the cave crawled forth a monstrous snake, five or six shaku across when lying in a coil, and fourteen or fifteen jō from head to tail when lying outstretched. The earth rumbled as it came slithering out. The needle that she had stuck in the collar of her lover's suit was now seen piercing the windpipe of the snake. The girl was struck by terror. Her attendants, who had accompanied her to the cave, shrieked with fear and fled.

The girl returned to her home and was soon delivered of a boy. He was taken care of by his great-grandfather, Daitayū. He grew up so fast that he was tall and huge before he was ten years old. At seven his coming of age was celebrated, and he was named Daita after his great-grandfather. As his hands and feet were raw and rough in winter and summer, he was nicknamed "Chapped Daita."

It is said that the monstrous serpent was an incarnation of the god of the Takachiho Shrine, who was worshiped in the province of Hyūga. Koreyoshi was the fifth-generation descendant of this god's formidable offspring, the warrior Daita. When he circulated the governor's letter as an edict of the cloistered emperor, all chief warriors on the two islands of Kyushu obeyed him.

[1] A village in Tsukushi, Chikuzen Province.

[2] A remote village in Yamato Province. The Japanese word tōchi can also mean "far land."

[3] When Empress Saimei (A.D. 655–661) decided to lead an army to Korea, she built a temporary palace at Asakura in Chikuzen Province to serve as headquarters for her expedition.

[4] The Japanese for "gloom" is usa.

[5] The Japanese for "tax" is pronounced tsukushi, which is the ancient name for Kyushu.

CHAPTER IV

THE HEIKE'S FLIGHT FROM DAZAIFU

No sooner had the Heike decided on the site of a new capital at Dazaifu than they heard that Koreyoshi had turned against them. They were upset, but Lord Tokitada said: "Koreyoshi was once a retainer of Lord Shigemori. Perhaps his son, Sukemori, might go to negotiate a settlement with him."

Lord Sukemori quickly agreed to this suggestion. At the head of some five hundred horsemen, Sukemori crossed over the mountains to the province of Bungo. There he did his best to negotiate peace, but Koreyoshi paid his persuasions no heed. To make matters worse, he grew more and more insulting and drove Sukemori away with these angry words: "I could arrest you at this very moment, if I wanted to. To arrest you, however, is only a trivial matter before great ones. In any case, there is nothing you can do to thwart me. Go back to Dazaifu at once, join your main force and do as you please."

Shortly afterward Koreyoshi sent his second son, Koremura, to Dazaifu with this message: "Since we have received many favors from the Heike from generation to generation, we wish we could take off our helmets and bows to be at your side. However, inasmuch as we have been ordered by the cloistered emperor to drive you away, we cannot let you stay here. We advise you simply to leave Kyushu at once."

To meet Koremura, Lord Tokitada wore a formal robe, a hakama laced with scarlet cords, and a ceremonial hat. He roared at Koremura: "The emperor whom we uphold is the forty-ninth-generation descendant in the pure line of the Sun Goddess, Amaterasu, and the eighty-first earthly sovereign since Emperor Jimmu. There is no other but our emperor capable of receiving holy support from the Sun Goddess and the great bodhisattva Hachiman. Above all, our late Priest-Premier destroyed the rebels both in the

Hōgen and Heiji eras. And it was he who summoned you, the men
of Kyushu, to the capital and gave you the opportunity to serve
at court. The barbarians of the north and east, in obedience to
Yoritomo and Yoshinaka, have raised a number of rebellions. They
may have promised to give you some provinces or manors as a
reward if you would side with them. Now understand how unreasonable you are to forget our ancestral favors and obey the
commands of that damnable Big-Nose Bungo !"

At that time the stewardship of Bungo Province belonged to
Lord High Marshal Yorisuke, whose nose was so large that he was
thus spoken of. Koremura returned to Bungo and reported Tokitada's resistance to his father, who exclaimed: "What? Old times
are old times. The present is the present. If the Heike react to
my advice in the same way as Tokitada, we must lose no time in
driving them out of Kyushu."

Upon hearing that Koreyoshi was gathering forces, two warriors of the Heike—Suesada and Morizumi—set out at the head of
three thousand horsemen to attack Koreyoshi, thinking that his
evil influence should not go unpunished.

As soon as they arrived at Takano-no-Honsho in Chikugo Province, they began a furious fight that continued for a day and a
night. Unable to hold their position against the repeated attacks of
Koreyoshi's soldiers, they were obliged to withdraw.

Some time afterward the Heike heard that thirty thousand horsemen of Koreyoshi had set out to attack them, and so, terrified,
they abandoned Dazaifu. Their hearts sank when they were obliged
to give up their abode at the shrine of Usa, for they had depended
upon the powers of the god of the shrine. As there were neither
proper palanquin for the emperor nor carriers, the emperor was
helped into a smaller palanquin that was barely more than a stretcher.
The court ladies of high rank, beginning with the mother of the
emperor, tucked up their skirts, and the nobles and courtiers, beginning with Minister Munemori, tucked up their robes as they
set out from Mizukinoto in Dazaifu and hurried to the port of
Hakozaki. The rain fell like shafts; the wind whirled up the sand.
Tears and raindrops rushed down their cheeks in torrents. When
they saw the shrines of Sumiyoshi, Hakozaki, Kashii, and Muna-
kata at some distance along the way, they offered prayers to each
of them, making their wishes as one—that the emperor might be

able to return to the capital. Crossing over the steep mountain of Tarumi and the vast dunes of Uzura-hama, their feet became torn and bloodied, for they were unaccustomed to walking on the rough roads. The blood stained the sand, and deepened the color of their skirt hems, turning them to red.

Long ago a Chinese priest named Hsüan-tsang[1] suffered great hardships in the desert and on the high mountains that lay to the north of India. But it seemed that his suffering had not been so severe as that of the Heike. Hsüan-tsang was able to endure it, for he was seeking a way to Buddhahood, not only for his own benefit but also for the salvation of mankind. The Heike, for their part, found it more than their flesh and blood could bear, since they had already suffered at the hands of their enemies. It seemed as if they were undergoing the first tortures of hell in this world, before entering those regions beyond the grave. Although they wished to go as far as Shiragi, Kudara, Kōrai, and Keitan, and even to the end of the sea and the sky, the wind and waves rose to oppose them. Now they were led by Hidetō, a descendant of Fujiwara Takaie, to take shelter at the castle of Yamaga. But, as they heard that the enemy had set out to attack them there, they got into small boats and fled by night to the beach at Yanagi in the province of Buzen. On the beach they hoped to set up the court. However, as the beach was narrow and their money was insufficient, they were unable to do so. And again they heard that the Genji were advancing toward them from Nagato, and so they boarded small fishing boats and wandered over the waves.

Major General Kiyotsune, the third son of Lord Shigemori, was a man of sensitive and meditative nature. One moonlit night he said to himself: "At the approach of the Genji we were obliged to flee from the capital. Driven out of Kyushu by Koreyoshi, we are now like a school of fish trapped in a net. To what land can we escape? There is no chance of living long."

So saying, he calmed his mind under the moon, standing by the gunwale of the boat playing the flute and singing rōei. Then, quietly chanting a sutra, he threw himself into the waves. All the men and women of the Heike lamented the self-destruction of Kiyotsune in vain, for he had already entered the world from which no traveler can return.

The province of Nagato was the fief of Lord Tomomori, the

[473]

new councilor. His deputy was Province Marshal Michisuke. Hearing that the Heike were forced to flee in small fishing boats, he chose a hundred larger vessels and presented them to the Heike, who re-embarked and sailed to Shikoku.

In Shikoku there was a warrior on the side of the Heike named Shigeyoshi. Because he was influential in that district, the Heike took advantage of his name to recruit more soldiers there. Then, on the shores of Yashima in Sanuki Province, they built huts from logs and planks so that the imperial rituals could be carried out. Even at a time like this the humble house of a commoner could not suffice as a temporary palace.

Thus it was that the emperor remained on board a boat; his seaborne abode creaked with each passing wave. The nobles and courtiers, including Minister Munemori, were obliged to spend their days and nights in the thatched huts of fishermen.

All of the Heike sank into melancholy, their hearts too heavy to be carried away on the ebb tide bathed in the moonlight. They trembled like frost-laden reeds, fearing that the wind's next breath would snap their fragile lives. At dawn the clamor of the sea plovers over the sand bar deepened their sorrow. At night, when the boats drew near the bluffs, the sound of the oars pierced their hearts. Seeing a flock of white herons in the distant pines, they were terrified, wondering if they were the white banners of the Genji. They shuddered at the cry of wild geese in flight, wondering if it was the sound of the enemy's boats. Exposed to the sea breeze, their black brows and handsome faces lost their radiance. Gazing at the blue sea, they recalled their bygone grandeurs in the capital. The jade green hangings over their scarlet bedchambers in former days were now replaced by reed hangings in crude cottages. In place of the fragrant smoke from their incense burners rose the briny flames from fishermen's driftwood. All these changes brought the ladies of the court infinite sorrow and endless tears. Eyebrows that had glistened grew dull from weeping. Beauty that had shone faded into nothing.

---

[1] (A.D. 597–662). Having studied in India for ten years, he returned to China at the age of 39 and translated 75 sutras (1330 vols.) into Chinese.

CHAPTER V

EDICT OF THE CLOISTERED EMPEROR

Thus, as the tale tells us, Yoritomo, who had remained at Kamakura, without making a trip to the capital, was to receive an imperial edict proclaiming him commander-in-chief against the barbarians.[1] It is said that the envoy was the secretary of the Left, Yasusada. On the fourteenth day of the tenth month, Yasusada arrived at Kamakura.

"Years ago I was punished by the emperor," said Yoritomo. "However, now that my fame as a military man has been established, I am honored by the title of commander-in-chief against the barbarians. I do not think it proper to receive an imperial edict at a private residence. Let me receive it at the new shrine of Hachiman."

Hachiman Shrine was located at Tsuruga-oka. It was very similar to Iwashimizu on Mount Otoko-yama, with long corridors and two-story gates. The paved path that led from the front gate to the location of the main image of the shrine was some ten chō long. A council was held to discuss who should first receive the edict. This honor went to Miura-no-suke Yoshizumi, for, in addition to the prestige of being a scion of Miura no Heitarō Tametsugi, he was a warrior of the highest skill in the art of the bow, renowned in all the twelve provinces of the Kantō District. His father, Yoshiaki, had fought to the death in battle for his master, Yoritomo. Yoritomo and his retainers had wished to brighten the dark path for Yoshiaki in the world beyond, and so bestowed this honor upon his son.

The envoy, Yasusada, was accompanied by two of his family retainers and ten of his warrior-retainers. The edict had been kept in the letter bag that one of his retainers had hung round his neck. Yoshizumi was also accompanied by two of his family retainers and ten of his warrior-retainers. The family retainers were Munezane and Yoshikazu. The warrior-retainers were men who had been summoned suddenly by the ten local lords under the command of Yoshizumi. To receive the edict, Yoshizumi wore armor laced with black silk cords over a brown battle robe and carried a sword in a black lacquered sheath. His quiver held twenty-four arrows feathered black and white. Each feather had a black bar in the center. Under his arm he held a black lacquered bow bound with rattan. He took off his helmet, hung it on his shoulder cord, and bowed as he received the edict.

"Who is to receive the edict?" asked Yasusada. "Let him declare his name and title."

At this request, Yoshizumi did not declare his real name and title, but improvised that of Miura no Arajirō Yoshizumi.[2] He did so, because he knew that the name and title of a warrior given by the provincial lord would mean nothing to a formal envoy from the capital. He received the edict in a casket woven of rattan and carried it to Yoritomo. After a short interval the casket was returned to Yasusada. Feeling it to be extremely heavy in his hands, he opened it, and found that the casket contained a hundred ryō of gold dust. Yasusada was then offered some saké in the outer oratory of the shrine. Meals were prepared by the aide to the chief official at the Kamo Shrine, Chikayoshi, and were carried to the banquet hall by a courtier of the fifth court rank. The food was rich; the tableware was elegant.

Yasusada was also presented with three horses. One of them was saddled and led by Suketsune, the former squad chief of the Guard of the Grand Empress Dowager. An ancient house, thatched with rushes, was refurbished to serve as a special lodging for Yasusada. In this house, upon opening an oblong lacquered chest, he found more gifts—two ryō of heavy silk and ten short-sleeved kimonos. In addition, a thousand rolls of white linen, some beautifully dyed with indigo patterns, were piled up as gifts for Yasusada.

The next day Yasusada paid a visit to Yoritomo at his mansion. Within and without the mansion grounds, he saw two large buildings, each about twenty jō long. In the outer building were ranked a great number of Yoritomo's retainers, sitting shoulder to shoulder, cross-legged. In the inner one the upper seats were occupied by all the lords of the Genji and the lower seats by all the lords summoned from the eastern provinces. Yasusada was seated at the head of the lords of the Genji. After a while he was led into one of the inner chambers, which was laid with fine straw mats edged with black and white brocade. The adjoining wide veranda was laid with similar mats edged with purple brocade. When Yasusada was seated there, a curtain was raised to disclose Yoritomo. He was dressed in a plain court robe and a high lacquered bonnet. His head was disproportionately large for his small body. He had a remarkably handsome countenance; his speech was that of an educated man.

"The Heike," began Yoritomo, "in fear of my power, fled from the capital. After they had gone, however, Yoshinaka and Yukiie took their places. Becoming proud and ambitious in their own ways, they demanded higher rank and position than they deserved, and showed their likes and dislikes for the provinces given them by the cloistered emperor. This was presumptuous! Hidehira and Taka-yoshi were appointed governors of Mutsu and Hitachi respectively. They have become arrogant and ignore my commands. Therefore I wish I could obtain an edict from the cloistered emperor to destroy them without delay."

"I understand," replied Yasusada. "I wish I could write my pledge to obtain the edict for you now. I am, however, still on duty as an envoy of the cloistered emperor, and so I cannot do so. As soon as I return to the capital, I will write to you. My younger brother, Shigeyoshi, will assist me in this matter."

"In my present position," replied Yoritomo, "I have no intention of receiving such a pledge from you and your brother. If I am to receive the pledge, it will be at your convenience."

Yasusada then said that he wanted to start back for the capital on that very day; however, he was persuaded to stay at Kamakura one more day.

The next day Yasusada visited Yoritomo. He was presented with more gifts: armor laced with light green silk cords, a sword studded with silver, a rattan-bound bow with a set of hunting arrows, and thirteen horses, three of which were accoutered. Furthermore, his twelve retainers received battle robes, short-sleeved kimonos, hakamas, and saddles. The horses that carried these gifts numbered more than thirty. At each station, from Kamakura to Kagami in Ōmi Province, they were supplied with ten koku of rice. Because it was much more than they could eat, it is said that they gave away some to the poor as they proceeded.

[477]

[1] Originally a temporary title given to Ōtomo Otomaro in 791 during his expedition to repulse the Ainu, the title became hereditary and effective for life after Yoritomo. Later its abbreviation *shōgun* ("commander") was used.

[2] His title, Miura-no-Suke, means "Aide to the Chief of the Miura Clan"; the name he improvised, "Violent Second Son of the Miura."

CHAPTER VI

LORD NEKOMA

As soon as Yasusada returned to the capital, he presented himself at the Cloistered Palace. Kneeling before the cloistered emperor in the courtyard, he reported all that had taken place in the east. The nobles and courtiers as well as the cloistered emperor were deeply impressed with his report. So lordly was Yoritomo that Yoshinaka, the present guardian of the capital, looked markedly inferior to him. Yoshinaka's conduct was rude; his speech was rustic. How could anyone who had been brought up in a wild mountain village like Kiso and who had spent most of his life in the provinces be expected to be any better?

One day a vice-councilor named Mitsutaka, who lived at Nekoma, or "Cat Room," paid a visit to Yoshinaka, hoping to discuss a certain problem with him. When he arrived at the mansion, one of Yoshinaka's retainers announced: "Lord Nekoma is here to see you, my lord."

Upon hearing his name, Yoshinaka exploded into a roar of laughter, saying: "A cat wants to see a man?"

"It is," replied the retainer, "a courtier with the title of vice-councilor from Nekoma, my lord. I understand that Nekoma is the name of the place where he lives."

" Well, then, show the knave in !" exclaimed Yoshinaka. Even after Lord Nekoma had been led into his presence, he still called him "Lord Neko" instead of his proper title. After a while he called to his retainer: "We don't see much of Lord Neko around here. Bring him some food."

Lord Nekoma politely declined his kind offer, saying: "No, thank you. I cannot eat just now."

"What's the matter? You came at mealtime, why will you not eat?"

Now Yoshinaka ordered his retainer to prepare a meal. To

Yoshinaka fresh food was anything unsalted. "Ah! Unsalted mushrooms! What a treat! Bring them quickly!" he bellowed.

His retainer, Koyata, in his provincial manner, served a mountainous load of rice in an extremely large deep bowl, three dishes of fish and vegetables, and, of course, a bowl of mushroom soup. When the feast was brought in before Yoshinaka, he immediately seized his chopsticks and began to eat. Lord Nekoma lost his appetite at the sight of the filthy bowls. He could not take the first bite. Seeing his reluctance, Yoshinaka urged him to eat: "These are the bowls I use in ceremonial banquets—not ordinary bowls, do you understand?"

Fearing that he might be rude to Yoshinaka if he ate nothing, Lord Nekoma took up his chopsticks and pretended to eat, only poking at the offered food. Yoshinaka, however, perceived this, saying: "Lord Neko, you have a small appetite. They say that a cat has the habit of leaving a meal unfinished. I see now that this is true. Eat, you fool!"

Lord Nekoma was now in no mood to stay, and so he begged his leave in haste, without mentioning what he had wished to discuss.

Inasmuch as Yoshinaka had been listed on the scroll of visitors at court, he was well aware that he should wear a ceremonial dress for his attendance there. But clad in the hakama and high formal hat, Yoshinaka appeared stiff and clumsy. One day Yoshinaka went to the Cloistered Palace dressed in this awkward manner. He entered an ox-drawn carriage and lounged carelessly as the carriage proceeded. In contrast to Yoshinaka's splendid demeanor in battle dress, this slumping figure appeared truly ridiculous.

The carriage and its ox tender had belonged to Lord Munemori of the Heike before he fled to the western provinces. Since it was common practice that one should yield to a victor, this ox tender was now in attendance upon Yoshinaka. But in his heart he was not pleased with Yoshinaka's rustic manners. The ox had not been driven for some time, and so, once out of its shed, it was easily agitated. To make matters worse, the ox tender cracked a mighty whip as they passed through the gate. Indeed this was inexcusable, for they flew off at a gallop. As the carriage jerked forward, Yoshinaka lost his balance and toppled onto his back. He struggled again and again to get up, with the long sleeves of his ceremonial robe spreading out on each side like the wings of a huge butterfly confined in a cage. Instead of calling his ox tender by his proper name, he cried out: "You, stupid calf tender! You simple swine!"

Hearing these words, the ox tender misunderstood Yoshinaka. Because of his master's provincial accent he thought that he was being ordered to spur on the ox, and so they continued at a gallop for about five or six chō. Yoshinaka's retainer, Kanehira, whipped his horse to overtake them and shouted to the ox tender: "What do you mean by driving so wildly?"

"I suppose," replied the ox tender, "the ox is afraid of its own nose, sir." Then wishing to reconcile with Yoshinaka, he shouted into the carriage: "Please hold on to the handrail at your side, my lord."

"That is an idea! Here we go!" replied Yoshinaka. "You there, calf tender! Tell me, is this your own idea? Or is this the way your former master used to do things?"

Upon arriving at the Cloistered Palace, the ox was released. When Yoshinaka was to get down, however, he tried to step from the rear of the carriage. Seeing this, one of his servants who was a native of the capital corrected him: "My lord, it is proper to enter from the rear. But when alighting, it is proper to get down from the front."

"This is only a carriage," replied Yoshinaka as he stepped out at the rear, "but how can I pass through it without paying my respects to the place where I came in?"

CHAPTER VII

THE FIGHT AT MIZUSHIMA

Now that the Heike had settled down at Yashima in Sanuki Province, they dispatched their armies to the fourteen neighboring provinces. Eight armies along the Sanyō-dō highway and six along the Nankai-dō had succeeded in subjugating them all. When these defeats were reported, Yoshinaka became angry and ordered more than seven thousand horsemen to set out immediately to destroy the Heike. They were led by the commander-in-chief, Yoshikiyo, who was assisted by a general, Yukihiro.[1] They first went along the Sanyō-dō highway to the bay of Mizushima, where they prepared boats to cross the Inland Sea to Yashima. Now they were ready to sail at any time.

On the first day of the tenth month of the year, there appeared on the waves in the bay of Mizushima a small craft. It was being rowed straight toward the Genji. At first, they thought it was only a fishing boat, but they soon found it was from the Heike and was carrying a letter of challenge. The boats of the Genji had been drawn up on the shore, and so they hurried to push them into the water, shouting: "Yo-heave-ho! Yo-heave-ho!"

The Heike appeared with a fleet of a thousand. Their commanders were Tomomori, at the head of the fleet, and Noritsune, at the rear. Now Noritsune cried out to his men: "Hear this, fellow seamen! A fight can be as quick as lightning. Let me see how brave you are! May you suffer in shame if you are taken alive by those uncivilized boors of the north! Advance together! Go closer to each other. Fasten your boats alongside each other."

At this command, they linked their boats tightly with hawsers at bow and stern, and over the hawsers stretched planks for moving about. Thus it was that the whole fleet was like a field spacious enough for battle.

Now the Genji and the Heike shouted their war cries and let

fly their turnip-headed arrows. The battle raged as their boats drew closer. The distant foe were shot; those nearby were slain with swords. Some used long rakes to pull their opponents into the water. Some grappled with each other and fell into the waves. Some stabbed each other.

After a while the Genji general, Yukihiro, was killed. Seeing his general dead, the commander-in-chief of the Genji, Yoshikiyo, sprang into a small boat with six of his retainers and advanced to the forefront of the battle. Thus was he fighting gallantly when his boat suddenly sank and all on board were drowned. The Heike had brought with them saddled horses; and so, as they approached the beach, they pushed them overboard. Then, jumping onto their horses, the Heike warriors galloped into the enemy with a shout. The Genji were dismayed by the deaths of their commanders. Overwhelmed by the horses of the Heike, they became confused and fled. With this victory, the Heike wiped away the shame of their former defeats.

[1] A son of Yukichika, a native of Shinano Province.

CHAPTER VIII

THE DEATH OF SENO-O NO KANEYASU

When Yoshinaka heard of the Genji defeat at Mizushima, he was incensed and hurried to the province of Bitchū with ten thousand horsemen. On the side of the Heike, Kaneyasu, a native of Bitchū Province, lay in wait for the Genji at Bizen.

Some time before, during the battle at Kurikara, Kaneyasu had been taken alive by Narizumi of the Genji, a native of Kaga Province, and had been under the custody of Narizumi's younger brother, Nariuji. Since he was a valiant warrior of great strength, Yoshinaka commended him and did not put him to death, exclaiming: "How can we let such a man die in vain!"

Nariuji too was pleased to get acquainted with a man of such high caliber as Kaneyasu, and so he treated him warmly. To stay alive as a captive far away from home, however, was a source of deep sorrow even in ancient days. In China, for instance, Ssu Wu of Han was captured by the barbarians of Hu Kuo and suffered many trials and hardships. Another captive, Li Hsiao-ch'ing, was unable to return to Han in the end. Kaneyasu protected himself from the wind and rain with tanned leather sleeves and a rug. He overcame thirst and hunger with the milk and meat of wild beasts, and he possessed great spiritual determination. Outwardly he tried to serve the enemy's whims, leading a life scarcely different from that of a woodcutter or farmer. Inwardly he waited day and night for a chance to kill them and return home to see his master once more. One day Kaneyasu met with Nariuji and said: "Since the fifth month of the last year, my worthless life has been preserved. I think I am now able to choose my own master at my own will. If a war breaks out, I am determined to rush to the forefront of battle to give my life to Lord Yoshinaka. My manor, Seno-o, in the province of Bitchū, is abundant with grass, most suitable for feeding horses. You can tell your master that I am willing to turn over my manor to you if I can return there."

When Nariuji reported this offer to Yoshinaka, he was impressed and said: "What he says is reasonable! Take him with you as your guide. Go down to Seno-o ahead of me, before I move out with my main force. Let him prepare grass for the horses." This command was solemnly received by Nariuji, who immediately departed with Kaneyasu for the province of Bitchū.

At that time Kaneyasu's eldest son, Muneyasu, was still on the side of the Heike. When he heard that his father had been set free, he gathered some fifty faithful retainers under his command and came galloping to meet him. They met at the capital of Harima Province, and from there they continued on together. At the post station of Mitsuishi[1] in Bizen, Kaneyasu's former retainers appeared with some saké to celebrate his homecoming. Kaneyasu eagerly offered it to Nariuji and his thirty retainers. As the night wore on, Nariuji and his men fell into a stupor; Kaneyasu sprang at them and killed them all. From the time that the Genji prevailed over the Heike, the province of Bizen was the fief of Yukiie of the Genji, and so Kaneyasu proceeded to attack Yukiie's deputy at the provincial capital and put him to death also.

Now Kaneyasu sent messengers to all his retainers in the provinces of Bizen, Bitchū, and Bingo with this proclamation: "I, Kaneyasu, have been set free. Those who remember old favors that they have received from the Heike are requested to come to me. Now take to arms and follow me! Let us lie in wait for Yoshinaka and shoot an arrow of challenge at him."

Almost all of the young warriors in these provinces, however, had already been recruited by the Heike at Yashima. Foot soldiers, horses and weapons had also been gathered. Thus it was that only old, retired warriors stood up again at Kaneyasu's summons. They were clad in faded yellow battle robes dyed with persimmon juice. Some had put on short-sleeved kimonos and tucked them up into their girdles. They wore mended, worn-out or damaged body armor and had provided themselves with homemade bamboo quivers that held but few arrows.

This contingent of some two thousand men gathered at Kaneyasu's fortress near Fukuryūji-Nawate[2] in Bizen Province to prepare

[485]

it for battle. There they dug moats, two jō wide and two jō deep. They set up barricades of sharpened stakes and constructed high towers within the walls. With their arrows ready to loose, they could fight at a moment's notice.

Meanwhile, when the deputy governor of Bizen Province had been killed by Kaneyasu, his retainers fled to the capital. They met Yoshinaka and his army at Funasaka on the border of Harima and Bizen. When Yoshinaka heard what had happened, he fumed: "This is intolerable! I should have put Kaneyasu to death."

"Indeed," replied Kanehira. "I saw treachery in his face, and so I advised you a thousand times to cut off his head, but you spared his life. Well, the mistake is now in the past. He is no greater than other mortals. Now let me pursue him—to the death. I must begin at once. To whimper over our lost chances is a waste of time." With these words, Kanehira galloped to Fukuryūji at the head of three thousand horsemen.

The road that led to Kaneyasu's hideout was but one bow length wide.[3] On each side of this narrow road lay deep rice fields, where horses could not gain a foothold. Daring and dashing though the warriors were, they had to control their spirited horses as they went.

When Kanehira's army arrived at Fukuryūji, Kaneyasu climbed the tower of the fort, stood at the top, and roared at the enemy throng below: "From the fifth month of last year until recently, I was your captive. You were kind enough to spare my worthless life. For each and every one of you I have prepared a slight token of my thanks. Take this!"

These words had hardly been uttered when a hundred powerful bowmen, standing in rank, let fly a shower of arrows. The men of the Genji could not counterattack. Kanehira, however, took no heed of the arrows and galloped forward into the fray. He was followed by Chikatada, Koyata, Miyazaki, Suwa, and Fujisawa, each of whom could match a hundred men in strength. They bent low over their horses as they galloped forward so that the neckplates of their helmets might protect them. As men and horses were felled by arrows, they were replaced by others in seemingly endless succession. They plunged recklessly into rice fields till their horses sank up to their chests and bellies.

The battle raged all day long. When night had fallen, Kaneyasu found that most of his men had been killed or mortally wounded.

The fortress upon which he had relied was a shambles. Unable to put up further resistance, he made a retreat to the Itakura River in Bitchū Province. There he erected barricades of shields as he awaited the enemy. Kanehira soon followed and renewed the attack. The men under the command of Kaneyasu fought till their supply of arrows ran out. When they had no more, they fled.

As Kaneyasu was fleeing with only two of his retainers along the river to Mount Midoro, Narizumi appeared in pursuit of him. It was Narizumi who had captured Kaneyasu at the battle of Kurikara in the north. Since his younger brother, Nariuji, had been killed by Kaneyasu, he now wished to avenge him; so he whipped his horse, saying to himself: "I cannot let him flee. He is a scoundrel, if anyone ever was. I must take him alive again at all costs!"

He outdistanced all the others as he galloped on. Coming to within one chō of Kaneyasu, he called out in a loud voice: "You there! It is cowardly for a warrior to show his back to a foe. Turn back!"

At this point Kaneyasu was halfway across the river to the west. Upon hearing Narizumi's shouts, he halted his horse in the shallows and waited, facing his enemy. Narizumi charged him, grappled with him, and fell with him to the ground. They were both men of great strength, and so they rolled over and over, first one on top and then the other, until they came to a brink from which they fell into deep water. Narizumi was barely more than a stone in the water, while Kaneyasu was an excellent swimmer. Thus it was that Kaneyasu pressed Narizumi to the bottom, drew a dagger from his girdle, pulled up the skirt of his opponent's armor, and stabbed him so deeply three times that even the hilt and his fist went into Narizumi's belly. The struggle was over when Kaneyasu cut off the head of his enemy. Since his horse was exhausted, he mounted Narizumi's horse and rode off.

Kaneyasu's eldest son, Muneyasu, was only twenty-two years old, but he was so stout that he could run no more than one chō. His horse lost, Muneyasu was running away on foot with his retainer when his father overtook him. Because of his great bulk Muneyasu finally exhausted himself; so even without his armor and weapon, he could neither run nor walk. Kaneyasu felt obliged to leave him behind. After he had ridden on more than ten chō, however, he regretted forsaking his son and said to one of his retainers: "I,

Kaneyasu, have fought many times. At each and every fight I feared no man. The sun shone upon my fighting spirit! But today I feel terribly sad, for I have left my son behind. Everything is growing dark before my eyes. Even if I manage to escape alive and join my friends on the side of the Heike, I know they will rebuke me, saying, 'Kaneyasu is now already sixty years old. How many years more can he live? To cling to the short road of life, he has fled, leaving his only son behind.' I would be very much ashamed of this."

"That is what I told you, my master," replied the retainer. "I told you that you should share the fate of your son. Please go back to him."

Without hearing his retainer to the end, Kaneyasu galloped back to his son. Muneyasu was lying on his back by the road, his feet grossly swollen.

"Cheer up, my son!" said Kaneyasu, as he alighted from his horse, "I have come back to stay by you. See, I am here to die with you."

"Such a worthless fellow I am!" replied Muneyasu, weeping bitterly. "I must kill myself. If you put an end to yourself, my father, on my account, I will be guilty of committing one of the Five Cardinal Crimes of the Buddha's Law. I pray you, leave here at once."

"I have made up my mind. I cannot leave." So saying, Kaneyasu was about to sit down by his son, when Kanehira galloped up to them at the head of some fifty horsemen. Kaneyasu still had eight arrows in his quiver. Fixing them to his bow one after the other without pause, he shot down five or six men. Then, drawing his long sword, he first cut off the head of his son, and then dashed into the crowd of his enemy. He fought desperately, brandishing his blade, cutting off many heads, until at last he fell. His two retainers, though badly wounded, fought gallantly, in no way inferior to their master. Although they tried to kill themselves, they were taken alive. The day after the next they died. The heads of Kaneyasu and his two retainers were exposed to the people at the wood of Sagi in Bizen Province. When Yoshinaka inspected them, he said to himself: "Indeed, he is a man who deserves the honor of being called 'a match for a thousand!' I have failed in not sparing the life of this great warrior, a man who shall never be forgotten."

[1] Located near the border of Okayama and Hyōgo prefectures.
[2] The northern part of present-day Okayama City.
[3] The standard bow length is 2.3 m.

CHAPTER IX

THE BATTLE AT MURO-YAMA

Thus, as the tale tells us, Yoshinaka had been reorganizing his force at Manju-no-shō[1] in Bitchū Province. He was ready to move on to Yashima when he received a messenger from Kanemitsu, one of his protégés, whom he had left in charge of his mansion during his absence from the capital.

"I have come with news of Yukiie," said the messenger. "There is no one who should be more faithful to you, my lord. Yet he has coerced one of the favorite retainers of the cloistered emperor into defaming you. Please lay aside your expedition in the west for a while and return to the capital immediately."

Recognizing the importance of this report, Yoshinaka galloped day and night back to the capital. Yukiie admitted his offence and tried to avoid a clash with Yoshinaka. He therefore set out from the capital for the province of Harima by way of Tamba. Yoshinaka came back to the capital through the province of Settsu.

Meanwhile, the Heike crossed the Inland Sea aboard a thousand boats with the intent of launching another attack on Yoshinaka's army. A force of twenty thousand commanded by Tomomori, Shigehira, Moritsugi, Tadamitsu, and Kagekiyo entered Harima Province and occupied a position on the hill of Muro-yama. Now Yukiie, in Harima, must have thought that he would be able to regain Yoshinaka's favor if he attacked the Heike, so he advanced to Muro-yama with five hundred horsemen. The Heike divided their force into five armies. The first army, with two thousand horsemen, was commanded by Moritsugi; the second, with another two thousand, by Ienaga; the third, with three thousand, by Tadamitsu and Kagekiyo; the fourth, with another three thousand, by Shigehira; and the fifth, with ten thousand, by the commander-in-chief, Tomomori.

Yukiie's five hundred mounted soldiers made a thunderous assault upon their enemy. In receiving this attack, however, all the armies of the Heike, from the first to the fifth, merely pretended to fight seriously in order to let the enemy penetrate deep into their ranks. Then they planned to surround them with their vast numbers. After completely besieging them, the Heike began their charge upon the Genji with a roar. Although Yukiie found himself trapped, he was not daunted but was determined not to give up ground until he drew his last breath.

Many men of the Heike raced one another to catch Yukiie, yelling, "Let me grapple with the commander of the Genji," but none of them could gain on him. Among Tomomori's most trusted warriors, Kishichi-zaemon, Kihachi-zaemon, and Kikujūrō were killed by Yukiie.

Of the Genji, however, five hundred men had been reduced to only thirty. Enemy soldiers enveloped them like a thick fog. Though there was no hope for his escape, Yukiie dared to go back through the enemy lines and came out unscathed. Some twenty of his retainers survived the battle by retreating, but most of them were wounded. They took a boat from Takasago in Harima and sailed to Izumi. From there they crossed to the province of Kawachi and confined themselves in the stronghold of Nagano.[2]

With triumphs over the Genji in the battles of Mizushima and Muro-yama, the Heike increased their strength.

---

[1] One of twenty-eight manors belonging to the new Kumano Shrine, it was located in the north of present-day Kurashiki City, Okayama Prefecture.

[2] Present-day Kawachi-Nagano City at the western foot of Mount Kongō.

CHAPTER X

CAPTAIN TSUZUMI

Now a growing number of Genji warriors occupied every corner of the capital and began to pillage as they pleased. They even violated the sacred precincts of Kumano and Yahata and reaped the crops to feed themselves and their horses. They broke into storehouses to forage as they wished. Becoming more and more violent, they attacked citizens on the streets and robbed them of their clothing. Thus it was that the people in the capital said: "When the Heike ruled the capital, we only had a vague fear of the Priest-Premier. The men under his command did not strip us of our clothing. The Genji are now worse than the Heike."

To put an end to such violence the cloistered emperor sent a messenger to Yoshinaka. The message was borne by the captain of the Police Commissioners Division, Tomoyasu, who was the son of the governor of Iki Province, Tomochika. Because Tomoyasu was an excellent player of the *tsuzumi* drum, he was commonly known as Captain Tsuzumi. When Yoshinaka met him, he did not say anything in reply to the cloistered emperor's message but inquired: "Tell me why they call you Captain Tsuzumi. Is it because you have been beaten or slapped by so many people?"

Silenced by this blunt inquiry, he said nothing further to Yoshinaka but hurried back to the Cloistered Palace and said to Go-Shirakawa: "Your Majesty, Yoshinaka is an ignorant scoundrel. I believe he will become an enemy of the imperial house at any moment. I pray you to punish him at once."

Upon hearing of Yoshinaka's insolence, the cloistered emperor made up his mind to destroy him. Instead of warriors of high reputation, however, he summoned the notorious monks of Mount Hiei and Mii-dera through the intermediation of their chief priests. The nobles and courtiers also did their best to muster volunteers, but those who responded to the summons were such ne'er-do-wells as pebble shooters, begging priests, and prowling street loafers. When it was rumored that Yoshinaka was no longer favored by the cloistered emperor, the warriors of the five provinces of the Kidai District, who had first obeyed Yoshinaka, turned against him and stood by the cloistered emperor. The acting vice-governor of Shinano Province, one of the Genji's kinsmen, a man named Murakami no Saburō Motokuni, also abandoned Yoshinaka and went over to Go-Shirakawa.

Kanehira advised Yoshinaka: "You have terrible intentions, which we cannot take lightly. Your opponent this time is none but the cloistered emperor who has mastered the Buddha's Ten Precepts. How dare you stand against him? Out of due respect, take off your helmet and throw yourself at his feet."

At this admonition, however, Yoshinaka sprang up in a rage and exclaimed: "Since I set off from the province of Shinano, I have never turned my back on my enemies. I have won battles at Ōmi, Aida, Tonami, Kurosaka, Shiosaka, and Shinohara in the north, and at Fukuryūji, Sasa-no-Semari, and Itakura in the west. Even though it means that I must put myself in opposition to the sacred ruler who has mastered the Buddha's Ten Precepts I cannot, by any means, take off my helmet and bring myself to Yoritomo's knees. For a man who is ordered to guard the capital, what can be wrong with feeding a horse or taking a mount? The rice fields around the capital are abundant. Why can we not reap some of them to feed our horses? There is not sufficient rice for military use, so some of our young men go to the outskirts of the capital to forage from time to time. Can they be accused of wrongdoing? If they break into the mansions of ministers and princes, we cannot leave them unpunished. Should the cloistered emperor take up a trivial matter like this? It must be that Captain Tsuzumi has intrigued to overthrow me, Yoshinaka. Beat the damnable drum till it bursts. Lord Yoritomo will perhaps be interested in hearing of this. Fight gallantly!"

Most of Yoshinaka's soldiers had gone to the western provinces to fight against the Heike, and so there remained in the capital only six or seven thousand. Following Yoshinaka's usual superstitious habit, his force was divided into seven armies. The first, with ten thousand horsemen led by Kanehira, set out for Imagumano to attack the rear flank of the foe. The other six armies were ordered to move from the west to the east on the narrow roads in the central area of the capital until they were united at Shichijō on the banks of the Kamo River.

It was on the morning of the nineteenth day of the eleventh month that the fight broke out. At the Cloistered Palace at Hōjū-ji more than twenty thousand soldiers had remained waiting for Yoshinaka's force. For identification they wore pine branches on their helmets. When Yoshinaka arrived at the Cloistered Palace, he saw Captain Tsuzumi standing at the top of a clay wall on the west side of the palace with a ceremonial spear in one hand and an iron mace tipped with bells in the other. He was obviously the commander of the imperial force. That day he wore a red battle robe but was daring enough not to protect himself with armor. On his head, however, was a helmet, the front of which was decorated with the figures of the four sacred guards of the Buddha's Law.[1] From time to time he danced, swinging his iron mace. The bells on it rang as it swung. At this sight, the young nobles and courtiers burst into laughter, saying: "He lacks elegance! He must have been possessed by an evil spirit, a tengu."

Captain Tsuzumi cried out: "In days past, when an imperial edict was read, even the mute grasses and trees were reborn with flowers and fruit, and even the devils and demons brought themselves to the emperor's knees. Though imperial power is little esteemed in this degenerate age, how dare you shoot arrows against the cloistered emperor who has mastered the Buddha's Ten Precepts? You will find that your arrows fly back to your own bodies and your swords fall back upon you."

Yoshinaka ordered his men to shout a war cry to drown out Tsuzumi's words, adding: "Keep him quiet!"

At the roar of this war cry, Yoshinaka's army, stationed at Imagumano, rushed to the rear of the Cloistered Palace. They set fire to the heads of turnip-headed arrows and shot them into the palace. The wind was blowing hard at that moment, so the flames immediately shot up toward heaven and the whole sky sparkled. Captain Tsuzumi was the first to take to his heels. When the twenty thousand men of the imperial force saw their commander running away, they were seized with terror and followed him. They fled, on each other's heels, leaving their gear behind. They were so confused that those who took bows forgot to take arrows, and those who took arrows forgot to take bows. There were some who gripped the shafts of their sickle-bladed halberds upside down, piercing their own legs with the sharp blades as they dashed out and striking the earth with them. There were many whose bows became entangled in their swords and armor, so they abandoned them.

When they fled to Shichijō, another misfortune awaited the imperial force. This area had been guarded by the Genji from Settsu Province, who had sided with the imperial force. They had been ordered by the cloistered emperor to fall upon any of Yoshinaka's men fleeing from the palace. Therefore, they had taken up positions on rooftops, protected by shields and provided with heavy stones and missiles to throw down on the heads of the enemy. Thus when the fugitives of the imperial force came headlong in flight, they began to hurl stones at them.

The fugitives cried out: "We are on the side of the cloistered emperor. Make no mistake!"

"Be quiet!" retorted the Genji from Settsu Province. "We have an imperial order!" And then they shouted: "Let us kill them! Kill them all!"

The shower of stones fell without pause. Some fell from their horses and managed to crawl away; but others were killed, their heads and backs crushed.

The eastern end of Hachijō had been guarded by the monks of Mount Hiei. Among them, those who respected their own fame died in battle, and those who were shameless fled.

The lord chamberlain of the imperial ceremonies, Chikanari, clad in body armor laced with light green silk cords over a light blue hunting suit, was in flight upstream along the Kamo River when Kanehira came galloping up and loosed an arrow at him. It flew straight through his Adam's apple. Upon his death, however, the people commented: "A learned man such as Chikanari should not wear armor to meet such an ignominious end."

The acting vice-governor of Shinano Province, Motokuni, who had turned against Yoshinaka and had gone over to the cloistered emperor, was also shot down. Many men of high rank on the side of the imperial force, such as Tamekiyo, Nobukiyo, Mitsunaga, and his son Mitsutsune, were killed. Major General Masakata, the grandson of Councilor Sukekata, who went to do battle in armor and a high lacquered bonnet, was taken alive by Kanemitsu. Arch-

[495]

bishop Mei-un, the chief priest of the Tendai sect, and the princely abbot Enkei of Mii-dera had been staying at the Cloistered Palace; but when it became enveloped in flame and smoke, they fled on horseback to the banks of the Kamo River. There Yoshinaka's warriors let fly a shower of arrows at them. Mei-un and Enkei fell under this barrage, mortally wounded. They were then set upon, and their venerable heads were severed.

Yoshisuke, the lord high marshal and governor of Bungo Province, who held the third court rank, had also been staying at the Cloistered Palace. When it began to burn, he hastened away to the Kamo River. However, a warrior of low rank under the command of Yoshinaka stripped him of all rich garments and left him stark naked on the river beach. It was the morning of the nineteenth day of the eleventh month. The cold wind from the river pierced him to the bone. His elder brother-in-law, the priest Shōi, who had gone out to see the battle, happened to come up, noticed Yoshisuke in this plight, and ran straight to his side. Since he was wearing a priest's robe over two layers of short sleeved kimonos, he should have given Yoshisuke not only his priest's robe but one of his kimonos as well. Instead, he took off only his priest's robe and threw it upon Yoshisuke. Since Yoshisuke covered even his head with the robe, it was very short. Despite his miserable appearance, however, he walked slowly with his brother-in-law and some monks clad in white robes and stopped here and there, asking, "Whose house is that?" or "Whose mansion is this?" or "Where am I now?" Seeing this peculiar band of monks, all passers-by clapped their hands and burst into laughter.

As for the cloistered emperor, he was put into a palanquin and taken for refuge to some other palace. Not knowing who was in the palanquin, the warriors began to shoot arrows at it. Major General Munenaga from Bungo Province, who was escorting the cloistered emperor, cried out: "This is an imperial trip! Make no mistake!"

Hearing his warning, all the warriors dismounted from their horses and made obeisance. Upon His Majesty's inquiry, one of them stood forth and declared his name: "I am Yukitsuna, a native of Shinano Province."

He then escorted the palanquin to the palace at Gojō, where he kept the cloistered emperor under strict guard.

The child emperor, Go-Toba, was playing with the court ladies in a boat upon the pond at the Cloistered Palace. Unaware of the emperor's presence on board, the warriors shot many arrows at the boat. The lord chamberlain, Nobukiyo, and the governor of Kii Province, Norimitsu, were in the boat, and so one of them stood up and cried: "His Majesty, the emperor, is in this boat! Do not harm him!"

Immediately all the horsemen dismounted and bowed to the emperor. They then escorted him to the Leisure Palace. The sight of this imperial procession was wretched beyond description.

[1] The Kings of the Four Quarters.

CHAPTER XI

THE FIGHT AT HŌJŪ-JI

Among the men of the imperial force was the governor of Ōmi Province, Nakakane. He was guarding the western gate of the Cloistered Palace with some fifty horsemen when Yoshitaka, one of the kinsmen of the Genji from Ōmi Province, came galloping up and said: "Who is it that you are guarding here? The cloistered emperor and the reigning emperor have already gone to other places."

Upon hearing this, Nakakane spurred his horse with a shout and penetrated deep into the enemy lines. He fought desperately until his soldiers were cut down to eight. One of them was a warrior-priest of the Kusaka clan named Kaga-bō. He was riding a moon white horse with a hard mouth. He said to his master: "My horse is so spirited that I can hardly manage him."

To this complaint, Nakakane replied: "Take mine! He rides well."

Nakakane himself took a remount. It was a chestnut steed, whose tail was white at the tip. The eight warriors dashed with a thunderous battle cry deep into the army of two hundred horsemen under the command of Koyata, who had been lying in wait at Kawara-zaka. There they fought until only three of the eight were left alive. During the assault Kaga-bō, who had remounted his master's horse, met his end.

Among the family retainers of Nakakane was a warrior from Shinano Province, a man named Nakayori. While he was fighting recklessly, he lost sight of his master. He could see only a chestnut steed with a white-tipped tail galloping along without a rider, and so he asked his servant: "I understand this chestnut belongs to my master. He must be dead by now. We have pledged each other to die together. What a pity it is that we must die separately! Where was my master fighting?"

"He must have charged upon the enemy at Kawara-zaka," replied the servant, "because it is from that direction that his horse has come."

"Now listen to me," Nakayori said to the servant. "Get out of this fight. Go home and tell my wife and children how I have met my end."

Nakayori then dashed alone into battle and roared: "I am Shinano no Jirō Kurando Nakayori, the second son of the governor of Shinano Province, Nakashige, and the ninth-generation descendant of Prince Atsumi,[1] twenty-seven years old. Is there any one among you who thinks himself a great warrior? Let him stand forward!"

With these words of challenge, Nakayori fought, galloping back and forth, left and right, like a spider's legs, and then in the form of a cross. After he had killed many, he himself was killed.

His master, Nakakane, however, was still alive. Unaware of the gallant death of Nakayori, he galloped off toward the south with two retainers, one of whom was his own brother, Nakanobu. When they came to Mount Kohata, they happened to overtake the sesshō, Motomichi, on his way to refuge at Uji. The sesshō was frightened and stopped his carriage to ask their identities. Upon this inquiry, they gave their names.

"Frankly," said the sesshō, "I thought you might be some of those terrible warriors of Yoshinaka. Now I am pleased to meet you. Come close and guard me!"

Nakakane and Nakanobu escorted the sesshō as far as the Fuke Palace at Uji, and after parting from him, they fled to the province of Kawachi.

The next day, the twentieth, Yoshinaka went out to the banks of the Kamo River at Rokujō and inspected the heads of the fallen enemy. There were more than six hundred and thirty. Among them he found those of the chief priest of the Tendai sect, Mei-un, and the princely abbot of Ninna-ji, Enkei. Seeing the heads of these noble priests exposed for identification, the spectators wet their sleeves with tears. After his inspection, Yoshinaka ordered his seven thousand men to turn the heads of their horses toward the east and then to shout a cry of triumph three times. The heaven echoed; the earth rumbled. The people of the capital were again seized by

[499]

terror; however, it was soon known that it had been only a shout of triumphant joy.

State Councilor Naganori, the son of the late council secretary, Shinzei, went to visit the cloistered emperor at the palace at Gojō. He said to the guard: "I have something to tell the cloistered emperor. Make way!"

But the guard did not allow him to enter the palace. Unable to force his way in, he turned back to a small house nearby, which he knew well. In the house he cut off his hair and changed into the black robe of a recluse. He then went again to the palace, and said: "Since I am now a monk, you can have no objection. Now let me in!"

This time the guard gave in to his demand. When he entered into the august presence and reported to His Majesty all those who had been killed in the fight, Go-Shirakawa wept bitterly and said: "I had never thought that Mei-un would meet such a violent end, for he has been innocent of all sins in this world. Since my shameful life was endangered, he must have put an end to himself for my sake."

Yoshinaka summoned all his retainers and held a council, in which he exclaimed: "I, Yoshinaka, have raised my hand to His Majesty, the cloistered emperor, and I have triumphed over him. If I wished, I could be the emperor or cloistered emperor. To be an emperor, however, I must change my hair style to that of a child. That would be distasteful to me. To be a cloistered emperor, I must expose the shaved pate of a priest. That is also hateful. What else can I be? Ah, yes—the kampaku, that is what I would like to be!"

On this matter his secretary, Kakumei, advised him: "The kampaku is a hereditary title that belongs to the Fujiwara family in the pure line of Fujiwara no Kamatari. My lord, you belong to the Genji family. Therefore you cannot hold this title."

"Then let us forget it," Yoshinaka replied.

Thus it was that the council ended with the decision that Yoshinaka would become superintendent of the stables at the Cloistered Palace and receive the stewardship of Tamba Province. Foolishly Yoshinaka was ignorant of the fact that an abdicated emperor could be called a cloistered emperor only after entering the priesthood, and was unaware that the present emperor looked like a child only because he had not yet celebrated his coming of age. After a time he called for a daughter of the former kampaku, Fujiwara Motofusa, and made her his wife.

On the twenty-third day of the eleventh month of the year [1183], Yoshinaka imprisoned forty-nine nobles and courtiers after dismissing all of them from their offices. Under the control of the Heike the number of dismissals had not gone beyond forty-three. This proved that Yoshinaka was more tyrannical than Kiyomori.

Yoritomo, at Kamakura, had ordered his brothers, Noriyori and Yoshitsune, to go up to the capital in order to chastise Yoshinaka. When they arrived at Owari on their way to the capital, they heard a rumor that the Cloistered Palace had been burned and Yoshinaka had driven the world into darkness. This unexpected news made it difficult for them to carry out Yoritomo's original plan. Thinking it unwise to hurry on to the capital, they decided to bide their time at the Atsuta Shrine in Owari Province. As they were preparing a message for Yoritomo, two guards of the Cloistered Palace, Kintomo and Tokinari, galloped up to the shrine to tell them of all that had taken place in the capital.

"I think you had better go down to Kamakura yourself to report to Lord Yoritomo," Yoshitsune said to Kintomo. "A messenger bearing this kind of news must be well informed of the incident. Otherwise Lord Yoritomo will be unable to make fair judgment of the situation."

Thus advised, Kintomo galloped on to Kamakura. He was accompanied only by his son, Kinmochi, a boy of fifteen. All of his other retainers had fled in fear of war.

When they arrived at Kamakura and related circumstances in the capital, Yoritomo was greatly shocked, but he composed himself and said: "First, Captain Tsuzumi is to be accused of causing the burning of the Cloistered Palace and the death of the noble priests by his presumptuous agitation. He is an offender of the Imperial Law! If the cloistered emperor keeps him at his side, he will soon bring another calamity upon himself."

He immediately sent a message to the cloistered emperor, expressing his anger. Then, Captain Tsuzumi, to establish his innocence, galloped day and night to Kamakura and demanded a private audience with Yoritomo. But Yoritomo shouted to his retainer: "Keep him away! Do not allow him to enter!"

Captain Tsuzumi, not frightened by this heated refusal, went day after day to the mansion of Yoritomo. After all these vain efforts, he was greatly humiliated and started back to the capital. It is said that he went to Inari and secluded himself from the world to sustain the dewdrop of his life.

Meanwhile, Yoshinaka sent a message to the Heike: "You are welcome to return to the capital. Let us unite and attack the east."

Munemori rejoiced at this request, but Tokitada and Tomomori expressed their opposition: "Though we are suffering hardships, how can we obey Yoshinaka and return to the capital? We must not forget that we still hold Antoku, who has mastered the Buddha's Ten Precepts and has risen to the supreme place of honor as emperor. You must reply to Yoshinaka with this command, 'Take off your helmet and surrender to the emperor!'" When the command reached the capital, however, Yoshinaka ignored it.

The former priest-kampaku, Motofusa, summoned Yoshinaka and said: "Kiyomori was an evil man, but he mitigated the punishment of the gods and the Buddha by means of charities. He contributed part of his personal income for the repair of the great pagoda on Mount Kōya and built the lighthouse island off the shore of Fukuhara. This was why he was able to maintain peace on land and sea for more than twenty years. The world cannot be ruled only by power. You must pardon all the nobles and courtiers who were dismissed from their offices for a slight offence to you."

Though Yoshinaka had seemed to be a man of nothing but violence, he gave in to Motofusa's advice and pardoned all the nobles and courtiers, allowing them to resume their offices. At the time Moroie, the son of Motofusa, was still only a lieutenant general and vice-councilor, and so Yoshinaka elevated him to be the minister and sesshō. The general of the Left, Jittei, had enjoyed the position of state minister, but he had been forced to resign from the office in favor of Moroie. It was thus that the people called Moroie the Indebted Minister.

On the tenth day of the twelfth month of the year, the cloistered emperor changed the court from the palace at Gojō to the mansion of the lord high chamberlain of the imperial household, Naritada, at Rokujō Nishi-no-Tōin. On the thirteenth day of the month, the year-end ceremonies were held, and then the ceremonies of conferment were performed. In these ceremonies Yoshinaka took the law unto himself.

Thus, as the tale tells us, the western provinces were ruled by the Heike, the eastern provinces by Yoritomo, and the capital by Yoshinaka. The circumstances were very similar to those during the dynasties of the first and second Han, when Wang Mang usurped the throne and ruled the country for eighteen years. The gates of all checkpoints around the capital were closed, and so the provincial tribute, be it official or personal, was no longer brought into the city. The people of the capital, high and low, therefore were like a school of fish in a pool where the water was decreasing day by day.

The years of calamity had passed, and the Juei era advanced into its third year.

¹ A son of Emperor Uda.

BOOK NINE

" After all his men had fled, . . . [Tomomori] made his way to the *beach* to retreat
. . . ."
—Book 9, Chapter XVII, page 564

CHAPTER I

THE HORSE IKEZUKI

On the first of the New Year days of the third year of the Juei era [1184], the New Year ceremonies were not held at the cloistered palace. Since only a temporary palace at Naritada's mansion at Rokujō Nishi-no-Tōin was available, the nobility could not perform court rituals in the traditional manner. Thus it was that none of the nobles and courtiers attended court, even at the palace of the reigning emperor.

The Heike too were unable to perform the traditional ceremonies. They were obliged to let the old year pass without them, far away from the capital, at Yashima in the province of Sanuki. Despite the presence of the emperor, the three consecutive New Year days were spent without celebration. No New Year banquet was held. The emperor offered no prayer to the Sun Goddess of the Great Ise Shrine. The ceremony of presenting the first trout of the year from Dazaifu to the emperor was not performed. The men traditionally sent from Kuzu in Yoshino did not come to play flutes and sing songs in celebration of the New Year. The men and women of the Heike lamented: "In times past whatever confusion came to the capital, we never passed as miserable a New Year as this."

Now, when the sun had increased its brilliance, when the winds over the shore had died, and when the aroma of spring had begun to fill the air, the Heike still shivered like tropical birds in frozen climes. They could do nothing but wait for a better turn of events and sigh, reminiscing about their elegant life in the capital. Soon on the banks of the Kamo River, the buds would spring out on the willow trees, and from south to north, in the fields and mountains around Kyoto, the plum trees would begin to bloom. The Heike remembered that they had spent the prime of spring among flowers or under trees. Bathed in the morning sunshine or evening moonlight, they had competed with one another in contests of football[1] and archery, writing poems and painting fans, identifying grasses and insects, or playing flutes and stringed instruments. As they lingered over their recollections of these bygone delights, their hearts sank into sorrow.

On the eleventh day of the first month of the year, Yoshinaka visited the cloistered emperor and declared that he would go to the western provinces to destroy the Heike. On the thirteenth day of the month, he was about to set off when he received news that Yoritomo had dispatched several thousand soldiers to punish him for his lawlessness in the capital, and that these armies had already arrived at the provinces of Mino and Ise. Frightened by this news, Yoshinaka immediately sent his armies to the bridges of Uji and ordered them to tear out the bridge planking. At that time, however, many of Yoshinaka's men had been sent to the west to fight the Heike, and so his forces remaining in the capital were much smaller than usual.

The Seta Bridge was to be attacked by Yoritomo's main force. For this reason Yoshinaka sent his most reliable retainer, Kanehira, at the head of eight hundred horsemen. Five hundred horsemen were sent to the Uji Bridge under the command of Nishina, Takanashi, and Yamada no Jirō. And to Imoarai, he sent his uncle, Yoshinori, at the head of three hundred horsemen.

Yoritomo ordered his brother Noriyori to lead the main force of the Genji and his other brother, Yoshitsune, the rear force. Their sixty thousand horsemen under the command of thirty renowned generals rushed to the two bridges.

Yoritomo had two peerless steeds called Ikezuki and Surusumi. Of the two, Ikezuki had been earnestly sought by Yoritomo's retainer Kagesue before he set off from Kamakura. Instead of Ikezuki, however, Yoritomo gave him Surusumi, saying: "I wish to keep Ikezuki for emergencies. Surusumi is also a fine horse, in no way inferior to Ikezuki."

But when Takatsuna visited Yoritomo, he, unbeknownst to anyone, presented Takatsuna with Ikezuki and said: "There are many men who covet the horse. Remember this and take him with you."

"I promise," replied Takatsuna, "that I will be the first to ford the Uji River. If you hear that I died during the fight at the river, assume that I was overtaken by another. If you hear that I am still alive, then you will know that I have succeeded in fording it in the lead."

All the warriors, from large or small estates, who happened to be with him at the time, whispered to one another: "He knows no modesty!"

The great force of Yoritomo marched on, one part crossing the mountains of Ashigara and the rest over Mount Hakone. Arriving at the dunes of Ukishima in the province of Suruga, Kagesue took up an elevated position from which he could view the great procession of horses below while Surusumi rested. Each horse was caparisoned with colorful trappings of his rider's choice. Some were led by the bridle, and some by the bit. Viewing this endless line of horses, a sense of contentment welled up in his heart, for he was able to find none superior to Surusumi. Then his eyes fell upon a horse that looked like Ikezuki, wearing a gold-studded saddle and trappings decorated with tassels. The horse was foaming at the mouth and uncontrollable, though it was led by many grooms. As the horse sprang into his sight, Kagesue dashed forward and inquired: "Whose horse is that?"

"The horse of Lord Takatsuna, sir," replied one of the grooms.

"My master is not fair!" exclaimed Kagesue. "I have been determined to die in battle, fighting with Yoshinaka's four greatest warriors and with the soldiers of the Heike renowned in the western provinces. But if my master wishes to treat me this way, I must change my mind. I shall fight Takatsuna instead and kill us both. May the deaths of two such valiant warriors bring woe to the force of our master, Yoritomo."

Knowing nothing of this, Takatsuna approached on another horse. Kagesue pondered his strategy: should he attack from behind and wrestle Takatsuna from his mount or should he charge him head on to make him fall? Wanting to speak to him, however, he cried out: "Takatsuna! Ikezuki has been given to you, has he not?"

Yoritomo's warning flashed through Takatsuna's mind. Kagesue too must have coveted Ikezuki.

"Yes, he is truly mine," replied Takatsuna. "I knew that our foes would destroy the bridges at Uji and Seta when they heard we were on our way up to the capital. To ford either of these rivers requires a stronger horse than I possessed. I thought of asking our master for Ikezuki, but when I heard that your request for him had been turned down, I gave up that idea. I then said to myself that if I could only have that horse, I would accept any punishment in the future. On the night before my departure from Kamakura, I won over his grooms and succeeded in stealing this peerless steed, Ikezuki. What do you think of that?"

Kagesue roared with laughter, satisfied by this explanation. "What a shame! I did not think to steal him myself!" he said, making way for Takatsuna.

¹ *Kemari*, a court game played with a deerskin ball.

CHAPTER II

RACE AT THE UJI RIVER

The horse given to Takatsuna was a dark chestnut, very well fed and stout. Because of the habit of snapping at anyone who approached, the horse was called Ikezuki, or "Mortal Eater." It is said that Ikezuki was a full two hands higher than ordinary horses. The horse given Kagesue was extremely bold and completely black. For this reason, it was called Surusumi, or "Charcoal." Both were superior animals, difficult to distinguish in quality.

When Yoritomo's force arrived at the province of Owari, it was divided into two. The main body was led by Noriyori. At the head of these more than thirty-five thousand horsemen marched the valiant warriors Nobuyoshi, Tōmitsu, Tadayori, Kanenobu, Shige-nari, Shigetomo, Naozane, and Noritsuna. They soon reached Noji and Shinohara in the province of Ōmi. The rear force was led by Yoshitsune. At the head of these more than twenty-five thousand horsemen marched Yoshisada, Koreyoshi, Shigetada, Kagesue, Ta-katsuna, Arisue, Shigesuke, and Shigesue. They reached the Uji Bridge by way of Iga Province. As expected, Yoshinaka's men had torn up the bridge planking, hammered piles into the riverbed, fastened nets to the piles, and built barricades of sharpened stakes.

It was now past the twentieth day of the first month. The snow on the high mountains of Hira and Shiga was gone, and the ice in the valleys had melted. The streams rushed in torrents. The Uji River rose high. The white capped waves surged against the banks, and the raging waters ran fast, roaring like a waterfall. Though daybreak had come, it was so dark that men could not be distinguished from horses, nor armor from saddles. The commander, Yoshitsune, stood by the river, looking over the running waters. Trying to read the hearts of his men, he asked: "What shall we do? Do we have to go over to Yodo or Imoarai, or should we wait here till the waters subside?"

In answer, Shigetada, who was then only twenty-one years old, stood forth and exclaimed: "Did we not discuss the problems concerning this river many times? Had an unknown sea or river suddenly risen before us, we would have indeed been dismayed. The waters of this river come directly from the lake in Ōmi Province, and so they will never subside, however long we may wait! Who can build a bridge in a flood like this? During the battle that was fought here in the Jishō era, Tadatsuna darted across the river like a man possessed. Let me, Shigetada, test the waters!"

Now Shigetada and five hundred horsemen of the Tan family[1] were ranged along the bank, ready to plunge into the stream when two warriors, whipping their chargers at breakneck speed, emerged downstream of Tachibana-no-Kojima-ga-saki in the direction of the Byōdō-in temple. One was Kagesue and the other Takatsuna. To the eyes of Shigetada's warriors, the two were galloping together in seeming companionship, but in reality they were racing each other to gain the lead. Kagesue was some six ken ahead when Takatsuna shouted at him: "This is the greatest river in all the western provinces. So be careful! Your saddle girth is loose. Tighten it!"

Heeding his warning, Kagesue dropped his reins, kicked his feet from the stirrups, leaned forward in the saddle, loosened the girth and tightened it afresh. While he was doing so, however, Takatsuna spurred his charger harder, gained the lead, and dashed into the river. Kagesue perceived that he had been tricked, so he sprang in after him, crying: "Takatsuna! You are thirsty for fame, but make no mistake—at the bottom of this river lies a net of ropes. Watch out!"

Takatsuna drew his sword, and as he advanced, cut the ropes that caught the feet of his charger. Ikezuki was the finest steed in the land. Undaunted by the swift current of the Uji River, the horse pushed ahead and leaped onto the opposite bank. Surusumi, however, was swept up halfway across and landed some distance downstream.

Now Takatsuna, rising high in his stirrups, cried out in a loud voice: "I am Sasaki no Shirō Takatsuna, the fourth son of Sasaki no Saburō Hideyoshi,[2] who was the ninth-generation descendant

of Emperor Uda. I am the first rider in the charge on the Uji River!
He who thinks himself worthy of accepting my steel—stand forth!
Let me fight him!" With this declaration, he dashed toward the
enemy position.

Shigetada had by this time ridden his horse into the waters.
The five hundred horsemen followed him. His horse, however, was
hit in the forehead by an arrow that had been loosed by Yamada
no Jirō from the far bank. The horse weakened, and so Shigetada
dismounted, using his bow as a pole to vault from the saddle.
Though the rushing waters swirled through his armor, he was
not deterred. Diving into the waves, he reached the far bank. He
was climbing the bank when someone caught him tightly from
behind. Shigetada demanded his name. "Shigechika," replied the
man.

Shigetada wanted to make sure, for his relationship to Shigechika was as a headgear father to his son. He asked again: "Are
you really Shigechika?"

"Yes, I am," replied Shigechika. "The waters are rushing so
fast that I followed, holding on to you."

"You can always rely on a man like me," said Shigetada, as he
grabbed him and tossed him to the bank.

Standing up, Shigechika cried out: "I am Ogushi no Jirō Shigechika, a native of Musashi Province. I am the first to ford the
Uji River on foot."

Hearing this boast, his friends and foes burst into great laughter.
Then Shigetada mounted a passing horse and sprang onto the bank.
At that moment there appeared in front of him a warrior wearing
armor laced with scarlet silk cords over a twilled silk battle robe
with a design of fish and waves. He rode a dapple gray with a gold-
studded saddle. Shigetada inquired: "Who is coming up to meet
me? Let me have your name!"

"I am Nagase no Hangan Shigetsuna," replied the man, "one
of Lord Yoshinaka's retainers."

"Let me cut off your head and make it the first sacrifice today
to the god of war!"[3] So said Shigetada, as he whipped his charger
alongside of Shigetsuna, grabbed him, threw him down to the
ground, twisted his head, and cut it off. He then had one of his
retainers, Chikatsune, hang the sacrifice from his saddle.

As the battle raged, Yoshinaka's men defended well for a while. But pressed by the great army of Yoritomo, they soon scattered and fled to Mount Kohata and Fushimi.

Meanwhile, Yoshinaka's army defending the Seta Bridge was also destroyed by the main force of Yoritomo under the command of Noriyori. One of his strategists, Shigenari, had made it possible to ford the river downstream at Kugo in Tanakami.[4]

[1] One of the seven large military clans in Musashi Province.

[2] A military man living at Sasaki-no-shō in Ōmi Province, he supported the Genji in the Hōgen and Heiji insurrections. When Yoritomo raised the standard of rebellion against the Heike, Hideyoshi sent his four sons to the headquarters of the Genji in Kamakura.

[3] It is not known if here, and elsewhere in the text, this is a reference to Hachiman.

[4] Whitebait caught in the shallows at Tanakami, at the southern end of present-day Ōtsu City, used to be served at the emperor's table. Hence this shallow area was called Kugo, or "Emperor's Table."

CHAPTER III

BATTLE ON THE RIVER BANK

As soon as the fight ended in defeat of Yoshinaka's force, a messenger was sent to Kamakura with a report for Yoritomo. Before reading the record of the battle, however, Yoritomo asked the messenger: "What did Takatsuna do?"

"He was the first rider in the charge on the Uji River, my lord."

Yoritomo unrolled the report and read: "The first rider in the charge on the Uji River was Takatsuna. The second was Kagesue."

When Yoshinaka heard that his armies at the Uji and Seta Bridges had lost their positions, he rode off to the Cloistered Palace at Rokujō to say farewell to the cloistered emperor. Within the palace the emperor and his retinue wrung their hands in terror, saying: "All is lost! What shall we do?"

They were making vows to the gods and the Buddha, as many as they could think of, when Yoshinaka arrived at the gate. It was then that Yoshinaka heard the enemy had already advanced to the Kamo River. Giving up the idea of bidding farewell to Go-Shirakawa, he turned away from the gate.

At that time there lived at Rokujō Takakura a lady with whom Yoshinaka had lately fallen in love. He went to her house for a visit. Unwilling to part from this lady, he did not leave her at once. Seeing that Yoshinaka was reluctant to depart, one of his retainers, Iemitsu, became irritated and called out to his master: "My lord, how can you relax at a time like this? The enemy is already on the banks of the Kamo River. If you stay here any longer, you will die a dog's death!"

Yoshinaka, however, paid no heed to this warning, and so Iemitsu decided to kill himself in protest.

"You have ignored my warning, my lord. Now let me go before you to the next world and lay myself on Mount Shide[1] to wait for

[515]

you." With these words on his lips, he cut open his belly and died.

At the death of his retainer, Yoshinaka regained his senses and said: "Iemitsu has killed himself to encourage me!" Abandoning his lady, he rushed out of the house.

Yoshinaka's soldiers now numbered only a hundred. At their head rode a native of Kōzuke Province named Hirozumi. When they rode toward the banks of the Kamo River at Rokujō, they saw coming to meet them some thirty horsemen of Yoritomo's force led by two warriors, Korehiro and Arinao. Korehiro proposed: "Let us not fight until we are supported by our main force."

"Inasmuch as the front lines of the enemy have already been destroyed," Arinao replied, "the rest of them must be demoralized. They will soon give in. Forward!"

Arinao then galloped into the enemy lines with a great shout. The battle raged. Yoshinaka fought desperately, determined to die that very day. Yoritomo's men vied with one another to put an end to Yoshinaka.

Meanwhile, Yoshitsune was worried about the safety of the cloistered emperor, so he left the fight to his retainers and urged his horse toward the palace at the head of five horsemen in full armor. At the Cloistered Palace, Naritada, the chamberlain of the Imperial Household, was standing on the top of the eastern wall watching the battle at a distance to see which side would gain the upper hand; his whole body was trembling in a fit of terror. Now he saw a few warriors galloping up to the palace. Their helmets were tied securely, and their bow-arm sleeves flew in the wind; they held the white banners of the Genji. A thick cloud of dust rose behind them.

"Yoshinaka is coming back. What are we to do?" Shouted Naritada. All at the palace were terrified. They thought their last moment had finally come.

But the voice of Naritada was heard again: "My report was wrong. These are the warriors of the east who entered the capital today. They wear an insignia different from Yoshinaka's."

Hardly had these words been spoken when Yoshitsune arrived at the gate. He alighted from his horse, and, pounding on the door, cried out: "Kurō Yoshitsune, a brother of the former aide to the chief of the Imperial Guard, Yoritomo, has come from the east. Please open the gate."

Hearing this, Naritada sprang up in delight. As he scrambled down the wall he slipped and hurt his back. But so great was his joy that though he could not walk, he crawled on all fours to report to Go-Shirakawa. His Majesty was so pleased that he immediately ordered his retainers to throw open the gate.

That day Yoshitsune wore armor laced with purple silk cords, shaded deeper at the bottom, over a red brocade battle robe. His helmet was decorated with a pair of golden horns. The sword at his side was studded with gold, and the arrows on his back were feathered black and white. He carried a bow bound with red lacquered rattan. A strip of white paper wound around one end indicated that he was a commander.

Coming out to the middle gate, the cloistered emperor viewed the warriors through the lattice window and exclaimed: "Gallant and reliable fellows! Let me hear their names."

At this command, Yoshitsune, Yoshisada, Shigetada, Kagesue, Takatsuna, and Shigesuke, declared themselves in loud voices. Though the colors of their armor varied, none was inferior to the other in bravery. Through Naritada the cloistered emperor ordered them to sit in the courtyard next to the wide veranda and speak about the battle. Yoshitsune made his obeisance to Go-Shirakawa and reported: "The lawless conduct of Yoshinaka greatly surprised my brother, Yoritomo, and so he has sent Noriyori and Yoshitsune at the head of some thirty warrior-generals[2] and sixty thousand horsemen to the capital to punish Yoshinaka. Noriyori is not yet here, but he is coming into the capital by way of Seta. I, Yoshitsune, have defeated one of Yoshinaka's armies at Uji and have been the first to hurry here to protect His Majesty. Yoshinaka is now running away to the north along the Kamo River. Since I ordered my men to attack him, his head must have been cut off by now."

At these brief straightforward words, the cloistered emperor was moved to great joy: "These warriors are to be highly commended! I fear that the remnants of Yoshinaka's band will come here again to do violence. Now let me see that this palace is well guarded."

Yoshitsune received this command respectfully and at once ordered his men to stand guard at every gate. Before long the number of his men around the palace increased to ten thousand.

Yoshinaka at first thought of seizing the cloistered emperor and taking him to the western provinces to join the force of the Heike. In preparation for this last resort, he ordered twenty servants of great strength to come along as bearers for the palanquin of the cloistered emperor. However, upon hearing that Yoshitsune had already placed his men on guard at the Cloistered Palace, he abandoned his plan and galloped into a crowd of Yoshitsune's soldiers with a great shout. Again and again he was faced with imminent death, but he galloped on. Tears rushed down his cheeks as he exclaimed: "If I had known of this catastrophe, I would never have sent Kanehira to Seta. Since childhood he has been my most trusted friend. We swore to each other that we would die together. Now it seems that we will fall separately. What a pity! Where is he now? I must find him."

In search of Kanehira he rode off to the north, from Rokujō to Sanjō, along the Kamo River, but attackers rushed him again and again. He made five or six charges into the swarming cloud of soldiers. With a small band of his own warriors, he finally succeeded in fording the Kamo and reaching Matsuzaka by way of Awataguchi.

In the previous year, when he had set off from Shinano Province, he had marched at the head of more than fifty thousand horsemen. Today, however, he was running away from the capital along the riverbank near Shinomiya[3] with but six retainers. So pitiful was his flight that it seemed as if he were already lost in that nether world in which travelers wander without destination for forty-nine days.[4]

---

[1] Literally "Death Journey." It is believed by Buddhists that the dead, whipped by the jailers of hell, cross over this mountain within seven days after death.

[2] *Samurai-taishō*, warrior-generals, were not authorized by the central government. They were usually the heads of small provincial military clans in the service of a more powerful family like the Heike or Genji.

[3] This river has since dried up.

[4] It is a Buddhist belief that when one dies, the soul departs the body to wander for forty-nine days before being reborn in the next world.

CHAPTER IV

THE DEATH OF YOSHINAKA

Yoshinaka had brought with him from Shinano Province two beautiful women, Tomoe and Yamabuki. Of the two, Yamabuki had become ill and had remained in the capital.

Tomoe was indescribably beautiful; the fairness of her face and the richness of her hair were startling to behold. Even so, she was a fearless rider and a woman skilled with the bow. Once her sword was drawn, even the gods and devils feared to fight against her. Indeed, she was a match for a thousand. Thus it was that whenever a war broke out, she armed herself with a strong bow and a great sword, and took a position among the leaders. In many battles she had won matchless fame. This time too she had survived, though all her companions had been killed or wounded. Tomoe was among the seven last riders.

At first the men of Yoritomo's force had thought that Yoshinaka would take the Tamba Road through Nagasaka or would cross over the Ryūge Pass toward the north. Instead, taking neither of these, Yoshinaka urged his horse toward Seta in search of Kanehira. Kanehira had held his position at Seta until Noriyori's repeated assaults had reduced his eight hundred men to fifty. He then ordered his men to roll up their banners and rode back toward the capital to ascertain his master's fate. He was galloping along the lakeshore of Uchide when he caught sight of Yoshinaka ahead of him at a distance of one chō. Recognizing each other, master and retainer spurred their horses to join each other. Seizing Kanehira's hands, Yoshinaka said: "I would have fought to the death on the banks of the Kamo at Rokujō. Simply because of you, however, I have galloped here through the enemy swarms."

"It was very kind of you, my lord," replied Kanehira. "I too would have fought to the death at Seta. But in fear of your uncertain fate, I have come this way."

"We are still tied by karma," said Yoshinaka. "There must be more of my men around here, for I have seen them scattered among the hills. Unroll the banner and raise it high!"

As soon as Kanehira unfurled the banner, many men who had been in flight from the capital and Seta saw it and rallied. They soon numbered more than three hundred.

"Since we still have so many men, let us try one last fight!" shouted Yoshinaka jubilantly. "Look! That band of soldiers over there! Whose army is that?"

"I hear," replied one of Yoshinaka's men, "that it is Tadayori's army, my lord."

"How many men are there in his army?"

"About six thousand, my lord."

"Just right!" cried out Yoshinaka. "Since we are determined to fight to the death, let us ride neck and neck with our valiant foes and die gallantly in their midst. Forward!"

Shouting, Yoshinaka dashed ahead. That day he wore armor laced with twilled silk cords over a red battle robe. His helmet was decorated with long golden horns. At his side hung a great sword studded with gold. He carried his quiver a little higher than usual on his back. Some eagle-feathered arrows still remained. Gripping his rattan-bound bow, he rode his famous horse, Oniashige.[1]

Rising high in his stirrups, he roared at the enemy: "You have often heard of me. Now take a good look at the captain of the Imperial Stables of the Left and governor of Iyo Province—Rising-Sun General Minamoto no Yoshinaka, that is who I am! I know that among you is Kai no Ichijōjirō Tadayori. We are fit opponents for each other. Cut off my head and show it to Yoritomo!"

At this challenge, Tadayori shouted to his men: "Now, hear this! He is the commander of our enemy. Let him not escape! All men—to the attack!"

Tadayori tried to seize Yoshinaka by surrounding him with his many men. Yoshinaka fought desperately, urging his horse into the six thousand, galloping back and forth, left and right, like a spider's legs. When he had dashed through the enemy, he found that his three hundred men had been cut down to fifty. Then he encountered another army of two thousand led by Sanehira. He continued on, attacking several other small bands of one or two hundred here and there, until at last his men were reduced to four. Tomoe was among the survivors.

Yoshinaka called her to his side and said: "You are a woman— leave now for wherever you like, quickly! As for me, I shall fight to the death. If I am wounded, I will kill myself. How ashamed I would be if people said that Yoshinaka was accompanied by a woman in his last fight."

Tomoe would not stir. After repeated pleas, however, she was finally convinced to leave.

"I wish I could find a strong opponent!" she said to herself. "Then I would show my master once more how well I can fight." She drew her horse aside to wait for the right opportunity.

Shortly thereafter, Moroshige of Musashi, a warrior renowned for his great strength, appeared at the head of thirty horsemen. Galloping alongside Moroshige, Tomoe grappled with him, pulled him against the pommel of her saddle, and giving him no chance to resist, cut off his head. The fight concluded, she threw off her armor and fled to the eastern provinces.

Among the remaining retainers of Yoshinaka, Tezuka no Tarō was killed, and his uncle, Tezuka no Bettō, took flight, leaving only Kanehira. When Yoshinaka found himself alone with Kanehira, he sighed: "My armor has never weighed upon me before, but today it is heavy."

"You do not look tired at all, my lord," replied Kanehira, "and your horse is still fresh. What makes it feel so heavy? If it is because you are discouraged at having none of your retainers but me, please remember that I, Kanehira, am a match for a thousand. Since I still have seven or eight arrows left in my quiver, let me hold back the foe while you withdraw to the Awazu pine wood. Now I pray you to put a peaceful end to yourself."

No sooner had he spoken to his master than another band of soldiers confronted them. "Please go to the pine wood, my lord," said Kanehira again. "Let me fight here to keep them away from you."

"I would have died in the capital!" replied Yoshinaka. "I have come this far with no other hope but to share your fate. How can I die apart from you? Let us fight until we die together!"

With these words, Yoshinaka tried to ride neck and neck with Kanehira. Now Kanehira alighted from his horse, seized the bridle of his master's mount, and pleaded in tears: "Whatever fame a warrior may win, a worthless death is a lasting shame for him. You are worn out, my lord. Your horse is also exhausted. If you are surrounded by the enemy and slain at the hand of a low, worthless retainer of some unknown warrior, it will be a great shame for you and me in the days to come. How disgraceful it would be if such a nameless fellow could declare, 'I cut off the head of Yoshinaka, renowned throughout the land of Japan!'"

Yoshinaka finally gave in to Kanehira's entreaty and rode off toward the pine wood of Awazu. Kanehira, riding alone, charged into the band of some fifty horsemen. Rising high in his stirrups, he cried out in a thunderous voice: "You have often heard of me. Now take a good look. I am Imai no Shirō Kanehira, aged thirty-three, the foster brother of Lord Yoshinaka. As I am a valiant warrior among the men of Lord Yoshinaka, your master, Yoritomo, at Kamakura must know my name well. Take my head and show it to him!"

Kanehira had hardly uttered these words when he let fly his remaining eight arrows one after another without pause. Eight men were shot from their horses, either dead or wounded. He then drew his sword and brandished it as he galloped to and fro. None of his opponents could challenge him face to face, though they cried out: "Shoot him down! Shoot him down!"

Sanehira's soldiers let fly a shower of arrows at Kanehira, but his armor was so strong that none of them pierced it. Unless they aimed at the joints of his armor, he could never be wounded.

Yoshinaka was now all alone in the pine wood of Awazu. It was the twenty-first day of the first month. Dusk had begun to fall. Thin ice covered the rice fields and the marsh, so that it was hard to distinguish one from the other. Thus it was that Yoshinaka had not gone far before his horse plunged deep into the muddy slime. Whipping and spurring no longer did any good. The horse could not stir. Despite his predicament, he still thought of Kanehira. As Yoshinaka was turning around to see how he fared, Tamehisa, catching up with him, shot an arrow under his helmet. It was a mortal wound. Yoshinaka pitched forward onto the neck of his horse. Then two of Tamehisa's retainers fell upon Yoshinaka and struck off his head. Raising it high on the point of his sword, Tame-hisa shouted: "Kiso no Yoshinaka, renowned throughout the land of Japan as a valiant warrior, has been killed by Miura no Ishida Jirō Tamehisa!"

Kanehira was fighting desperately as these words rang in his ears. At that moment he ceased fighting and cried out: "For whom do I have to fight now? You, warriors of the east, see how the mightiest warrior in Japan puts an end to himself!" Thrusting the point of his sword into his mouth, he flung himself headlong from his horse so that the sword pierced his head.

Yoshinaka and Kanehira died valiant deaths at Awazu. Could there have been a more heroic battle?

[1] Literally "Gray Demon."

CHAPTER V

THE EXECUTION OF KANEMITSU

K anehira's elder brother, Kane-
mitsu, had gone to the castle of Nagano in Kawachi Province to
destroy Yukiie. But upon arriving there, he discovered that Yukiie
had already fled to Nagusa in Kii Province. As Kanemitsu was
chasing Yukiie to Kii, he heard that war had broken out in the
capital. He immediately turned back toward the capital. Upon arriving at the bridge of Owatari at Yodo, he met one of Kanehira's
retainers, who inquired: "Where are you going, Your Excellency?
The war in the capital is over! I regret to report that our master,
Yoshinaka, was killed and my master, Kanehira, put an end to himself."

Kanemitsu burst into tears and said: "Hear this, everybody!
Any among you who wishes to show his loyalty to our lord, Yoshinaka, may leave here and go wherever he pleases. Take the tonsure,
carry a begging bowl, practice austerities, and pray for our lord's
peace and happiness in the afterlife. I, Kanemitsu, will go up to
the capital to fight to the death, hoping that I will again wait upon
our lord in the world beyond."

With these parting words, Kanemitsu rode toward the capital.
As he rode, however, his followers gradually departed one by one.
By the time he passed through the south gate of Toba, his force
of a hundred horsemen had been reduced to some twenty.

When the men of the east heard that Kanemitsu had come
back to the capital, several select groups of Yoritomo's soldiers
rushed to the gates of Shichijō, Shujaku, and Yotsuzuka to meet
him. One of Kanemitsu's retainers, Mitsuhiro, galloped into the
great mass of guards at the gate of Yotsuzuka and roared: "Are
there any present among you who are the retainers of Tadayori, a
native of Kai Province?"

At this inquiry, great laughter arose, and the guards replied:

"Why must you fight with none but the retainers of Tadayori? Take anyone! Do not choose your opponents!"

In answer to their contemptuous laughter, Mitsuhiro raised his voice again: "Do not misunderstand me! I am Chino no Tarō Mitsuhiro, a son of Chino no Taifu Mitsuie, a native of Suwano-Kami-no-Miya of Shinano Province. I do not mean to select my opponents from among the retainers of Tadayori alone, but my younger brother, Chino no Shichirō, is a member of his band. In my home province I have two children. When they grieve at the news of my death, they may still wonder how their father died, honorably or dishonorably. This is why I want to fight to the death before the eyes of my younger brother, Shichirō, so that he may tell my little ones how gallantly their father died. Among my opponents there is none whom I fear!"

Mitsuhiro galloped back and forth, left and right, and cut down three challengers. Riding alongside a fourth, he grappled with him, and fell with him to the ground. Then they stabbed each other to death.

The men of the Kodama clan had formerly been on close terms with Kanemitsu. Now they gathered together and said: "We men of bow and sword like to have a wide circle of friends. Even in time of war when we are obliged to stand against each other, we can still hope to be friends during a lull or spare each other's lives in the heat of battle. Kanemitsu used to be one of us. Why do we not extend aid to him now? As reward for our distinguished services in recent battles, we can plead with our lord for his life."

They then sent a messenger to Kanemitsu with the following note: "In times past you were renowned as one of the two greatest warriors of Yoshinaka, with no equal but for Kanehira. Your master, Yoshinaka, is dead. It is not your fault. Do not worry. Admit that you are beaten and join our ranks. We shall receive some reward from our lord for our great contribution in recent battles. In exchange for this, however, we will plead with him for your life. Then, if he spares your life, you may enter the priesthood and pray for your master's better fortune in the world beyond."

Valiant warrior though he was, thinking his life was drawing to an end, he surrendered to the Kodama clan. This was reported immediately to the commander, Yoshitsune, who, in turn, sent a petition on his behalf to the cloistered emperor.

The nobles and courtiers as well as the court ladies in attendance upon the cloistered emperor were unanimous in protesting against the petition: "At the time Yoshinaka's army stormed the palace at Hōjū-ji, they made a thunderous war cry, terrified His Majesty, set fire to the palace, drove us into the fire of hell, and put many men and women to death. The names of Kanehira and Kanemitsu were heard in every corner of the palace. It would be a terrible mistake to spare the life of such a devil."

On the twenty-second day of the month, the new sesshō, Moroie, who had been raised to that office by the tyrannical Yoshinaka, was forced to surrender his office to the former sesshō, Motomichi. Moroie was astounded by his sudden dismissal. The power he had dreamed of had been snatched away—after just sixty days. Of old, however, the kampaku Michikane had been in office for but seven days before he died. In comparison Moroie was fortunate. Even during his short span he was able to attend the ceremonies of the New Year and conferment; these would be sources of pleasant memories in his later days.

On the twenty-fourth day of the month, the heads of Yoshinaka and his four main retainers were brought into the capital and paraded through the streets. Though Kanemitsu had already been imprisoned, he begged again and again to accompany his dead master in the parade. This was permitted, and he walked behind the heads of his master and companions. The next day he was put to death.

It is said that Noriyori and Yoshitsune interceded for his life in every way possible, but the cloistered emperor had closed his heart and took no heed of their petitions, exclaiming: "Yoshinaka was proud of his four most valiant retainers, Kanehira, Kanemitsu, Chikatada, and Koyata. To spare the life of one of them is as dangerous as to keep a tiger at large. Kanemitsu must be put to death."

In China, when the power of Ch'in[1] declined and all provincial lords rose in rebellion like a swarm of bees, P'ei Kung was the first to enter the capital and occupy the palace of Hsien-yang. Even so, anticipating another fight with Hs'iang-yü, he made a greater effort to fortify the checkpoint of Han Ku. He neither sought beautiful women to indulge in carnal pleasures nor collected gold, silver, or polished gems for luxuries. Only after such austerity was he able to bring the whole country under his rule. Had Yoshinaka acted in accordance with Yoritomo's commands, he might have secured his position as did P'ei Kung.

Thus, as the tale tells us, the Heike had departed from the shore of Yashima in Sanuki Province in the winter of the previous year, and had crossed the Inland Sea to the bay of Naniwa in Settsu Province. Taking up their residence again at the old capital of Fukuhara, they built a stronghold at Ichi-no-tani as their rear gate to the west and another one at the woods of Ikuta as their main gate to the east. In these places—Fukuhara, Hyōgo, Itayado, and Suma —were encamped all the forces of the eight provinces of the Sanyō-dō District and those of the six provinces of the Nankai-dō District. They numbered a hundred thousand in all.

The area called Ichi-no-tani, with mountains to the north and a bay to the south, was an ideal military site. The entrance of the bay was extremely narrow, but the shore, along which stood steep cliffs, was spacious. The cliffs rose so high and straight that they looked like a standing screen. From the shallows of the bay to the cliffs, barricades of stones and sharpened stakes formed the first line of defense. In the deep water beyond the barricades were anchored great vessels, spread out like a shield. On the towers within the fort were stationed a throng of soldiers from Shikoku and Kyushu in full armor with bows and swords at the ready. This throng seemed as a storm cloud ready to burst, so great was its mass! Below the towers stood a legion of their saddled horses. Ceaseless was the roll of their war bells and drums. The silhouettes of their bows were like crescent moons, and the gleam of their blades like the shimmer of hoar frost in autumn. The red banners flowing aloft in the spring breeze seemed as the flames of a monstrous bonfire.

---

[1] The Ch'in dynasty.

CHAPTER VI

SIX BATTLES

After the Heike had moved to Fukuhara, their followers in Shikoku began to think of desertion. To begin with, the subordinate officials in the provinces of Awa and Sanuki wished to go over to the Genji in open rebellion against the Heike. They said: "We wonder if the Genji will believe our sudden change, for we have been on the side of the Heike up to now. First, we should take a few shots at the Heike. Thus proving our hostility to our former allies, we will go over to the Genji".

Upon hearing that the Vice-Councilor by the Main Gate, Norimori, and his two sons, Michimori and Noritsune, had occupied positions at Shimotsui in Bizen Province, the traitors set sail aboard ten boats to attack them.

When Noritsune learned of this, he was incensed: "What repulsive wretches they are! Till yesterday these fellows were no more than grass cutters, feeding our horses. Now they have turned traitor, have they not? Yes, they have! Kill them all! Let none escape!"

He pushed on into the sea with his men in a number of small boats to challenge the traitors. The men of Shikoku had only intended to shoot a few arrows as proof of their rebellion, so they at once made a prearranged retreat. Nevertheless they suffered heavily. Unable to flee to the capital, they arrived at the port of Fukura in Awaji Province.

In this island province there were two famous warriors of the Genji, Yoshitsugi and Yoshihisa. They were the youngest sons of the late captain of the Police Commissioners Division, Tameyoshi. Under their leadership the rebels fortified their stronghold in wait for the enemy. This war plan, however, was soon found useless under the relentless onslaught of Noritsune. Yoshitsugi was killed in the raging day-long battle. Yoshihisa, seriously wounded, cut open his own belly. The heads of the rebels numbered more than a hundred and thirty. Noritsune sent a messenger with a list of their names to Fukuhara to convey word of his victory.

Norimori set off for Fukuhara, while his two sons, hoping to deal with Kōno no Shirō Michinobu of Iyo Province, who had not answered the Heike's summons, made their way in the opposite direction and crossed over to Shikoku. The elder son, Michimori, arrived at the castle of Hanazono in Awa Province, and the younger son, Noritsune, at Yashima in Sanuki Province.

Upon hearing of the Heike's return to Shikoku, Michinobu crossed to the province of Aki to seek aid from his maternal uncle, Nuta no Jirō. When Noritsune learned of this, he wasted no time in setting sail from Yashima. Within the same day he arrived at Minoshima in Bingo Province. The next day he was before Nuta's castle, upon which he immediately made a violent assault. Nuta no Jirō and Michinobu encouraged each other to stamp out Noritsune's force. The battle raged all day and all night. Nuta no Jirō could see no hope of winning, so he laid down his arms and surrendered.

Michinobu, however, held on to his position until his five hundred men were cut down to fifty. He then began a retreat. Seeing Michinobu withdraw, one of Noritsune's warriors, Tamekazu, led two hundred horsemen in pursuit of him. Surrounded, Michinobu fought until his men were reduced to six. As they were retreating along a narrow path to the shore in order to escape by boat, Yoshinori, who was the son of Tamekazu and renowned as a powerful bowman, caught up with them and shot down another five men in the twinkling of an eye. Now only Michinobu and his retainer remained alive. Yoshinori then urged his horse alongside Michinobu's retainer, grappled with him, and they fell to the ground together. Michinobu loved this retainer above all others. He would have truly laid down his own life for his sake. At the moment that Yoshinori pressed him down and was about to cut off his head, Michinobu turned and saw the deadly struggle. Springing to his retainer's aid, he chopped off the head of Yoshinori as he was bending to deliver the final blow. He flung the severed head into a deep rice field nearby and shouted in a thunderous voice: "I am Kōno no Shirō Michinobu, aged twenty-one. You have just watched the way I fight! Are there any among you who think themselves great warriors? Let them come forward and stand in my way!"

Eluding his enemies, he carried his retainer on his shoulders, and dashed out of sight of his pursuers. Michinobu then escaped in a small boat to Iyo Province. Noritsune, though he had been unable to capture Michinobu, returned triumphantly to Fukuhara, dragging Michinobu's accomplice Nuta no Jirō.

At that time there was another traitor in the island province of Awaji, a man named Awa no Rokurō Tadakage. With a few men, he sailed for the capital on board two large boats loaded with weapons and provisions. When Noritsune learned of this, he set out in pursuit of Tadakage and overtook him off the shore of Nishinomiya. Tadakage turned back with his men to fight, but they were soundly defeated. Unable to put up any resistance, he escaped to the beach of Fukei in the province of Izumi.

Another traitor, in the province of Kii, a man named Tadayasu, heard of Tadakage's plight and galloped to his aid with a hundred horsemen. Noritsune soon made an assault on the united forces of Tadakage and Tadayasu. They fought for a full day and a full night. Seeing no chance of winning, Tadakage and Tadayasu fled to the capital, leaving their men behind to fend for themselves. Noritsune beheaded more than two hundred of the traitors and after exposing the heads to public view, returned to Fukuhara.

Shortly afterward Michinobu, who had fled to Iyo Province, joined two natives of Bungo Province, Koretaka and Koreyoshi and crossed over to the province of Bizen with more than two thousand soldiers. There they shut themselves up in the castle of Imagi and awaited the Heike attack. Noritsune soon set off from Fukuhara and galloped down to Imagi with three thousand horsemen. This time, however, Noritsune did not make an all-out, decisive assault, but meditated upon his war plan. "These rascals are tough!" he thought. "I must send for a larger army."

When Noritsune's plan was reported to the army entrenched in the castle, they thought that many tens of thousands of horsemen would be sent against them. By this time they had already fought enough to win fame and gain booty, and so they decided to withdraw, saying: "Our opponents are numerous! We are but a small army, hopeless to triumph over them. Let us retreat and rest."

Koretaka and Koreyoshi went by boat to Kyushu, and Michinobu crossed over the Inland Sea back to Iyo Province.

"No enemy stands before us now!" declared Noritsune, as he turned back to Fukuhara. Munemori and the rest of the Heike were all greatly pleased with Noritsune's repeated victories.

CHAPTER VII

MUSTER AT MIKUSA

On the twenty-ninth day of the
first month, Noriyori and Yoshitsune paid a visit to the cloistered
emperor and expressed their intention of marching into the western
provinces to destroy the Heike. Go-Shirakawa himself came out to
meet them and commanded: "Our court has maintained the Three
Sacred Treasures from the days of our ancestral gods. They are
the seal, the mirror, and the sword. Be careful! Bring them back
safely!"

At this command, Noriyori and Yoshitsune bowed respectfully
and left the palace.

On the fourth day of the second month of the year, the Heike
at Fukuhara quietly performed a Buddhist service to commemorate
the anniversary of Kiyomori's death. Days and months had passed
in struggle; the mournful spring that had deprived them of their
only leader, Kiyomori, in the preceding year, seemed to return.
If times had been better, they would have erected a great pagoda
and made lavish offerings to the priests and the Buddhas. But now
all they could do was lament their miserable fate in tears. There
still remained many men and women of the Heike who had once
flourished with high rank and title at court. Taking advantage of
the Buddhist service, they had a ceremony of conferment, thereby
promoting both priests and laymen. When the Vice-Councilor by
the Main Gate, Norimori, heard from Munemori that he would
be appointed councilor with the senior grade of the second court
rank, he refused these positions and titles and composed the following poem:

Like a pale mirage
My life passes before me.
I must be dreaming.

[532]

Promotion is nothing more
Than a dream of empty dreams.

The vice-governor of Suhō Province, Morozumi, the son of the
court secretary Moronao, was appointed court secretary. The aide
to the chief of the Munitions Division, Masaakira, was appointed
archivist of the fifth court rank.

Of old, when Masakado held sway over the eight eastern provinces and built the capital in the county of Sōma in the province
of Shimōsa, he called himself a prince of the blood in the line of
the Heike and established a court that consisted of a hundred officials. However, the office of the chief of the Calendars and Records
Division was left vacant. Unlike Masakado, the Heike at Fukuhara
had the right to perform the ceremonies of conferment: though they
had abandoned the capital, they had carried away with them the
reigning emperor of the pure line of the throne and the Three Sacred Treasures.

It was rumored that the Heike had already returned to Fukuhara
and would soon fight their way up to the capital. Their families,
who had been left behind in Kyoto, were greatly encouraged and
regained confidence. Prince Shōnin,[1] the chief priest of Entoku-in,[2]
had from time to time exchanged letters with Senshin Sōzu, a foster
son of Kiyomori, who had accompanied the Heike in their flight.
In one of these letters, Shōnin expressed sympathy with his old
friend in refuge: "It makes my heart bleed when I think of you
roaming homeless under the remote sky. Even so, no peace has
been restored to the capital." He then wrote the following poem at
the end of the letter:

My yearning for you
Is always hidden 'neath my face,
Be it ever great.
How I long to be with you
On the moon going westward.

When Senshin read this poem, he pressed it to his face and
burst into tears.

With the passage of days and months, Lord Koremori, the
lieutenant general of the third court rank, became preoccupied,
longing for his wife and children in Kyoto. Once in a while he was

able to communicate with his wife through traveling merchants. Her letters were full of complaints, telling of the misery of her life in the capital. Though he eagerly wished to live with her, fears of many hardships that would await his wife on the waves prevented him from sending for her. He was perpetually plagued by this dilemma—yearning for reunion, yet suppressing this desire.

Meanwhile, the Genji had first intended to attack the Heike at Fukuhara on the fourth day of the second month. However, because it was the anniversary of Kiyomori's death, they allowed the day to pass without executing their plan and gave the Heike time to perform a memorial service. The next day, the fifth, was an unpropitious day, for, according to the zodiac, the gate to the west was closed. The sixth day was also bad, for the calendar prohibited them from any venture or activity. Thus it was that they fixed the hour of the hare [6: 00 A.M.] on the seventh day to release the arrows declaring war upon the Heike at the gates of Ichi-no-tani.

Despite their decision to wait until the seventh day to begin the fight, the Genji on the fourth day, assuming it was a more propitious time for their departure, divided their force into two, the main and rear armies, and set out from the capital for the west. The main army was commanded by Noriyori and his aides, Nobuyoshi, Tōmitsu, Nagakiyo, Noriyoshi, and Yoshiyuki. They were assisted by Kagetoki and his three sons, Kagesue, Kagetaka, and Kageie, as well as Shigenari, Shigetomo, Yukishige, Tomomasa, Munemasa, Tomomitsu, Hirotsuna, Michitsuna, Sukenobu, Tokitsune, Shigeharu, Shigekage, Hiroyuki, Tadaie, Takaie, Yukihira, Shigemitsu, Takanao, Morinao, and Yukiyasu. At the head of more than fifty thousand horsemen, they set out at the hour of the dragon [8: 00 A.M.] on the fourth day and arrived at Koyano in Settsu Province at the hour of the monkey [5: 00 A.M.] on the same day.

The rear army was commanded by Yoshitsune and his aides, Yoshisada, Koreyoshi, Yasuyuki, and Nobutsuna. They were assisted by Sanehira and his son Tōhira, Yoshizumi and his son Yoshimura, Shigetada and Shigekiyo of the Hatakeyama clan, Yoshitsura, Yoshimori, Yoshimochi, and Munezane of the Wada clan, Takatsuna, Yoshikiyo, Naozane and his son Naoie, Yoshiharu and his son Mitsuyoshi, as well as Sueshige, Naotsune, Sukeyoshi, Kiyomasu, Ietada, Chikanori, Kiyotada, Kiyoshige, Tsuneharu, Hirotsuna, Yoshimori, Tsuginobu, Tadanobu, Genzō, Kumai Tarō, and Musashi-bō Benkei. With more than ten thousand horsemen, they set out at the same time as Noriyori's main army. They marched down the Tamba Road in a single day, rather than the two days needed by regular travelers, and arrived at Yamaguchi and Onobara to the east of Mount Mikusa on the border of Harima and Tamba.

[1] The seventh son of Go-Shirakawa.
[2] Founded first at Sakamoto at the eastern foot of Mount Hiei, it was relocated in 1130 on the present site of Sanzei-in, Ōhara.

CHAPTER VIII

THE BATTLE AT MIKUSA

On the side of the Heike, more than three thousand horsemen commanded by Sukemori, Arimori, Tadafusa, Moromori, and the generals in the field, Kiyoie and Morikata, marched to Yamaguchi to the west of Mount Mikusa, a distance of some three ri from Onobara.

At the hour of the dog [8:00 P.M.], Toshitsune summoned Sanehira and inquired: "The Heike have gone to Yamaguchi to the west of Mount Mikusa, three ri from here. Shall we attack them tonight or shall we fight tomorrow in the daylight?"

Nobutsuna, who was with Sanehira, stood forth and said: "The Heike will be reinforced by tomorrow. Their army is now only three thousand, while ours is ten thousand. We far outnumber them! We must attack tonight!"

Nobutsuna was a scion of Tametsuna, the vice-councilor and governor of Izu Province. His mother was a wife of Mochimitsu, but Mochimitsu was not his real father. Nobutsuna was born illegitimately from her liaison with a descendant of Tametsuna. He was raised by his maternal grandfather to be a man of the bow and the sword. His ancestry can be traced to the fifth generation of the prince of the blood Sukehito, who was the third son of Emperor Go-Sanjō. Born of aristocratic lineage, Nobutsuna was indeed a splendid warrior.

Sanehira agreed with Nobutsuna, exclaiming: "Nobutsuna is completely right! Let us attack!"

All the warriors under the command of Yoshitsune sprang on their horses and moved forward. Some soldiers complained of the darkness that enfolded them, and so Yoshitsune suggested: "Let us use an immense torch!"

"That is a good idea!" replied Sanehira. He immediately ordered his men to set torches to the houses of Onobara. The grasses and trees on the plains and mountains also went up in flames. The whole sky was lit up like broad daylight. The distance of three ri was now only a matter of a few steps.

The Heike never dreamed that the Genji would attack by night. Thus their commanders ordered the soldiers to sleep: "It is certain that we will have to fight tomorrow. Sleep is important. If you are drowsy, you cannot use your full energy. Sleep well and fight well!"

Of course some of their vanguard stood watch, but all in the rear lay stretched out in deep sleep, taking for pillows their helmets, or sleeves of their armor, or their quivers. They were entirely unprepared for a sudden attack.

At about midnight a thunderous war cry rang out. The ten thousand Genji swept down the western slope of Mount Mikusa. The soldiers of the Heike were so confused that those who took bows forgot to take arrows, and those who took arrows forgot to take bows. In fear of being trampled under the horses' hooves, they scattered. The Genji galloped right through their ranks, chasing them in all directions. In an instant five hundred men of the Heike were killed, and many others were wounded. Ashamed of this defeat, the commanders of the Heike—Koremori, Arimori, and Tadafusa—boarded boats at Takasago in Harima Province and fled to Yashima instead of returning to Fukuhara. Kiyoie, accompanied by Morikata, made his way back to Ichi-no-tani.

CHAPTER IX

THE OLD HORSE

Now Munemori sent his retainer Yoshiyuki as a messenger to all kinsmen of the Heike with a command: "Come immediately to our assistance! Yoshitsune has attacked our outpost at Mikusa and occupied it. Our hillside position is now in danger."

But all declined this summons, so Munemori called Noritsune to him and said: "Since you have already fought so many battles, perhaps this is more than you can bear to accept, but will you go to the front once again?"

"War can be won," replied Noritsune, "only when a soldier takes it as a serious matter of his own. It is not fun like hunting or fishing. He who chooses a comfortable position and refuses a dangerous one will never know victory. I do not care how often I have been sent to war. I am always prepared to undertake any dangerous engagement. Leave it to me. Trust in my dealing with Yoshitsune and set your mind at rest!"

Munemori was pleased with Noritsune's confidence and put Moritoshi's army of ten thousand horsemen at his disposal. Noritsune set out with Michimori for a hillside position near the Hiyodorigoe Pass. When they had encamped there, however, Michimori took his wife into Noritsune's tent, wishing to spend the night with her as a tender farewell before battle.

Upon learning of this, Noritsune was incensed and rebuked him: "The position we are taking is against a most ferocious enemy. This is why a veteran such as I, Noritsune, has been sent here. We will no doubt have a terrible fight. If the enemy were to scramble down the hill and fall upon us at this moment, you would be greatly confused. You may take a bow, but unless you fix an arrow to the string, a bow means nothing. Even if you nock an arrow, unless you draw the bow, the arrow means nothing. As long as you are so frivolous as to make love at such a crucial time, neither bow nor arrow will do you any good."

These words cut Michimori deeply. He immediately armed himself and dismissed his wife.

At dusk on the fifth day of the second month, the Genji set off from Koyano and moved on toward the woods of Ikuta. When the Heike looked out over the pines of Suzume and Mikage and Koyano, they could see the enemy camping everywhere. They had kindled their campfires,[1] which, as the night grew darker, flashed like stars in the cloudless sky. Roused by a spirit of rivalry, the Heike kindled campfires in and around the woods of Ikuta. Toward dawn they brightened the sky like the moon rising over mountains. In times past literary men gazed into the distance toward the ocean and composed poems as they looked at torches of fishing boats burning on the waves, for these torches reminded them of fireflies glimmering over the marshes. And so, the men on the side of the Heike who loved elegance and poetry must have remembered some of these ancient poems.

As the Genji calmly rested and fed their horses, they seemed to have courage in reserve. Their confident manner only heightened the fear and anxiety of the waiting Heike soldiers.

At dawn on the sixth day, Yoshitsune divided his army of ten thousand men into two. First, he sent Sanehira to the west of Ichi-no-tani at the head of seven thousand horsemen. Then he himself, commanding the remaining three thousand horsemen, went round by way of Tamba to attack the rear of the enemy. From there he intended to risk descending the precipice of Hiyodorigoe on horseback. Alarmed by this proposal, the men of Yoshitsune said to one another: "According to everyone, this is a place of great danger. We want to die facing the enemy, but not falling over a cliff. Does anyone know a path that will lead us out of the mountains?"

After listening to their complaints, Sueshige stood forth and exclaimed: "I know these mountains very well."

"Ridiculous!" replied Yoshitsune. "You were brought up in the eastern provinces. You are seeing these mountains in the west for the first time today. I cannot believe you."

"Your Excellency, it is quite unlike you, the commander of an army, to say that!" retorted Sueshige. "A poet knows the cherry blossoms of Mount Yoshino and Hatsuse without actually seeing them. A warrior of quality knows how to reach the rear of his enemy's stronghold."

After this audacious speech, a young warrior of eighteen named Kiyoshige, a native of Musashi Province, stood forth and said: "My father, Priest Yoshishige, once told me, 'If you are lost in mountains, while hunting or fighting, take an old horse, tie the reins, throw them on his neck, and drive him onward, and you will surely find a path.'"

"Your father was a wise man!" replied Yoshitsune. "They say that an old horse will find his way out even when buried in the snow!"

They then took an old dapple gray outfitted with a gold-studded saddle and a well-polished bit, tied the reins, threw them on its neck, and urged the animal forward. Then they followed as the horse plunged into the unknown mountain.

It was the beginning of the second month. The snow had melted here and there on the peaks. The snow remaining on the twigs looked like flowers. At times the notes of nightingales in the valleys could be heard somewhere in the mist. High above stood peaks crowned with white clouds. Far below gaped green and craggy hollows. The moss grew thick under the snow-laden pines. The snowflakes that whirled in the mountain gale looked like plum blossoms. They whipped their horses eastward and westward to follow the tracks of the old lead horse until, at last, the falling dusk compelled them to camp for the night in the depths of the mountain.

When they had halted, Musashi-bō Benkei came with an old man into the presence of his master, Yoshitsune.

"Who is this old man?" inquired Yoshitsune.

"He is a hunter on these mountains, Your Excellency," replied Benkei.

Yoshitsune turned to the old man and said: "Since you are a hunter here, you must know every corner of these mountains. Speak honestly!"

"Yes, I do, Your Excellency!"

"Then, what do you think of my plan to ride down these mountains into the stronghold of Ichi-no-tani?"

"Ah," replied the old man, "you cannot succeed, Your Excellency. These craggy hollows are all fifteen to thirty jō deep. No mortal can get down from here. Impossible! How much more foolish with horses! I cannot even conceive of this sort of reckless attempt, Your Excellency."

But Yoshitsune continued to inquire: "I know how reckless I am. But tell me if stags pass here."

"Yes," replied the old man, "They pass here. Truly they do. In spring they come from Harima Province in search of rich grass in Tamba Province. In winter they go back to Harima where the snow lies light."

"Good!" cried out Yoshitsune. "This is a fine riding ground upon which to train our horses. Where stags can pass, horses can. Be a guide to take us down the mountains!"

At this command, the old man was taken aback, but he replied: "Because I am getting on in years, I cannot be your guide. I am sorry."

"Do you have any children?"

"Yes, I have."

With this reply, the old man took his leave, and after a while he came back with his son Kumao, a boy of eighteeen. Yoshitsune then performed the ceremony of his coming of age and gave him the name of Washio no Saburō Yoshihisa after his father's name, Washio no Shōji Takehisa. Immediately after the ceremony, Yoshitsune took the boy as a guide on the ride down to Ichi-no-tani. Later, when the Heike had been overthrown and when Yoshitsune had fallen into disfavor with his elder brother, Yoritomo, Washio no Saburō Yoshihisa accompanied his master, Yoshitsune, in flight to Mutsu Province, where, at last, he shared his master's tragic fate.

---

[1] These fires were not used for cooking or as gathering places by the soldiers but were beacons lit to indicate the size of the army.

CHAPTER X

FIRST TO ENGAGE THE ENEMY?

Until midnight of the sixth day, Naozane and Sueshige rode with the rear army under the command of Yoshitsune. Then Naozane called his son, Naoie, to his side and said: "This is rough ground. If we travel with this army, we will not be among the first in making the assault on the enemy. Let us join the army of Sanehira and see if we can be the first against the enemy at Ichi-no-tani."

"A splendid idea, father!" replied Naoie. "That is what I also thought. Let us go before others do the same."

"You are right, my son," said Naozane. "But remember Sueshige is in this army. He does not like to compete with a crowd of his friends in a fight. Keep your eye on him!" Naozane then sent his servant to see how Sueshige fared.

As expected, Sueshige had already decided to leave his companions, saying to himself: "I do not know how others feel, but I cannot bear to be second in any assault. Never!"

Sueshige's groom was hastily feeding his master's horse and grumbling: "Damnable horse! This beast takes too much time in stuffing himself."

Seeing his horse fed by force, Sueshige scolded his groom: "Let him eat alone. Be gentle to him, for this is going to be his last night."

Naozane's servant hurried back to his master and reported what he had seen and heard. The servant had barely finished speaking when Naozane sped off, his suspicion now confirmed.

That day Naozane wore armor laced with red leather over a dark blue battle robe. Around his neck he wore a red scarf. He rode a peerless chestnut steed called Gonda.¹ His son, Naoie, wore armor laced with blue and white straw-rope-patterned leather over a battle robe decorated with water plantains and rode a cream colored horse called Seiro.² Naozane's standard-bearer wore armor laced with yellow leather over a blue battle robe and rode a white horse with yellow splotches. Now these warriors retraced their steps, leaving the mountains and hollows to their left. They descended an old path called Tainohata that had long been unused and soon arrived at the beach of Ichi-no-tani.

The night had deepened. It was so dark that the seven thousand horsemen led by Sanehira stopped at Shioya near Ichi-no-tani and spent the night there. Naozane, accompanied by his son and a retainer, made a detour around them, passing by in the darkness. They then advanced to the western gate of the Heike stronghold. No sound came from within. Only the three warriors were to be seen outside the fort.

Naozane called his son to his side and said: "There must be many others who want to be the first in battle. Remember that one cannot be too cautious—do not be taken in. I am certain that some other men are already here, waiting for dawn. We must not waste time. Let us be the first to declare who we are!"

Naozane rode close to the enemy barricade and shouted: "We are Kumagai no Jirō Naozane and Naoie, father and son, from Musashi Province. We are the first in the assault on Ichi-no-tani!"

The Heike within the fortress heard this, but none came out to meet them. The Heike said to one another: "Keep silent! Do not accept their challenge! Let their horses be worn out! Let their arrows be used up!"

After a while Naozane heard someone coming from behind, so he hailed him: "Who comes?"

"I am Sueshige," was the reply. "Who calls me?"

"Can you not recognize my voice? I am Naozane."

"Oh ho! Naozane! Tell me how long you have been here."

"Since last night!"

"I too should have been here before," Sueshige said, "but I am late, for I was deceived by that devious Narita Gorō. He insisted that he would share death with me. That is the oath he swore. So I took him with me. While riding along, however, he said to me, 'Sueshige! You are rushing headlong into the first onslaught against the enemy. But remember that you must have some men behind you who will later prove your honor as the first. If you ride alone

[543]

into the enemy and happen to die, who will be able to justify your honor?' What he said seemed reasonable to me.

"When I reached the top of a small hill, I reined in my horse and waited for my friends. I had meant to ride slowly alongside Gorō to have a chat with him about tactics for the forthcoming battle. But that deceitful Gorō gained on me and passed by, throwing a sneering sideways glance at me. Obviously this was how he had planned to be first. I was completely taken in. He was galloping some five or six *tan*³ ahead before I regained my composure. I thought that his mount could not be as fast as mine. After giving my horse a few lashes, I was able to overtake him and roared at him, 'Gorō! You have made a fool of a great warrior, Sueshige.' Since I passed him, I have increased my lead, and so he must still be far behind. He cannot yet see us."

Naozane and Sueshige, with only three horsemen, stood in wait for dawn. Later, at the first gray light of daybreak, Naozane wanted to declare himself and his son again to the enemy in the presence of Sueshige. Riding up once more to the enemy barricade, he shouted: "Let us declare our names again! We are Kumagai no Jirō Naozane and Naoie, father and son, from Musashi Province. Are there any among you who think themselves worthy of receiving our steel? Stand forth! Let us fight!"

"Take them alive, that father and son of the Kumagai! They have been shouting their names throughout the night." So saying, some twenty horsemen of the Heike opened the gate and came out. They were led by Moritsugi, Tadamitsu, Kagekiyo, and Sadatsune.

That day Sueshige wore armor laced with scarlet silk cords and a hood to protect him against arrows coming from behind. His battle robe was made of tie-dyed silk. His mount was a fine chestnut with gray spots around its eyes called Mekasuge.⁴ His standard-bearer wore armor laced with black leather and a helmet from which hung many neckplates in layers and rode a dark cream colored horse.

"I am Hirayama no Sueshige, a native of Musashi Province. In the two battles of Hōgen and Heiji it was I who rode first into the enemy." So shouted Sueshige, as he galloped into the enemy with his standard-bearer. When Naozane withdrew, Sueshige made an onslaught. When Sueshige withdrew, Naozane advanced. Thus they competed with each other in abusing the men of the Heike.

With no hope of winning over Naozane and Sueshige, the Heike retreated into their stronghold and tried to shoot at them from within. When Naozane's horse was shot in the belly and reared in pain, he leaped to the ground and fought on foot. His son, Naoie, too, after declaring his name and age—he was sixteen at the time —fought his way ferociously into the midst of the opposition until the nose of his horse ran against the barricade. Then he was shot in the bow hand. Jumping from his horse, he stood near his father, who said: "Ah! Naoie! Have you been shot?"

"Yes."

"Close up the gaps in your armor, so arrows will not pierce them," warned Naozane. "Bend forward so that the neckplates of your helmet will protect your throat."

Throwing away the arrows that had struck his armor, Naozane glared at the enemy and shouted: "When I left Kamakura last winter, I pledged my life to my master, Yoritomo. I have come here with the firm determination that I would die on the battleground of Ichi-no-tani. Is there one among you named Etchū no Jirōbyōe Moritsugi, who is proud of his valiant fight at the battles of Muroyama and Mizushima? Are Kazusa no Gorōbyōe and Akushichibyōe here? Is there in your midst the governor of Noto Province, Noritsune? Know that your fame depends on your opponent. A worthless opponent gives you no chance of increasing your fame. Now stand forth and deal with a famous warrior, Naozane!"

At this challenge, Moritsugi dashed out from the Heike side. That day he wore armor laced with scarlet silk cords over a white and purple battle robe and rode a cream colored horse. Now he urged the horse toward Naozane. The Kumagai, father and son, held their swords up against their foreheads and walked shoulder to shoulder so their enemy could not gallop between them. They walked forward, not a step backward. There was no chance for Moritsugi to defeat them, and so he was obliged to withdraw.

Seeing his opponent turn back to the stronghold, Naozane rebuked him: "You there! I believe you are Moritsugi. Why do you shun me as your opponent? Come and grapple with me!"

"Not me! Not me!" replied Moritsugi, as he galloped back into the stronghold.

Akushichibyōe cried out to Moritsugi: "It is unmanly of you to turn your back on the enemy without declaring your name!"

Having spoken these words, Akushichibyōe started to rush from the stronghold. But Moritsugi grasped the sleeve of his armor and begged: "This is not the last fight for our lord, Noritsune. You must not die a worthless death at a place like this!" Thus persuaded, he did not fight Naozane.

Later Naozane, on a fresh horse, galloped back and forth shouting battle cries. Sueshige gave rest to his horse, while the Kumagai fought gallantly. Now they joined in another assault.

There were not many men on the side of the Heike who could fight on horseback. Most of them climbed towers and poured down a rain of arrows. But their targets were obscured by the overwhelming numbers of their comrades. "Ride neck and neck with the enemy! Grapple with them!" the men in the towers urged their fellow soldiers, but the horses of the Heike had been overridden or had been long kept tied on board ships without sufficient food and exercise, so they seemed weary. The well-fed horses of Naozane and Sueshige were in high spirits. Once spurred, they could shame all the horses of the Heike. Consequently none of the Heike dared come out on horseback.

Sueshige found that his faithful standard-bearer had been shot, so he galloped deep into the enemy lines and soon returned with the head of the bowman. Naozane too captured many heads.

Naozane had been the first in the assault, but as the enemy did not open the gate for him, he was unable to ride into the stronghold. However, the gate was opened for Sueshige, and he was able to ride in. Thus it was that a dispute arose afterward as to who had truly been the first, Naozane or Sueshige.

[1] Literally "Uncontrollable Boy."
[2] Literally "West Tower."
[3] One tan is 10.9 m long.
[4] Literally "Gray Spots around the Eyes."

CHAPTER XI

KAGETOKI'S TWO ENGAGEMENTS

In the meantime, Narita Gorō arrived at the battleground. Sanehira too galloped into the enemy at the head of seven thousand horsemen holding war banners aloft and roaring battle cries.

Among the men of the Genji's main force at the woods of Ikuta, there were two brothers of the Kawara family, Takanao and Morinao. Takanao called his younger brother to his side and said: "A warrior-lord of a large domain can increase his fame by the distinguished service rendered by his retainers. But a warrior-lord of a small domain, such as I, cannot be recognized unless he fights gallantly himself. I am becoming impatient waiting in front of the enemy. I want to slip across the lines and let arrows fly against them. I may have no chance of returning. Stay here and stand witness for my family so that you will be able to justify my honor after this fight."

"You speak so sadly," replied Morinao in tears. "We are the only sons. If you are killed and I stay alive, what glory shall I deserve? Let me die with you at the same place!"

Takanao gave in to his brother's plea, and so they summoned their retainers and ordered them to return home and tell of their courage to their wives and children. They deserted their horses, put on straw sandals, struck the ground with their bows, and jumping over the barricade of sharpened stakes, sprang into the enemy position. The colors of armor the brothers wore were indistinguishable under the dim light of the stars.

Suddenly the voice of Takanao rang out within the stronghold: "I am Kawara Tarō Kisaichi no Takanao and here with me stands my brother, Morinao. We are both natives of Musashi Province. Among the men of the Genji at the woods of Ikuta, we are first into the fray!"

Hearing this declaration, the men of the Heike said among themselves: "Warriors from the eastern provinces—what terrible creatures they are! But they are only two in the midst of our many. They can do no harm. Let us make fools of them!"

Although Takanao's challenge was not accepted, the brothers, both strong archers, loosed a great barrage of arrows. Their opponents countered the attack by calling on a warrior named Manabe no Gorō, a native of Musashi Province renowned for his archery throughout the western provinces. His brother, Shirō, was also a great bowman. However, he had been ordered to fight at Ichi-no-tani, and so Gorō alone was to do battle at the woods of Ikuta. Now, fixing an arrow to his bow and drawing with all his might, he let it fly with a great whizzing sound. The arrow pierced the breastplate of Takanao's armor and knocked him down. Takanao was stunned and barely supported by his bow. Seeing him in trouble, Morinao rushed to him, and putting Takanao on his shoulder, tried to climb over the barricade to make a retreat. But a second arrow caught him in the gap between the lower panels of his armor. Thus the two brothers came to rest on the same pillow. The retainers of Manabe no Gorō fell upon them and cut off their heads. When their deaths were reported to Tomomori, the commander of the Heike, he heaved a deep sigh: "Brave men! They are true warriors, each worth a thousand! I have failed to spare their lives!"

Now Takanao's retainer cried out: "The Kawara brothers made the first strike into the enemy position, but they have been killed!"

"Shame on the Kawara clan! They let the brothers die in vain! The time is ripe. Let us attack!" shouted Kagetoki, one of the Genji generals.

At this command, his men bellowed a war cry that immediately brought a resounding shout to the lips of the fifty thousand horsemen of the Genji. After having their foot soldiers remove the sharpened stakes from the barricade, five hundred of Kagetoki's horsemen galloped into the enemy with a roar. Seeing his son Kagetaka in a frenzy to be first in battle, Kagetoki sent a messenger to him with these words: "You will not receive any reward at the time of conferment for your first charge, unless you are witnessed by your comrades. This is what our commander, Noriyori, has told me."

Kagetake paused for a while and gave the following poem in reply to his father's advice:

Once an arrow flies
Shot from a catalpa bow,
It can ne'er return.
Having taken the first step,
How can I dare turn my back?

Murmuring this poem, he galloped into the enemy.

"Do not let Kagetaka fall! Follow him!" So shouting, his father and his brothers Kagesue and Kageie followed him. The five hundred men of Kagetoki fought their way through the enemy. When they had been cut down to fifty, they made a swift withdrawal, but Kagesue was not to be found.

"Where is my son Kagesue?" asked Kagetoki.

"He has gone too far into the other side," replied one of his retainers. "I am afraid he has been killed, my lord."

"I am living in this world only to see my children's happiness. If I have outlived my son Kagesue, the rest of my life will be worthless! Return and attack!"

Kagetoki galloped into the enemy and roared: "I am a descendant of Kagemasa. Long ago when Yoshiie attacked the castle of Kanazawa at Senbuku in Dewa Province during the war of Gosannen,[1] Kagemasa led his brave men to the attack. An arrow pierced his left eye and went through him to the neckplate of his helmet, but he was not daunted. The arrow Kagemasa let fly in return toppled his attacker. At that time he was a young man of but sixteen. He is still remembered as one of the most valiant warriors ever to don armor—one worth a thousand. Now before you rides Kajiwara no Kagetoki, a scion of Kamakura no Gongorō Kagemasa! Is there any among you who thinks himself worthy of receiving my steel? Stand forth! Take my head and show it to your commander!"

In reply to this challenge, the commander of the Heike, Noritsune, cried out: "Kagetoki is a valiant warrior, famous throughout the eastern provinces. Do not let him escape!"

At this command, the men of the Heike surrounded Kagetoki and engaged him. Kagetoki did not fear for his own safety, but sought out his son. He galloped back and forth, to the left and right,

[549]

like a spider's legs, and then in the form of a cross, shouting: "Kagesue! Answer me! Where are you?"

Kagesue was alive. His horse, however, had been shot from under him. With his back against a two-jō cliff, he was fighting desperately, protected by two retainers on his left and right. Catching sight of his son, Kagetoki rushed to his aid.

"Thank god, you are alive, my son! Your father is here! Kagesue, if you are to die, do not turn your back on your enemy!"

The Kajiwara, father and son, killed three and wounded two. After the fight, Kagetoki emerged from the enemy lines with Kagesue and warned him: "My son, a man of the bow and sword must remember this. To attack or retreat depends on the progress of the battle. You should have retreated."

In the years following, Kagetoki's two attacks in this battle came to be known throughout the land as "Kagetoki's Two Engagements."

---

[1] Takehira and Iehira of the powerful Kiyohara clan in Dewa raised a revolt against the provincial governor in 1086. The three-year conflict was resolved by Minamoto Yoshiie when he captured the castle.

CHAPTER XII

RIDING DOWN THE CLIFF

The ensuing battle became a melee, as the men of the military families—the Chichibu, Ashikaga, Miura, and Kamakura—and of the smaller clans—the Inomata, Kodama, Noiyo, Yokoyama, Nishi, Tsuzuki, and Kisaichi—galloped into the enemy in ceaseless flow. The shouts echoed among the hills. The sound of hooves was like thunder. The shafts fell like rain. Some withdrew, carrying the wounded on their shoulders. Some engaged in hand-to-hand combat, stabbing each other to death. As the battle rolled on, none could tell who was victorious. The Genji found they could not win with their main force alone.

Meanwhile, at dawn on the seventh day, Yoshitsune climbed the pass at Hiyodorigoe, which lay to the west of Ichi-no-tani. At the moment that they were about to ride down the steep mountainside, two stags and a doe, perhaps startled by the soldiers of the Genji, rushed out and fled over the cliff straight into the stronghold of the Heike at Ichi-no-tani.

"This is strange," exclaimed the men of the Heike on guard within the fortress. "The deer of this area should be frightened by soldiers. They should have run away from us into the mountains. It must be the Genji that frightened the deer. The enemy is falling upon us from above!"

As they were running about in confusion, Kiyonori, a native of Iyo Province, stood forth and said: "Whatever comes from the enemy's position should not escape."

He shot at the two stags, but let the doe escape. When another of the Heike tried to shoot at the doe, Moritoshi dissuaded him, saying: "What a foolish thing it is to shoot at the deer! Can you not see that one of those arrows might stop ten of the enemy in their rush upon us? Do not add sins to your karma by killing harmless beasts."

Yoshitsune had been looking down at the Heike position, thinking to himself: "I had better find out how the horses go down."

He then drove some of his saddled horses down the cliff. Some
lost their foothold halfway, breaking their legs; but others reached
the bottom, scrambling down safely. Three of them stood trembling upon the roof of the headquarters of the Heike warrior Moritoshi.

"If you guide them carefully," exclaimed Yoshitsune, "you will
be able to get them down. Let us go! I will show you how. Follow
me!"

At the head of thirty horsemen, he rode down the cliff. The rest
of his men and horses followed. The stirrups of the men behind
almost struck the helmets and armor of those before. Since the
cliff was sandy, they slid down about two chō and landed on level
ground halfway. There they rested. From there downward, however, plunged a great mossy, craggy bluff, a sheer fifteen-jō drop
to the bottom. It seemed that they could go no further, nor retrace
their steps upward. All of them halted there and thought that the
end had come.

At this point Miura no Sahara Yoshitsura stood forth and said:
"Back in our native place of Miura we ride down slopes like this
even in pursuit of a single bird. This is nothing but a race course
for me!"

Shouting these words over his shoulder, Yoshitsura started descending. All followed him. They grunted under the strain, as
they steadied their horses. The sight below was so horrible that
the riders closed their eyes. Their actions seemed more those of
demons than of men. They shouted their war cries even before they
reached bottom. Their cries echoed among the cliffs like those of a
hundred thousand.

The soldiers under the command of Yasukuni set torches to the
huts and houses of the Heike. Just then strong winds arose, in-
stantly turning the huts and houses to cinders. Wrapped in black
smoke, the men of the Heike rushed toward the sea in search of
escape. Many vessels had been drawn up on the beach. But there
was such confusion that four or five hundred or even a thousand
men in full armor jumped onto one; and when it was rowed some
three chō offshore it capsized. In this way two more large craft
sank before their eyes. Then it was commanded that only men of

high rank get on board. When men of low rank tried to embark, they were threatened by swords and halberds. Even so, they clung to the vessels and strove to drag themselves aboard. Their hands and arms cut off, their blood reddened the sea and beach.

Noritsune had made no mistakes in former battles. Now how did he feel when he mounted his charger Usuguro[1] and galloped away toward the west? He took a boat at Takasago in Harima Province and fled to Yashima in Sanuki Province.

[1] Literally "Light Black."

CHAPTER XIII

THE DEATH OF MORITOSHI

The battle raged throughout Ichi-no-tani. The warriors of Musashi and Sagami provinces, in the main and rear forces of the Genji, fought fiercely.

Tomomori, who had commanded the Heike at the wood of Ikuta, began fighting his way to the east. The Kodama clan of the Genji appeared along a nearby mountainside and sent a messenger down to Tomomori.

"Your lordship was governor of Musashi Province in years past," said the messenger. "For old acquaintance's sake, the Kodama clan has sent me to warn you. Please look to your rear."

Tomomori and his retainers turned their eyes to see clouds of black smoke billowing up behind them on the horizon. Realizing that their western force must have been defeated, they fled in terror.

Moritoshi, one of the Heike chieftains who fought on the cliffs at Ichi-no-tani, had finally conceded his own defeat. Finding no route of escape, he rested his horse, waiting for the enemy. Noritsuna of the Genji came riding alongside him and wrestled him from his mount, thinking he might be a warrior of high rank.

Noritsuna was renowned in all eight eastern provinces for his great strength. It was said that he could easily tear off the first and second branches of a stag's horns. Moritoshi too was reputed to have the strength of twenty or thirty ordinary men. His limbs were so powerful that he could pull a boat that normally required sixty or seventy men.

Thus it was that Moritoshi gripped Noritsuna and pinned him so he could not move. Noritsuna tried to reach for his sword, but his fingers were benumbed; despite great effort he could not grasp the handle. He tried to speak, but no words came forth. Though his head was about to be cut off, he remained undaunted; he was an impetuous man at heart. For a moment he held his breath and then gasped out these words: "Did you hear my name? When taking the head of an opponent you must give your name first and then let your victim give his. A head without a name—is that what you want?"

Accepting his protest, Moritoshi declared himself: "I am Etchū no Zenji Moritoshi, formerly one of the Heike courtiers but now a warrior with no court rank. Now who are you? Declare yourself!"

"I am Inomata no Koheiroku Noritsuna," replied the other. "As I examine the trends of this world, I can see that the Genji are winning over the Heike. Therefore even if you present an enemy head to your lord, you will be rewarded only when he is prosperous. I pray you to unbend and spare my life. In exchange for any honors I may receive at the conferment ceremony, I will plead for the lives of you and your retainers, if you let me go."

"Are you mad?" cried Moritoshi angrily. "However humble, I am still a Heike. I have no intention of pleading with the Genji for my life. I cannot believe that you, a Genji, would ask me to intercede with the Heike for your life. What disgraceful words you speak!"

As Moritoshi prepared the final blow, Noritsuna again pleaded: "Stop this absurdity! It is against all chivalry to cut off the head of a surrendered foe!"

At this, Moritoshi was taken aback. Releasing his grip, he helped Noritsuna to his feet. The ground on which they had been fighting was solid, but only a narrow path divided it from an expanse of swampy rice fields. The two warriors sat down to rest on this slightly elevated path.

After a few moments a warrior in black leather-laced armor galloped up on a cream colored horse. Seeing the caution in Moritoshi's eyes, Noritsuna hastened to explain: "He is a good friend of mine—Hitomi no Shirō. He is coming to see what is the matter with me. Would you mind if I spoke to him?" At the same time he thought to himself: "As soon as Hitomi no Shirō comes near enough, I will tackle this rascal again. Shirō will certainly help me kill him."

At first Moritoshi kept his eyes evenly on his two foes, but when the rider had advanced to within one tan, Moritoshi's attention centered on him. Noritsuna did not miss his chance. He sprang up and dealt Moritoshi a powerful blow on the breastplate with his fists. Losing his balance at the unexpected attack, Moritoshi fell backward into the swampy rice fields. As he tried to rise, Noritsuna leaped on him, grabbed his sword, pulled up the skirt of his armor, stabbed him three times so deeply that the hilt and his fist followed the blade into the body. He then cut off Moritoshi's head.

By this time Hitomi no Shirō had arrived at Noritsuna's side. Noritsuna suspected that at the conferment of honors he would try to claim he had assisted in the kill. Therefore to certify his single-handed victory over Moritoshi, he stuck the head on the point of his sword, held it high, and declared firmly: "The head of Etchū no Zenji Moritoshi, the most famous devil-warrior of the Heike, was this day taken by Inomata no Koheiroku Noritsuna!"

By this singular deed, Noritsuna was given the first place on the list of awards for the battle that day.

CHAPTER XIV

THE DEATH OF TADANORI

Tadanori was in command of the western flank of the Heike at Ichi-no-tani. That day he wore armor laced with black silk cords over a blue and gold brocade battle robe and rode a great black charger with a gold lacquered saddle. Escorted by a hundred horsemen under his command, he was unperturbed by the enemy's repeated attacks as he made his retreat. A warrior of the Genji, Tadazumi of the Inomata clan, saw him and thought he might be a famous general of the Heike. He whipped his horse to overtake him and cried: "I pray you—declare yourself! Who are you?"

"We are friends!" replied Tadanori, as he turned his eyes to the inquirer. At this moment Tadazumi caught a glimpse of his face and noticed that his teeth were blackened.[1]

"There is no one on our side who has blackened his teeth," he said to himself. "This must be one of the Heike courtiers." Tadazumi galloped alongside and grappled with Tadanori.

Seeing the two struggling, Tadanori's men fled in terror, leaving their leader to meet his fate. Only hired retainers recruited from various provinces, they felt no special bond of loyalty and fled without remorse.

"You knave! I said, 'We are friends.' How dare you fight me?" shouted Tadanori in rage.

Being a man of great strength and quick reflexes, Tadanori drew his sword and struck Tadazumi twice while he was still in the saddle. He struck again as they fell together to the ground. The first two blows, however, struck Tadazumi's armor and failed to pierce it. The third one had thrust inside his helmet to wound his face, but it was not a mortal wound. Now Tadanori pressed him down and was about to cut off his head when one of Tadazumi's retainers, who had been riding behind him, rushed to the spot, drew his sword, and chopped off Tadanori's right arm above the elbow. Tadanori realized he was doomed. He pushed Tadazumi from him about a bow's length, saying: "Keep away from me. I wish to chant the death prayer!"

He then turned toward the west and raised his voice chanting a few lines from a sutra: "O Amida Buddha! Thy light shines upon all the ten quarters of the world. Thou saveth all sentient beings who seek thee calling thy name."

Tadanori had hardly finished this prayer when Tadazumi approached him from behind and swept off his head. Though he was certain of having obtained a great prize, he did not know whose head it was. In searching for some identification, however, he found fastened to Tadanori's quiver a piece of paper, upon which was written the following poem entitled "A Flower at a Traveler's Inn":

> When the day is done
> I take a tree for my lodge.
> On my weary way,
> Lying under its broad boughs,
> A flower is my sole host.

Since the poet had signed his name, Tadazumi was able to recognize Tadanori as a true Heike courtier, the governor of Satsuma Province. Sticking the head on the point of his sword, he held it high and declared in a loud voice: "The head of one of the most prominent Heike courtiers, a lord named Tadanori, governor of Satsuma Province, has been obtained by Okabe no Rokuyata Tadazumi."

At this declaration, however, friends and foes alike wet their sleeves with tears and said: "What a pity! Tadanori was a great general, preeminent in the arts of both sword and poetry."

---

[1] Blackened teeth were the fashion for the nobles and courtiers.

CHAPTER XV

ARREST OF SHIGEHIRA

L
ieutenant General Shigehira was an aide to the commander-in-chief of the Heike force at the woods of Ikuta. Since his men had fled, only one of his retainers remained with him. Wearing armor laced with purple silk cords over a dark blue battle robe decorated with an embroidered design of sea plovers, he rode a stalwart mount known throughout the land as Dōjikage.[1] His retainer was his foster brother, Morinaga. He wore armor laced with scarlet silk cords over a tie-dyed silk battle robe and rode his master's favorite cream colored charger, Yomenashi.[2] They were retreating to the shore when Kagesue and Takaie, thinking that Shigehira and Morinaga might be great warriors of the Heike, came galloping up. Though there were many boats ranged along the shore waiting for them, Shigehira and Morinaga were so closely pursued by the enemy that there was no chance for them to join their companions.

Thus it was that they crossed the rivers of Minato and Karumo, passed the pond of Hasu on the right and the wood of Koma on the left, rode through Itayado and Suma, and urged their horses on and on to the west. Since theirs were fine horses, it seemed that the tired horses of the Genji would never gain on them. Growing impatient at losing ground, Shigehira's pursuer, Kagesue, stood high in his stirrups, drew his bow with all his might, and let fly. Though it was a long shot, the shaft flew true to its target and buried itself deep into the haunch of Shigehira's horse. Seeing the horse slacken its pace, Morinaga feared that his master would demand his mount, so he beat a hasty retreat.

"Morinaga!" exclaimed Shigehira. "Have you forgotten all that you promised? Where are you going? How dare you desert me?"

Without a reply, Morinaga tore the red insignia of the Heike from his armor and hastened to escape.

Dōjikage was weakening as the enemy drew near, so Shigehira, attempting to put an end to himself, plunged into the sea. But the water was too shallow, so he dismounted, cut off the belt of his armor, untied the strings of the breastplate, and stripped himself. He was thus about to cut open his belly when Takaie came up at breakneck speed, ahead of Kagesue, and dismounting, cried out: "Do not kill yourself! You need not die. Surrender as a captive."

Takaie put him on his own horse, bound him to the pommel of his saddle, and, riding a remount, escorted Shigehira back to the Genji camp.

Safe on the swift and tireless Yomenashi, Morinaga fled to Kumano and took refuge at the house of Priest Onaka. After the death of the priest, however, he returned to the capital with Onaka's widow who was to bring a lawsuit there. At that time there were still many people who could recognize Morinaga, so they scornfully said: "Shameless Morinaga! He received many favors from his master, Shigehira, but in an hour of need he would not risk his life and refused to help his master escape. How disgraceful he is to come back to the capital with the widow of Priest Onaka. This is an intolerable act!"

Thus jeered and mocked, Morinaga was so ashamed of himself that he was obliged to hide his face with his fan.

[1] Literally "Heavenly Youth Bay."
[2] Literally "No Night View."

CHAPTER XVI

THE DEATH OF ATSUMORI

Naozane, seeing overwhelming victory for his side, said to himself: "The Heike courtiers are running away to the beach to their boats. Ah, I wish I could challenge a great general of the Heike!"

As he was riding to the beach, he caught sight of a fine-looking warrior urging his horse into the sea toward a boat anchored a little offshore. The warrior wore armor laced with light green silk cords over a twilled silk battle robe decorated with an embroidered design of cranes. On his head was a gold-horned helmet. He carried a sword in a gold-studded sheath and a bow bound with red lacquered rattan. His quiver held a set of black and white feathered arrows, the center of each feather bearing a black mark. He rode a dapple gray outfitted with a gold-studded saddle. He was swimming at a distance of five or six tan when Naozane roared at him: "You out there! I believe you are a great general. It is cowardly to turn your back on your enemy. Come back!"

Naozane beckoned to him with his fan. Thus challenged, the warrior turned his horse around. When he reached the beach, Naozane rode alongside, grappled with him, and wrestled him to the ground. As Naozane pressed down his opponent and removed his helmet to cut off his head, he saw before him the fair-complexioned face of a boy no more than sixteen or seventeen. Looking at this face, he recalled his son, Naoie. The youth was so handsome and innocent that Naozane, unnerved, was unable to find a place to strike with the blade of his sword.

"Now tell me who you are," asked Naozane. "Declare yourself! Then I will spare your life."

"You? Who are you?" replied the youth.

"I am a warrior of little importance. A native of Musashi Province, Kumagai no Jirō Naozane, that is who I am."

"I cannot declare myself to such as you. So take my head and show it to others. They will identify me."

"Ah, you must be a great general, then," replied Naozane. But he thought to himself: "The slaughter of one courtier cannot conclusively effect this war. Even when I saw that my son, Naoie, was slightly wounded, I could not help feeling misery. How much more painful it would be if this young warrior's father heard that his son had been killed. I must spare him!"

Looking over his shoulder, he saw a group of his comrades galloping toward them. He suppressed his tears and said: "Though I wish to spare your life, a band of my fellow warriors is approaching, and there are so many others throughout the countryside that you have no chance of escaping from the Genji. Since you must die now, let it be by my hand rather than by the hand of another, for I will see that prayers for your better fortune in the next world are performed."

To this, the young warrior replied simply: "Then take off my head at once!"

So pitiable an act was it that Naozane could not wield his blade. His eyes saw nothing but darkness before him. His heart sank. However, unable to keep the boy in this state any longer, he struck off his head. Frenzied with grief, Naozane wept until the tears rushed down his cheeks.

"Nothing is so bitter as to be born into a military family! Were I not a warrior, I should not have such sorrow! What a cruel act this is!"

He covered his face with the sleeves of his armor and wept. But he could no longer stand there weeping. Then as he was wrapping the head in a cloth, he found a flute in a brocade bag tucked into a sash around the boy's waist.

"What a tragedy! At dawn I heard the sound of a flute from within the Heike lines. It was this youth who was playing. Among the hundred thousand warriors on our side, there is no one who has carried with him a flute to a battlefield. What a gentle life these nobles and courtiers have led!"

Murmuring these words, he returned to his own army. When he presented the head to Yoshitsune for inspection, all the warriors shed tears in sympathy. It was soon recognized as the head of Lord

Atsumori, only seventeen years of age, a son of the chief of the Palace Repairs Division, Tsunemori.

It is said that the flute had first been possessed by Emperor Toba who gave it to Atsumori's grandfather, Tadamori, an excellent player of the instrument. It was then passed on to his son Tsunemori, who in turn gave it to Atsumori, since his surpassing talent on the flute deserved his possession of it. This flute was known as Saeda.[1]

Even singing, an exaggeration of words and speech, can now and then cause enlightenment to awaken in a man. Simply the sound of this flute played by Atsumori inspired Naozane to pursue the way to the Buddha.[2]

[1] Literally "Small Branch."

[2] He became a disciple of Hōnen at Kurodani and called himself by the Buddhist name Rensei.

CHAPTER XVII

THE DEATH OF TOMOAKIRA

The chief of the Archivists Division, Narimori, the youngest son of the Vice-Councilor by the Main Gate, Norimori, was killed by a native of Hitachi Province named Shigeyuki. The aide to the chief of the Board of the Empress's Affairs, Tsunemasa, while fleeing to the shore to board a boat, was surrounded by a band of soldiers led by Shigefusa and put to death. His brothers, Tsunetoshi, Kiyofusa, and Kiyosada, galloped into the enemy positions, fought desperately, and beat down many foes before dying together.

Tomomori was in command of the Heike force at the woods of Ikuta. After all his men had fled, he made his way to the beach to retreat by boat. He was escorted by only two men, his son Tomoakira and one of his retainers, Yorikata. Catching sight of the three, about ten horsemen of the Kodama clan came galloping up with a shout. Yorikata, a strong bowman, let fly an arrow at the standard-bearer riding at the head of the band. The shaft pierced the standard-bearer's neck and toppled him from his horse. The leader of the band, urging his horse, started to gain on Tomomori. But Tomoakira, spurring his charger, thrust himself between them, grappled with his foe, fell with him to the ground, pressed him down, and cut off his head. While Tomoakira was getting to his feet, his opponent's retainer fell upon him and struck off his head. Seeing this, Yorikata attacked the retainer and killed him. After all his arrows had given out, he drew his sword and slew many of the attackers. But in the scuffle he took a shot in the kneecap. Unable to stand, he brandished his sword desperately, sitting erect even after he had breathed his last. During the fight Tomomori retreated, urging his fine charger to the beach, and made the horse swim some twenty chō until he reached the boat that Munemori had boarded. The boat was so crowded that Tomomori, finding no space for his horse, sent the animal back to the beach.

"Your horse will fall into the hands of the enemy. Let me shoot him!" said Shigeyoshi, standing forth and fixing an arrow to his bow.

Tomomori dissuaded him, saying: "Let anyone have him who will. That horse has saved my life. I cannot bear to see him die. Do not shoot!"

Tomomori's horse stubbornly refused to leave his master. He swam after the boat until it was rowed far off. The horse then swam back to the beach where his master was no longer to be found. On the beach he managed to stand and neighed two or three times, looking back toward the boat. As the horse was resting, Kawagoe no Shigefusa captured him. Later he presented the horse to the cloistered emperor, who had him put in his stables.

This horse had formerly been favored by the cloistered emperor and had been lodged in the First Imperial Stables. When Lord Munemori was promoted to the post of state minister, the horse was given to him as a commemorative token. Then the animal was put into the hands of Lord Tomomori. He soon became so fond of him that Tomomori offered a prayer on the first day of every month to the god of Mount T'ai[1] for his charger's long life. Perhaps because Tomomori did so, not only the life of this horse but also that of his master was thus prolonged. Because the horse was brought up in the country of Inoue in the province of Shinano, he was called Inoueguro, or "Inoue Black"; but after being presented to the cloistered emperor by Kawagoe no Shigefusa, he came to be called Kawagoeguro, or "Kawagoe Black."

Tomomori, in the presence of Munemori, grieved: "I have outlived my son Tomoakira and my retainer Yorikata. Everyone grudges his own death. But this particular son of mine grappled with his father's enemy to save him from death. His father, however, did not try to save his son during his death struggle, but deserted him only to save his own life. If I saw a scene like this taking place between other persons, how bitterly would I regard the cowardice of the father! I am terribly wretched. This is the first time that I have truly recognized the dearness of life. I am ashamed to face others when I think of how they must regard my son's tragic end and his father's unmanly behavior." He hid his face in the sleeve of his armor and wept bitterly.

"What a faithful son he was!" replied Munemori. "Tomoakira was indeed a great general, skilled in the arts of bow and sword and valiant of heart. He would be just sixteen years of age if he were still alive. As young as my son Kiyomune!" Munemori turned his eyes toward Kiyomune, who was on board the boat.

All men of the Heike, whether they had hearts or not, drenched the sleeves of their armor with their tears.

[1] A mountain in western Shantung, China, upon which it was supposed that the god of longevity resided.

CHAPTER XVIII

FLIGHT

The governor of Bitchū Province, Moromori, the youngest son of Lord Shigemori, boarded a small boat with his six retainers to escape the enemy. They were rowing their boat from the beach when one of Tomomori's retainers, Kinnaga, galloped to the water's edge and cried out: "That is the boat of the governor of Bitchū Province, is it not? Let me get on board."

At this request, the boat was rowed back. Now Kinnaga was a man of enormous size. It was easy to see what would happen if such a heavy man jumped from his horse into such a small boat. The tiny vessel rolled over at the shock. Thrown into the water, Moromori was struggling up and down in the waves. Chikatsune, one of the Hatakeyama's retainers, came galloping up with fourteen or fifteen horsemen, dragged him from the water with a grappling hook, and cut off his head. Moromori was then only fourteen years old.

Michimori was in command of the Heike army on the mountainside. His armor, laced with silk cords, was worn over a red battle robe. His ivory colored horse was outfitted with a silver-studded saddle. He had been separated from his troops and his younger brother, Noritsune. An arrow had pierced his helmet severely wounding him, so he made up his mind to kill himself at a quiet place. As he was riding his horse to the east, he was surrounded by seven soldiers of the Genji, including Naritsuna from Ōmi Province and Sukekage from Musashi Province, and put to death. His retainer had been with him, but at the moment of his death he was alone.

At the east and west gates of the fortress of Ichi-no-tani, the battle raged for about two hours. Scores of the Genji and Heike were killed. In front of the towers and under the sharpened stakes were layers of dead men and horses. The green of the Ozasa Plain had been changed to scarlet. Beyond count was the number of the Heike soldiers who had been injured or slain at Ichi-no-tani, at the wood of Ikuta, on the mountainside, and on the beach. The severed heads exposed to public view by the Genji numbered more than two thousand. Michimori and his younger brother, Narimori, Tadanori, Tomoakira, Moromori, Kiyofusa, Tsunemasa and his younger brother, Tsunetoshi, and Atsumori had all been killed.

How sad it was to see the Heike escape with the child emperor Antoku once again on board vessels driven by the wind and tide. Some were rowed to Kii; others rolled on in the offing beyond Ashiya; and yet others were steered along the shores of Suma and Akashi. Thus the Heike drifted here and there with no definite anchorage. They used sleeves for pillows and planks for couches. The dim light of the spring moon stirred them only into endless tears. Some crossed the strait of Awaji and drifted along the shore of Eshima. At the cry of the sea plovers that had lost their mates in their twilight flight over the waves, they reflected upon their own fate. Others still lay off the shore of Ichi-no-tani with their hearts too heavy to move on. All the men and women of the Heike gave themselves up to the winds and tides that would take them aimlessly from beach to beach, from island to island. They could hardly guess each other's fates. Yesterday they had had fourteen provinces under their control and a great force of a hundred thousand soldiers under their command. From Ichi-no-tani to Kyoto was a journey of a day, and so they must have thought of returning there to lead an elegant life once more. But with the destruction of their fortress at Ichi-no-tani, their hopes faded; their despondency deepened.

CHAPTER XIX

KOZAISHŌ

One of the warriors of Lord Michimori was an imperial guard named Tokikazu. In the aftermath of Ichi-no-tani he rowed out to the boat carrying the wife of his master and said to her: "My master was surrounded by seven of the enemy on the lower Minato River and was put to death. There were two men who drew their swords and wielded them upon him—Naritsuna from Ōmi Province and Sukekage from Musashi Province. I know it was they who killed my master, for I heard them declaring their names. I should have stayed with my master so that I could go with him to the world beyond. But I remembered what he had always said to me, 'If anything happens to me, do not throw away your life for my sake, but stay alive at all costs to find my wife and look after her.' This is why I have fled—to save my worthless life and come to you."

Hearing this, the wife of Lord Michimori gave no word in reply, but pulled her robe over her face to weep bitterly. At first she could not believe that her husband had been killed, for she still clung to the faint hope that Tokikazu's report may have been a mistaken one. She waited for Michimori for two or three days, as if waiting for one who had gone out for a short time and would soon return. But when four or five days had passed in vain vigil, her hope faded away, and she fell into deep sorrow. At that time she was attended only by her former wet nurse, who lay on the same pillow to share her tears of grief. From the late afternoon of the seventh day after she had heard the sad news until the night of the thirteenth day, she did not rise from her bed. The boat was to arrive at Yashima the next day, the fourteenth. Night wore on, a dead silence fell over the boat.

Michimori's wife lifted her head and said to her wet nurse: "Since I heard the sad news the other day till this evening, I have

[569]

dwelt upon the faint hope that my husband was alive. Now I feel differently. He is dead. Everyone says that he was killed on the lower Minato River—no one has appeared to tell me that he has been seen alive.

"On the night before the battle, I met my husband at a small hut. At that time he looked sadder than usual and said to me, 'I am certain that I shall be killed in the battle tomorrow. I wonder what will become of you after I am dead.' Since I had already grown accustomed to his many battles, I did not pay any special heed to his words. If only I had known that this was his last meeting with me, I would have promised to follow him to the world beyond. This is what grieves me most.

"Only one consideration remains. Up to that time I had concealed the fact that I was with child. To keep it secret from him seemed to be too reserved of me, and so I finally confessed it to him. He was extremely pleased to hear it and said, 'I, Michimori, have been without any children of my own till the age of thirty. But now that I am to have a child, I hope it will be a boy. He will then be a fine memento of myself in this fleeting world! Now tell me how many months you have been with child and how you feel. Our life is now aboard an ever-rolling vessel, so I must prepare a quiet place for your peaceful lying-in.'

"Ah, these words were spoken in vain! Is it true that under such difficult circumstances nine out of ten women in labor must die? How ashamed I shall be when I expose my great pain to others! How wretched I shall be when I meet my end after losing my composure! Again, if I bear a child and bring him up so that he may remind me of the form and features of my dead husband, my every glance at him will bring back the old memories only to cause me endless grief.

"I know that death awaits me at any moment. If I could with any luck hide myself, unharassed, from this perilous world, would I be certain of escaping the fate of a woman? Can I refuse thoroughly the temptation of being entangled in another love? Such a frail vessel is a woman!

"Even to think of this is unbearable for me. When I sleep, my husband appears in my dreams. When I awake, he stands before my eyes. As long as I live in this world, I cannot set myself free from my longing for him. Now there remains nothing more for me than to drown myself in the depths of the sea. My one regret is that you will be left here alone in grief. But I pray you to take all my robes to some priests so that they will cover the expenses of prayers for my husband's better lot and the Buddha's assistance to me in the world beyond. And here is a letter that I have written. Send it to the capital."

These words saddened her wet nurse terribly. Suppressing her tears, she advised her lady: "I pray you to think how fervently I have devoted myself to you. I have left my little ones and aged mother in the capital and have come this far to wait upon you. Yours is not the only tragedy of a woman losing her husband in the battle at Ichi-no-tani. After you have been delivered safely of a child, you must strive to bring him up, even among the rocks and trees. You may then become a nun and spend the rest of your life in offering prayers for your husband's better lot in the other world. Please remember that though you wish to sit on the same lotus as your husband, your meeting with him is not assured until you are reborn in the next world, where none can tell which path to take when passing through the Four Births and the Six Realms. If you fail to meet him there, what will be the use of casting away your life now? Yet another point—to whom shall I deliver this letter of yours in the capital? Upon whom can I depend? Please do not make me feel so sad."

The lady thought that her wet nurse had not understood her true wishes, and so she tried to comfort her: "You are the only one who can truly sympathize with me. Please understand that it is only natural for a woman who loathes her miserable lot in this fleeting world to drown herself. So forget what I have told you. If I had truly meant to end my life, I would have kept my intention secret from you. It is getting late. Let us sleep."

The wet nurse, remembering that her mistress had eaten nothing and had not even drunk hot or cold water for the last four or five days, concluded that her mind had truly been made up and that she would drown herself.

"If you are determined to drown yourself, let me follow you to the bottom of the sea. I intend to live not a moment longer if you die," said the wet nurse. She remained awake for some time and kept an eye on her mistress, but at last she fell asleep.

The lady had been waiting for this chance, and, slipping out quietly, ran to the rail of the vessel. For a while she gazed into the distance over the vast waters. Searching for paradise, she turned toward the mountain that hides the fading moon and calmly chanted "Hail Amida Buddha." The melancholy cry of the sea plovers on the distant sand bars and the dull creaking of the rudder mingled with her soft voice as she repeated the invocation of Amida a hundred times.

"Hail Amida Nyorai, the savior who leads us to the Pure Land Paradise in the west, according to thy Original Vow[1] unite my husband and me on the same petal of thy lotus—so that we may be inseparable forever!"

After she had beseeched Amida Buddha and Nyorai in tears, she flung herself into the waves, still invoking them on her lips.

It was already past midnight. Since it was the last night of the long journey from Ichi-no-tani to Yashima, all on board had fallen into deep sleep. At first no one noticed her. However, when she jumped overboard, the loud splash caught the attention of the helmsman, who alone had been awake.

"How terrible!" cried the astonished helmsman. "A lady overboard! A lady overboard!"

At this alarm, the wet nurse came to with a start and groped for her mistress in the dark. Feeling nothing by her side, she was lost in terror, repeating only: "Oh dear! Oh dear!"

Many men jumped overboard in search of the lady. At that moment the clouds converged, obscuring the moon. Even without the clouds, the sea had been murky this spring night. The men who dived into the waters could only grope blindly in the dark. After some time they discovered her and pulled her from the water; but her soul had already passed to the world beyond. When they laid her on the deck, the water streamed down from her white hakama and the double layers of her tie-dyed silk court robes. The drops glittered on her long raven locks. The wet nurse took her lady's hands in her own, and pressed her face to them, crying: "If you had determined to put an end to yourself like this, why did you not take me with you to the bottom of the sea? I pray you to speak to me but once more."

But the lady was already gone from this world. The breath that had just barely fluttered in her body had at last ceased forever.

Now when the wanton moon of the spring night had faded into

dawn, they could remain in grief no longer. They bound a suit of her husband's armor around her body so she would not rise again and returned her to the waters. The wet nurse attempted to leap after the body, but she was held back by the others. Having no way to demonstrate her unswerving faithfulness, she cut off her hair with her own hands in order to surrender her soul to the world beyond. A priest and vice-councilor, Chūkai, who was a younger brother of the late Lord Michimori, performed the ritual shaving of the head, bestowing upon her this symbol of penitence.

From of old many women had forsaken the world on the deaths of their husbands, but few had destroyed themselves to follow their husbands to the land of the shades. The death of the wife of Lord Michimori reminds us of a Chinese saying: "A loyal retainer will not serve a second master; a good wife will remain faithful to the memory of her husband."

The lady was the daughter of Lord High Marshal Norikata. She had been a famed beauty at court, where she was given the name Kozaishō and waited upon Shōsaimon-In. In the springtime of Angen, when Shōsaimon-In made a trip to the Hosshō-ji temple to view the cherry blossoms, Kozaishō accompanied her. She was sixteen years old at the time.

Michimori was still only the aide to the chief of the Board of the Empress's Affairs, and, accordingly, he was to accompany them to Hosshō-ji. The first time that he saw Kozaishō, he knew what it was to be in love. Her beautiful figure soon glided before his eyes day and night. From then on he continued to send his poems and letters to her, but they all went unanswered.

In this way three years went by. Then Michimori wrote a letter, which he determined would be his last, and sent it to her with his messenger. However, as bad luck would have it, the messenger was not able to find the court servingmaid who could hand the letter to Kozaishō. Unable to fulfill his master's command, he started to make his way back to his master's house. He met Kozaishō coming in a carriage from her home to attend court. Since he was obliged to deliver the letter to her, he ran to her carriage and pushed the letter through a gap in the curtains. She asked her attendants who had thrown it to her, but they could not tell who it had been. Upon opening the letter, however, she found that it was from Michimori. The letter could not be left in the carriage or thrown out on the road, so she thrust it into the sash of her hakama and entered court. Then, while she was engaged in waiting upon the princess, she happened to drop it in front of Her Highness. The princess at once picked up the letter and put it into the sleeve of her robe. After a while she summoned all her ladies-in-waiting and said: "Here is a strange letter that I have found. To whom does this belong?"

All of them swore by the gods and the Buddhas that they knew nothing about it. Only Kozaishō blushed terribly and said nothing. Now the princess confirmed her hunch that Michimori had given his heart to Kozaishō. She proceeded to open the letter to examine its contents. It was beautifully scented with musk incense. So fragrant was the letter that the princess was tempted to hold it tight in spite of herself. The strokes of Michimori's brush displayed skill that could be attained only after much practice.

"You are coldhearted. Even so, I cannot stop loving you . . ." began the letter, and the princess read until she came to the following poem, which concluded it:

> As a single log
> Over a small mountain stream
> Endures being trodden upon,
> I feel like that log and weep,
> Having no reply from you.

"This is a letter protesting that you never responded to him," said the princess, turning to Kozaishō. "If you remain too hardhearted, you will be liable to ill-fortune.

"Long ago there lived a woman named Ono no Komachi, renowned for her beauty and her talent at composing poems. What she lacked, however, was tenderness of heart. Many men approached her and wooed her, but they were all rejected, and finally everyone began to despise her. Her heart of stone brought inevitable retribution to her. She was then obliged to live alone in a desolate hut, hardly protected from the wind and rain. Her eyes, dimmed with tears, reflected the light of the moon and stars filtering through the chinks of the hut. She managed to sustain the dewdrop of her life by eating young grass in the fields and plucking watercress. This letter should be answered by all means."

So saying, she called for an ink stone and wrote as a reply in her own distinguished hand the following poem:

> Simply trust the log,
> Be it ever so slender,
> As strong is the core.
> Although trampled and splashed,
> It will stay over the stream.

This poem kindled the fire of passion that had been smoldering in the depths of Kozaishō's heart. Now it rose like smoke from the crater of Mount Fuji. Her tears of joy rushed down her sleeves like the lapping waves at the Kiyomi Checkpoint. Thus her flower-like beauty brought her happiness and led her to be the wife of Lord Michimori of the third court rank. The affection between them was so profound that they journeyed together even among the clouds over the western sea and even to the dark path in the world beyond.

The Vice-Councilor by the Main Gate, Norimori, outlived his eldest son, Michimori, and his youngest son, Narimori. Only two of his sons—the governor of Noto Province, Noritsune, and the priest and vice-councilor, Chūkai—survived the battle. He had eagerly wished to see Michimori's child, but this hope was carried away with his daughter-in-law Kozaishō to the regions beyond the grave. He now fell into deep sorrow.

---

[1] The vow of all Buddhas and bodhisattvas to save sentient beings.

BOOK TEN

" ' Am I [Korimori] still unable to rid myself of worldly *desire?* ' "
—Book 10, Chapter XII, page 623

CHAPTER I

PARADING THE HEADS THROUGH
THE CAPITAL

I t was on the twelfth day of the second month of the third year of Juei [1184] that the heads of the Heike cut off during the battle at Ichi-no-tani in Settsu Province were returned to the capital. All the men and women related to the Heike were filled with sorrow and wondered what fate now awaited them. One who was terrified was the wife of Lord Koremori, the lieutenant general of the third court rank, who had been hiding at Daikaku-ji.

She had been informed that a few of the Heike courtiers had survived the battle at Ichi-no-tani, and one noble, a lieutenant general of the third court rank, would be brought back as a captive to the capital. She was certain that this noble would be her husband, Koremori. Thus it was that she fell prostrate, covering her face with her sleeve. Then one of her maids came to her and said: "The lieutenant general of the third court rank is not your husband, but another lieutenant general, Lord Shigehira."

"Therefore," replied the lady, "my husband's head must be among the fallen ones. This is all that I can expect." Anticipating the worst, she could not set her heart at rest.

On the thirteenth day of the month, the captain of the Police Commissioners Division, Nakayori, went out to meet the soldiers of the Genji on the bank of the Kamo River at Rokujō to receive the fallen heads. Noriyori and Yoshitsune demanded of the cloistered emperor that they be allowed to parade the heads north on the wide street of Higashi-no-Tōin and then hang them on the trees to be exposed to public view. Go-Shirakawa was dismayed at this demand, so he summoned the sesshō, Motomichi, the ministers of the Left and Right, Tsunemune and Kanezane, the state minister, Jittei, and the councilor, Tadachika, and ordered them to hold a council. These five nobles unanimously concluded: "From of old there has been no precedent for this—that the heads of nobles and courtiers should be paraded on the streets of the capital. Above all, these people were related to the Emperor Antoku on his maternal side, and it is with this status that they have served the imperial family for many years. Therefore we think that it is advisable for His Majesty to reject the demand of Noriyori and Yoshitsune."

Despite this rejection at court, Noriyori and Yoshitsune sent their petition again and again to the cloistered emperor, saying: "These beheaded men of the Heike were the enemies of our grandfather Tameyoshi at the time of the Hōgen Insurrection, and of our father, Yoshitomo, at the time of the Heiji Insurrection. We obtained their heads at the risk of our lives to calm His Majesty's wrath and avenge our father and grandfather. If we are not allowed to parade them, how shall we be able to fight courageously against the rest of the Heike?"

The cloistered emperor could not refuse their demand any longer and finally allowed them to exhibit the heads. Many people looked on aghast. In times past, when the Heike flourished, they wore colorful ceremonial robes for their attendance at court and terrified these people. Their heads were now paraded before the people's eyes, only to arouse their sympathy and sorrow.

Saitō-go and Saitō-roku, the retainers of Lieutenant General Koremori, now in attendance upon his son Rokudai, had been worried about their master. Disguising themselves in humble clothes, they watched the procession for a while to see if the head of their master was to be found there. Although they felt some sense of relief at discovering their master's head was not among those paraded, their spirits were low. Tears rushed down their cheeks. In fear of suspicious eyes observing them, they hurried to Daikaku-ji to Koremori's wife.

"Come now! Tell me what you have seen," she exclaimed.

Urged by the lady, they replied: "Among the sons of Lord Shigemori, only the head of Lord Moromori[1] was found. As for the heads belonging to other lords of the Heike, they were too numerous to mention." However, at the request of the lady, they listed all the names of the beheaded that they had seen in the parade.

"Whoever they are," said the lady, "I cannot disregard them and act unconcerned."

Now Saitō-go, repressing his tears, said: "Since I have been

[580]

in hiding more than a year, it was fortunate that the other spectators did not notice me. I should have stayed longer to watch the parade till the end. But I did overhear someone speaking of the later activities of the Heike. He seemed to be well informed. This is what he said. 'At the recent battle the sons of Lord Shigemori occupied a position on Mount Mikusa, which lies on the border of Harima and Tamba. However, they were defeated by Yoshitsune's army, and so Lieutenant General Sukemori, Major General Arimori, and Lord High Chamberlain Tadafusa embarked at Takasago and fled to Yashima. I do not know why Lord Moromori alone was separated from his brothers and killed at Ichi-no-tani.'

"Then I asked him, 'Can you tell me how Lieutenant General Koremori fared in the battle?' His reply was, 'Before the battle he had been seriously ill, so he was obliged to stay at Yashima. That is why he did not take part.' This is about all the information I could gather."

"He must have become ill from long brooding over the grim realities of our lives," said the lady. "As for myself, when it is windy, I worry that he might embark in the teeth of a storm. When I hear there is war, I am terrified that he might be killed at any moment. Now he is ill! But who can attend him? Who can take care of him, leaving nothing for him to desire? Oh, you should have asked this stranger what his condition is now."

Her son and daughter too rebuked Saitō-go and Saitō-roku, saying: "Why did you not ask him from what ailment our father is suffering?"

Man has mysterious power to discern the thoughts of others far away. Koremori, at Yashima, heaved a deep sigh and said to himself: "I wonder if my family is worried about me. Though they will not find my head among the fallen they could think that I was drowned or killed and left unidentified on the battlefield. They would hardly believe that I am still alive. Now I must tell them that I have managed to sustain the dewdrop of my life."

Koremori wrote three letters and had one of his retainers deliver them to members of his family in the capital. The one that went to his wife read thus: "I understand how wretched you are in the capital, where all around you are enemies. You must be having a hard time hiding yourself from them. How much more difficult when you are not alone but with your two little ones. I wish I could

[581]

send for you, and we could live together and overcome whatever hardship may lie before us. But I cannot bear to think that you would have to share such a miserable life here."

Before closing, he added this poem:

> A seaweed loiters,
> Knowing nowhere to settle
> Away, off the shore.
> Take this as a memento,
> My writing on the seaweed.

He wrote a message to his children, inquiring: "I wonder how you are spending your weary days. Wait until I send for you soon."

These letters brought nothing but sorrow to his wife. The bearer of the letters stayed four or five days until he was to depart from the capital. Weeping, the lady wrote a reply for him to take. The son and daughter too wet their brushes with ink, and asked their mother what they should tell their father. But this was her only answer: "Tell him just what you have in your minds!"

Then they expressed their thoughts in these words: "Why have you not sent for us? We miss you terribly. Please send for us at once."

Bearing these letters, the messenger returned to Yashima and presented himself before his master. Koremori first read the letters from his little ones. Lost in deep sorrow, he murmured tearfully: "Now I do not think that I can take the tonsure and enter the priesthood. As long as my beloved ones dwell upon my heart in this world, I cannot help but give up the idea of attaining enlightenment in future priesthood. All I can do is dare to cross over the mountains to the capital and see my wife and children but once more. Then let me put an end to myself."

---

[1] The youngest son of Shigemori.

CHAPTER II

SHIGEHIRA'S LADY

O n the fourteenth day of the second month, Lord Shigehira, the lieutenant general who had been taken alive and brought back to the capital, was paraded east on Rokujō. The carriage in which he rode bore a design of lotus flowers. The bamboo curtains at the front and rear were lifted, and the windows on both sides were opened. Sanehira, clad in a vermilion battle robe and half armor,[1] rode at the head of some thirty horsemen accompanying the carriage at the front and rear. People, both high and low, in the capital saw Shigehira and said to each other: "What a pity! For what crime is he obliged to suffer this shame? Of the many courtiers of the Heike, such a fate has befallen none but Lord Shigehira! Since he was greatly loved by the Priest Premier and his wife, he was respected by all kinsmen of the Heike. Whenever he visited the palaces of the reigning emperor and the cloistered emperor, all courtiers, young and old, made way for him and honored him with special attention. Obviously his public humiliation is the punishment that the Buddha has brought upon him in retribution for his burning the temples at Nara."

The carriage proceeded to the east of the Kamo River and then turned back to the mansion of the late Vice-Councilor Ienari at Hachijō Horikawa. There Shigehira was confined and guarded by Sanehira.

The cloistered emperor sent the archivist Sadanaga as his envoy to Shigehira at Hachijō Horikawa. Sadanaga wore a red ceremonial robe and carried a sword and iron staff. In former times Shigehira had never been frightened by the presence of Sadanaga, but now he felt as if he were seeing Emma, the king of hell, in the world of the shades.

"His Majesty has decided thus," said the envoy. "If you wish to return to Yashima, send a message to the Heike and persuade them to return the Three Sacred Treasures to the capital. When this has been done, you will be set free to return to Yashima."

"This is truly how I feel about the matter," replied Shigehira. "All courtiers of the Heike, beginning with the state minister Munemori, will never agree to return the imperial regalia to the capital in exchange for my life or thousands upon thousands of lives. As for my mother, Nii-dono, she will never part with them, for it is the nature of a woman to be unwilling to dispense with anything. But I hate to reject the commands of the cloistered emperor without making any effort. I will therefore act as an intermediary for His Majesty to convey his commands to the Heike at Yashima."

Shigehira's hereditary retainer, Shigekuni, was designated messenger and was accompanied by Hanakata, one of the servants in attendance upon the cloistered emperor. Since they were not allowed to bear any personal letters, Shigehira could only entrust them with oral messages to various people of the Heike. One of them was to be conveyed to his wife: "Even during the journey of our escape from place to place we loved and consoled each other. Now separated, I can imagine how wretched you are! They say that the conjugal tie lasts for two existences. I surely will be reborn to meet you again in the next world."

Shigekuni heard this message and, in tears, set out for Yashima.

In former days among the retainers of Shigehira there had been a warrior named Tomotoki, aide to the chief of the Palace Repairs Division. After he had parted from his master, he waited upon Princess Hachijō. Now he came to see Sanehira and said: "I am Tomotoki who once served Lieutenant General Shigehira. Though I should have gone with him to the western provinces, I was unable to do so because I was in attendance upon the princess at that time. Today I saw my master paraded through the capital. He looked so miserable that I was unable to gaze at him long. I felt terribly sorry for him. If I may be allowed to see him, I shall be most obliged to you. I wish to console him by reminiscing of former days. Since I am a worthless man in the arts of bow and sword, I have never accompanied my master to battle. All I could do for him was to wait upon him morning and evening. Even so, if you still suspect me, I will leave my sword in your hand. Will you unbend and allow me to see him?"

Sanehira was a kindhearted man, and so he replied: "There is nothing wrong in having a private meeting with Lord Shigehira. I trust you, but let me keep your sword while you are with him."

With these words, Sanehira ushered him into the room where Shigehira was confined. Tomotoki, overjoyed at receiving permission to meet with his master, hurried into the room. But when he saw Shigehira in such a wretched state, tears rushed down his cheeks. Shigehira, for his part, felt as if he were dreaming a dream within a dream. Unable to find suitable words he simply cried.

After a while they began to speak about the past and present. Then Shigehira asked Tomotoki: "Do you remember a lady whom I used to meet when you acted as a messenger between us? Is she still attending court?"

"Yes, my lord," replied Tomotoki. "That is what I have heard."

"When I set out for the western provinces, I was unable to send a letter or message to her. I could hardly bear the pangs of remorse if she thought that all I had vowed to her had turned out to be nothing but a lie. Now I wish to send a letter to her. Can you take it?"

"Certainly, my lord."

Exhilarated by this reply, Shigehira wrote a letter and entrusted it to Tomotoki. The warriors on guard inquired of Tomotoki: "What kind of letter is it? Unless it is examined, we cannot let you go."

So, with Shigehira's permission, Tomotoki showed it to one of the guards. After reading it, the guard returned it to Tomotoki, saying: "You may take it with you."

Bearing the letter, Tomotoki went to court. But it was hard for him to hand it to the lady during the daytime without being seen by others, and so he went into a nearby cottage to let the day pass. Since the cottage stood next to the rear door of the waiting room for the court ladies, he was able to overhear some words spoken within. After a while, he heard a voice that he recognized as the lady's; she was weeping: "Of many courtiers of the Heike, Lieutenant General Shigehira alone was captured and paraded through the capital. What a pity it is! All the people say that this is the punishment the Buddha has brought upon him in retribution for burning the temples of Nara. Shigehira himself once told me, 'I did not order my men to set fire to the temples. However, there were many rascals among them, and they set their torches to the temples and towers.

When dewdrops on the leaves and twigs run together, they become the water that rushes down the trunk of a tree. Since I played the role of a trunk at that time, I cannot escape the blame. The fault was all mine!' What I feared for Shigehira has now come about."

Tomotoki was deeply impressed by her tenderness for Shigehira. Now he decided to speak up: "Excuse me, I have brought a letter to you."

"From whom?" asked the lady.

"My master, the lieutenant general."

The lady had long been reluctant to receive any visitors, but now she was so excited that she dashed out the door and cried: "Where do you have it? Where?"

She snatched the letter from Tomotoki and opened it. It described in detail how Shigehira had fared in the western provinces, how he had been taken alive, and what fate awaited him. At the end of the letter she read the following poem:

> The scorn of others
> Drifts down the river of tears
> On and on with me.
> Though I am about to die,
> I wish to see you again.

Choked with tears, the lady could say nothing. She put the letter into the folds of her robe and sobbed violently. She cried until she realized that crying could not assuage her sorrow. Finally regaining herself, she wrote in reply about how wretchedly she had spent the past two years, not seeing him, and added this poem:

> Though my name drifts down
> In disgrace because of you,
> On the same river
> I wish I could be with you
> To become dross in the depths.

Tomotoki returned to his master. The guard again demanded to inspect the letter. Since it seemed harmless, he allowed Tomotoki to hand it to his master. The lady's poem stirred Shigehira. Finding it difficult to suppress his longing for her, he begged a favor of Sanehira, saying: "There is a woman whom I visited for many years. I wish to be allowed to see her, for I have something to tell her."

Sanehira, being a gracious man, permitted this visit: "There is nothing wrong with your seeing the lady here. I have no objection."

Shigehira was delighted to obtain permission from Sanehira. He borrowed a carriage and sent it for the lady. Without a moment's hesitation, she threw herself into it and hurried to the house where Shigehira was confined. Upon arriving, the carriage was drawn up to the veranda. At the announcement of her presence, Shigehira ran to the carriage and said: "Do not alight, for the guards will see you."

He then drew aside the rear curtain of the carriage, thrust the upper half of his body inside, took her hands, and pressed his face to hers. The two remained speechless, only weeping. After a while he regained his composure and said: "When I set out for the western provinces, I desired to see you. But due to the confusion in the land, I was unable to send even a messenger. Since then I have long wished to send a letter to you and hear from you in return. But my homeless life in flight from place to place has deprived me of every opportunity to do so. Thus many days and months have passed in vain. That I was captured only to suffer such shameful hardships and to see you under such strange circumstances—these are but the whims of fate."

He covered his face with his sleeve and fell forward into the carriage. It was indeed a sad reunion of their souls. Night wore on.

"The streets at night are dangerous these days, so you should leave here before it gets late." Thus Shigehira urged her to depart. But when the carriage was about to leave, he caught the sleeve of her robe and improvised this poem:

> Seeing you briefly,
> The frail dewdrop of my life
> Sustained a pace—
> I cannot but suppose
> That this will be our last night.

Suppressing her tears, the lady composed the following reply:

> Since I bid adieu,
> Convinced that this is the end,
> My life's joy has passed.

Its dewdrop will disappear
An age before yours expires.

After she had returned to the palace, they were no longer permitted to meet. The most they could do was exchange letters from time to time.

This lady was a daughter of the priest Chikanori, who had once held the post of lord high chamberlain of Civil Administration. She was a famed beauty with a tender heart. Later, when she heard that Shigehira had been sent to Nara and executed there, she immediately took the tonsure and donned the black robe of a recluse to pray for his better fortune in the world beyond.

[1] The breastplate and arm and shin guards.

CHAPTER III

EDICT AT YASHIMA

Thus, as the tale tells us, the envoys of the cloistered emperor, Shigekuni and Hanakata, arrived at Yashima and presented an edict to the Heike demanding the return of the Three Sacred Treasures to the capital. The nobles and courtiers of the Heike, led by Lord Munemori, gathered in a solemn council and unrolled the scroll, upon which these words were written: "A few years have passed since Emperor Antoku set out from the capital for various provinces in the Nankai and Shikoku Districts, bearing with him the Three Sacred Treasures. The absence of the emperor and the imperial regalia from the capital is a great calamity for the imperial family and will perhaps bring the whole country to ruin. Lord Shigehira is a disloyal retainer of the imperial family who burned down the Tōdai-ji temple at Nara. It is the request of the emperor's retainer, Yoritomo, that Lord Shigehira be put to death. Separated from his kinsmen, he alone was captured. Now he is like a bird in a cage pining for the sky or like a wild goose that has lost his mate. His weary heart must be floating over the far away waves of the southern sea or flying across many layers of clouds to his lordship at Yashima. If the sacred treasures are returned to the capital, he shall receive the imperial pardon. This is truly the edict of the cloistered emperor, dictated by the lord high chamberlain of the Imperial Household, Naritada, to Councilor Tokitada of the Heike on the fourteenth day of the second month of the third year of the Juei era."

CHAPTER IV

THE ANSWER

Shigehira wrote to Munemori and Tokitada so that they would understand the purport of the edict. To his mother, Nii-dono, too he explained: "If you wish to see me again, alive, please entreat Munemori and see to it that the Three Sacred Treasures are sent back to the capital. Otherwise consider that you will never see me again."

Reading this, Nii-dono thrust the letter into the folds of her robe and then fell into a faint. How sad she was!

Meanwhile, all the nobles and courtiers of the Heike, led by Councilor Tokitada, held a council to discuss what reply would be made to the edict of the cloistered emperor. Nii-dono opened the sliding door that stood behind the nobles and courtiers and stumbling into the presence of Munemori, pressed Shigehira's letter to her face, fell prostrate, and said in tears: "Here is Shigehira's letter[1] from the capital. What a pitiful one it is! I can understand his feelings now. Munemori, please accept your mother's entreaty. I pray you to send back the Three Sacred Treasures to the capital!"

"I too think that I should do so," replied Munemori, "but I am afraid that it may be imprudent. For once they are possessed by the enemy, we shall no longer be able to exercise our power over the provincial warriors. Surely we would become the victims of Yoritomo. We must keep them in our hands at all costs. The very proof that the emperor is on the throne depends upon his maintenance of the imperial regalia. Even a mother's affection for her child must vary according to circumstances. How can you bring disaster to your other children and your friends for only one of your sons?"

Nii-dono, however, did not give up easily, but persisted, saying: "Although I have outlived the Priest-Premier, not a single day or hour have I desired to remain alive. I have sustained myself simply because I sympathized with the wretched state of the emperor on his journey and hoped to see you, my sons, flourish again in the capital. From the time that I heard that Shigehira had been taken alive at Ichi-no-tani, my soul has lived apart from my body, always to be by his side. Though I wish to see him but once more in this world, he does not even appear in my dreams. My breast and throat are choked, and so I can no longer drink even hot or cold water. At this very moment, holding his letter, I simply do not know where to place this sorrow of mine. If only I were to hear that Shigehira was no longer in this world, then I would follow him to the next world! Before I hear that he has been killed, I pray you to kill me so that I may be troubled no more."

Thus she cried and groaned in a loud voice, and so all who assembled there were moved to tears and looked down in embarassment. Vice-Councilor Tomomori then expressed his opinion: "Even if we send back the imperial regalia to the capital, the safe return of Shigehira will not be guaranteed. We must bring this up in our reply."

"Your suggestion is a most worthy one," replied Munemori, as he began to write. In tears, Nii-dono too wrote a reply to Shigehira. Lost in sorrow, she could hardly hold her pen. But her motherly love prevailed and soon she was able to regain firmness in her hand and describe her fruitless efforts. She then handed the letter to Shigekuni.

The wife of Shigehira could do nothing but weep bitterly. Not knowing what to say, Shigekuni wet the sleeves of his hunting suit with tears and took his leave.

Councilor Tokitada summoned the envoy and asked: "Are you Hanakata?"

"Yes, I am, Your Excellency."

"Since you have come this far upon the waves," said Tokitada, "I will give you a souvenir of your expedition, to carry with you your whole life." With these words, he had the two characters *nami* and *kata*[2] branded on the cheek of Hanakata with a hot iron.

When Hanakata returned to the capital, the cloistered emperor noticed them and burst into laughter, saying: "We can do nothing about the brand on your face. Let us leave it as it is and call you 'Namikata' from now on."

The Heike's answer to the cloistered emperor was as follows:

[591]

"The edict of the cloistered emperor dated the fourteenth day of this month arrived here at Yashima in Sanuki Province on the twenty-eighth day. We have respectfully read it. Now we wish to express our thoughts in reply. Many people of our house, including Lord Michimori, have already been killed at Ichi-no-tani in Settsu Province. How can we rejoice at a single pardon that may be granted to Shigehira?

"It is some four years since Emperor Antoku succeeded to the throne of the late Emperor Takakura. He was making august efforts to follow in the steps of his benevolent and virtuous predecessors and the ideal examples set by the wise rulers of Yao and Shun, when Yoritomo, a barbarian of the east, and Yoshinaka, a rebel of the north, united their forces and invaded the capital. Thus they caused the young emperor and his mother, Kenreimon-In, great anguish, and no small indignation to his maternal relatives and retainers. He was consequently obliged to stay away from the capital for a while, on the isles of Kyushu, in search of a peaceful life. How can the Three Sacred Treasures be separated from his august presence before he returns to the capital?

"A subject takes for a mind the emperor, and the emperor takes for a body his subjects. A sound body is assured by a sound mind. If the emperor is of one mind, living in peace, so will be the subject. If the subjects are at peace with one another, so will be the country. If the emperor above is troubled, the subject below will not rejoice. If the heart within is heavy, the body without will be cheerless.

"From the time that our ancestor Sadamori destroyed the rebel Masakado, all his successors have maintained a tradition of appeasing rebellions in the eight eastern provinces and punishing the enemies of the throne from generation to generation. We have thus devoted ourselves to the service of safeguarding the fate of the imperial family. At the battles of Hōgen and Heiji, for instance, our late father, the Priest-Premier, was concerned only with the imperial wishes and made light of his own life. As for Yoritomo, because of the treason of his father, the captain of the Imperial Stables of the Left, the cloistered emperor, in the twelfth month of the first year of Heiji, issued commands again and again to have him put to death. The late Priest-Premier, however, out of his merciful heart, pleaded for his life. Entirely unmindful of his former gratitude and obligation to our great favors, Yoritomo has raised a number of rebellions.

He is not aware of the fact that he is only a lean wolf. His offensiveness to our family is intolerable ! May he soon invite the punishment of the gods ! Defeat and destruction will be all that he deserves.

"Neither the sun nor the moon darkens their light for one creature, nor does the Buddha alter the Law for one man. A ruler should neither get rid of his worthy subject because of one evil act nor have a small blemish obscure great merit. If His Majesty, the cloistered emperor, had not forgotten our faithful services rendered to the imperial family throughout many generations and a great number of loyal deeds done by our late father, the Priest-Premier, in his service to the imperial family, Emperor Antoku would not have been transferred to Shikoku.

"Let an imperial edict be issued so that we may return once again to our ancient capital and wash away the shame of old defeats ! If not, we shall go to Kikai-ga-shima, or Korea, or China, or India. What a pity for the imperial family, if the imperial regalia, which has been handed down through eighty-one generations, were to be but vain ornament in an alien land ! Let these our wishes be brought openly before His Majesty, the cloistered emperor. With utmost respect and obeisance, on the twenty-eighth day of the second month of the third year of Juei. This is truly the answer of Munemori, junior grade of the first court rank."

[1] Although the text states that the envoy was not allowed to bear any personal letters, perhaps Shigehira's letters, the one to Munemori and Tokitada and the other to Nii-dono, were delivered by the envoy in the hope of securing the return of the imperial regalia.

[2] Literally "Wave Man."

CHAPTER V

HŌNEN'S COUNSEL

Upon hearing of the contents of the Heike's reply, Lieutenant General Shigehira expressed his disappointment: "That is what I expected. I know how little they think of me."

He had not really expected the return of the Three Sacred Treasures in exchange for his life. Nevertheless he had entertained a faint hope until the answer arrived. And when it was decided that he should be sent down to Kamakura, he was obliged to acknowledge that all hopes were gone. His heart was too heavy to bear the journey from the capital to the east. He called for the chief guard, Sanehira, and asked to be permitted to take the tonsure. But when this request was conveyed to Yoshitsune and then to the cloistered emperor, it was answered that no permission would be given to him until he saw Yoritomo at Kamakura.

"Then," said Shigehira to Sanehira, "may I be allowed to see a saintly priest whom I have long respected as my spiritual counselor? I wish to speak with him about my afterlife. What do you think?"

"Who is this saintly priest?" asked Sanehira.

"He is the priest Hōnen[1] of Kurodani,"[2] was the reply.

"There will be nothing wrong with your meeting him."

Shigehira was greatly pleased and called for the priest at once. Upon Hōnen's arrival, Shigehira said to him in tears: "Perhaps it is karma that I can meet you again after having been captured. Please tell me what fate awaits me now. When I had rank and office, I was so busy attending court and administering affairs of state that I was ambitious and haughty, unmindful of my fate in the world beyond the grave. Since confusion was brought to the land with the decline of our house, I have done nothing but fight here and there, my mind

devoted to the evil desire of killing others only to save my own life.
I have been utterly blind to Buddhahood!

"The worst event was the burning of the temples at Nara.
Unable to ignore the rules of this world, I was obliged to follow
the commands of the cloistered emperor and my father and go to
Nara to pacify the violent monks there. The burning of the temples
that followed was beyond my power. However, the fault was all
mine, for I was the commander-in-chief at that time. I am prepared
to receive any punishment, if the responsibility must fall upon one
person. I should accept any blame for my acts, for I know that all
is but retribution.

"Now I wish to shave my head and observe the Buddha's Ten
Precepts so that I may be able to devote myself to the way of the
Buddha. My only regret is this—however hard I may practice austerities, I shall not be able to attain salvation from even a single crime
of mine, for I am now a prisoner, threatened with execution at any
moment. When I reflect upon the conduct of my past life, my evil-
ness is greater than Mount Sumeru, while my goodness is smaller
than a speck of dust. If I die in such a wretched state of mind, I will
surely be reborn in hell, where await me the tortures of the pit of
fire, the blood pond of beasts, and the swords of hungry spirits.
And so I beseech you to be so kind as to extend your compassionate
hand to help an evil man like me and show me the way to salvation."

These words moved Hōnen to tears and rendered him speechless
for a while. Finally he said: "Though you have had the blessing of
wearing human flesh in this world, it seems you shall now fall into
hell. What a pity! But you have the sobriety of heart to renounce
the sinful world and desire the Pure Land in the world beyond. Inasmuch as you are awakened to Buddhahood, cleansing your mind
of evil and directing your mind to good, the Buddhas in the Three
Worlds will surely be overjoyed. Though there are many and various ways to Buddhahood, the supreme practice in this degenerate
age is to invoke Amida Buddha. The Pure Land is divided into nine
levels to receive people according to their good deeds in this world.
Recitation of prayers required in any one of these nine levels has
been simplified into three words—'Hail Amida Buddha.' Therefore
even the prayers recited by the ignorant will be accepted.

"However sinful you have been, do not deprecate yourself. Even to one who is an offender of the Buddha's Ten Precepts or a perpetrator of the Five Cardinal Crimes, once his mind is turned from evil to good, his rebirth in paradise shall be granted. However small your merit, do not give up your hope for Buddhahood. If you give all your heart to Amida Buddha and repeat the invocation of him ten times, surely he will come to meet you. At the moment when your first faith arises in you, your birth in paradise is determined. If you constantly recite 'Hail Amida Buddha' with firm conviction in your repentance, you shall certainly be forgiven. If you trust in Amida Buddha, the all-powerful, whose sword is so sharp as to cut you free from any evil passion, even King Emma of hell may not approach you. If you place all your faith in uttering the name of Amida Buddha, casting aside all other practices, your sins will be washed away. Truly this is the essence of the Pure Land sect.

"Thus I have summarized the whole doctrine for you. Now one gravely important point is that the attainment of paradise depends upon faith. Never doubt, but simply believe this teaching. If you do not neglect to recite 'Hail Amida Buddha,' putting your faith in it even during the four basic acts of walking, standing, sitting, and lying, at the instant when death comes, you will be delivered from this world of trouble to paradise, where you will be reborn into eternal bliss."

Shigehira was greatly encouraged, saying: "I wish to take advantage of this opportunity for receiving from you the Buddha's Ten Precepts, so that I may vow to observe them. But can I do this without becoming a monk, my venerable master?"

"Indeed, it is quite usual for a layman to observe the Precepts."

Hōnen immediately took a razor, laid it on Shigehira's forehead, and simply made a motion of shaving his head. In this manner the ceremony was performed for Shigehira, who received it with tears of joy. Hōnen too wept as he performed it. Shigehira then sent Tomotoki for an ink stone, which he had deposited with an intimate friend, and handed it to Hōnen, saying: "Please do not give this away to anyone, but keep it always by your side. And whenever you look at it, I pray you to remember me and recite 'Hail Amida Buddha.' If you would be so kind as to chant a volume of sutras for me from time to time, I shall be most happy."

Choked with tears, Hōnen could not utter any words of gratitude. He put the ink stone into the folds of his robe, and weeping bitterly, returned to Kurodani.

This ink stone was the one that the emperor of the Sung dynasty had sent to Shigehira's father, the Priest-Premier, in return for his gift of gold dust. It was inscribed: "To the Priest-Premier of Wada in Japan." People called it Matsukage, or "Pine Shadow."

[1] Also called Genkū (1133–1212). Born in Mimasaka Province, he entered the monastery of Enryaku-ji at fifteen. Dissatisfied with orthodox teachings of the Tendai sect, he became a convinced Jōdo ("Pure Land") advocate and taught that the only salvation was to invoke the name of Amida Buddha. For this radical teaching, he was exiled to Tosa in Shikoku in 1207. In 1211 he was permitted to return to Kyoto.

[2] One of the temples belonging to Enryaku-ji, it is located northeast of Kyoto.

CHAPTER VI

SHIGEHIRA IS SENT TO KAMAKURA

Finally Yoritomo, at Kamakura, requested the cloistered emperor to send Shigehira there. First he was escorted by his guard, Sanehira, to the mansion of Yoshitsune, and then, on the tenth day of the third month, he was ordered to set out. This time he was accompanied by Kagetoki. He had already suffered the shame of being sent as a captive from the western provinces to the capital. How pitiful that he was made to travel through the eastern provinces—the length of the road to Kamakura —in disgrace.

When he came to the banks of the Shinomiya River, he remembered a thatched hut belonging to Semimaru,[1] the fourth son of Emperor Daigo, near the Osaka Checkpoint. It had been there that Semimaru had calmed his mind in the mountain breeze to play the biwa. Lord Hiromasa of the third court rank went to listen to his biwa at this spot day after day, night after night, for three long years. He made these trips on windy days or calm, on rainy nights or fine. Thus pacing up and down, or standing near the hut, he strained his ears and mastered the three secret melodies. Now a sense of profound pathos welled up in Shigehira as he passed this area.

Soon after he had crossed over Mount Ōsaka he found himself on the bridge at Seta, where the sounds of horses' hooves echoed. Riding onward, he saw a skylark winging over the village of Noji,[2] Shiga in the quiet mood of spring, the village of Kagami-yama[3] in the mist, and the lofty peak of Hira to the north. Then Mount Ibuki rose up a short distance before him.

Riding further, he arrived at the Fuwa Checkpoint. In his previous experience, a checkpoint had been simply a place where a carriage and its passengers were stopped for investigation. But now he found beauty here, and he felt reluctant to leave, for the di-

lapidated eaves of the checkpoint house held a certain charm. The
ebbing tide of the bay of Narumi[4] sadly suggested his future, and so
his sleeves were wet with tears. As he came to Yatsuhashi[5] in Mikawa
Province, he thought of Arihara no Narihira, who had paused at
this spot during his journey and, while viewing iris, had composed
a famous poem in yearning for his wife left behind in the capital. It
was also there that Shigehira saw the waters divide and pass around
the small islands, and likewise his thoughts ran in many directions.

As he crossed the bridge over the outlet of Lake Hamana,[6] the
wind blew through the pines. The waves of the lake lapped at the
shore. Even without these mournful sounds, the journey would
have been melancholy for him—a captive under guard on his way
to execution.

The evening was well advanced when he arrived at the station
of Ikeda.[7] That night he was lodged at the house of a certain lady-in-
waiting, a daughter of the mistress of the women entertainers at
the station. When the lady had had a look at him, she was surprised
at what turns fate could take and said to herself: "In times past he
was so high a personage that I was unable to find a way of showing
my affectionate feelings through even a proper intermediary.
How surprising that I find him staying at such a place today!"

Then she composed the following poem and presented it to
him:

> When on a journey
> You are thus obliged to stay
> In humble lodgings,
> How fondly you must think of
> Your home in the capital.

To this poem, Shigehira replied:

> Though on a journey,
> I do not miss my old home
> In the capital.
> For it does not yet provide
> Eternal comfort for me.

After a while Shigehira inquired of the guard, Kagetoki: "Who
is the author of this poem? It must be a person of some elegance."

"Perhaps you do not know," replied Kagetoki, "but this lady is one who was summoned to wait upon Lord Munemori when he was the governor of this province. Because he gave his true love to her, he took her back to the capital. She had left her aged mother here, and so she begged Lord Munemori for leave to see her again. But as he obstinately refused, she composed the following poem and presented it to him in the early part of the third month:

> Though truly I miss
> The joyful beauties of spring
> In the capital,
> My heart flies back to the east
> Where a flower is dying.

"After reading this poem, Lord Munemori finally granted her leave. In all the provinces along the Tōkai-dō highway, there are none who can surpass her in elegance and poetry."

Many days had passed since Shigehira's departure from the capital. Half of the third month was already gone, and spring was past its prime. The cherry blossoms on the faraway mountains looked like unmelted snow. While viewing the mist over the shores and islands, Shigehira brooded over his past and future and wept, saying to himself: "What karma in my former life has brought this miserable lot to me?"

His mother and wife had often regretted that he had no children, and they had prayed fervently to the gods and the Buddhas that he might be rewarded with a child, but they had received no sign. Mindful of this, Shigehira said to himself: "It is now a relief for me that I have no child of my own. If I had had one, how many times more miserable I would feel!"

When he came to Saya-no-Nakayama,[8] his heart sank, for he remembered the melancholy poem that had been composed by the priest Saigyō at this very spot:

> After I have grown
> Bent under the weight of years
> I am here again
> —Saya-no-Nakayama—
> I have lived beyond my span.

He proceeded along the ivy-covered path of Utsu-no-Yamabe[9] to the time-honored station of Tegoshi.[10] Then, far off to the north, appeared a mountain covered with snow. Upon inquiring,

Shigehira was told that it was Kai-no-Shirane, the white peak of Kai Province. Repressing his tears, he expressed his sorrow in this poem:

> Through this futile life
> I have passed from day to day,
> Death a step behind.
> Now I see as my reward
> The forlorn white peak of Kai.[11]

Passing by the Kiyomi Checkpoint, he entered the plain at the foot of Mount Fuji. To the north the pine trees rustled in the wind. Beyond them lay the green slope of the mountain. To the south, the waves lapped at the beach. Vast was the blue ocean.

When he passed over Mount Ashigara,[12] Shigehira remembered that the god of the shrine on this mountain had seen his wife after three years of separation and had divorced her, saying: "If you are truly in love with me, you must keep thin. Since you have grown stouter, I do not believe that you love me any longer."[13]

Then Shigehira came to the woods of Koyurugi[14] and the Mariko River,[15] and the shores of Koiso and Ōiso. He went on along the shore of Yatsumato,[16] the Togami Plain, and the Mikoshi Peninsula.[17] He was not required to press on, and so many days passed until at last he arrived at Kamakura.

---

[1] Historians challenge his imperial birth and assert that he was a servant of the prince of the blood Atsuzane (897–966), son of Emperor Uda. Semimaru was blind but excelled in composing poems and playing the biwa.

[2] Present-day Kusatsu, Shiga Prefecture.

[3] Located in the western part of Gamō-gun, Shiga Prefecture.

[4] Present-day Narumi, Aichi Prefecture.

[5] Present-day Chiryu, Aichi Prefecture.

[6] A lagoon in Tōtōmi Province, present-day Shizuoka.

[7] Present-day Ikeda, Toyota, Shizuoka Prefecture, west of the Tenryū River.

[8] The sloping hillside from Kakegawa City to Kanaya in present-day Shizuoka Prefecture.

[9] A mountain on the border of Shizuoka City and Shida-gun.

[10] Located in the present-day city of Shizuoka.

[11] A pun: *kai* also means "reward."

[12] Located in Kanagawa Prefecture.

[13] According to legend, the god Ashigara set out on a journey to China and left his wife at home. When he returned three years later, he found that she had grown fat and sleek during his absence, and so he said: "If you had been worried about me,

you would have become thin. The fact that you are fat and beautiful proves that you no longer love me." He immediately divorced her.

[14] The shores southeast of Ōiso, Kanagawa Prefecture.

[15] Presently called the Sakawagawa.

[16] Present-day Fujisawa, Kanagawa Prefecture.

[17] The ancient name of Inamura-ga-saki, east of Kamakura City.

CHAPTER VII

SENJU NO MAE

Immediately after his arrival, Shigehira was brought into the presence of Yoritomo. Yoritomo exclaimed: "Since I made up my mind to ease the wrath of His Majesty, the cloistered emperor, and avenge my father, my plan to overthrow the Heike has been fairly successful. However, I never expected to see you here under these circumstances. Your presence here enables me to anticipate the honor of receiving the state minister, Munemori, as well. As for the burning of the temples at Nara, tell me whether it was done at the command of the late Priest-Premier or at your own order on the spur of the moment. Either way it was an unpardonable crime."

"It was neither the command of the Priest-Premier nor my own," replied Shigehira, "but it happened by accident in the course of operations that we undertook at the time to appease the violence of the monks. Truly it was beyond my control.

"In former days the Genji and the Heike always stood by the throne, though in rivalry, on its right and left, and so the imperial family enjoyed nothing but peace. Some time ago the fortunes of the Genji declined and our family, since the days of Hōgen and Heiji, has frequently destroyed the enemies of the imperial family. Our services have been rewarded beyond measure. Since we became relatives of the emperor through Kenreimon-In, more than sixty members of our family have been promoted to extremely high positions at court. Nothing has stood in our way to glory and happiness for some twenty years.

"But now we are in a decline. It is indeed an unfortunate turn of events that I have been brought down here as a captive. What I most regret is this. Everyone believes that he who serves in war against an enemy of the throne is entitled to receive the imperial favor for as many as seven generations. But I can prove that this

[603]

is false. Over and over again the late Priest-Premier endangered his life for the safety of the throne, but it was in his generation alone that his family was able to bask in the imperial favor. His children have been forgotten and deserted in a wretched state, as you can see. Our men have become resigned to their fate and are now determined to expose their corpses on the mountains and plains, or drift upon the waves of the western sea.

"Never had I dreamed of being taken alive and brought here. Truly this must be a retribution for misdeeds that I committed in a former life. In China King T'ang of the Yin dynasty was captured by King Chieh of Hsia and imprisoned at Hsia-t'ai, and King Wen of the Chou at Yeo-li. Wise rulers though they were, they met the fate of imprisonment in good times past, and so it is quite natural that a worthless man such as I be captured and imprisoned in this degenerate age. It is not a disgrace at all for a man of bow and sword to fall into the hands of his enemy and be put to death. Now I pray you to cut off my head at once."

After he had said this, he shut his mouth and would not talk. Deeply impressed by his resolution, Kagetoki exclaimed: "Indeed he is a great general!"

All the warriors in attendance wet their sleeves with tears. Yoritomo too was moved to compassion and exclaimed: "It is far from my wish to regard the Heike as my personal enemies. I ask you to understand that I am simply carrying out the imperial order. Now what I fear is that the monks of the south capital will never forget you but will demand of us that we send you into their hands."

He then ordered that Shigehira be placed in the charge of Kano no Suke Munemochi, a native of Izu Province. Shigehira's status in the custody of Yoritomo and his men seemed just like that of a criminal, who, after committing crimes in this world, is sent to hell and is passed from demon to demon ten times for periods of seven days each.

His new guard, Munemochi, however, was a compassionate man who never treated him severely. He first offered Shigehira a hot bath. In this bath Shigehira thought that he might wash away the dust and grime of the long journey and purify himself to meet the end that could come at any moment. In such sad preoccupation, he was just entering the bath when the door of the bathhouse opened and there appeared a beautiful lady of some twenty years. Her complexion was exquisitely white against her raven locks. She was clad in an unlined silk robe and a blue patterned overwrap, and attended by a maid of fourteen or fifteen, whose hair hung to her waist. The maid was also wearing an unlined white silk robe and a blue patterned overwrap; she carried some combs in a wooden basin. The lady waited upon Shigehira as he bathed. Then, after she had bathed herself and washed her own hair, she took leave of him.

As she was going out, she said to Shigehira: "It was my master, Yoritomo, who sent me to serve you here. He sent a woman, because had he sent a man he would be considered lacking in elegance. He also ordered me to ask if there might be anything that he could do for you. Perhaps he thought that a man would have some difficulty, but that a woman could manage this better."

"Since I am a captive, I must not expect to receive favors," replied Shigehira, "but there is one thing I desire—to take the tonsure and become a monk."

When this request was conveyed to Yoritomo, he replied: "Impossible! This would be acceptable only if he were my personal enemy. Inasmuch as he has been given into my hands as an enemy of the throne, I am powerless to grant him permission."

The lady brought Yoritomo's reply and left. Shigehira asked his guard the name of this elegant visitor.

"She is the daughter of the mistress of the women entertainers at Tegoshi," replied the guard. "Since she is extremely graceful in form and figure and disposition, she has been in attendance upon our master, Yoritomo, for about two years now. Her name is Senju no Mae."

That night it rained a little, and everything appeared faint, weary, and sad, when the lady, Senju no Mae, returned with a biwa and a koto. Munemochi too came in with ten of his retainers and brought saké for Shigehira. Senju no Mae served it to him. Shigehira drank some but still remained in low spirits.

"Perhaps you are already aware of my master's wishes," Munemochi said. "He ordered me to wait upon you most cordially so that you would feel comfortable here. If you feel sad because of my negligent service, he will not forgive me. I am a native of Izu Province and only a sojourner at Kamakura, but I will do all that I can for you."

[605]

He then turned to Senju no Mae and requested: "Say something that may please my guest and serve him more saké."

At this request, Senju no Mae laid aside the saké bottle for a moment and chanted a rōei once, then again:

> I am angry with the weaving girl
> Who made the dancer's robe too heavy.
> I am angry with the piper
> Whose melody never ends.
> I am trying to entertain you.
> Why must you look so sad?

"Michizane swore to protect anyone who sang the song," said Shigehira. "But I am one who has already been forsaken by him. I am now entirely helpless in this world. What merit could there be in joining you to chant it through? If it is one that might lighten my guilt, I will be glad to join you."

Senju no Mae then chanted another rōei:

> Even an offender of Buddha's Ten Precepts
> Shall be taken by Buddha to paradise.
> Buddha will come and help you
> Faster than a puff of wind,
> Piercing through mist and cloud.

And she added the following imayō, singing four or five times:

> Let all who desire paradise call
> Upon the name of Amida Buddha.

Her melody was so expressive that Shigehira drained his saké cup and handed it to her. She took the cup and passed it to Munemochi. This time, while he was drinking, she played the biwa.

"This is an ancient Chinese piece composed merrily by Shun for the purpose of invoking the gods, a melody called 'Gojōraku',"[1] said Shigehira, "but now, to my ears, it sounds like 'Goshōraku',[2] a melody that we will hear in the world beyond the grave. So let me play the last verse of T'ang's 'Ōjō-no-kyū',[3] hoping that I may be taken to paradise soon."

After introducing these puns, Shigehira took the biwa and tuned it. He then began to play the melody of "Ōjō-no-kyū." The night wore on; his mind and heart became tranquil. After a time he said:

"Who would expect to find a lady of such elegance in the eastern provinces?"

He requested Senju no Mae to sing another song. Then, perfectly composed, she sang the following imayō:

> A sense of close companionship
> Can grow out of such brief encounters—
> Such brief interludes—
> Two strangers may stand close together
> Under a tree to take shelter from a summer shower,
> Or they many share a drink at the same spring.
> This is the fulfillment of a promise
> Made in a former life.

Shigehira too sang a rōei called "The Tears of Consort Yü When the Light Grew Dim." This song has the following story. In ancient China, when Kao-tsu of Han and Hs'iang-yü of Ch'u contended for the throne, Hs'iang-yü triumphed in seventy-two battles, but he was defeated in the end, his army surrounded. Admitting defeat, he sprang onto his piebald, renowned for its birdlike swiftness when galloping a thousand miles a day, and intended to escape with his consort, Yü. Then, strangely enough, the horse set its feet firmly and refused to move. Hs'iang-yü said in tears: "My power is gone. There remains no way out of the enemy encirclement. I do not care about their attacks. My only regret is parting with this lady." He wept all night. As the lamp grew dim, Yü's heart sank. She too wept. The night wore on. The enemy came shouting down on all sides. Later this pitiable scene was represented by State Councilor Hirosuke[4] in one of his poems. Shigehira must have connected this story with his own fate, and it was a sign of his artistic sensitivity that he had chosen it to sing on this occasion.

The banquet continued until day was about to break. When the warriors took leave of Shigehira, so did Senju no Mae.

The morning after, as Yoritomo was chanting the *Lotus Sutra* before his family shrine, Senju no Mae came to see him. He turned to her with a smile and said: "Do you not think that it was very thoughtful of me to arrange a meeting for you with a man of such elegance?"

His retainer, Chikayoshi, who was writing something in his presence, could not understand the meaning behind these words, so he asked Yoritomo, who replied: "For the last few years the men of the Heike were used to fighting all the time, and so it has been my understanding that they knew nothing but the arts of bow and sword. Yesterday, however, Shigehira sang and played the biwa so skillfully and beautifully that I stood all night out in the garden listening to him. He is truly a great artist."

"I too would have liked to hear him," said Chikayoshi, "but unfortunately I was sick last night, and so I could not. Henceforth, however, I will not miss the chance to do so. I must admit that the Heike have produced many talented musicians and artists. Last year, when we talked about the Heike, comparing them to flowers, we honored Shigehira as the peony among them."[5]

Shigehira's singing and playing on the biwa were so impressive that Yoritomo often remembered him and admired him long afterward.

Senju no Mae could not forget him. Later, when she heard that he had been sent to Nara and put to death there, she at once took the tonsure, donned the black robe of a recluse, and, giving her heart up to the Buddha at Zenkō-ji in Shinano Province, prayed for Shigehira's better lot in the world beyond. Thus it was that she fulfilled her wishes and attained Nirvana.

---

[1] Literally "Five-Pleasure Melody."

[2] Literally "Afterlife Melody."

[3] A quick melody, urging one to die with unswerving faith in Amida Buddha.

[4] A fifth-generation descendent of Tachibana Moroie, the minister of the Left at the time of Emperor Shōmu; he died in 890 at fifty-six.

[5] A peony denotes radiant beauty. An old Japanese proverb says: "She is like a lily while standing up, and like a peony while sitting down."

CHAPTER VIII

YOKOBUE

Thus, as the tale tells us, Lord Koremori of the third court rank was now at Yashima and eagerly sought a chance to return to the capital. The image of his wife left behind in Kyoto remained with him. He could not forget her even for a moment. At dawn on the fifteenth day of the third month of the first year of Genryaku [1184], he said to himself, "I can no longer live this worthless life," and slipped out of the fortress of Yashima. He was accompanied by two young servants, Shigekage and Ishido-maru, and a warrior-retainer, Takesato. Takesato was chosen because he was an excellent oarsman. They boarded a small boat at Yūki[1] in Awa Province and rowed across the strait of Naruto toward Kii. They steered along the shores of Waka and Fukiage, places near the Tamatsushima Shrine, where Sotōrihime was worshiped. Passing by Nichizen and Kokuken, they arrived at the port of Kii.

"Though I wish to take a mountain route up to the capital and see my loved ones but once more, I would hate to be found by the enemy and have my blood shed upon the corpse of my father. This would only add to Lord Shigehira's shame, for he was taken alive and paraded through the streets of the capital. And I hear that he was recently sent down to Kamakura." As he spoke these words, Koremori's heart was heavy. Suppressing his fervent desire to return to the capital, he did not take the route to Kyoto but headed for Mount Kōya.

Atop the mountain lived a certain priest with whom Koremori had been acquainted many years before. He was a son of the chief guard of the Imperial Gate of the Left, Mochiyori, and had formerly been an imperial guard and a retainer of Lord Shigemori. His name was Tokiyori. When he was thirteen years old, he went to visit the office of the Archivists Division. It was there that he happened to see in attendance upon Kenreimon-In a maid of low rank, a girl named Yokobue. Tokiyori was at once captivated by her charms. Upon hearing of his infatuation, his father became angry and advised him strictly, saying: "I have plans for you. It is my wish to find a good match for you, a girl of an influential family, who might help you obtain a high position at court. Take heed of your father's advice and stop loving such a lowly maid!"

"Of old there lived a maiden in China named Hsi Wang-mu," replied Tokiyori, "but she is alive no longer. There also lived a hermit named Tung-fang Shuo, but he is nothing more than a name now. To die old or to die young—that is a trivial accident of nature, ephemeral as a spark from a flint. However long a life one may wish to live, it is but seventy or eighty years at most, and of these years the prime of life is twenty years more or less. In this world of dreams and illusions, why should a man be burdened even for a moment with an ugly woman whom he dislikes? But if I choose the one I love, I will be condemned as a disloyal son to my father. This is a moment when I must open my eyes to find a way to Buddhahood. Now let me renounce this fleeting world!"

Tokiyori cut off his topknot and secluded himself at the Ōjō-in temple[2] in Saga. He was then only nineteen years old.

When Yokobue heard that Tokiyori had renounced the world, she said: "It is all right that he deserted me, but I regret that he became a monk. And when he decided to renounce the world, why did he not first come and tell me so? However firm his resolve or however closed his heart, I will dare to go visit him and let him hear my complaint."

One evening Yokobue set off from the capital. She walked, without firm command of direction, toward Saga. It was now past the tenth day of the second month. The spring breeze over the village of Umezu was fragrant. The plum blossoms blooming there sent her their graceful scent on the wind. The moon, half-hidden by the drifting mist, was reflected dimly on the waters of the Ōi River. As she walked on, her heart sank. She asked herself over and over again for whom did she feel such anguish. Arriving at the precinct of Ōjō-in, Yokobue was obliged to search for her loved one, for all she had heard of his whereabouts was the name of the temple. She did not know in what part of the temple he was living. After a long search, she came to a rough cell and from within heard a voice chanting a sutra. Yokobue recognized the voice as Tokiyori's, and so she ordered her maid to deliver a message to him: "It is I, Yokobue. I have come this far to see how you have changed in the priesthood."

This message made Tokiyori's heart beat fast. He peeped through a chink in the sliding door and saw her standing outside, exhausted from her strenuous search. Even for the most fanatic devotee of the Buddha, it was a sight that could not fail to restore earthly affection. But Tokiyori only sent someone out to say in reply: "The person for whom you are looking is not here. You must have come to the wrong place."

For Yokobue there was nothing more to say, and so, suppressing her tears, she turned back. As she staggered homeward, her heart was almost too heavy to bear.

Tokiyori said to the monk who dwelt with him in the same cell: "This is a quiet place where nothing interrupts me in offering prayers to the Buddha. But the girl whom I loved has already discovered my whereabouts. I managed to steel my heart to avoid her once. However, if she should come again, I might not resist but melt. I must leave here."

With these words, he departed from Saga and went up to Mount Kōya. There he entered the Shōjōshin-in temple[3] to practice his austerities. And it was there, after a time, that he heard that Yokobue too had renounced the world to become a nun, so he composed the following poem and sent it to her:

> Sorrow had I felt
> Till I heard you shaved your pate
> To become a nun.
> Glad are we in the same way,
> Like two arrows—no return.

Yokobue answered:

> Once I shaved my head,
> There was nothing to regret
> In this fleeting world,
> For I was unable to grasp
> Your heart—a flown-off arrow.

Perhaps her sad memories of the past never ceased to dwell in her heart, even though she had given herself up completely to the Buddha at the Hokke-ji temple in Nara, for it was not long before she became ill and passed away. When Tokiyori was told of her death, he redoubled his austerities. Thus it was that his father forgave his unfilial conduct, and all who became acquainted with him placed their trust in Tokiyori and called him the Saint of Kōya.

Now Koremori tried to seek out Tokiyori, and, after a search, finally found him. There appeared before Koremori a priest, seemingly old and thin, dressed in the black robe of a recluse and a somber colored stole. It was none other than Tokiyori, who must have been still less than thirty years of age. This was, after all, Koremori's first meeting with him after Tokiyori had renounced the world. Koremori remembered how rich and manly he had been in the capital, attired in hunting suit and high lacquered bonnet, his hair carefully dressed. And yet Koremori envied him now, for he looked like a sage, unswervingly devoted to the Buddha, even more venerable than the Seven Sages[4] of Tsin in the Bamboo Grove or the Four Whitebeards[5] of Han on Mount Shang.

[1] Present-day Yuki-chō, Umibe-gun, Tokushima Prefecture.
[2] Established by Nembutsu-bō, a disciple of Hōnen.
[3] Literally "Purification of Heart." This temple is located north of the Great Pagoda within the monastery of Kōya.
[4] These seven sages—Chi-K'ang, Yüan Chi, Yüan Hsien, Shan T'ao, Lin Ling, Wang Jung, and Hsiang Hsiu—secluded themselves from the world in the Bamboo Grove and found solace in a simple life and academic discussions.
[5] Four old men—Tung-yüan-kung, Ch'i-li-chi, Hsia-huang-kung, and Lu-li Hsien-sheng—denied the violent rule of Ch'in and took refuge on Mount Shang.

CHAPTER IX

ON MOUNT KŌYA

When Tokiyori saw Koremori, he cried: "Am I dreaming? Now tell me how you managed to escape and come here all the way from Yashima?"

"Let me explain why I am here," replied Koremori. "When I left the capital for the western provinces, as did all the men of the Heike, I could not set my mind at rest even for an instant, thinking of those whom I had left behind. Though I said nothing about this to others, trying hard to conceal my wretchedness, my face betrayed me. Lord Munemori and Nii-dono sensed my true feelings, and suspected that I would turn traitor like Lord Yorimori. I knew that I had been worthless in battle. Reluctant to stay longer at Yashima, and yet having no definite plans in mind, I left there and came this far. I am eager to take a mountain route up to the capital and see my loved ones once more, but the shameful example set by Lord Shigehira has discouraged me. I think I should give up everything. I would rather take the tonsure and devote myself to the torturous austerities of fire and water. The first thing that I wish to do is pay a pilgrimage to the Kumano Shrine. This has been my long-cherished desire."

"Your anxiety and hardship in this world of dreams and illusions are of but little account," replied Tokiyori, "for real pain awaits you on the long and dark path in hell."

Tokiyori then led him around to offer prayers at all the temples and pagodas until at last they arrived at the innermost temple of Mount Kōya.

Mount Kōya lies at a distance of two hundred ri from the capital, far from the bustle of the city. The only sound that breaks its stillness is the mountain wind that now and again rustles the branches of the trees. Calm are the trees' shadows thrown by the setting sun. With eight peaks and eight valleys, it is truly a sacred mountain that purifies the hearts of all men. Beneath the misty forests the flowers bloom; among the cloud-capped hills echo the temple bells. On the roof tiles the pine shoots grow; over the clay walls is thick moss. A time-honored place!

In the Engi era [901–922], Emperor Daigo had a dream in which he received a sign from the saintly priest Kobo Daishi. In reply to the priest's request, the emperor sent a dark red robe to him on Mount Kōya. When the imperial envoy, Lord Suketaka, taking Bishop Kangen of Hannya-ji as his guide, climbed the mountain and opened the doors of the cell to put the robe on Kōbō Daishi, a thick mist arose and hid his body. And so, bursting into tears, Kangen said: "Ever since I was born out of the womb of my merciful mother and allowed to become a disciple of my venerable master, I have offended none of the Buddha's Precepts. Why am I not permitted to see Kōbō Daishi?"

He prostrated himself and wept bitterly. The mist then faded away and Kōbō Daishi appeared like the moon through the rifts in the clouds. Now, weeping for joy, Kangen clothed him in the robe that he had carried with him from the capital and then shaved the saint's hair, which had grown extremely long. What an inspiring sight!

The imperial envoy and the bishop had thus been able to see and adore the saintly priest, but their attendant priest, Junyū from Ishiyama Temple, who was the bishop's disciple, was unable to enjoy the same privilege as his master. He was so saddened that the bishop took his hand and placed it upon the knee of Kōbō Daishi. It is said that, because of this event, his hand remained fragrant thereafter, and that this scent has remained on all the sutras at the Ishiyama Temple for years upon years.

Kōbō Daishi wrote to Emperor Daigo the following words: "Many years ago I met Kongō Satta[1] and from him I learned all the secrets of hand signs that indicate various ideas while chanting the mystic syllables. I took upon myself an unparalleled vow to propagate Buddhism in Japan. That is why I have stayed here, far away from India. I plead day and night for the Buddha's mercy upon all the people of this land. I have done my best to bring forth the Ten Great Vows of Fugen Bodhisattva.[2] Giving up all of myself to the fulfillment of this task, while still sustaining my flesh on Mount Kōya, I look forward to seeing Maitreya Bodhisattva."

[614]

Kōbō Daishi could be compared to one of the Buddha's ten disciples, Mahākāshyapa, who made his abode in the cave of Kukhrita, where he waited for the appearance of Maitreya Bodhisattva in this world after his descent from Tusita Heaven. On the twenty-first day of the third month of the second year of Shōwa [835], at the hour of the tiger [4: 00 A.M.], Kōbō Daishi entered Nirvana. That was three hundred years ago, and so he still had five billion six hundred and seventy million years to wait until Maitreya Bodhisattva would come down to this world to hold ceremonies three times under the dragon-flower tree.

¹ Skt. Vajrasattva. According to esoteric Buddhism, Mahavairocana transmitted the Law to Vajrasattva, who in turn compiled it in a series of sutras that he put in an iron stupa in South India. Nāgārjuna opened it and obtained the secrets of the Law. Kōbō Daishi is said to be an incarnation of Nāgārjuna.

² His ten great vows are: to pay respect to all the Buddhas; to admire all tathagatas; to propagate the veneration of the Buddha; to repent evil karma; to rejoice at virtuous acts; to crush all illusions; to request all the Buddhas to appear in the world; to study the teachings of the Buddha; to respond to the wishes of all creatures; and to turn one's merit to the attainment of Buddhahood.

CHAPTER X

KOREMORI TAKES THE TONSURE

"**I** am plagued by the perpetual torture of anxiety, for I know that death awaits me perhaps today or certainly tomorrow," Koremori said in tears. "I feel like a tropical bird trapped in frozen climes, trembling and crying."

Tanned by the sea breeze and emaciated from constant worries and sorrows, he looked different from what he had once been. Even so, there remained in his face something elegant, something superior to ordinary men.

That night he stayed in Tokiyori's cell and talked with him all night of things both past and present. In Tokiyori's religious life he was able to see a virtuous example that would move one toward Buddhahood. At the boom of the bells, at the hour of the tiger [4: 00 A.M.] and again at the hour of the hare [6: 00 A.M.], he heard Tokiyori chanting sutras wholeheartedly. Indeed, Tokiyori was leading a life of austerities in which he was already liberated from the law of life and death. Koremori thought that he should take the tonsure and enter this pure life in order to set himself free from his miserable lot in this world. When morning came, he sent for a venerable priest named Chikaku Shōnin and expressed his wish to become a monk. He also summoned his servants, Shigekage and Ishidō-maru, and said: "I have long brooded over my beloved wife and children, driving myself to desperate straits, but I do not think that I will be able to sustain my life much longer. Whatever becomes of me, you must not put an end to yourselves. At the present time there are many men who, though formerly on the side of the Heike, are now enjoying high positions in government office. Therefore after I have met my end, you two make your way up to the capital and try hard to establish yourselves in the world. Marry and settle down. Be good husbands to your wives. Be good fathers to your children. And pray for my better lot in the world beyond."

The two servants wept bitterly, unable to utter a word. After a while Shigekage suppressed his tears and said: "During the Heiji Insurrection, my father, Kageyasu, the captain of the Imperial Gate of the Left, followed your father, Lord Shigemori. At that time he grappled with Masakiyo at Nijō Horikawa, and it was there that he fell by the hand of the wicked Genta Yoshihira. I too am not reluctant to sacrifice myself in my service to you, my lord. I am in no way inferior to my father. Since I was only two years old at the time, I remember nothing about his death. I was seven years old when my mother followed my father to the world beyond. I was then left alone in this world. There was no relative of mine who would care for me. Then your father, Lord Shigemori, took compassion on me, saying, 'This boy is the son of the one who gave his life for me.' Thus it was that I was brought up in your house.

"When I was nine years old, on the same night as you celebrated your coming of age, I was also privileged to bind up my hair. I still remember what your father said to you at that time, 'The character *mori*[1] in my name is the hereditary sign of our house. Now I give it to you and hereafter call you Koremori.' He then turned to me and said, 'As for another character, *shige*, in my name, I give it to you and hereafter call you Shigekage.' As a result of the gallant death of my father, I was able to receive such a great blessing from your father. Furthermore all of his retainers were extremely kind to me.

"When he was dying, Lord Shigemori said no more of earthly trifles, for he had already thrown away each and every matter of this fleeting world. But he summoned me to sit close by his side and said to me, 'You have regarded me as your father, and I have looked after you in memory of your father, Kageyasu. It had been my intention at the next conferment to raise you to be the captain of the Imperial Gate of the Left, the same rank and office as your father held. In this way I had hoped you would always be by my side. But this hope of mine is all in vain. After I have died, I ask you to remain loyal to my son, Koremori.'

"Now I cannot understand what makes you bid farewell. Do you think that I will desert you and run away to save myself? I cannot be such a shameless man. You say that there are many men who are now enjoying high positions in government office, though they were formerly on the side of the Heike. In reality, however, they

[617]

are nothing but retainers of the Genji. After you have become a god or a Buddha, whatever you might be in the world beyond, what pleasure can I have, staying alive in this world? Can I live as long as a thousand years? If I were to live for ten thousand years, I would nevertheless die in the end. There is no better lesson than this realization to help one to gain enlightenment himself."

After he had spoken these words, Shigekage cut off his hair and then received the tonsure from Tokiyori. Ishidō-maru too cut off his hair and had his head shaved by Tokiyori. He had been with his master since he was eight years old, and Koremori's favor for him was no less than that for Shigekage. When Koremori saw their lack of hesitation in renouncing the world, he felt extremely sad. Now he could delay no longer, and so he began to recite one of the Buddhist texts: "As long as one is continuously reborn in the Three Regions, he cannot sever the bonds of affection that tie him to his wife and children. Only one who renounces his earthly affection and becomes a monk can be awakened to true affection." Thus repeating the text three times, Koremori submitted his head to the tonsure.

"Ah, I had thought to see my loved ones but once more before I took the tonsure. Had I been able to do so, I might have nothing to look back on in regret." These words revealed Koremori's lingering desire for this world, sinful enough to hinder him from salvation. Both Koremori and Shigekage were twenty-seven years old at the time, while Ishidō-maru was only eighteen.

Koremori summoned his warrior-retainer, Takesato, and said: "Do not go up to the capital but return to Yashima at once, for one simple reason. I think that in the end the news of my death cannot be concealed. But if my wife were to hear of it now, she would no doubt renounce the world. When you arrive at Yashima, tell the Heike leaders as follows, 'As you can see, everything in the world is now in turmoil, and it is likely that you will have an increasing number of uncontrollable troubles. That is why I have hidden myself from your presence without a word. The lieutenant general of the Left, Kiyotsune, fell in the western provinces. The governor of Bitchū Province, Moromori, was killed at Ichi-no-tani. I can imagine how you will be saddened and discouraged when you are informed of what I have done, and it causes me to feel sorrow for you. Here is a set of armor, Karakawa,[1] and a sword, Kogarasu, which after nine generations have been handed down to me from the general Taira no Sadamori. If the world becomes favorable for our house again, please entrust them to my son, Rokudai.'"

Takesato replied to Koremori: "Only after I have seen how you meet your end, my lord, will I set out for Yashima."

Thus it was that Koremori was obliged to take him, as well as the two servants, and together, disguised as mountain priests, they set out from Mount Kōya for Sandō in Wakayama. Tokiyori went with them as their guide to salvation.

They first worshiped at the Fujishiro Shrine, and then at many other shrines along their way of pilgrimage. When they arrived at the gate of the Iwashiro Shrine, north of the shore of Senri-no-hama, they encountered seven or eight horsemen garbed in hunting suits. Koremori feared that they might be the men of the Genji coming to arrest him and that he could not escape. Thus Koremori and his attendants put their hands on the daggers at their sides, ready to slit open their own bellies. The band of warriors, however, showed no sign of attacking Koremori. Indeed, alighting from their horses, they bowed politely to him and passed on.

"They must not be strangers to us. I wonder who they are," said Koremori, as he quickened his steps to go away from the strangers.

The leader of the horsemen was Munemitsu, the son of a native of Kii Province named Muneshige. When he was asked by one of his retainers who was the monk to whom he had bowed, he replied in tears: "It may be imprudent of me to speak about him, but he is actually Lieutenant General of the Third Court Rank Koremori, eldest son of the late Lord Shigemori. I wonder how he has escaped to this province from Yashima. And he has already become a monk! Two of those accompanying him are Shigekage and Ishidō-maru, who have also renounced the world! I wanted to step forward, closer to him, and say a few words of greeting. But I did not do so, for I thought he would be embarrassed. So I passed on. What a pity!"

With these words, he wept, pressing his sleeve to his face. All of his retainers too wet their sleeves with tears.

---

[1] Literally "Chinese Leather."

CHAPTER XI

PILGRIMAGE TO KUMANO

Hurrying on, Koremori and his retainers finally arrived at the Iwata River. It was said that whoever crossed this river would be cleansed of all evil karma and concern for earthly trifles. Koremori remembered the great legend of this river and he was encouraged by it.

Going to the Shōjō-den of Hongū, he knelt before the main image of the shrine. After chanting sutras, he looked around the sacred mountains of Kumano. The magnificent sight silenced both mind and tongue. It was there that the Buddha's great wish to save all sentient beings was transformed into the mist rolling over the mountains; his matchless spiritual power to purify every man became manifest in the clear water of the Otonashi River. Unhindered by clouds was the light of the moon, shining over the bank of the river, where people chanted the *Lotus Sutra*, the most effective sutra for attaining Nirvana. No dew of evil illusions fell over the garden where repentance was made for the Six Roots of Offence[1] to the Buddha. Everything there provided him with clear inspiration. The night wore on and was silent as he offered his prayer to the god of the shrine. He remembered wistfully that at this shrine his father had once prayed to the god to shorten his life and grant him happiness in the afterlife. Now Koremori prayed: "Thou art the manifestation of Amida Nyorai. I believe in thy vow to save all of us and lead us to the Pure Land Paradise. Let me beseech thee to bring peace and safety to my wife and children in the capital."

He had already renounced this world to enter the true path to Buddhahood, and yet he was unable to free himself from earthly trivialities. A sad fate!

The next day, he boarded a boat for Shingū, where he worshiped the holy rock atop Mount Kan-no-kura. On the cliffs towered lofty pine trees, which rustled in the mountain winds and awakened men from their illusions. In the river ran the clear water that washed away all the dust and mire of this world. After he had worshiped at the Asuka Shrine[2] and passed by the shore of Sano, where the pine trees stood in impressive array, he came to the Nachi Shrine. The water of the three-tier waterfall roared a few thousand jō above. At the top stood a holy statue of Kannon, which made him think of Mount Potalaka[3] in India. Far below the mist he heard the chanting of the *Lotus Sutra*, reminding him of the Vulture Peak, where Sakyamuni gave his sermons.

Since the time that the god of Nachi manifested himself upon this mountain, all people, high and low, rich and poor, of our country have come up here to bow their heads and clasp their hands. By so doing, they have enjoyed the grace of the god. Consequently a great number of halls have been built in the precinct, roof to roof, where both priests and laymen sit sleeve to sleeve to practice austerities. In the summer of the second year of Kanwa [986], the cloistered emperor Kasan, who had mastered the Buddha's Ten Precepts and had graduated to the place of supreme honor as emperor, came here to pray for his rebirth in the Pure Land Paradise. Just outside of the cell where he stayed stood an old cherry tree in bloom, reminiscent of his pious austerities.

Now among the monks who were staying at Nachi, there was one who had often seen Koremori. As other monks wondered who the newcomer was, he explained: "At first I was unable to believe my eyes, but now I am certain that he is Lieutenant General of the Third Court Rank Koremori, eldest son of Lord Shigemori. In the summer of the second year of Angen [1176], there was a celebration of the fiftieth birthday of the cloistered emperor Go-Shirakawa at Hōjū-ji. At that time Koremori was still only major general of the fourth court rank. His father, Lord Shigemori, was state minister and general of the Left. His uncle, Lord Munemori, was the councilor and general of the Right. Besides these nobles, attendant upon the celebration that day were Lieutenant General of the Third Court Rank Tomomori, Lieutenant General Shigehira, and all the nobles and courtiers of their house, at the height of their glory and splendor.

"From among the flute players sitting in a circle near the stage came this young noble, Koremori, holding up a branch of a cherry tree in bloom, to dance a piece called Seikaiha.[4] He swayed like a dew-sprinkled flower, his sleeves floating gracefully on the breeze.

[621]

He was dazzling to the spectator's eyes, brightening the earth and illuminating the sky. Then the imperial consort, Kenshunmon-In, sent a robe of honor as a present in the hands of the kampaku, Motofusa. Koremori's father, Lord Shigemori, left his seat, came forth to receive it, and placed it on the right shoulder of his son. All the while Koremori made obeisance to the cloistered emperor.

"This was indeed a great honor for Koremori, an honor that few could equal, and for which his fellow courtiers must have been envious. Some court ladies admired him, saying, 'He is a plum tree among ordinary trees deep in the mountains.' At that time I thought he would rise swiftly to be a minister and general of the Imperial Guard. And today I see him so emaciated and wretched. Who would have ever expected to see him in such a sad condition? Impermanence is a rule of the world, but this is indeed too cruel a reality to recognize."

With these words, he pressed his sleeve to his face and wept bitterly. The monks at Nachi too wet their sleeves with tears.

[1] The five senses and intellect.

[2] One of the branch temples of Shingū.

[3] Cf. footnote 10, p. 142. During the 11th to 14th centuries some Japanese Buddhists believed it to be a paradise located far off the shores of Kumano. Many sailed off in search of Potalaka and eventually disappeared. Some suggest that Koremori drowned himself off the Kumano shore (Chapter XII) while trying to reach Potalaka.

[4] Literally "Blue Waves."

CHAPTER XII

KOREMORI DROWNS HIMSELF

Now Koremori, having completed the pilgrimage to the three shrines of Kumano, boarded a small boat near the shrine of Hama-no-miya.[1] The boat was rowed out into the open sea, where far offshore there was an island called Yamanari.[2] The boat was directed to this island, and Koremori and his attendants disembarked and strode onto the shore. Koremori peeled some bark off a large pine tree and on the trunk he wrote his name and genealogy: "Lieutenant General of the Third Court Rank Koremori, Jōen by Buddhist name, twenty-seven years of age, the son of Lord Shigemori, state minister and general of the Left, Jōren by Buddhist name, and the grandson of Lord Kiyomori, premier, Jōkai by Buddhist name, drowned himself off the shore of Nachi on the twenty-eighth day of the third month of the third year of the Juei era."

After writing thus, he boarded the boat, which was rowed away from the shore. He was determined to put an end to himself, yet he was sad when it came to the last moment. The mist rolling over the distant waters made him feel dreary. Even on an ordinary spring day, twilight shadows drive one into melancholy. How much more so when it is the last evening one spends in this world! Far offshore a fishing boat was seen bobbing up and down on the waves. When Koremori saw it, he could not but compare the motion to his fate. A line of wild geese, their cries echoing, was flying back to the north. Koremori wished to ask one of them to deliver a message to his home. Perhaps he remembered Ssu Wu, in China, who had been captured by the barbarian army. It was he who had sent words to his native land on the wings of a wild goose.

"What is the matter with me? Am I still unable to rid myself of worldly desire?"

Reproving himself, he turned to the west and joined his palms.

He began to repeat the name of Amida Buddha but earthly thoughts came again to his mind: "Since my loved ones in the capital cannot know that I am now putting an end to myself, they will continue waiting for tidings of me. Even at this moment they must be hoping anxiously. Someday, however, news of my death will reach them. I have no conception of how terrible their sorrow will be!"

Having spoken these words in his heart, he ceased to invoke Amida Buddha and put down his hands. He then turned to the priest Tokiyori and said: "Ah, what a burden it is to have a wife and children! They are not only a cause of sorrows in this world but also a hindrance to enlightenment and salvation in the other world. Even at this moment my wife and children are present in my mind. As long as I still talk with such lingering affection for my loved ones, I know I shall be unable to attain Buddhahood. Tokiyori, these are sinful feelings of which I must rid myself."

Tokiyori was moved to compassion, but outwardly he remained impassive. He feared that Koremori would not drown himself if he showed any sign of weakness. Wiping away his tears, Tokiyori said: "What you have said is reasonable! The bonds of affection seem beyond your control. Above all, it is karma that predetermines as many as a hundred lives before a man and woman can place their pillows together even for a single night. Deep indeed is the karma of the past. But all living creatures must die. Those who meet must part. It is the law of this fleeting world. A dewdrop on the tip of a leaf is no different from that on the trunk of a tree. One must go before the other, or one must die before the other. This is only a trivial accident of nature. All must pass away in the end.

"Hsüan-tsung's promise of eternal love to Yang Kuei-fei on an autumn evening at the Li-shan Palace became nothing but their sorrow in the end. Wu Ti had a painter draw the portrait of his loving consort Li on the wall of the Kan-chüan Palace. His love too had to meet an end. Even the hermits Ch'ih-sung-tze and Mei-fu were not able to live forever. Moreover the bodhisattvas next in rank to Sakyamuni were also obliged to obey the law of birth and death.

"You may live long and become proud of your longevity. Even so, you will still regret your parting from this world. Mara, the king of evil, rules the Six Heavens of Desire[3] at his whim. As he despises seeing the sentient beings of this world awaken to enlightenment, he appears in the form of wives or husbands to hinder

[624]

them from salvation. On the other hand, all the Buddhas in the Three Worlds regard them as their own children and lead them to the Pure Land Paradise. For countless numbers of years, wives and children have been fetters to bind men to the Wheel of Birth and Death. Consequently the Buddha strictly forbids your affection to wives and children.

"Nevertheless, simply because you have been bound to your loved ones, do not abandon yourself to despair. Long ago an ancestor of the Genji, a man named Yoriyoshi, received an imperial edict to destroy Sadatō and Munetō,[4] the rebels in Mutsu. He was engaged in this campaign for twelve years. During these years he killed more than a million beasts on the mountains and plains and fish in the rivers. However, when his last moment came, a fervent desire for Buddhahood arose within him, and it is said that even he was able to attain a seat in paradise.

"Now you must be aware of your new status as a monk, which is so virtuous that all the sins of your previous lives will be washed away. Even if one built a pagoda of seven precious stones to rise above the thirty-third heaven, his merit would not be as great as a monk for a single day. Or again, if one offered feasts of fattened beasts to a hundred arhats for thousands upon thousands of years, his merit would not be as great as yours as a monk for a single day. This is truly what the Buddha teaches us. In the case of Yoriyoshi, though he was a sinful man, he sought a true path so ardently that he was able to attain Nirvana. Since you are not as sinful as he was, you will certainly be led to the Pure Land Paradise.

"Furthermore the god of the Kumano Shrine is an incarnation of Amida Buddha. Each and every one of his forty-eight vows implies the salvation of all sentient beings. Of these the eighteenth vow says, 'When I become a Buddha, when all sentient beings believe in me, and when they invoke my name ten times, if they still cannot attain rebirth in the Pure Land Paradise, this may mean that I have not yet enlightened myself!' Therefore, your utterance of his name, one to ten times, will enable you to attain your rebirth in the Pure Land Paradise. Believe in him and do not doubt. Whether you invoke his presence once or many times, Amida Buddha will diminish his immeasurable height to only sixteen shaku and come forth to meet you from the eastern gate of paradise with the sounds of a celestial orchestra and chorus and surrounded by a countless number of Buddhas and bodhisattvas, led by Kannon and Seishi. Your body may sink to the depths of the sea, but your soul will rise up into the purple clouds. And when you have become a Buddha and attained liberation, you may come again to this fleeting world and lead your wife and children to the true path to salvation. Without doubt, you will succeed."

Having spoken these words, Tokiyori struck the bell and urged Koremori to invoke Amida Buddha. Realizing that this was his last chance for Buddhahood, Koremori cast away all vain thoughts and repeated "Hail Amida Buddha" a hundred times. Then, with the word "Hail" still on his lips, he sprang into the sea. His servants, Shigekage and Ishidō-maru, followed their master to the world beyond.

¹ A shrine belonging to Nachi.

² Literally "Mountain Fulfillment."

³ The last of the Six Realms is heaven, which is divided into six parts: the heaven of the Kings of the Four Quarters; the heaven of the Thirty-Three Gods; the heaven of Yama; the Tusita Heaven; the Nirmānarati Heaven; the Paramirmita-vesavartin Heaven.

⁴ The insurrection, called Zen-kunen-no-eki, was brought about by the provincial warrior Yoritoki and his sons Sadatō and Munetō when they refused to pay taxes to the government. The war lasted nine years (1056–64).

CHAPTER XIII

YORIMORI TRAVELS TO KAMAKURA[1]

Takesato was also about to fling himself into the water, but Tokiyori prevented him, saying: "What a weak little fellow you are! How dare you disobey your master's last command? However wretched you may be, do at least pray for his better lot in the world beyond!"

To this tearful admonition, Takesato gave in. However, his heart was torn with the grief of being left behind. Forgetting his obligation to pray for his master's afterlife, he cast himself down to the bottom of the boat and wailed loudly.

Long ago, when Sakyamuni was still only Prince Siddhartha, he went deep into Mount Dantalikagiri[2] in search of enlightenment. At that time Sakyamuni gave the horse that he had ridden, Kanthaka, to his retainer, Tchandaka, and ordered him to return to the palace. Tchandaka wept bitterly at the sorrow of parting from his master. Takesato's grief seemed to be even greater than that of Tchandaka.

For a while Tokiyori and Takesato rowed about to see if the three would come to the surface, but they did not, having sunk deep into the waters. Tokiyori and Takesato then chanted the sutras and repeated "Hail Amida Buddha" for the rebirth of the three departed souls in the Pure Land Paradise. The sun set; the sea grew dark. With their hearts almost too heavy to bear, they rowed back —their boat lightened by the loss of the three men. Tears rushed down Tokiyori's face. So torrential were his tears that they mingled indistinguishably with the splashes of sea water upon his sleeves.

Now Tokiyori climbed back up Mount Kōya, and Takesato went weeping back to Yashima. Takesato delivered a letter from his master to his master's younger brother, Sukemori.

"Oh, this is terrible!" exclaimed Sukemori, when he unrolled the letter. "I regret that Koremori was unable to understand how much

I relied upon him. Lord Munemori and Nii-dono thought that he had followed the example set by Yorimori and headed for the capital to go over to Yoritomo. Because of his escape, they became watchful of us, his brothers. How sad that he drowned himself in the sea off the shore of Nachi! He is to be blamed, for he did not take us all with him to die together. Did he give you any more words for us besides this letter?"

"Yes, he did," replied Takesato. "He asked me to say this, 'The lieutenant general of the Left, Kiyotsune, fell in the western provinces. The governor of Bitchū Province, Moromori, was killed at Ichi-no-tani. I can imagine how you will be saddened and discouraged when you are informed of what I have done, and it causes me to feel sorrow for you.'"

As Takesato talked of his master's armor, Karakawa, and sword, Kogarasu, he felt more and more miserable. Tears choked his throat. Sukemori resembled Koremori so much that people pictured Koremori and wept. Munemori and Nii-dono lamented: "We thought that Koremori had turned traitor and had gone over to Yoritomo, but we were wrong. He must have died in deep sorrow!"

On the first day of the fourth month, Yoritomo was elevated from the lower junior grade of the fifth court rank to the lower senior grade of the fourth court tank. This promotion was an extraordinary honor, for he was allowed to skip five grades as a reward for his distinguished services in destroying Yoshinaka.

It had been decided that Emperor Sutoku was to be raised to the status of a god. On the third day of the same month, a new shrine was built at the east end of Ōi-no-Mikado, the site of the battle during the Hōgen Insurrection; there he was enshrined. It is said that the ceremony was performed by the order of the cloistered emperor. The reigning emperor was not informed of this event at all.

On the fourth day of the fifth month, Yorimori set out for Kamakura. Previously he had received many letters from Yoritomo, which usually included these words: "I always wish well for you, for I am especially grateful to your late mother, Ike no Zenni. Let me repay you for her kindness."

Trusting these words, Yorimori had turned away from the Heike and remained in the capital. Even so, he had been possessed by fear, for he had wondered if the favorable regards of Yoritomo alone could be complete assurance of his safety—what would the rest of the Genji do to him? But recently a messenger from Yoritomo had come bearing these words: "I would like you to come down here as soon as possible, for I wish to see you. Since I regard you with as much respect as I paid to your late mother, Ike no Zenni, I will receive you warmly." Yorimori set out at once.

Now among the retainers of Yorimori was a warrior named Munekiyo. He was the most faithful of the family's retainers. This time, however, he refused to go with Yorimori. When he was asked the reason, he replied: "My lord, it is all right for you to go down to Kamakura. But when I think of the others of our house who are still adrift upon the waves of the western sea, my heart aches and my mind is restless. Only when I have calmed myself, shall I join you."

Displeased and abashed, Yorimori said: "That I parted from the rest of my house, I admit, was a dishonorable act. Life was dear to me and hard to give up, so I stayed here. I dared to remain alive. Inasmuch as I remained here, I must now heed the summons of Yoritomo. I am going on a long journey. Why do you not escort me? You cannot refuse to come with me. I regret only this. When I decided to part from the rest of my family, why did you not speak up and oppose the decision? You are the one I used to consult on every matter, be it great or small."

Munekiyo answered: "To all men, high and low, life is dear, my master. They say that it is easier for them to become monks than to throw away their lives. I am not blaming you at all. Yoritomo has attained his present glory only because his life was spared. When he was sent into exile, I escorted him, at the bidding of Ike no Zenni, as far as the post station of Shinohara in Ōmi Province. I hear that he has not forgotten this kindness of mine. So if I accompany you to Kamakura, I will certainly receive a warm welcome and many gifts from him. But I would not like to receive this kind of favor from Yoritomo. When I think of my friends and the noblemen of our house drifting upon the waves of the western sea, I would feel greatly ashamed to receive such preference. This is the reason why I wish to stay here. Inasmuch as you parted from the rest of the Heike and stayed in the capital, you must go down to Kamakura sooner or later.

[629]

"Of course I am worried about the length of your journey. If you were going to attack the enemy, I would never hesitate to be the first to do battle. In this journey, however, there will be no danger. I do not think you will need my service. If Yoritomo inquires about me, please tell him that I was ill at the time of departure."

Hearing this, all the soldiers who had hearts wept. Yorimori too was sad and ashamed, but he had to go down to Kamakura.

On the sixteenth day of the month, Yorimori arrived at Kamakura. Yoritomo immediately came out to receive him and inquired: "Where is Munekiyo? Is he not escorting you?"

"At the time that I set out," replied Yorimori, "he was ill, so he could not come with me."

"How can that be?" exclaimed Yoritomo. "What illness is he suffering? I wonder what might be troubling him? Many years ago, when he escorted me to Kamakura, he was so kind and courteous to me that I cannot forget him even now. I have been looking forward to seeing him again. What a pity it is that he did not accompany you!"

Since Yoritomo had prepared for Munekiyo a grant of many manors and such presents as horses, saddles, and armor, he was greatly disappointed. So were all the lords of the eastern provinces who also had prepared similar presents, competing with each other to do him honor. All the lords, high and low, expressed their regret at Munekiyo's absence.

On the ninth day of the sixth month, Yorimori started on his return journey to the capital. Although Yoritomo pressed him to stay longer, Yorimori feared that his family and retainers in the capital would be concerned about him, and so he begged his leave. Yoritomo then sent a request to the cloistered emperor that all the fiefs and lands that had once belonged to Yorimori be returned to him without exception, and that he resume his former title of councilor. In addition Yoritomo presented Yorimori with thirty saddled horses, thirty unsaddled, and thirty long chests containing feathers, gold, and rolls of plain and dyed silk. Seeing Yoritomo's bountiful gifts to Yorimori, all the lords of the eastern provinces made him presents also, and the horses alone amounted to three hundred. Thus it was that Yorimori set out on his return journey not only with his head safely on his shoulders but with a great stock of wealth.

On the eighteenth day of the month, when Yorimori arrived at

Ōmi Province, he was attacked by a band of the Heike warriors. They were the natives of Iga and Ise Provinces, commanded by Sadatsugu, an uncle of the governor of Higo Province, Sadayoshi. The Genji of Ōmi Province rushed to rescue Yorimori, and a battle raged. All of the men of the Heike were killed—not a single one survived. They had remained loyal to their hereditary master and had attacked their traitor, Yorimori. Although they were heroic, their attempt was a pathetically blind act without regard for consequences. This was what is now called the Three-Day Rule of the Heike.

The wife of Koremori was constantly worried about her husband. Many days had passed since she had received his last letter. As she was used to receiving a letter from him once a month, she waited apprehensively for some word from him. When spring was gone and summer past its prime, she heard a rumor that he was no longer at Yashima. She became so anxious about him that she sent a messenger to Yashima to inquire. For a long time the messenger did not return. Summer advanced into autumn. At the end of the seventh month,[3] the messenger returned. Koremori's wife ran to meet him, saying: "Tell me how he is. Oh, tell me."

To this hasty inquiry, the messenger replied: "At dawn on the fifteenth day of the third month, my master set out from Yashima and went to Mount Kōya. There he took the tonsure and then made a pilgrimage to the Kumano Shrine. After he had prayed for his afterlife, he drowned himself off the shore of Nachi. This is what I heard from Takesato."

"Ah, how sad," sighed Koremori's wife. "I knew something terrible had happened to him, for I had received no word from him for such a long time."

She fell prostrate and covered her face with her kimono sleeve. The children too wept bitterly. Her son's wet nurse, weeping unabashedly, said: "This is not a matter of great surprise! You have long brooded over such sad news. To be taken alive, like Lieutenant General Shigehira, only to be exposed to public disgrace in the capital—ah, how much more miserable that must be than death! Our master took the tonsure on the holy mountain of Kōya and made a pilgrimage to the sacred shrine of Kumano. To know that he was able to pray for his afterlife and then put a peaceful end to himself should be a source of joy in the midst of sorrow. You must set your mind at rest. I pray you to be unshaken and strong—to bring up your children in the face of any hardship, even though taking refuge among rocks and trees."

These words of encouragement, however, were only vaguely heard by the lady, for there remained in her heart nothing but reminiscences of her deceased husband. It seemed as if she would be able to live no longer. Soon afterward she took the tonsure, performed a Buddhist rite for her departed husband, and prayed for his better lot in the world beyond.

[1] The title in the original version is "The Three-Day Rule of the Heike." However, because of the lack of emphasis on the resurgence of the Heike, the translator altered it.

[2] Located in North India.

[3] According to the ancient Japanese calendar, autumn begins in July.

CHAPTER XIV

FUJITO

At Kamakura, when Yoritomo heard of the suicide of Koremori, he was deeply grieved: "What a pity that he did not come and throw himself upon my mercy. I would certainly have spared his life. I still remember his father, Lord Shigemori, with a feeling of great respect, for it was he who, as a messenger of Ike no Zenni, pleaded with Kiyomori to reduce my sentence to exile. Because of this special favor, I could never be cruel to his children. Since he had become a monk, there would have been nothing wrong with my saving him."

After the Heike had crossed over to Yashima, they heard that a new force—scores of thousands of horsemen—had arrived at the capital from the eastern provinces to march against them, and that the clans of Usuki, Hetsugi, and Matsuura had been united in Kyushu to attack them. This news was unfavorable and discouraging to their ears. Their hearts sank. They had already lost many men at Ichi-no-tani—almost half of their warriors had been killed there. Those who had survived were dispirited. The only power that they could now rely on was the force of Shigeyoshi and his brother, who were confident of being able to recruit more soldiers from Shikoku and Kyushu. In the eyes of the Heike, this force appeared to be as unassailable as a high mountain or a deep sea against the Genji's attacks.

On the twenty-fifth day of the seventh month, the court ladies gathered, lamenting their fate: "On this day of last year we left the capital. How quickly time flies past us!" They remembered how hastily they had been obliged to move from place to place. As they reminisced, some wept and some laughed.

On the twenty-eighth day of the month, the accession ceremony for the new emperor, Go-Toba, was held at the capital. It is said that this was the first time in eighty-two generations, since the reign of Emperor Jimmu, that an accession ceremony was performed without the Three Sacred Treasures.

On the sixth day of the eighth month, Noriyori was appointed governor of Mikawa Province. Yoshitsune was made captain of the Imperial Gate of the Left. In addition Yoshitsune received an edict from the cloistered emperor that promoted him to captain of the Police Commissioners Division.

The chill wind began to blow through the bush clover. The dew hung heavily on the lower branches. The hum of insects was heard as a complaint of the arrival of autumn. The rice stalks rustled in the wind. Leaves began to fall from the trees. Even to a traveler freed from the odds and ends of daily life, the sky of autumn is one cause of melancholy thoughts. How much more so it must have been for the men of the Heike! In times past they had played among the flowers in the imperial garden, but now they lamented their sad fate under the autumn moon by the shore of Yashima. They wished to compose poems, unable to forget the carefree manner of bygone evenings in the capital. But each day was dreary and tearful. Yukimori composed a poem of lament:

> As long as we have
> The honor of upholding
> His august presence,
> The moon is bright above us
> And still we think of Kyoto.

On the twelfth day of the ninth month of the year, Noriyori, in command of more than thirty thousand horsemen, set out for the western provinces to destroy the Heike. He was assisted by Yoshikane, Nagakiyo, Yoshitoki, and Chikayoshi. There were many more generals in this action: Sanehira, Tōhira, Yoshizumi, Yoshimura, Shigetada, Shigekiyo, Shigenari, Shigetomo, Yukishige, Tomomasa, Munemasa, Munetō, Moritsuna, Tomoie, Akimasu, Sanehide, Tōkage, Tomomune, Yoshikazu, Ienaga, Shōgen, and Shōshun. They soon arrived at Muro in Harima Province.[1]

The command of the Heike was assumed by Sukemori, Arimori, and Tadafusa. The generals in the field were Kagetsune, Moritsugi, Tadamitsu, and Kagekiyo. Having more than five hundred boats under their command, they set sail for Kojima in Bizen Province.

Upon receiving news of the Heike's movements, the Genji

left Muro and occupied positions at Fujito in Bizen Province. Separated by the strait, the two forces faced each other at a distance of five chō. Since the Genji had no boats, they could do nothing but lie in wait for their seaborne enemy's attack. From the Heike, however, some young warriors of impetuous spirit rowed out now and again in small boats and waved their fans at the Genji. They beckoned and shouted: "Why do you not come over here?"

"Their insolence is intolerable!" exclaimed the Genji. "What shall we do?"

On the twenty-fifth day of the ninth month, when it grew dark, Moritsuna of the Genji sought out a native of the shore and bribed him with a short-sleeved kimono, a hakama, and a silver-studded sword that had no guard, asking: "Can you show me the way to the shallows, so I can cross the strait on horseback?"

"Many men live along this shore," replied the man, "but very few know of the shallows. I am one who can lead you to them. At the beginning of the month they are to the east. At the end of the month they are to the west. The two shallows are separated by a distance of ten chō. Through either of them you can easily cross on horseback."

Moritsuna was pleased by this information. Without telling any of his retainers about his plan, he slipped out of his camp with only the guide. They took off their clothing and thus, stark naked, they crossed the shallows that the guide had pointed out. Indeed, they were not deep. In some spots the water was up to their knees or waists or shoulders. In some spots it wet their hair. At the deep spots they swam from shallow to shallow.

"To the south," said the guide, "it is much shallower. There your enemies are waiting with bows ready to shoot at any moment. As we are naked, we would be able to do nothing. Let us turn back."

Moritsuna had started back with the guide when he thought to himself: "This coarse fellow might betray me at any time. He might be wheedled by someone else into showing the same shallows, but I wish to be the only one who knows them." To ensure the guide's silence, Moritsuna stabbed him to death, cut off his head, and threw it away.

At the hour of the dragon [8:00 A.M.] on the twenty-sixth day of the month, the Heike rowed out again in small boats and tried to provoke the Genji to fight. Seeing this challenge, Moritsuna advanced toward the enemy, for he knew how to cross the strait. That day he wore armor laced with black silk cords over a tie-dyed battle robe and rode a dapple-gray steed. At the head of seven retainers on horseback, he sprang into the water. As Moritsuna charged into the water, the commander-in-chief, Noriyori, exclaimed: "Do not let him fight! Stop him!"

At this command, Sanehira whipped and spurred his horse to overtake Moritsuna, shouting: "Moritsuna! What is this madness? Obey your master's command! Stop there!"

Moritsuna, however, rode on as though he had heard nothing. Unable to stop him, Sanehira also rode with him. Their horses sank up to their breasts, and bellies, and saddles. When they came to the deep spots, they let their horses swim from shallow to shallow. Seeing this, Noriyori exclaimed: "Moritsuna cheated us. The water is shallow. After him, cross!"

At his command, the entire army of thirty thousand horsemen plunged into the sea. The Heike were frightened. They launched their boats, drew their bows, and shot showers of arrows at the Genji. Not at all daunted, the soldiers of the Genji bent forward to protect themselves and sprang into the boats of the Heike. The battle raged. Many men of the Heike tumbled out of the boats to their deaths. Some were thrown out as the boats capsized. They continued to fight all day. When night came, the Heike withdrew from the shore, and the Genji landed at Kojima to give rest to their men and horses. After a time the Heike rowed back to Yashima. The Genji, though eager to follow to do battle again, were unable to pursue them, for they had no boats.

"From of old there were many men who crossed rivers on horseback, but I do not know if there was anyone who crossed a strait on horseback in India and China. I do know there have been none in our country. This is an extraordinary feat. Therefore the fief of Kojima in Bizen Province will be given to Moritsuna as a reward for his distinguished service." This is how Yoritomo inscribed his order to Noriyori.

On the twenty-seventh day of the month there was the conferment of offices in the capial. Yoshitsune was promoted to captain of the Police Commissioners Division and given the fifth court rank.

The year advanced into the tenth month. At Yashima the wind

blew hard and the waves rolled high. The Heike, consequently, expected no attack from the Genji. Even the number of merchants sailing to Yashima decreased, and so there was little communication with the capital. The sky was dark and hail fell. Melancholy overcame them.

In the capital the ceremony of offering the first crops to the gods after the new emperor's enthronement was to be held. First, Emperor Go-Toba went in procession to the Kamo Shrine to purify himself in preparation for the main ceremony. The ceremony of purification was conducted by Lord Jittei, who was state minister at the time.

On the occasion of the same ceremony performed two years before for Emperor Antoku, Lord Munemori of the Heike had officiated. The stateliness with which he had carried himself was remarkable. In front of the tent set up for the ministers he had unfurled a large ceremonial flag with a design of a dragon. The elegance with which he had worn his high lacquered bonnet and long trailing robes was startling to the eyes of the spectators. And what could have been more dignified than the sight of the Imperial Guard in array under the command of Tomomori and Shigehira?

On this day, however, the procession was accompanied by Yoshitsune. Unlike Yoshinaka, he was a stately looking courtier. Even so, he looked far inferior to even the lowliest of the Heike.

On the eighteenth day of the eleventh month, the ceremony was performed; however, it was done only as a matter of form. This was because the people, since the eras of Jishō and Yōwa, had been continually harassed by a series of wars. They found it difficult to sow seed in spring and reap harvest in autumn. Many of their houses and kilns had been destroyed or deserted. How was it possible to celebrate this great festival as lavishly as in normal times?

If Noriyori had pursued the Heike into the sea, he could have destroyed them. Instead he remained at Muro and Takasago. He spent the days and months of inactivity amusing himself with entertainers and women of pleasure. Under his command, eager to fight, were many lords, great and small, from the eastern provinces. But inasmuch as Noriyori issued no order, they could do nothing. The enormous wealth of the country had been squandered, causing pain to the people. In this way the year ended.

[1] Present-day Murotsu, Hyōgo Prefecture.

CHAPTER XV

THE IMPERIAL PILGRIMAGE TO MOUNT KŌYA

Here is a story about Mount Kōya. During the time of the abdicated emperor Shirakawa, a series of lecture-and-discussion meetings on the Buddha's Law were held at his palace.

"I have heard," Shirakawa said, "that Nyorai appeared in person in a western country called India, where he gave most valuable sermons. Are we all to travel to India to hear his sermons?"

The nobles and courtiers expressed a fervent wish to go to India. Ōe Masafusa, however, said: "Others may go, but I do not care to. It is not so difficult for us to travel over the sea from our country to China. But a vast desert and high mountains lie between China and India. They are all places of great danger. First, there is a mountain called Ts'ung-ling,[1] which is connected to the Himalayas in the northwest and which has bluffs that jet out to the ocean in the southeast. This mountain, Ts'ung-ling, divides the land. China lies to the east, India to the south, Shih-ch'iao[2] to the west, and Hu Kuo to the north. The path over the mountain is eight thousand ri long—no grass grows there and no water flows. Among the peaks, the highest is Keihara-saina.[3] You will have to spend twenty days among the rocks above the white clouds. Atop the mountain the whole world is spread open before you, and Jambu-dvipa lies below your feet.

"Next, lies a wide river called Liu-sha.[4] The winds blow hard in the daytime, causing showers of sand. Evil spirits run about at night, bearing awesome torches in their hands. You will have to spend eight days crossing this river, stream after stream, bank after bank. Hsüan-tsang, a venerable priest of the T'ang dynasty, once traveled there. He was on the brink of death as many as six times. Drifting down the stream, he came alive again, and later he was able to transfer the Buddha's Law from India to China. Without having to undertake such a hazardous journey to India or China, you may find an incarnation of Dainichi Nyorai on Mount Kōya in our country. Rather than paying a visit to this holy mountain, why should I dare to travel thousands upon thousands ri over mountain and sea to reach the Vulture Peak. Sakyamuni in India and Kōbō Daishi in Japan both attained Buddhahood while still alive."

"During the reign of Emperor Saga," Masafusa continued, "the learned priests of Mahayana Buddhism, each representing one of four sects—Hossō, Sanron, Tendai, and Kegon—were ordered to assemble at the Seiryō-den hall of the Imperial Palace and discuss the doctrines of their esoteric austerities. At that time Gennin represented the Hossō sect, Dōshō the Sanron, Gishin the Tendai, and Tō-ō the Kegon.

"Gennin of the Hossō sect exclaimed, 'Our sect upholds the theory of dividing Sakyamuni's lifelong teachings into three views—yū, kū, and chū.'[5]

"Dōshō of the Sanron sect proclaimed, 'Our sect considers Sakyamuni's lifelong teachings in respect to Nirvana, which is beyond the realms of birth and death. We embrace the teachings of both Mahayana and Hinayana.'

"Gishin of the Tendai sect clarified his stand, saying, 'Our sect teaches all the doctrines of Buddhism contained in the text of Ssu-chiao-i[6] and the five periods[7] of the Buddha's teachings.'

"Tō-ō of the Kegon sect said, 'Our sect views Buddhism through five doctrines—Hinayana, primitive Mahayana, gradual enlightenment, instantaneous enlightenment, and perfection.'

"After a while, Kōbō of the Shingon sect declared, 'Our sect teaches how to attain Buddhahood in this world by practicing mystic finger signs and esoteric prayers.'

"To this, Gennin countered, 'If we examine the teachings of Sakyamuni, we see that Buddhahood can only be attained through many cycles of life and death. There is no description of such an immediate attainment as you proclaim. If there is any scripture that gives evidence for your words, show it to us all so that we may be able to rid ourselves of doubts.'

" 'Truly,' replied Kōbō, 'the scriptures you uphold promise no immediate attainment of Buddhahood.'

" 'Show us,' Gennin demanded again, 'scriptural evidence, if any.'

[639]

Thus challenged, Kōbō excerpted a passage from *Treatise on the Mind Tending toward Enlightenment*[8] and recited, 'If one attains enlightenment after vigorous search for the Buddha's wisdom, he who still bears the body given from his parents will be able to reach the holy status of Nirvana.'

"Gennin, not yet satisfied with this passage, demanded that Kōbō show a living example of one who had attained Buddhahood within a single life.

" 'Those who attained Buddhahood in this world in ancient times were Dainichi Nyorai and Kongō Satta. And I am truly a modern example of one who has attained Buddhahood in this world.' With these words, Kōbō performed a variety of sacred finger signs and prayers. He then transformed himself into a golden image of the Buddha. His head was crowned with an aureole that shone brighter than a shaft of sunlight. The entire court shone like a jewel, as if the Pure Land of Dainichi Nyorai had suddenly appeared. Dazzled by Kōbō's transformation, Emperor Saga withdrew from his dais and bowed to Kōbō. All the nobles and courtiers as well as the priests knelt and bowed, with their heads touching the ground. Tō-ō and Dōshō were astounded by the practical force of Kōbō's theories. Gennin and Gishin were silenced by Kōbō's mysterious power of transformation. The four sects—Hossō, Sanron, Tendai, and Kegon—were now obliged to revere Kōbō. So was the imperial court, which from this time began to learn from him. His teachings concerning the sacred finger signs and esoteric performances of prayers spread over the nation and purified the hearts of all. His virtue gave light to the darkness that had long ruled the world. Even after his death he continued to sustain his flesh in wait for the appearance of Maitreya Bodhisattva."

This speech by Masafusa deeply impressed the abdicated emperor Shirakawa. Regretting that he had been unaware of Kōbō's greatness, he wished to visit Mount Kōya and declared that he would set out the next day.

"Your Majesty, your decision is too abrupt." Masafusa advised again. "The Buddha's sermons on the Vulture Peak used to be attended by sixteen kings of sixteen kingdoms[9] of India. For their travels to the peak, they all paid special attention to ceremonial manners. They wore dresses made of gold and silver brocade and crowns adorned with precious stones. They caparisoned their horses richly. They did so, because they wished to show their deep gratitude to the Buddha for blessing them with such rare opportunities. So let us regard our Mount Kōya as the Vulture Peak and likewise Kōbō as the Buddha. I beg you to prepare a gorgeous procession for your journey to Mount Kōya."

Shirakawa, agreeing to Masafusa's proposal, postponed his departure for five days. At the end of that time, all the nobles and courtiers accompanied the imperial procession attired in new silk and dazzling brocade. Shirakawa was the first emperor to make a pilgrimage to Mount Kōya.

[1] The Pamirs, where the Hindu Kush, Tien Shan, and Himalaya ranges converge.

[2] Present-day Chekiang in western China.

[3] Located in present-day Kabul, Afghanistan.

[4] Literally "Shifting Sands," it is supposed to be in the Turkestan Desert.

[5] Yū teaches how one can awake from ignorance; kū enables one to comprehend the truth that all is void; chū trains one's mind to ignore yū and kū so that he can obtain a complete unification of the two views.

[6] This text teaches the important and fundamental doctrines of the Tendai sect. The abstract was written by T'ien-t'ai-tashih Chih-i in 575 and later compiled by Taikan of Korea.

[7] The five periods of development leading to enlightenment are divided according to the following sutras expounded by the Buddha—(1) the *Āvatamsaka*, (2) the *Agarua*, (3) the *Vaipulya*, (4) the *Prajnā*, (5) the *Saddharma-Pundarika* and *Nirvana*.

[8] A work attributed to Nāgārjuna, it clarifies the functioning of the Buddha mind and enlightenment.

[9] Of the many kingdoms of India, sixteen pledged their devotion to the Buddha.

BOOK ELEVEN

" . . . all is vanity and *evanescence.*"
—Book 1, Chapter II, page 5

CHAPTER I

OARS AT THE BOW

On the tenth day of the first month of the second year of the Genryaku era [1185], Yoshitsune paid a visit to the Cloistered Palace and reported to the cloistered emperor through the finance minister, Yasutsune: "The Heike have been forsaken by heaven and the imperial family. Driven from the capital, they are now fugitives, no more than exiles drifting upon the waves. But it is my great regret that they were not completely destroyed over the past three years. Many provinces are still under their control. This time I, Yoshitsune, am determined to follow them anyplace —Kikai-ga-shima, Korea, India, or China—until I succeed in annihilating them. I shall not return to the capital until I fulfill this goal."

The cloistered emperor was deeply impressed with Yoshitsune's resolution and replied: "Make your war plans with great care. Fight well and fight to win!"

When Yoshitsune returned to his mansion, he said to the warriors from the eastern provinces: "I, Yoshitsune, represent Lord Yoritomo in receiving the edict from the cloistered emperor to overcome the Heike. As far as the legs of our horses can go on land, and as far as the oars of our boats can make headway at sea, we shall fight. Anyone who cherishes his own life—away from us at once!"

At Yashima time passed quickly. The New Year celebrations were completed, and the second month came. The spring grass died, and the winds of autumn unnerved the Heike. And when the winds died down, the spring grass sprouted again. In this manner three springs passed. Then a rumor spread that the Genji force at the capital, reinforced by thousands of horsemen from the eastern provinces, were prepared to advance toward Yashima. Some said that the clans of Usuki, Hetsugi, and Matsuura had united in Kyushu, ready to sail to Yashima. Each and every report received was frightening to the Heike. Tense with apprehension, they gathered here and there to lament their fate.

The ladies-in-waiting, among them Kenreimon-In and Nii-dono, said: "We do not know what new misfortune awaits us. What further sad news must we hear?"

"The warriors of the northeastern provinces," said Tomomori, "received many favors from our house, but they forgot their obligation to us and deserted to Yoritomo and Yoshinaka. Since I feared that our hardships would be the same in the western provinces, I advised Lord Munemori that we should stay in the capital and make a last stand there. But this single objection of mine was powerless. My spirit weakened, I left the capital with no destination in mind. Now I regret my actions, which have brought us only misery." His words were pathetic, for he spoke the truth.

On the third day of the second month of the year, Yoshitsune set out from the capital and proceeded to Watanabe[1] in Settsu Province. It was there that he collected a large fleet of boats to carry his many soldiers over to Yashima. Now Yoshitsune was ready to sail.

On the same day, Noriyori too set out from the capital and proceeded to Kanzaki.[2] There he was provided with boats to make a voyage offshore paralleling the route of the Sanyō-dō highway.

On the thirteenth day of the second month, imperial envoys were dispatched to the great shrines of Ise, Hachiman, Kamo, and Kasuga, to present them with new on-pei-shi. An imperial order was issued to all the officials of the Rituals Division and to the Shinto priests, commanding that they offer prayers at their shrines for the safe and swift return of Emperor Antoku and the Three Sacred Treasures to the capital.

On the sixteenth day of the month, the forces of the Genji at Watanabe and Kanzaki were about to sail, when a violent storm arose. The north wind blew so fiercely that many trees were uprooted; great waves slapped and battered the boats unsparingly. Instead of putting out to sea, the Genji were obliged to remain in port and pass the day in repairing their vessels.

At Watanabe the many lords, of both large and small domains, held a council and complained: "We have not been trained at all for a fight at sea. What shall we do?"

Kagetoki stepped forward and said: "To do battle at sea this time, I think it most advisable to have oars at the bow."

"What do you mean by 'oars at the bow'?" asked Yoshitsune. "What are they?"

"When you ride a horse," replied Kagetoki, "you can easily turn right or left by using the reins. But to turn a ship around quickly is a very difficult matter. So, if we fix oars at both bow and stern, instead of having them only at the stern, and put a rudder on each side, then we shall be able to turn about as easily as we wish."

"It is of the utmost importance in battle," exclaimed Yoshitsune, "to maintain a fighting spirit. Without retreating, we must dart and dash among the enemy until the battle is finished. Though we wish never to retreat, it is a common tactic to withdraw when the odds are unfavorable. But what is the meaning of preparing for a retreat even before we set out for a fight? This is an ill-omened proposal for the start of a voyage ! You lords may fix a hundred or a thousand extra oars at the bow, fasten 'turn-back oars' or whatever you like to your boats, but I shall put out to sea with no more than the normal number of oars !"

"A good general," retorted Kagetoki, "is one who advances at the proper time and withdraws at the proper time, continually securing his position until he wins. Being overly daring in battle is the act of a wild boar—it can be of no help."

"A wild boar?" Yoshitsune cried out. "Wild boar or wild stag—I do not care what you may call me. But at the moment of victory, the greatest joy comes from having made relentless assaults."

The warriors did not dare to laugh openly, for they were afraid of Kagetoki's wrath. They muttered to each other under their breath, making signs of warning with their eyes. After a while, however, they whispered: "Yoshitsune and Kagetoki will have to fight someday."

The sun was down and the sky was dark when Yoshitsune said: "The boats have been repaired. Well done ! My lords, let us feast and drink in celebration."

This, however, was but a pretense. By thus distracting Kagetoki with a banquet held on the boats, he had his men load all weapons, horses, and provisions aboard. After this was completed, he ordered the seamen and helmsmen to set sail at once.

"We have the wind behind us, but it is too strong. The sea will be very rough. How can we put out to sea in such a storm?" they whimpered.

Yoshitsune was incensed: "We are not going into the teeth of the wind! The wind is behind us, only a little more brisk than usual. That is all. At such a critical moment, do you suppose that I would abandon plans of putting out to sea because of a slight breeze? Men-at-arms! Shoot these seamen if they will not follow orders!"

At this command, Tsuginobu and Yoshimori sprang forward with arrows fixed on their bows, shouting: "What is the use of argument? Obey our lord's command! Sail at once, or we will shoot every one of you!"

Thus threatened, the seamen and helmsmen cried out: "To be shot to death here or to drown out there, in the sea, is all the same. If the wind is strong, let it push us at breakneck speed even if it carries us to death! All you seamen! Set sail!"

Of the two hundred boats, however, only five actually put out to sea. They were commanded by Yoshitsune, Nobutsuna, Sanemoto and his son Motokiyo, Ietada and his brother Chikanori, and Tadatoshi. The rest remained on shore, perhaps because they feared the wind, or Kagetoki. Out on the waves, Yoshitsune said: "Even though the others have not set off, there is no need for us to quit. If the sea were calm, the enemy would be on the lookout for our attack. In a storm like this, they would not expect us. A surprise attack will assure us of victory.

"If the enemy see many lights at sea, they will be on the alert. So light no torches on any of the boats except mine. This is your flagship. Keep your eyes on the torch at the stern of my boat."

In this manner they sailed all night. Though it was usually a three-day voyage, they were able to make it in only four hours. It had been at the hour of the ox [2:00 A.M.] on the sixteenth day of the second month that the Genji set sail from Watanabe and Fukushima in Settsu Province.[3] At dawn, at the hour of the hare [6:00 A.M.], a strong wind blew them toward the shore of Awa Province.

[1] Present-day Naniwa-ku, Osaka City.

[2] Present-day Kanzaki, Amagasaki City.

[3] The text here is inconsistent; it states earlier that the Genji were at Watanabe and Kanzaki.

CHAPTER II

KATSUURA BEACH AND ŌSAKA PASS

It was daybreak. Here and there on the beach red banners were fluttering in the breeze. Yoshitsune roared when he saw them: "Look! They are welcoming us. If we sail close together, deck to deck, to unload the horses, we shall be fat targets for their arrows. Now hear this! While we are still some distance from the shore, put the horses overboard and let them swim tethered to the boats. As soon as their hooves touch the bottom and the water reaches only the saddles, then mount and gallop ashore."

In the five boats were piled the weapons, armor and provisions, and so there was little room for the horses; there were no more than fifty. All were put overboard. As instructed, when Yoshitsune's soldiers drew near the shore and found the water shallow enough, they sprang onto the horses and galloped away from the boats with a great whoop. The Heike on the beach numbered about a hundred on horseback. At the sudden violent onslaught of the Genji they could put up little resistance and withdrew at once about two chō inland.

Arriving at the beach, Yoshitsune rested his men and horses and summoned Yoshimori: "I can see one among those soldiers who seems to have some authority. Go and fetch him. I wish to question him."

At this command, Yoshimori galloped alone into the enemy lines, and though nobody knew how, returned with a man of about forty, clad in armor laced with black leather cords, who had removed his helmet and loosened his bow strings in submission.

"Who are you?" inquired Yoshitsune.

"A native of this province named Chikaie, Your Excellency."

"Whoever he may be, keep your eye on him," Yoshitsune ordered his retainers. "Do not let him take off his armor, for he will be my guide to Yashima. If he tries to escape, kill him."

Then turning to Chikaie, he asked: "What is the name of this place?"

"Your Excellency, this is Katsuura," replied Chikaie. "It is easier for a mean fellow, with his dialect, to pronounce it 'Katsura', but it is written in two characters *katsu*, or 'victory', and *ura*, or 'beach'."

"Oh, no flattery is needed," chuckled Yoshitsune, who turned to his retainers in delight. "Listen, my men! Is it not a good omen that we have landed at Katsuura, the 'Victory Beach', for a fight?"

He turned again to Chikaie and asked: "Are there any around here who support the Heike, who might attempt an attack from the rear?"

"There is Yoshitō, a younger brother of Shigeyoshi, the chief official of the civil government of Awa Province," was the reply.

"Well then, let us go and attack him first!"

Yoshitsune selected some thirty horsemen from the hundred under the command of Chikaie and added them to his own force.

When Yoshitsune's men arrived at Yoshitō's stronghold, they discovered that it had a swamp on three sides and a moat on the other. They approached the moat and shrieked their war cry. The soldiers within the stronghold stood in rank and let fly showers of arrows without pause. Undaunted, the men of the Genji bent forward to protect themselves and rushed shouting into the enemy lines. Perhaps Yoshitō conceded his defeat—for as his retainers shot arrows in his defense, he sprang on his stallion and escaped.

Yoshitsune beheaded some twenty bowmen who had shot to defend their master, and offered their heads to the god of war with a shout of triumph: "What an auspicious beginning for our campaign!"

He then summoned Chikaie and asked, "How many men are there in the Heike force at Yashima?"

"No more than a thousand horsemen, Your Excellency," replied Chikaie.

"Why is it that there are so few?"

"This is because the Heike have stationed bands of fifty or a hundred horsemen at every beach and island around Shikoku. In addition an army of three thousand horsemen under the command of Noriyoshi, the eldest son of the chief official of the civil government of Awa Province, Shigeyoshi, has left for Iyo to destroy Michinobu, who has paid no heed to their recent summons."

"Indeed! Our attack will be opportune. Now tell me, how far is it to Yashima?"

"It is a journey of two days, Your Excellency."

"Then let us make haste to arrive before they have a premonition of our attack."

They set forth for Yashima, riding their horses all night—sometimes at a trot, sometimes at a walk, sometimes at a gallop, sometimes in check. Thus they crossed the Ōsaka Pass at the border of Awa and Sanuki.

At midnight, while still on the mountain, they caught up with a man bearing a letter wrapped in a large white handmade envelope. Because it was dark, he was unable to recognize them as his enemy and must have thought that they were men of the Heike returning to Yashima, for he began to talk freely to them.

Yoshitsune asked: "You are carrying a letter. Tell me, who is it for?"

"I am taking this to Lord Munemori," was the reply.

"Who is it from?"

"From his lady at the capital."

"I wonder what she has written."

"Nothing particularly important. I think she reports the recent activities of the Genji and that their boats are at the mouth of the Yodo River."

"That may be true! We are also going to Yashima, but we are strangers around here. Can you guide us?"

"Certainly. Since I go there quite often, I know the way very well. Let me accompany you."

At this point Yoshitsune turned to his retainers and ordered: "Seize that letter! Bind him!"

As they took the letter, he added: "Do not cut off his head, for that would be a useless crime."

So they bound him to a tree in the mountains and passed on. When Yoshitsune opened the letter, he found that it was indeed from Munemori's lady in the capital, and he read thus: "Yoshitsune is a man of keen and quick action. He will never be cowed by the strong winds or great waves; I believe he will dare to attack you. Do not scatter your force and be on your guard!"

"This is a letter sent from heaven! Surely, it will be a credit to my gallantry in the days to come. I will keep it to show Lord Yoritomo," said Yoshitsune. He tucked the letter deep in the folds of his robe.

The next day, the eighteenth, at the hour of the tiger [4: 00 A.M.], Yoshitsune and his men galloped down the mountain to a place called Hiketa[1] in the province of Sanuki. After resting their horses for a while, they pressed on, passing by Nyunoya[2] and Shirotori,[3] toward the castle of Yashima.

Yoshitsune again summoned Chikaie and asked: "What kind of sea is it that surrounds the palace of Yashima?"

"Your Excellency, you are understandably concerned, having never been there before. But the sea is very shallow. At low tide the water between the mainland and Yashima is only up to the belly of a horse."

"Then let us attack at once!"

At Yoshitsune's command, they set fire to the houses of Takamatsu[4] and galloped straight to Yashima.

Meanwhile, Noriyoshi had gone from Yashima to Iyo at the head of three thousand horsemen to punish Michinobu. This expedition, however, ended in failure, for Michinobu escaped. From Iyo about a hundred and fifty heads of Michinobu's retainers were sent to the palace of Yashima. But as it was not proper to inspect the heads of rebels at the palace, Munemori had them carried to his headquarters. They were being examined one by one, when suddenly the Heike soldiers began to shout: "Fire! Takamatsu is burning!"

"In the daytime a fire like this cannot be accidental," said the soldiers. "It must have been set by the enemy. Be on your guard! The enemy is here in great strength! If we are closed in, we will be able to do nothing. Come now! Come! Let us get into our boats!"

Yashima was roused into action. The men and women of the Heike scrambled aboard the boats moored in rows along the beach in front of the main gate of the palace. Emperor Antoku was accompanied by his mother, Kenreimon-In, his grandmother, Niidono, the wife of the sesshō, Naozane, and the ladies-in-waiting.

They were escorted aboard the imperial vessel. Munemori and his son boarded another. The rest scrambled aboard any boat that had room for them.

When the seamen had rowed them out to a distance of one chō, seventy or eighty horsemen of the Genji, in full armor, galloped to the beach in front of the main gate of the palace. The area was a tidal bay, and at that moment the tide was at its ebb. The water was only up to the hocks or bellies of the horses in some spots, and still shallower in others. As they dashed through the waves, splashes and sprays mingled with the mist of spring. Through the mist could be seen fluttering white banners.

The Heike had been outwitted, for they thought the Genji were attacking with a great army. This deception had been well calculated, for Yoshitsune, wishing his army to appear larger, had divided it into small groups of five to ten horsemen each. They sprang up before the eyes of the Heike, squad after squad.

[1] Located in present-day Ōkawa-gun, Kagawa Prefecture.
[2] Present-day Ouchi-chō, Ōkawa-gun, Kagawa Prefecture.
[3] Located northeast of Hiketa.
[4] A small village located south of Yashima.

CHAPTER III

THE DEATH OF TSUGINOBU

That day Yoshitsune wore armor laced with purple silk cords over a red brocade battle robe. At his side hung a sword in a gold-studded sheath. In his quiver were black and white feathered arrows. Now, gripping his rattan-bound bow at its middle and glaring at the ship, he roared: "I am Minamoto no Yoshitsune, the captain of the Police Commissioners Division with the fifth court rank. I am here as an envoy of the cloistered emperor."

Following Yoshitsune's lead, all the Genji chieftains, Nobutsuna, Iesada, Chikaie, and Yoshimori, declared their names and titles. Still others—Sanemoto and his son, Motokiyo, Tsuginobu and his brother Tadanobu, Genzō, Kumai-Tarō, and Benkei—declared themselves.

"Shoot! Fight them to the death!" cried the Heike, letting fly showers of arrows all along the shore. But the Genji dodged right and left to avoid the deadly shafts. The boats that had been beached and deserted by the Heike were used as shields, behind which the Genji rested their horses. In the meantime, Sanemoto, a veteran warrior of the Genji who did not take part in the fight on the beach, proceeded to the palace and set it afire. The palace went up in flames in the twinkling of an eye.

Munemori summoned his retainers and inquired: "How many men are there in the Genji force?"

"No more than seventy or eighty, my lord. This is all we have counted so far," was the reply.

"What a shame!" exclaimed Munemori. "Even if the hairs of their heads were counted one by one, the total would not equal our force! Why did we not stand fast and destroy them? Instead, at the first sight of the enemy we ran to our boats. We even allowed them to burn down the palace. Is not Lord Noritsune here? Let him land and do battle!"

At this command, Noritsune had small boats rowed back to the shore carrying a band of warriors under the command of Moritsugi, and they took up a position in front of the burned out main gate of the palace. In response, Yoshitsune drew his eighty men within shooting range. Now Moritsugi stood on the deck of his boat and roared at the Genji: "I know you have already declared your names and titles, but far from the shore I could not hear you well. Which were they, real names or assumed ones? Who is the commander with whom I deal today?"

"It is needless to repeat our names and titles!" Yoshimori shouted back. "What a fool you are! Our commander is the captain of the Police Commissioners Division, Yoshitsune, a younger brother of Lord Yoritomo, a tenth-generation descendant of Emperor Seiwa."

"Oh, I remember him," retorted Moritsugi. "He is little more than a child. When his father was killed during the Heiji Insurrection, he was left orphaned with no hope but to become a temple serving boy at Kurama, and then he ran away to Mutsu carrying baggage in attendance upon a gold merchant."

"How your tongue rattles!" replied Yoshimori. "You shall pay for your impudent insult to our lord! Remember! Was it not you who was kicked down the mountain of Tonami a few years ago and had a narrow escape staggering along the Hokuroku Highway, begging and weeping your way home to the capital?"

"I am a retainer of a bounteous master, satisfied with his great favors. Why should I be a beggar?" Moritsugi cried back. "Now, what about yourself? Are you not ashamed to make your living and keep your family by robbing and thieving in the mountains of Suzuka in Ise?"

At this point Ietada cut in: "Stop this nonsense! What is the good of playing with words? Any fool can do that! Simply remember what you saw at Ichi-no-tani last spring! You saw what our valiant young warriors of Musashi and Sagami can do!"

Ietada had hardly spoken these words when his brother, Chikanori, took an arrow twelve handbreadths and three fingers long, fitted it to his bow, and drew it with all his might. The arrow flew hissing straight at Moritsugi and pierced his breastplate and chest. This put an end to the oratorical warfare!

"Let me show you how to fight a sea battle!" exclaimed Noritsune, the governor of Noto Province. That day he was not wearing a battle robe but a tie-dyed short-sleeved kimono, over which was armor laced with twilled silk cords. At his side hung a long sword in a magnificent sheath. Over his shoulder was slung a quiver containing twenty-four arrows plumed with black and white feathers from a hawk's tail. His left hand held a rattan-bound bow. He was a powerful bowman renowned throughout the land; no one within range could escape his shafts. Now he marked Yoshitsune for a single shot. The Genji were aware of his intention, and so Tsuginobu and his brother Tadanobu, Yoshimori, Hirotsuna, Genzō, Kumai-Tarō, and Benkei—each renowned as a match for a thousand—rode neck and neck in front of their master to protect him. Noritsune could not draw a bead on his well-guarded target.

"Get out of the path of my arrows, you worthless beggars!" screamed Noritsune. Drawing his bow again and again, he shot down ten or so armored Genji horsemen in an instant.

Tsuginobu had been in the vanguard of the Genji, and so an arrow had pierced him through from the left shoulder to the right armpit. Mortally wounded, he pitched headfirst to the ground. One of Noritsune's servants, Kikuō, a young man of great strength grasping a long sickle-bladed halberd with an unlacquered wooden shaft, darted to take the head of Tsuginobu. He was about to fall upon the body when Tsuginobu's brother Tadanobu drew his bow and sent an arrow through the back joint of Kikuō's body armor. Staggered by this shot, Kikuō fell and began to crawl away. Seeing Kikuō in danger, Noritsune sprang from his boat and still holding his bow under his left arm, he seized Kikuō with his right hand and dragged him aboard. Kikuō's head was saved from the enemy, but he soon died from his wound.

This young man, aged eighteen, had formerly been in attendance upon the governor of Echizen Province, Michimori, but since the death of his lord, he served Michimori's brother, Noritsune. Noritsune felt such grief at the death of Kikuō that he lost the heart to do battle.

Yoshitsune ordered his men to carry Tsuginobu to the rear.

Alighting from his horse, Yoshitsune took the wounded soldier by the hand and said: "Tsuginobu, revive yourself!"

"But I am dying, my lord," replied Tsuginobu faintly.

"Are there any last words you wish to say?" asked Yoshitsune.

"Nothing, my lord," replied Tsuginobu. "The only thing I regret is that I shall not live to see you flourish. Except for this, I have no desires. It is the fate of a man of bow and sword to fall by the shaft of an enemy. I am content with this death, for they will say in the days to come that Tsuginobu died in place of his master at the battle on the beach of Yashima in Sanuki Province during the war between the Genji and the Heike. This is a great honor for a warrior, and it is something that I will carry with me on the shaded path to the world beyond."

As the valiant soldier's breath began to fail, Yoshitsune wept bitterly and ordered his men to seek a reputable priest. When they found one, Yoshitsune instructed him: "This wounded man is dying. I wish you to gather as many of your disciples as possible and let them write out a copy of a sutra within a day and pray for this soldier's better lot in the next world."

With this request, Yoshitsune presented to the priest a fine black horse and a gold-studded saddle. This was the horse that Yoshitsune had given the name Tayūguro[1] at the time that he had received the fifth court rank with the title of captain of the Police Commissioners Division. Also, it was on this horse that Yoshitsune had galloped down the precipitous slope of the Hiyodorigoe Pass behind Ichi-no-tani.

Now, when all the warriors, led by Tsuginobu's brother Tadanobu, saw their master's gracious act, they were moved to tears and exclaimed: "For the sake of our lord, we shall not hesitate to risk our lives. In comparison to his, ours are as trivial as dust and dew."

---

[1] Literally "Black Captain."

CHAPTER IV

NASU NO YOICHI

As the fight wore on, the warriors of Awa and Sanuki Provinces who had formerly sided with the Heike abandoned them and, in small bands of fifteen or twenty, left their hiding places in the hills and caves to join the Genji. Thus reinforced, Yoshitsune soon found himself in command of some three hundred horsemen.

"Night is falling. For now, let us have no more fighting." So said the men of both armies who began to withdraw. Suddenly from the offing, a small well-equipped and beautifully decorated boat was seen rowing toward the Genji. When it approached within seven or eight tan of the water's edge, it swung around, broadside to them. Then a court lady of eighteen or nineteen, wearing a five-layer white robe lined with blue over a scarlet hakama, took a red fan emblazoned with a gold rising sun and fixed it on top of a pole. She then stood the pole on the gunwale and beckoned to the Genji.

Intrigued, Yoshitsune summoned Sanemoto and asked: "What does that mean?"

"It may be a mark for us to shoot at, my lord," replied Sanemoto. "But there must be some treachery behind this. I think they would like you to step out of our ranks to look at that beauty. Thus enticing you out to the boat, they plan to shoot you, my lord. We must have one of our men hit that fan."

Yoshitsune inquired: "Who is our best archer? Is there anyone who can bring down that fan?"

"We have quite a number of skilled bowmen, but the best one is Nasu no Yoichi, the son of Nasu no Suketaka, a native of Shimotsuke Province. He is a small man but a most skillful archer."

"How can you prove it?"

"In a contest of shooting down birds in flight, he can always hit two out of three, my lord."

"Then call him!"

On command, Yoichi stepped forward. This young warrior was but twenty years old. He wore armor laced with light green silk cords over a deep blue battle robe. The collar of the robe and the edges of the sleeves were decorated with red and gold brocade. At his side hung a sword in a silver-studded sheath. In his quiver were the black and white feathered arrows that remained from the day's battle and a turnip-headed arrow fashioned from a stag horn and fletched with feathers from a hawk's wing. These could be seen protruding from behind his head. Under his arm he carried a rattan-bound bow. With his helmet slung on his back, he came into the presence of Yoshitsune and made obeisance.

"Well, well, Yoichi!" said Yoshitsune. "Can you hit that fan in the center and show the enemy how skillful we are at archery?"

"My success is not certain, my lord," replied Yoichi. "If I happen to fail, it would be a disgrace for my lord and all the men of the Genji. Would it not be better to entrust this to someone who is confident of his success?"

Yoshitsune was incensed at his reply and roared: "All of you who have come with me from Kamakura to the western provinces must obey my commands! Any who do not—away with them at once!"

Yoichi knew that he was already committed to shooting down the fan, so he said: "I am still uncertain of my success, but inasmuch as this is my lord's command, I shall try."

After he had retired from the presence of his master, he mounted a fine black horse with a lacquered, shell-inlaid saddle and a tasseled crupper. Holding his bow firmly, he gripped the reins and rode toward the sea.

The warriors on his side, seeing him off from the camp, exclaimed: "This young fellow will surely bring down that fan!" Yoshitsune too was convinced of his success.

The fan was too far off for him to make a shot from the beach, so Yoichi rode about one tan further into the water. The target still seemed very distant.

It was the hour of the cock [6:00 P.M.] on the eighteenth day of the second month. Dusk had begun to fall. The north wind was blowing hard, and the high waves were lapping the beach. As the boat rolled and pitched, the fan atop the pole flapped in the wind.

Out on the offing the Heike had ranged their ships in a long line to watch the spectacle. On land the Genji lined up their horses neck to neck in anticipation.

Now Yoichi closed his eyes and prayed: "Hail to the great bodhisattva Hachiman! Hail to all the gods of my native land Shimotsuke! Hail to the god Utsu-no-miya of Nikkō! Grant that I may hit the center of that fan! If I fail, I will break my bow and kill myself. Otherwise how can I face my friends again? Grant that I may once more see my native land! Let not this arrow miss its target!"

When he opened his eyes, the wind had subsided a little, and the fan looked easier to hit. Taking the turnip-headed arrow, he drew his bow with all his might and let fly. Small man though he was, his arrow measured twelve handbreadths and three fingers, and his bow was strong. The whirring sound of the arrow reverberated as it flew straight to its mark. It struck the fan close to the rivet. The arrow fell into the sea, but the fan flew up into the air. It fluttered and dipped in the spring winds, and then suddenly dropped into the water. When the red fan, gleaming in the rays of the setting sun, bobbed up and down on the white crests of the waves, the Heike offshore praised Yoichi by beating on the gunwales of their boats, and the Genji on the shore applauded him by rattling their quivers.

CHAPTER V

THE DROPPED BOW

Yoichi's feat was so exciting that a warrior of some fifty years of age, unable to restrain himself, sprang up on the boat and began to dance near the place where the fan had been hoisted. He wore armor laced with black leather and carried a sickle-bladed halberd with an unlacquered wooden shaft.

Yoshimori rode into the sea and came up behind Yoichi, saying: "Our lord has commanded that you shoot that fellow too."

This time Yoichi took one of his sharpest arrows, drew his bow, and let fly. The shaft flew true, hit the dancer in the neck, and knocked him headfirst down to the bottom of the boat. The Heike were silent, while the Genji rattled their quivers again. Some applauded, saying: "A fine shot!" But some criticized, saying: "That was a cruel thing to do!"

Enraged, three Heike warriors came out, one with a shield, another with a bow, and another with a halberd. Dashing onto the shore, they protected themselves with the shield and beckoned to the Genji.

Yoshitsune bellowed: "Young men on strong horses! Drive them away!"

At this command rode forth five horsemen—Shirō, Tōshichi, and Jūrō from Mionoya[1] in Musashi, Shirō from Nifu[2] in Kōzuke, and Chūji from Kiso in Shinano. To counter this onslaught, the bowman behind the shield loosed a great black feathered lacquered shaft, which flew whizzing and hit the horse of Jūrō, galloping in the lead. The arrow pierced the horse's chest up to the notch, so that the animal collapsed like an overturned screen. The rider at once threw his left leg over the horse, flung himself off the right side, and drew his sword. Then he saw another of his opponents advancing from behind the shield to meet him with a long sickle-bladed halberd poised over his head. He thought his sword would be too short to

[661]

counter it, so he attempted to withdraw. The others immediately followed him. It seemed that the unhorsed Jūrō would be cut down with the halberd. Instead the Heike warrior placed the halberd under his arm and tried to seize Jūrō by the neckpiece of his helmet. Jūrō dodged his grasp and ran. Three times he escaped, but on the fourth attempt he was caught. For a moment the neckpiece stayed with the helmet, but it was wrenched off as Jūrō ran desperately. The four other Genji wished to spare their horses, and so did not run to his rescue but continued watching the struggle. Jūrō took shelter behind a friend's horse to recover his breath. His opponent followed him no further, but, striking the earth with the shaft of his halberd and holding the neckpiece high, he cried out: "You must have heard of my fame as a valiant warrior. Now you see me before you. I am Akushichibyōe Kagekiyo—a name familiar to even the children of the capital!"

Thus Kagekiyo had avenged the cruelty done to his fellow warrior, and now he had frightened the enemy. Encouraged by his bravery, the men of the Heike cried out: "Let not Kagekiyo be killed! Come now, men! To his rescue!"

This time some two hundred men of the Heike landed on the shore and set up their shields in a row, overlapping one another like the feathers of a hen's wing. Then they beckoned to the Genji.

"I cannot tolerate such insolence!" exclaimed Yoshitsune. With these words, he himself rode out at the head of eighty horsemen: in the lead were Sanemoto and his son Motokiyo, Ietada and his brother Chikanori; on his left and right, Tadanobu and Yoshimori; and at the rear, Nobutsuna. They charged upon the Heike with a great shout. Since most of the Heike soldiers were on foot, they feared being trampled, and so they hastened back to their boats. Their abandoned shields were kicked in all directions. Flushed with success, the men of the Genji raced into the sea in pursuit until the water was up to the bellies of their horses.

Yoshitsune too, fighting among the boats, penetrated the enemy line. With wooden-shafted grappling hooks the Heike tried to seize Yoshitsune by the neckpiece of his helmet. Two or three times the hooks rattled about his head. His retainers rushed to rescue their leader and tried to ward off the hooks with their swords and halberds. During the struggle Yoshitsune's bow was pulled away into the water by one of the hooks. He leaned out of his saddle to try to pick it up, nudging the bow with his whip. His men urged him to let it go, but he would not, and at last he managed to recover it. He then rode, laughing, back to the beach. His veteran retainers, however, disapproved of their master's act.

"Our lord, you did a careless thing! However valuable a bow may be, can it be compared with our lord's life?"

"It was not because I grudged the loss of the bow," replied Yoshitsune. "If it were one that required two or three men to bend, a bow like that of my uncle Tametomo, then I would gladly let it fall into the hands of the enemy. But if a weak one like mine were taken by them, they would laugh at it and say, 'Is this the bow of Yoshitsune, the commander-in-chief of the Genji?' That would be unbearable. I had to recover it even at the risk of my life!"

These words deeply impressed them all.

Night fell, and the Genji withdrew. They made their way inland and positioned themselves at a mountain village called Mure in Takamatsu. For two nights and three days they had not slept nor even lain down. The two previous nights they had sailed the rough sea from Watanabe and Fukushima. Tossed by the storm, they could not even doze. The past night they had galloped into the mountains after the fight at Katsuura in Awa. And this day too the battle had raged all day long. They were exhausted. Taking for pillows their helmets or quivers or the sleeves of their armor, they slept as if dead. But Yoshitsune and Yoshimori did not sleep. Yoshitsune climbed to a high place to stand guard. Yoshimori hid himself in a small hollow, lying in wait for the enemy. At a moment's notice he could put an arrow into the belly of an enemy horse.

The Heike, for their part, had made preparations for a night attack with a force of five hundred horsemen under the command of Noritsune. But as Moritsugi and Morikata prolonged their debate to decide which of the two would take the lead in the attack, the day dawned with nothing having been accomplished. If they had made an attack, how could the Genji have endured it? That they did not carry out their plan indeed spelled the end for the Heike.

[1] Located in present-day Kawashima, Hiki-gun, Saitama Prefecture.
[2] Present-day Kanra-gun, Gumma Prefecture.

CHAPTER VI

THE FIGHT AT SHIDO

When morning came, the Heike returned to the bay of Shido in the province of Sanuki. Yoshitsune selected some eighty horsemen from his force of three hundred and made a sortie against them.

The Heike were exultant and cried out: "Their numbers are few! Let us surround them!"

To meet the Genji attack, the Heike sent a thousand men ashore. The roar of battle filled the bay. The Genji who had been left behind at Yashima suddenly came galloping to the battleground.

When the Heike saw them, they panicked: "Who knows how many tens of thousands may be on their way? If we are surrounded, we can do nothing."

So saying they again boarded their boats and fled aimlessly at the mercy of wind and tide. Soon afterward all the provinces of Shikoku surrendered to Yoshitsune. The Heike knew that they could not go to Kyushu in search of shelter. Their wretched fleet looked like a departed spirit wandering on the border between this world and the next.

On the beach at Shido, Yoshitsune alighted from his horse and examined the heads of the fallen Heike. He then summoned Yoshimori and said: "Noriyoshi, the eldest son of Shigeyoshi, went out to Iyo at the head of three thousand horsemen to punish Michinobu for his disobedience to the Heike's summons. He failed to destroy Michinobu but sent back to the palace of Yashima the heads of a hundred and fifty of Michinobu's soldiers. I hear that Noriyoshi himself will be coming back today. Now go and meet him! Do your best to make him surrender to me. Use any tactics, but be sure to return with him."

Yoshimori solemnly received this command and set out with a small band of sixteen horsemen. They wore white kimonos, pretending to mourn the Heike defeat. Yoshimori unfurled the white banner that he had received from Yoshitsune and galloped off.

Before long Yoshimori and his men encountered Noriyoshi. When they approached within two chō the white and the red banners ceased to move for a moment. Then Yoshimori sent a messenger to Noriyoshi, saying: "I am Ise no Saburō Yoshimori, a man in the service of Yoshitsune, the commander-in-chief of the Genji. I have come to meet you, for I have something to tell your lordship. Since I am not here for a fight, I am wearing no armor nor carrying weapons. I pray you to make way for me so that I may be able to see your lordship."

At this request, Noriyoshi's three thousand horsemen opened their ranks and let Yoshimori and his men pass. Coming alongside Noriyoshi, Yoshimori spoke: "As your lordship has certainly heard, my master, Yoshitsune, the younger brother of Lord Yoritomo, has received an edict from the cloistered emperor to destroy the Heike and is now on a campaign in the western provinces. The day before yesterday he arrived at Katsuura in Awa and defeated your uncle Yoshitō. Yesterday he advanced to Yashima and burned down the palace. Munemori and his son were taken alive, and Noritsune put an end to himself. All the other nobles and courtiers of the Heike fought to the death or threw themselves into the sea. This morning at the bay of Shido, those who remained alive at Yashima were killed or captured. Among them, your father, Lord Shigeyoshi, was taken alive and entrusted to my charge. All last night he mourned his fate and lamented, 'How pitiful! My son, Noriyoshi, could never dream of my plight. Tomorrow he will come and do battle only to be killed!' I was deeply moved, and so I have come this far to bring you this news. Now that I have told you everything, whether you fight to the death or lay down your arms, hoping to see your father again, is all up to your lordship."

As he listened to Yoshimori, Noriyoshi, renowned warrior though he was, saw his fortune at an end. "What you have told me confirms the rumor I have already heard," he replied. He then removed his helmet, unfastened the string of his bow, and handed both to his retainers. Inasmuch as their commander had yielded, his three thousand soldiers could do nothing but give up their arms. They all surrendered to Yoshimori and with no sense of shame, went with him and his sixteen men to the knees of Yoshitsune. The retainers were ordered to keep the helmet and armor of Noriyoshi, and the defeated warrior was put into Yoshimori's charge.

"You carried that out splendidly!" said Yoshitsune to Yoshimori in admiration. "But what shall we do with this great army?"

"These provincial warriors care nothing about choosing a master," replied Yoshimori. "They are simply ready to follow anyone capable of bringing peace to the world."

"You are no doubt right!" agreed Yoshitsune, who decided to take the entire army of three thousand horsemen under his command.

At the hour of the dragon [8: 00 A.M.] on the twenty-second day of the second month, the two hundred boats under the command of Kagetoki of the Genji, which had remained at Watanabe and Fukushima, arrived at Yashima. Seeing their delayed arrival, people along the shore of Yashima laughed: "Since all the provinces of Shikoku have already been conquered by Yoshitsune, there is nothing left for them to do. They are like flowers that bloom after a festival."

After Yoshitsune had set out from the capital for Yashima, the chief priest of the Sumiyoshi Shrine, Nagamori, paid a visit to the Cloistered Palace and reported to the cloistered emperor through an intermediary of Finance Minister Yasutsune: "At the hour of the ox [2: 00 A.M.] on the sixteenth day of this month, the whizzing of a turnip-headed arrow flying west was heard in the third hall of my shrine."[1]

Go-Shirakawa, pleased at receiving this good news, presented Nagamori with a sword and other treasures to be dedicated to the patron spirits of the shrine.

Long ago, when Empress Jingū set out on an expedition to Korea to subjugate Shiragi, the vengeful spirits of two shrines, Sumiyoshi and Suwa, accompanied her from the Great Ise Shrine. The two spirits took positions on the bow and stern of her boat and enabled her to humble Shiragi. When the war was over and she had returned to her native land, one of the spirits made his abode at Sumiyoshi, and the other at Suwa in Shinano. This is how Sumiyoshi and Suwa came to be worshiped in our land.

"The gods of Sumiyoshi have not forgotten their former expedition. They must be moving again to destroy the enemies of the emperor," exclaimed the cloistered emperor and his retinue in thankful exultation.

[1] The sound of this arrow indicated that the gods of Sumiyoshi Shrine would take action against the enemies of the emperor.

CHAPTER VII

THE COCKFIGHT AND
THE FIGHT AT DAN-NO-URA

Thus, as the tale tells us, Yoshitsune crossed the Inland Sea to Suhō, where he joined the force of his elder brother, Noriyori. The Heike, vanquished at Katsuura and Yashima, took up positions on Hiku-shima, or "Retreat Island." At the same time the victorious Genji established themselves on the beach of Oitsu, or "Chasing Beach." This was indeed a strange irony.

Meanwhile, the superintendent of the Kumano Shrine, Tanzō, wavered over his decision as to which side he should support this time, the Heike or the Genji. Hoping to receive a sign from the god of Imagumano, he had the kagura performed at the shrine at Tanabe. The oracle advised him to side with the white banner—the Genji. Still unsettled, he had a cockfight held in front of the god of the shrine, choosing seven white cocks for one side and seven red ones for the other. None of the red cocks won. They all ran away. As a result of this cockfight, Tanzō at last made up his mind to join the force of the Genji and summoned all his clansmen. At the head of two thousand men on board two hundred boats, he sailed for Dan-no-ura. In his boat he set up the image of Nyaku-ōji, the incarnation of the Sun Goddess, and on the top of his standard he inscribed the name of Kongō-dōji, the guardian of the three shrines of Kumano. Thus when his boat approached Dan-no-ura, both the Genji and Heike saluted it with reverence. But when Tanzō went over to the Genji, the Heike's hearts sank.

In addition Michinobu, a native of Iyo Province, appeared with a hundred and fifty boats to join the Genji. These reinforcements were greatly encouraging to Yoshitsune since his fleet now numbered three thousand in all, while the Heike had one thousand. But among the boats of the Heike there were some extremely large ones. Even so, compared with the increasingly greater fleet of the Genji, the Heike navy seemed to be shrinking.

The day of battle was agreed upon by the two sides. At the hour of the hare [6: 00 A.M.] on the twenty-fourth day of the third month of the second year of the Genryaku era, they would shoot the first arrows from both sides, and the fighting would begin.

Shortly before the fight, however, a dispute arose within the Genji camp. Yoshitsune and Kagetoki were on the point of an open breach. The quarrel had begun with Kagetoki's request to Yoshitsune: "Let me make the first onset against the enemy today."

To this, Yoshitsune retorted: "Can you not see that I am here to do it?"

"You cannot, my lord," answered Kagetoki. "You are the commander-in-chief of our force."

"Not I!" replied Yoshitsune. "I have never thought of myself in that position. My brother, Yoritomo, is the true commander-in-chief. I am no more than a leader of one of his armies. I am equal to you in rank."

Thus rebuffed, Kagetoki thought that he could no longer press his request. Disgusted, he muttered under his breath: "By nature his lordship has no talent for taking command of warriors."

Overhearing him, Yoshitsune was incensed and laid his hand on the hilt of his sword, exclaiming: "You are the biggest fool in our land!"

"See that I respect and serve none but Lord Yoritomo!" replied Kagetoki, as he too laid his hand on the hilt of his sword.

Then Kagetoki's sons, Kageyasu, Kagetaka, and Kageie, leaped up with drawn weapons to support their father. Yoshitsune's retainers, Tadanobu, Hirotsuna, Genzō, Kumai-Tarō, and Benkei perceived what danger their master was in and sprang forward to surround Kagetoki. Yoshitsune, however, had a retainer named Yoshizumi, who now caught hold of his master, beseeching him: "If you split with Kagetoki before an important battle, the Heike will have a chance to gain strength. Such a quarrel among ourselves will not be countenanced by Lord Yoritomo."

Kagetoki was restrained in the same manner by his retainer Sanehira. Thus it was that Yoshitsune and Kagetoki were obliged to calm their anger. From this time on, however, Kagetoki bore a grudge against Yoshitsune, and it is said that his slanderous reports to Yoritomo in later days led to the destruction of Yoshitsune.

At last the Genji and the Heike faced each other over the water at a distance of some thirty chō. A strong tide was running through the strait of Moji and Akama from the direction of Dan-no-ura. Rowing against the current, the Genji were carried backward despite their desperate attempts to advance. The Heike, though, were able to move with the tide, since the current was much stronger offshore.

Kagetoki ordered his boat rowed close along the beach and had his men catch the passing enemy vessels with grappling hooks. At the head of fourteen or fifteen of his sons and retainers, he sprang from boat to boat, brandishing his sickle-bladed halberd. During his rampage he seized many weapons. Later in the battle record of that day his distinguished service was the first to be described.

In the meantime, the ships of the Genji and the Heike had taken up positions opposite each other. Their battle cries went up even to the paradise of Bonten and down to the palace of the Dragon King. The gods and the Buddhas in those regions must have started in amazement.

Now Munemori's brother, Tomomori, sprang onto the deck of his boat and roared at his men: "All of you, my brave men! Hear this! This is your last fight. No retreat! There have been many famous generals and valiant warriors in India and China as well as in our country. When their destiny was at hand, knowing there was no alternative, they accepted it without complaint. Do not fear death, but think of your honor! What else have we to live for? Do not tremble before these damnable warriors of the eastern provinces! This is all I wish to say."

This speech was repeated by his retainer Kagetsune to all the men of the Heike. Then Kagekiyo, one of the chieftains of the Heike, stood forth and said: "The soldiers of the eastern provinces can be proud of their skill at fighting on horseback, but they do not know how to do battle at sea. While they are helpless, let us pick them up one by one and dump them into the water."

"If we must fight, let us first mark the commander-in-chief, Yoshitsune," added another chieftain, Moritsugi. "He is a little fellow with fair complexion. It may be difficult for you to distinguish him from the others, but I hear that his front teeth stick out, so you can recognize him by that. He often changes his clothes and armor during a fight, so be on your alert lest he escape!"

"Valiant though he may be," exclaimed Kagekiyo again, "he is a puny little man. Let us tuck him under our arms and then throw him into the sea!"

Then Tomomori approached Munemori. "Our fellow soldiers are in high spirits today. The only one whose allegiance I doubt is the chief official of the civil government of Awa Province, Shigeyoshi. Shall I have him executed?"

"Without clear evidence, how can we behead him?" replied Munemori. "Up to now he has served us well. Summon him!"

When Shigeyoshi appeared before Munemori, he wore armor laced with pale red leather over a vermillion robe.

"What troubles you, Shigeyoshi?" inquired Munemori. "You look depressed today. Now rouse your men from Shikoku for a good fight! Are you really in such low spirits?"

"Why should I be in low spirits, my lord?" he said curtly and took his leave.

In the meantime, Tomomori had been standing by, gripping the hilt of his sword so tightly it seemed as though it would break. He cast his eyes toward Munemori in anticipation of some signal to attack. But as Munemori gave no sign, he could do nothing.

The Heike divided their thousand boats into three fleets. In the vanguard was Hidetō at the head of five hundred boats. After him came the Matsuura clan with three hundred. Bringing up the rear came the nobles and courtiers of the Heike on board two hundred vessels.

Hidetō had made his mark as one of Kyushu's foremost warriors. Now he chose five hundred strong archers and placed them shoulder to shoulder at the bow and stern of each boat. In unison they unleashed a barrage of arrows against the Genji.

At the outset the Genji fleet of three thousand seemed clearly superior. Their advantage, however, was weakened by careless shooting. Yoshitsune himself charged to the front, but his attack was thwarted by a rain of arrows sent down upon his shield and armor. The Heike, convinced they had made great gains, beat their war drums and shouted thunderously.

CHAPTER VIII

DISTANCE SHOOTING

One of the Genji chieftains, a man named Kotarō Yoshimori, from Wada in Sagami Province, did not board a boat. Remaining on the beach, he mounted his horse and sat firmly in the saddle with his feet deep in the stirrups. Taking up some arrows and drawing his bow with all his might, he let fly. His arrows flew deep into the ranks of the Heike, more than three chō away. Yoshimori requested that one of these shafts, the one that had flown the farthest, be shot back. Hearing this request, Tomomori called for the arrow and examined it. It was a plain bamboo shaft fletched with the white wing feathers of a crane mixed with those of a stork; it measured thirteen handbreadths and two fingers long. At a distance of a handbreadth from the lashing on the neck, the owner's name was inscribed in lacquer: "Kotarō Yoshimori of Wada."

Though there were many strong bowmen on the side of the Heike, few could shoot such a distance. The Heike chose Chikakiyo, a native of Iyo Province, and ordered him to shoot the arrow back to shore. Chikakiyo unleashed a mighty shot. The arrow flew like lightning more than three chō from boat to beach and buried itself in the bow hand of Ishizakon no Tarō of the Miura clan, who was standing several ken behind Yoshimori.

Impressed by this feat, the men of the Miura clan baited Yoshimori: "Yoshimori was so proud of his archery that he thought no one could equal him in distance shooting. What a pity that he has been put to shame so openly! See how angry he is!"

In a rage, Yoshimori then sprang into a small boat and had it rowed into the midst of the enemy vessels, while he sent forth an endless stream of arrows that killed or maimed more than a score of Heike soldiers.

At the same time a plain bamboo shaft came whizzing into the boat in which Yoshitsune stood. The Heike requested that this arrow too be shot back. When Yoshitsune had the arrow brought to him for inspection, he noted that it was fletched with the tail feathers of a pheasant and measured fourteen handbreadths and three fingers long. The name of the bowman was painted in lacquer: "Nii no Kishirō Chikakiyo, a native of Iyo Province."

Yoshitsune summoned Sanemoto, saying: "Do we have any among us who can shoot this back to the sender?"

"We have Yoshinari of Kai Province," replied Sanemoto. "He is truly a mighty bowman, my lord."

When Yoshinari came into the presence of his master, Yoshitsune handed him the arrow and said: "This came from the enemy with a request that we return it. Can you shoot it back?"

"May I first examine the shaft, my lord?" he replied, taking the arrow and examining it with his fingers to note its length and strength.

"This shaft is a little weaker than mine, my lord," said Yoshinari, "and a little shorter. If I must shoot, I would prefer to use one of my own."

With these words, he took from his quiver a great lacquered shaft, more than fifteen handbreadths and three fingers long, feathered in black. Fixing it to his nine-*shaku* lacquered rattan-bound bow, he drew it with all his might. It whistled through the air for more than four chō and struck Chikakiyo in the middle of his chest as he stood at the bow of one of the larger vessels. Mortally wounded, he fell headfirst to the bottom of the boat.

Yoshinari was indeed a powerful bowman. Firm of hand, he never missed his mark. It was said that, without fail, he could shoot a running stag at a distance of two chō.

After this feat both the Genji and the Heike fought desperately, heedless of their lives. It was difficult to say which side held the advantage. The Heike were possibly more courageous, for they had kept Emperor Antoku with them. Perhaps this is the reason the battle seemed to be going against the Genji. Suddenly a white cloud came drifting over the two fighting fleets. Soon it appeared to be a white banner floating in the breeze, and it drifted down onto the bow of one of the Genji boats. The loop of the banner draped around the prow. Strangely enough, it was a banner that none of the Genji had ever seen.

"This is truly a sign from the great bodhisattva Hachi-man!" rejoiced Yoshitsune, as he washed his hands, rinsed his mouth, and made obeisance to the banner. His men all followed him.

Another curious thing occurred. A large school of dolphins appeared near the fleet of the Genji and swam toward that of the Heike. When Munemori saw them, he summoned the diviner Hare-nobu and inquired: "There are always dolphins around here, but I have never seen so many before. What does it mean? You must tell me at once!"

"If the dolphins turn back with their mouths open," replied Harenobu, "the Genji will be destroyed. But if they continue toward us and swim under our ships from one side to the other, we will be in danger."

No sooner had he spoken than the dolphins swam straight under the ships of the Heike and passed on. Seeing this, Harenobu exclaimed: "The end of the world is at hand."

For the past three years Shigeyoshi had fought loyally and bravely against the Genji. But when his son, Noriyoshi, was captured by the Genji, he felt he could no longer rely upon the Heike. Because he had lost faith in the Heike cause, he suddenly deserted his position and went over to the Genji.

The strategy of the Heike was to put men of high rank on board small war boats and the men of low rank on board large, impressive, well-outfitted vessels. The Genji would be induced to attack the large ones, believing them to hold generals. The entire Genji fleet could then be surrounded and destroyed by the less imposing boats. The Heike fleet had already been formed according to the plan when Shigeyoshi deserted and revealed it to the Genji. Consequently the Genji ignored the large boats of the Heike and persisted in violently attacking the small ones, aboard which were the Heike of high rank disguised as lowly foot soldiers.

"I should have cut off the head of that wretch Shigeyoshi!" wailed Tomomori in regret. But a thousand of his regrets were of no use. Soon afterward all the men of Shikoku and Kyushu turned traitor and went over to the Genji. Those who had been faithful retainers of the Heike now loosed their arrows against their lords and drew their swords against their masters. Some of the Heike tried to beach their boats to take refuge. But on one shore the cliffs rose high and the waves repulsed them, and on the other the enemy's arrows sought them out.

This battle was the decisive one between the Heike and the Genji. Its outcome would spell doom for one side, power and glory for the other.

CHAPTER IX

DROWNING OF THE EMPEROR

Genji warriors had overrun all of the Heike boats and had slain the helmsmen. The Heike defenses had degenerated into complete collapse—escape was no longer possible. As his soldiers flung themselves in panic to the bottoms of their boats, Tomomori could feel death approaching. Boarding a small boat, he rowed to the imperial vessel.

"We are in the midst of a catastrophe! Destroy everything and throw it into the sea!" he ordered. "We must ready ourselves to meet our end."

The vessel was scoured from the stem to stern, swept and mopped to leave nothing graceless in the wake of death. All the while court ladies questioned Tomomori: "Vice-Councilor, how goes the battle?"

"You will soon receive some men of the east as your unexpected guests!" he answered with a bitter laugh.

"How can you make fun of us at a time like this?" they wept.

Nii-dono had determined to destroy herself; no fear showed in her face. Calm, unlike the others, she put on a double outer dress of dark gray mourning color, tucked up her glossy silk skirts, secured the sacred jewel under her arm, and placed the sacred sword in her sash. Then she took the emperor in her arms and said: "Though I am a woman, I shall not fall into the hands of the enemy. I shall accompany His Majesty. Any among you who remain faithful to him follow me!" With these words, she made her way to the gunwale of the imperial vessel.

The emperor was then eight years old but looked much older. He was so handsome that it was as if an aura of light glowed around his head. His long raven locks flowed loosely down his back. With a puzzled expression on his face, he inquired: "Where are you going to take me, grandmother?"

Nii-dono turned her gaze to him and suppressing her tears, replied: "Your Majesty cannot know what this is all about! Since you had mastered the Buddha's Ten Precepts in a former life, you were blessed to ascend to the supreme place of honor as the emperor in this world. But the day of this destiny is over, and now an evil karma is about to carry you away to the world beyond. I pray you—first turn to the east to bid farewell to the Sun Goddess of the Great Ise Shrine, and then to the west to repeat 'Hail Amida Buddha,' so that Amida will welcome you to the Pure Land Paradise in the west."

Thus instructed by Nii-dono, the emperor put on a parrot green silk outer robe and had his hair bound up at the sides. Tears rushed down his cheeks as he joined his little palms. He first turned to the east to bid farewell to the Sun Goddess and then to the west to repeat "Hail Amida Buddha."

Nii-dono took the emperor in her arms and consoled him, saying: "In the depths of the waves you will find a capital!" With these words, she plunged with him to the bottom of the sea.

What a pity it was that the fleeting spring breeze should carry away the sacred flower, and that the uncompassionate waves of life and death should thus engulf the jeweled person! His abode in the capital was called Long Life Hall, and the gate of his palace Eternal Youth, through which nothing of great age was allowed to pass. In spite of this, before he reached the age of ten he became but mud at the bottom of the sea. How transient his life—that he was obliged to abandon the throne rewarded him for his mastery of the Buddha's Ten Precepts! The dragon above the clouds suddenly plunged below the surface of the sea only to become a fish. In times past he had resided in a heavenly palace as great as that of the king of the Paradise of Bonten or the Palace of Correct Views of Ten-taishaku,[1] and had been waited upon by kinsmen, courtiers, and ministers. After such an elegant life at court, he had been deprived of his comfort and was forced to live rudely on board a tossing boat until at last he met an ignominious end beneath the waves.

[1] The palace located atop Mount Sumeru in the Tusita Heaven. Ten-taishaku, one of the tutelary gods of Buddhism, resides there.

CHAPTER X

THE DEATH OF NORITSUNE

When Kenreimon-In, the emperor's mother, saw what had become of her son, she put ink stones and warming stones into each sleeve of her robe and leaped overboard. Not recognizing the lady, Mutsuru of the Watanabe clan of the Genji, approaching in a small boat, caught her long raven locks with a wooden-shafted grappling hook and dragged her on board.

The court ladies cried out in horror: "That lady is the emperor's mother!"

Heeding their words, Mutsuru reported to Yoshitsune and hurried to escort the lady into the imperial vessel. Here, however, the wife of Lord Shigehira was preparing to leap overboard with the casket containing the sacred mirror, one of the imperial treasures. Just as she was about to jump, an arrow pinned the lower part of her hakama to the side of the boat, causing her to stumble and fall. Several Genji soldiers rushed up to her and held her back. Snatching the casket and breaking the chain and lock, they were trying to remove the lid when suddenly they were blinded and blood gushed from their noses.

Tokitada, a councilor of the Heike, who had been captured during the battle, was sitting nearby. Now he exclaimed: "This casket contains one of the imperial treasures! No commoner dares open it without suffering!"

The warriors drew back from the casket. Later, when Yoshitsune consulted Tokitada about the treasure, he was advised to tie the casket properly with a cord. Yoshitsune restored it to its former state with utmost care.

Kiyomori's brothers, Norimori and Tsunemori, hung anchors from the shoulder pieces of their armor and sprang overboard hand in hand. Shigemori's sons, Sukemori and Arimori, and their cousin Yukimori—they too leaped hand in hand into the waves. In this manner most of the kinsmen of the Heike ended their lives. But their leader, Munemori, and his son Kiyomune were not inclined to jump. Standing at the gunwale and looking absently about, they seemed quite at a loss as to what to do. The warriors under their command were greatly ashamed of their master's cowardice, and, merely pretending to pass by him, pushed Munemori into the sea. At the moment he saw his father fall, Kiyomune flung himself overboard.

All the warriors wore armor and carried heavy objects on their backs or under their arms, so that they would sink deep into the water. But wearing neither armor nor weapons, Munemori and Kiyomune floated. Moreover they were able to swim. As they drifted upon the waves, Munemori depended on his son for survival. If only Kiyomune would not sink, then he would be able to persevere. Kiyomune, for his part, depended upon his father for survival. Thus father and son gazed hopefully into each other's eyes as they swam. Soon, however, Yoshimori approached, rowing a small boat, and caught Kiyomune with a grappling hook and hauled him in. Seeing that Kiyomune had been taken on board, Munemori could not allow himself to drown. He too was captured.

Now Munemori's foster brother, Kagetsune, steered a small boat up to them and sprang into Yoshimori's boat, saying: "Who is he that has captured my master?"

Kagetsune drew his sword and rushed toward Yoshimori. He was holding him at sword's point when Yoshimori's servant came between them to ward off the attack against his master. Kagetsune's sword struck the servant's helmet, cutting it in two. The second blow cut off his head. Yoshimori was still in danger, so from a nearby boat Chikatsune drew his bow and took aim at Kagetsune. The arrow found its way through a gap in his helmet, staggering him. Then Chikatsune rowed his boat toward Yoshimori's, and, flinging himself into it, he grappled with Kagetsune. Chikatsune held his opponent down while one of his family retainers, who had rushed to his master's side, lifted a panel of his armor and stabbed Kagetsune twice. Though he was a man of great strength, his destiny was death. His enemies were many; his wound was fatal. Finally he breathed his last. Munemori watched as his foster brother was beheaded. How helpless Munemori must have felt at the sight of Kagetsune's violent end!

Because Noritsune was renowned as an archer, no one dared come within his range. But now his arrows were spent. With his sword and halberd, he resolved to fight on until overtaken by defeat. That day Noritsune wore armor laced with twilled silk cords over a red brocade battle robe. With a great gold-studded sword in one hand and a long sickle-bladed wooden-shafted halberd in the other, he cut and slashed at the foes that surrounded him. None could stand before his assaults.

When Tomomori saw how recklessly Noritsune fought, he sent a messenger, saying: "Noritsune, do not be so cruel! The slaughter of many men of little fame will only add to your sins."

"Then I will grapple with the commander-in-chief!" was his reply. Noritsune, gripping his short sword, cut his way through the opposition, leaping from one boat to the other, attacking any well-armed warrior. Although he did not know how to recognize Yoshitsune, he assumed the great chieftain would be wearing splendid armor and a fine helmet. Finally Noritsune jumped into Yoshitsune's boat prepared to spring upon the famous warrior. Perhaps Yoshitsune thought he would have no chance of winning if attacked, for he stuck his long sickle-bladed halberd under his arm and in a great arc leaped over to an allied boat about two jō away. As Noritsune was not deft at such tricks, he could not follow.

In disgust, Noritsune threw his sword and halberd into the sea, took off his helmet, and tore off the sleeves and skirts of his armor. Now wearing only his body armor, he stood on the gunwale, arms outspread. His hair hung loose and it ruffled in the wind. He roared at the enemy: "Let any among you who thinks himself worthy of a fight with me come and grapple with me. Take me alive if you can! I wish to go down to Kamakura and have a word with Yoritomo. Who will come and try? Stand forth!" He seemed to be an incarnation of the god of war, so no one dared to approach him.

Now there was a Genji warrior named Sanemitsu, the son of the head of Aki County in Tosa Province, Saneyasu. He was famous for possessing the strength of twenty or thirty ordinary men. He had a retainer who was in no way inferior and a brother named Jirō, also a man of extraordinary strength. Sanemitsu stood forth and said to his brother and retainer: "However sturdy Noritsune may be, he will fall if we three attack him together. Even a demon ten jō tall would fall to our assault."

Then the three men brought a small boat alongside Noritsune's. With a shout they sprang onto their opponent's boat. Bending forward and holding their swords high, they advanced shoulder to shoulder to face Noritsune. Noritsune was undaunted, and when they drew near, he kicked Sanemitsu's retainer into the water. He then clasped Sanemitsu under his left arm and his brother under his right. After he had given them a mighty squeeze, he flung himself, into the sea, still clasping them, and shouting: "You cowardly fools! Follow me to Mount Shide!"

CHAPTER XI

THE SACRED MIRROR RETURNED
TO THE CAPITAL

"Now I have seen everything in this world there is to see," said Tomomori. "Let me put an end to myself. Ienaga, is it not time for us to die together as we promised?"

"Certainly, my lord," replied his foster son, as he assisted his master into a double set of armor. Ienaga also donned armor, and the two warriors in their heavy garb leaped into the sea hand in hand. Some twenty of their companions followed them at once.

Several Heike generals—Moritsugi, Tadamitsu, Kagekiyo, and Shirō-Byōe—managed to avoid capture, though it is unknown how they made their escape.

Since the Heike had abandoned their red banners to the waves, the sea resembled the Tatsuta River in autumn, when maple leaves, torn away by the mountain gales, can be seen drifting in the current. Even the waves lapping the beach became red. Masterless boats drifted aimlessly with the wind and tide.

Among those taken alive were the former state minister, Munemori; the councilor, Tokitada; the captain of the Imperial Gate of the Right, Kiyomune; the chief of the Finance Division, Nobumoto; a lieutenant general, Tokizane; the lower secretary of the Ordinance Division, Masaakira; and Munemori's son Yoshimune. The advisory priests of the Heike—Senshin, Nōen, Chūkai, and Yūen—were also captured. Thirty-eight Heike warriors were captured, most notably, Suesada, Morizumi, and Shigeyoshi[1] and his son Noriyoshi. Takanao and Tanenao had already laid down their arms and surrendered to the Genji before the battle. Forty-three court ladies were likewise taken alive. Chief among them were Kenreimon-In, and the wives of Motomichi, Kanemasa, Shigehira, Tokitada, and Tomomori. Now, at dusk on this day in the spring of the second year of Genryaku, the emperor rested beneath the waves, and his retainers drifted upon the sea. What an ill-omened day and what a star-crossed year—so many lives had been carried away to the world beyond!

The mother of the emperor and her ladies-in-waiting were delivered into the hands of the rough warriors of the east. How sad it must have been to set out on the return journey to the capital—as captives in the midst of enemies. They must have felt great shame, comparing their fate to that of Chu Mai-chen, who wore a splendid brocade robe on his homecoming day, or perhaps they sympathized with the great resentment of Wang Chao-chün,[2] who was sent to the barbarian land of Hu Kuo.

On the third day of the fourth month of the year, Yoshitsune sent a report of his triumph to the Cloistered Palace. Hirotsuna relayed it to the cloistered emperor, saying: "On the twenty-fourth day of the third month at Dan-no-ura, to the east of the strait between Moji and Akama, the Heike were completely destroyed. The sacred mirror and the sacred seal were safely recovered."

Those gathered in the Cloistered Palace clamored in delight at this report. Hirotsuna was allowed to sit in the courtyard while he gave details of the battle. Go-Shirakawa was so pleased that he promoted Hirotsuna to aide to the chief of the Imperial Guard of the Left.

The next day the cloistered emperor ordered his guard, Nobumori, to hurry down to the western provinces to make sure that the sacred treasures were being returned to the capital. After receiving this command, Nobumori did not even go back to his own home to prepare for the journey, but made his way straight to the west. Since he had been given a fine horse from the Imperial Stables, he swiftly departed.

Yoshitsune was meanwhile making his return trip to the capital with the captives. On the sixteenth day of the fourth month, they arrived at the shore of Akashi in Harima Province, a famous scenic spot. As night deepened, the moon shone as clearly as the harvest moon of September. The court ladies gathered in groups, and, gazing at the moon, they wept, saying: "The last time we were here, we never thought our lives would become as wretched as this."

The wife of Lord Tokitada sank deep into despair. Her weeping was so violent that her bed was wet with tears. As she wept, she composed these poems:

> Sinking in sorrow,
> I see the moon reflected
> In tears on my sleeve.
> Tell me a tale of my home,
> The place of my longing.
>
> Though my life changed,
> Yet the moon remains the same
> As it was before.
> When I gaze on its clear light,
> My melancholy deepens.

The wife of Lord Shigehira expressed her thoughts in this poem:

> In tears I lie down
> On the shore of Akashi
> As I journey home.
> The moon spends the night with me,
> Casting its light on the waves.

Yoshitsune was a stout-hearted warrior in battle, but in times of peace he could understand elegance and poetry, and so he too felt melancholic.

"How painful it is for these ladies to recall their days of glory!" he sighed.

On the twenty-fifth day of the month, the cloistered emperor received a report that the caskets containing the sacred mirror and the sacred seal had arrived safely at Toba. To receive them, he at once dispatched to Toba Vice-Councilor Tsunefusa, Lieutenant General Yasumichi, Secretary of the Right Kanetada, Aide to the Chief of the Imperial Gate of the Left Chikamasa, Lieutenant General Kintoki, and Major General Noriyoshi. The warriors who escorted them were Yorikane, Yoshikane, and Aritsuna. That same night at the hour of the mouse [midnight], they returned to the capital with the sacred mirror and the sacred seal and handed them to the officials of the Grand Ministry.

The sacred sword was not returned, for it had been lost during the battle. As for the sacred seal, it at first sank with Nii-dono but had soon floated to the surface, where, it was said, the seal had been recovered by Tsuneharu.

[1] Shigeyoshi actually deserted the Heike to join the Genji forces.

[2] A court lady in the early Han dynasty. Beautiful though she was, she happened to be painted as an ugly woman by a court portrait artist. This caused an unfair judgment, and she was included among the enslaved concubines dedicated to the barbarian king.

CHAPTER XII

THE SACRED SWORD

In our land, from generation to generation since the days of the gods, three imperial swords have been handed down to posterity. They are the Ten-Hands Long Sword, the Rope-Cutting Sword, and the Grass-Slashing Sword. The first sword is enshrined at the Isonokami Shrine in Yamato Province, the second at the Atsuta Shrine in Owari, and the last is maintained at the imperial court. It was the Grass-Slashing Sword that was lost during the battle of Dan-no-ura. Several stories concerning this sword have been passed down to us.

Of old, when Susano-o-no-Mikoto built his palace at Soga[1] in Izumo, he composed a poem to celebrate the clouds of eight different colors that always hung over the palace:

Piles of clouds rise high
O'er the fences of my home
Here in Izumo.
I am making more fences
As protection for my bride.

This was the first poem ever composed in our land in waka form. It was from this poem that the province came to be called Izumo, or "Rising Clouds."

Once, when Susano-o-no-Mikoto was traveling along the Higawa River, he met an old couple named Ashinazuchi and Tenazuchi. With them was their beautiful daughter, Inada-hime. They were weeping so bitterly that he was moved to inquire why.

"I had eight daughters before," replied the old man, "but all except this one were eaten by a great serpent, and the time is approaching when he will come again to take the last. The serpent has eight heads and eight tails, and is so monstrous that it spans eight valleys and eight mountain peaks. Gnarled old trees grow on its

[686]

back. The serpent is more than a thousand years old. Its eyes shine like the sun and moon. It comes to our village each year to eat human flesh. Because of the serpent, children grieve for the loss of their fathers or mothers and parents grieve for the loss of their children. Never in this village does the crying cease."

Susano-o-no-Mikoto was deeply moved and made preparations to fight the serpent. He first transformed the girl into a comb with five hundred teeth and inserted it into his hair. He then filled eight barrels with saké. Next he built a statue of a beautiful girl on a high hill and placed the barrels around the statue, so the reflection of the girl was cast in the saké. The serpent, believing the reflection was a real girl, drank and drank until the barrels were drained. In a drunken stupor he lay down and slept. Then Susano-o-no-Mikoto unsheathed his sword, which was ten hands long, and hacked the serpent into pieces. In one of the tails, however, the blade of his sword hit something as hard as adamant. Thinking this strange, he thrust the blade along the sinew of the tail, which, when sliced open, revealed a mysterious sword. He took the sword as a gift to his sister, the Sun Goddess, Amaterasu.

When she saw it, she said in amazement: "This is the sword that I left at Takama-ga-hara[2] many years ago."

During the time that the sword was lodged in the tail of the serpent, billowing clouds used to hover over the village. This is why the sword was called Ame-no-Murakumo, or "Village Clouds under Heaven." The Sun Goddess designated it a treasure of her palace, Ame-no-miya.[3] Later, when she dispatched two of her descendants, Izanagi and Izanami, to Toyoashihara-no-Nakatsukuni, she presented to them the sword and the mirror. These treasures were kept at the imperial palace until the time of the ninth emperor, Kaika.[4] The tenth emperor, Sujin, however, was in awe of the mysterious power of the sword. Therefore when he built a shrine to worship the Sun Goddess at Kasanui in Yamato, he transferred it from the palace to the shrine. At this time he had a copy of the sword made and kept it at his side as an amulet. For about three generations, from the emperor Sujin to the emperor Keikō, the original was maintained at the shrine of the Sun Goddess.

In the sixth month of the fortieth year of Emperor Keikō's reign, however, the barbarians of the east[5] revolted against the imperial family. In an attempt to placate the rebels, Emperor Keikō presented the sword to his son, Yamato-Takeru-no-Mikoto, through Itsuki-no-Mikoto, the superintendent of the Great Ise Shrine. "Keep this with you as your most valued weapon!" Keikō commanded.

When Yamato-Takeru-no-Mikoto, a stout-hearted man of great strength, arrived at Suruga, the rebels tried to deceive him into accompanying them to a plain, saying: "There are many deer in this province. It would be great fun for you to go deer hunting." On the plain they set fire to the grass in order to trap him. The flames were about to engulf him, when he unsheathed the sword, Ame-no-Murakumo, and slashed at the grass around him. All the grass within one ri suddenly disappeared. This is why the sword is also called the Grass-Slashing Sword. Yamato-Takeru-no-Mikoto then set fire to the grass near the rebels, and the flames ran with the wind to their side, so that they were burned to death.

Yamato-Takeru-no-Mikoto went deep into the east and spent three years there subjugating the rebels. On his way back to the capital with many captives, however, he became ill, and in the seventh month of his thirtieth year he died at Atsuta in Owari Province. His spirit ascended into heaven in the form of a white bird. According to his will, the captives were presented by his son, Takehiko, to the emperor, and the Grass-Slashing Sword to the Atsuta Shrine.

In the seventh year of the reign of Emperor Tenchi [668], a Korean named Dōgyō stole the sword, hoping to make it one of the treasures of his country, and concealed it on board a boat bound for his homeland. During the voyage, however, a violent wind arose and the waves curled high. The boat was about to sink when Dōgyō realized the spirit of the sword had caused the storm, and so, begging pardon of the spirit, he returned the sword to the shrine.

In the first year of Shuchō [686], Emperor Temmu sent for it and placed it at court.

Indeed, the sword had mysterious power. While Emperor Yōzei was suffering from a long illness, he unsheathed it one night. The sword flashed like lightning in the darkness. Stunned with terror, he threw it away from him. With a click, the sword returned by itself to its sheath.

So great was the sword's mysterious power that even though the sword sank with Nii-dono to the bottom of the sea, the cloistered emperor could not believe it was lost forever. To search for it, many divers were summoned, and many priests of high virtue were ordered to confine themselves in their shrines and temples to offer fervent prayers and many gifts to the gods and the Buddhas. Despite all these efforts, the sword never reappeared.

Many learned men at the time offered an opinion, saying: "Of old the Sun Goddess, Amaterasu, swore to save a hundred generations of her descendants, so we should not think that she has changed her mind. Inasmuch as the water continues to run in the stream of the Yahata Shrine, her influence on earth is still greater than all others. However degenerate this age may be, it is not so bad that the fortunes of the throne will be brought to an end."

Among these scholars was one who divined this story: "The great serpent that was killed by Susano-o-no-Mikoto long ago at the upper part of the Higawa River must have borne a grudge because of the loss of the sword. Therefore with his eight heads and eight tails, he has entered into the eight-year-old emperor after eighty generations, and has taken the sword back to the depths of the sea."

Inasmuch as the sword had been carried away by the holy dragon to the bottom of the sea, a thousand fathoms down, people thought that it would never be recovered by any man of this world.

[1] Present-day Suga, Ōhara-gun, Shimane Prefecture.

[2] Literally "Plain of the High Sky." A home of heavenly deities, it is a mytho-religious location rather than an actual place.

[3] Literally "Palace of Heaven."

[4] (157–98 B.C.)

[5] The aboriginal inhabitants of Japan; ancestors of the Ainu.

CHAPTER XIII

THE HEIKE PARADING THROUGH THE CAPITAL

The second son of the late Emperor Takakura made his return journey to the capital with the triumphant force of the Genji. As a welcome, the cloistered emperor sent an imperial carriage to carry him. He was the prince who had been carried off by the Heike to the western provinces and forced to drift upon the waves for about three years. His mother and wet nurse, therefore, had been constantly worried about him. Now, upon his safe return to the capital, all his relatives gathered; their rejoicing was mixed with tears.

On the twenty-sixth day of the fourth month, the Heike captives arrived at the capital. They rode in carriages decorated with designs of small lotus flowers. The curtains in front and rear were rolled up, and the windows on the right and left were also opened so that the people could see them. Munemori was wearing a white hunting suit. In the rear of his carriage rode Kiyomune, wearing a white battle robe. The carriage in which Tokitada rode was also in the procession. His son, Tokizane, was supposed to accompany him, but due to an illness, he was allowed to remain away from the parade. Since Nobumoto had been seriously wounded, he was quietly escorted into the capital along a side path.

In days past Munemori had been a very handsome noble, but now he was so emaciated that he appeared to be a different man. Nevertheless he looked about showing no feelings of shame. His son Kiyomune never raised his head but cast his eyes downward. His pride had been deeply wounded. These nobles of the Heike were escorted by Sanehira's soldiers. Some thirty horsemen rode at front and rear.

The spectators, both young and old, came from far and wide, from city and country, from mountains and temples. These people, thousands upon thousands, poured into the area along the way from the south gate of the North Palace of Toba to Yotsuzuka. So great was the crowd that once they entered this area, they were unable to move about or change the direction of their carts. Famines in the Jishō and Yōwa eras and constant wars in the east and west had taken the lives of a great number of men, and yet there still appeared such masses. It seemed as though men could survive any misfortune.

According to the calendar, the Juei era was in its fourth year, but actually only a little over twenty months had elapsed since the Heike had abandoned the capital. The people, therefore, clearly remembered the days of Heike splendor. The men of the Heike, who only a few years ago had terrified them, now appeared so wretched that they could hardly believe their eyes. Even humble men and women, who had been little concerned with the Heike, were moved to tears. How much more affected were those who had been on good terms with them! Some men had received favors from the Heike from generation to generation; many of them, however, had allied with the Genji simply to spare their own lives. To forget old favors was not an easy matter. Immeasurably saddened, they pressed their sleeves to their eyes, unable to raise their heads to see the parade.

The ox tender who drove the carriage of Munemori was Jirō-maru, whose younger brother, Saburō-maru, had been executed by Yoshinaka for driving rudely. Jirō-maru had celebrated his coming of age when he had been with the Heike in the western provinces. Now, at Toba, he had begged Yoshitsune for permission to drive the carriage of his former master, Munemori, saying: "Since I am only an ox tender, I know I have no right to make this kind of request of you. But I cannot forget the favors that I received from Lord Munemori. If it is not too much to ask, I pray you to allow me to drive his carriage as my last service to him."

Jirō-maru's petition was so sincere that Yoshitsune was moved to compassion and granted his request. Greatly delighted, Jirō-maru took a driving rope from the folds of his robe and led the carriage. Blinded by tears, he could not see where he was going. He simply let the ox find its own way.

The cloistered emperor had the imperial carriage stopped at Rokujō-Higashi-no-Tōin and from there viewed the procession. All who passed drew alongside to pay their respects to His Majesty.

Since Go-Shirakawa had been served by nobles and courtiers of the Heike until recent times, he too felt compassion for their miserable condition.

"Who would ever have dreamed," said the spectators, "that these men of rank would suffer so wretchedly? Their influence was once so great that we were grateful even for a word or glance from them."

A few years ago, when Lord Munemori had come in procession to the Cloistered Palace to express his thanks to the emperor for his appointment as state minister, he was accompanied by twelve nobles led by Councilor Tadachika, and sixteen courtiers headed by Chief of the Archivists Division Chikamune. Among the courtiers had been such high officials as four vice-councilors and three lieutenant generals of the third court rank, who had worn their best ceremonial robes to honor the occasion. Tokitada too had ridden with them. Splendid was the sight when Tokitada was summoned into the august presence and entertained magnificently with many gifts. Today the Heike nobles were accompanied by none but twenty of their soldiers who had been captured by the Genji at Dan-no-ura. They were all clad in white battle robes and were bound by ropes to the saddles of their horses.

After they had been paraded through the streets to the banks of the Kamo River at Rokujō, Munemori and his son were taken to the mansion of Yoshitsune at Rokujō-Horikawa. Though food was brought before Munemori, he could eat nothing, for his throat was choked with emotion. Not a word was uttered between father and son—the most they could do was exchange tearful glances from time to time. Even when night fell, they would not put on different robes, but lay as they were, resting their heads on their elbows. Concerned about his son, Munemori covered him with his sleeve. Although such fierce warriors as Hirotsuna, Genzō, and Kumai-Tarō were standing guard, they were moved to compassion: "Regardless of rank and title, there is nothing more touching than affection between father and son. To spread his sleeve over Kiyomune is an act of little effect. Even so, this shows how tender is his heart toward his son!"

CHAPTER XIV

THE MIRROR

O n the twenty-eighth day of the
fourth month, Yoritomo was promoted to the junior grade of the
second court rank. This was extraordinary, for he was allowed to
skip three grades at once. To skip even two grades was an unusual
advancement, so his case was indeed exceptional. He was given
this great honor because the cloistered emperor wished to surpass
the precedent of the two-grade advancement set by the Heike.

That night at the hour of the mouse [midnight], the sacred
mirror was transferred from the office of the Grand Ministry to
the Unmei-den hall for proper installation. The emperor himself
appeared at the hall, and it was there that the kagura was performed
for three nights. A court musician, the superintendent of the Imperial Guard of the Right, Yoshikata, received a special order to play
two of the sacred melodies, 'Udachi' and 'Miyōdo'.[1] These sacred
melodies had been cultivated and maintained by his family alone.
The pieces he was to perform had been kept secret by his grandfather Suketada. Suketada, however, had been so anxious to keep
them to himself that he did not even pass them on to his own
son Chikakata. Fortunately before he died, Suketada played the
secret pieces for Emperor Horikawa. Emperor Horikawa then
passed them on to Chikakata after his father had died. Chikakata,
in turn, passed the pieces on to his son Yoshikata. What a wise
ruler Horikawa was to enable the court musicians to retain their
authority !

There is a story concerning the mirror installed that night at
the Unmei-den hall. Of old, when the Sun Goddess, Amaterasu,
decided to shut herself in the Heavenly Rock Cave, she had a mirror made, wishing to keep her reflection upon it forever so that
her offspring would be able to see her from generation to generation. The first mirror, made by a blacksmith, did not satisfy her.

Another was cast. The former was enshrined at the Nichizen-Koku-ken Shrine in Kii Province, and the latter was given to her son, Ame-no-Oshihomimi-no-Mikoto. Upon presenting it to him, she said: "Keep this with you at your palace."

When she hid herself in the Heavenly Rock Cave, the whole world was covered by darkness. The myriad gods and goddesses assembled in divine council and performed the kagura in front of the Heavenly Rock Cave. The Sun Goddess could not suppress her curiosity. In order to see why the gods were so joyous, she slightly moved the great rock at the entrance of the cave and peered through the crevice. Light was restored. The laughing faces of the gods and goddesses shone white in the dim light. This is how the ideographs *omo* and *shiro*, or "face white" came to imply "interesting."

Finally a god of great strength named Tejikarao-no-Mikoto forced open the door. This is how the word *taterarezu*, or "cannot be shut," came to imply "open."

Afterward the sacred mirror was maintained by successive emperors at the Inner Palace until the time of the ninth emperor, Kaika. But the tenth emperor, Sujin, fearing the mirror's mysterious power, had it transferred to another hall. It was then installed at the Unmei-den.

During the reign of Emperor Murakami, one hundred and sixty years after the relocation of the capital from Nara to Kyoto, at the hour of the mouse [midnight] on the twenty-third day of the ninth month of the fourth year of the Tentoku era [960], a fire broke out in the palace. It started at the Imperial Gate of the Left, near the Unmei-den. Since it was midnight, the court ladies in charge of the sacred mirror were not on duty, and there was no one to remove it to a place of safety.

Lord Saneyori hurried to the hall, but when he saw the flames, he cried out in tears: "The sacred mirror has been reduced to ashes! This is truly the end of the world."

While he was weeping, however, the sacred mirror sprang by itself out of the conflagration and into the branches of a cherry tree in front of the Shishin-den. It lit up as though the morning sun were rising above the mountain.

When Lord Saneyori beheld this spectacle, he cried again in tears: "The world has been saved from destruction!" With tears rushing down his cheeks, he made obeisance to the sacred mirror. His right knee on the ground, he extended his left sleeve and spoke to the sacred mirror: "Of old the Sun Goddess, Amaterasu, swore to protect the next one hundred generations. If her vow has not yet been revoked, I pray thee to come down upon my sleeve."

These words had hardly been spoken when the sacred mirror descended from the tree to his sleeve. Lord Saneyori wrapped it in his sleeve and carried it to the office of the Grand Ministry. Now, again, the sacred mirror is kept at the Unmei-den hall.

In a degenerate age such as this, no one would be able to address the sacred mirror. The sacred mirror, for its part, would not fly down to a man's hand. Those bygone days were incomparably superior to the present!

¹ Literally "Bowstand" and "Courtiers." These two melodies were based on the songs sung at court banquets during the reign of Emperor Sujin.

CHAPTER XV

THE LETTERS

Lord Tokitada and his son were also prisoners, near the mansion of Yoshitsune. Inasmuch as things had gone counter to the Heike's plans, it seemed proper for Lord Tokitada to abandon himself to his fate. Yet, despite his worsened circumstances, he clung to a faint hope of remaining alive. He said to his son, Tokizane: "Yoshitsune has confiscated a box of our secret letters. If they are sent to Kamakura for Yoritomo's examination, not only our lives but those of our family will be lost. What can we do to avoid this?"

"Yoshitsune is a man of compassionate nature," replied Tokizane. "If a woman, therefore, pleads with him in tears, he will be unable to give her a cold refusal. Since you have many daughters, let one of them go to him. After she has won his favor, why not let her plead with him on our behalf?"

"When I flourished in the world," Tokitada said, weeping, "I hoped that my daughters would be court ladies or imperial consorts. Never had I thought of sending one to a commoner!"

"In a time like this," replied Tokizane, "you must not speak of lost grandeur. Send him the one who is now eighteen years old, the daughter of your present wife."

Tokitada was not willing to part with her and chose another daughter, a girl of twenty-three. She was a daughter by his former wife. Mature, beautiful, and tender, she captivated Yoshitsune.

Though he already had a wife, a daughter of Shigeyori, Yoshitsune rearranged his mansion for Tokitada's daughter and allowed her to live with him. To please her, he had her chamber beautifully decorated.

Thus when she requested the return of the secret letters to her father, Yoshitsune did not even open the box but sent them at once to Tokitada. Greatly relieved at the recovery of the letters, he wasted no time in burning them. This only whetted people's curiosity about their contents.

Now that the Heike had been completely destroyed, peace was restored to all the provinces as well as to the capital. No longer in fear, people were able to travel freely. Thus it was that they began to say: "There is none greater than Yoshitsune throughout our land. Yoritomo at Kamakura—what did he do? We wish Yoshitsune to govern the country."

When Yoritomo heard of this, he roared: "What absurdities they speak! It was I alone who took command of the entire army. Can they not understand that it was my outstanding war plans that enabled us to bring about our overwhelming victory over the Heike? How can Yoshitsune alone rule the country? Flattered by parasites, he thinks he already holds the world in his palm. Despite the fact that there are many women in the world, he dared choose a daughter of Tokitada for his wife. That he treats Tokitada warmly for this reason is intolerable! Tokitada is also to be blamed! In a time when he must observe strict self-control, how can he have his daughter married? When Yoshitsune comes back to Kamakura, I am certain that he will wield power beyond measure."

CHAPTER XVI

THE EXECUTION OF YOSHIMUNE

It was rumored that on the seventh day of the fifth month Yoshitsune would set out from the capital for Kamakura with the captives of the Heike. When Munemori heard this news, he sent a message to Yoshitsune: "I have learned that you will depart from the capital tomorrow. I am worried about my son Yoshimune, for, as you are aware, deep is the affection between father and son. Is he still alive? He is listed in the record of the captives as an eight-year-old boy. I wish I could see him but once more before I set out for Kamakura."

To this petition, Yoshitsune replied: "As you say, affection between father and son is so deep that it is quite natural for you to make this kind of request."

Yoshimune had been placed in the charge of one of Yoshitsune's retainers, a man named Shigefusa. Now Yoshitsune ordered him to escort Yoshimune to Munemori's temporary dwelling. Accompanied by two female attendants, he was placed in a carriage. As Yoshimune arrived, he saw his father from a distance, and his eyes beamed with delight.

"Come! Run to me!" Munemori cried out.

Yoshimune raced up to him and climbed onto his knee. Caressing him, Munemori wept and said: "Listen! This child has no mother. Though she was safely delivered of him, she soon became ill. At that time she said to me, 'Perhaps you will have more boys by other ladies, but I pray you to give your constant love to this boy of mine and keep him always by your side in remembrance of me. Do not send him away to a wet nurse.' Her last words were pathetic but so earnest that I sought for words to cheer her. I told her that I would call him 'Vice-Commander,' while my eldest son, Kiyomune, would be called 'Commander.' I gave these titles to them in preparation for the future, when they would be engaged in war against the enemies of the emperor. She was so pleased that she continued to call Yoshimune 'Vice-Commander' until she breathed her last. Every time I see him, he reminds me of his mother's last moment. I can never forget it."

Hearing him reminisce, all the guards wet their sleeves with tears. Kiyomune wept. Yoshimune's wet nurse and lady attendant too wept bitterly. After a while Munemori said: "Now, Vice-Commander, you must return home! It has been a joy to see you."

But Yoshimune would not take leave of his father. Seeing his reluctance, Kiyomune said in tears: "Vice-Commander, my dear! You had better leave early tonight. Your father is expecting some other guests. Be of good cheer, for you may come again tomorrow evening."

These tender words were meant to entice him to depart, but Yoshimune clung to the sleeve of his father's white robe and kicked his feet in a tantrum, crying: "No, I do not want to leave. No, I do not."

Time passed pitilessly. The veil of night had fallen when the wet nurse took Yoshimune in her arms and climbed into the carriage. The wet nurse and the lady attendant pressed the sleeves of their robes to their eyes and left Munemori in tears. Seeing the carriage off, Munemori thought that his former affection for Yoshimune could not be as great as what he now felt. To have seen him was much sadder than not to have done so.

Munemori had followed the wishes of his wife. He had never sent his son away but had kept him always by his side. When the boy reached the age of three, a ceremony[1] was performed to bestow upon him a ceremonial hat and the name Yoshimune. As a child, he was so handsome and sweet-natured that Munemori grew more and more attached to him. Consequently he always took him everywhere, even on the journey upon the waves of the western sea. This day, however, was the first time since the defeat of the Heike that Munemori had seen him.

Now Shigefusa went to visit Yoshitsune and inquired: "What shall I do with Yoshimune, the son of Munemori?"

"We will not take him down to Kamakura," replied Yoshitsune. "You may do whatever you think fit."

Upon returning to his home, Shigefusa spoke to Yoshimune's two attendants: "Lord Munemori has been ordered to set out for

Kamakura, but he is not allowed to take your little lord with him. He must stay in the capital. To escort Lord Munemori, I am also going down to Kamakura. Therefore I must put your little lord in the charge of Koreyoshi. He is to prepare to leave in a carriage at once."

When the carriage was readied, Yoshimune, without knowing the real circumstances, climbed into it. He must have had a vain hope that he would be taken again to his father's side. The carriage, however, was headed east on Rokujō. The ladies soon realized they were moving in the wrong direction. Tense with apprehension, they were wondering where they were to be taken when some fifty or sixty horsemen surrounded the carriage and led it to the dry river-bed of the Kamo. There the carriage was ordered to stop. As soon as a deer skin was laid upon the riverbed, Yoshimune was requested to get down. Coming out of the carriage, he perceived something strange, and so he asked his attendants: "Where are they taking me?"

The two ladies were so upset that they could not reply. One of Shigefusa's retainers was already stepping round behind Yoshimune from the left side. With his sword ready to strike, he hid it behind his body so that Yoshimune would take no notice of the weapon. However, at the moment when Shigefusa's retainer was about to sweep off his head, Yoshimune realized he was in danger and ran into the arms of his wet nurse. The retainer hesitated to drag him out, for he too was humane. The wet nurse held her little lord firmly in her arms and fell prostrate on the ground, weeping bitterly. Shigefusa too wept in sympathy. After a while he said to the wet nurse: "Your little lord cannot escape this by any means."

Then, turning to his retainer, he commanded: "Execute him at once!"

The retainer dragged Yoshimune out of the arms of the wet nurse, pressed him down, drew a short sword that had no guard, and cut off his head. All the warriors wept. Brave and violent though they were, they were neither wood nor flint, and so felt pity for Yoshimune and his attendants.

When the head of Yoshimune was carried away to Yoshitsune's mansion for his inspection, Yoshimune's attendants ran after it, barefoot,[2] and pleaded with Yoshitsune: "Since our little lord is already dead, we pray you to allow us to take back his head with us. We wish to pray for his afterlife."

At this request, Yoshitsune was moved to tears and granted it to them: "Your request is reasonable. It is most appropriate for you to pray for the better lot of your little lord in the world beyond. Take leave with the head at once."

Weeping, the ladies left Yoshitsune's mansion with the head of their little lord. The wet nurse held it in the folds of her robe.

A few days later the drowned bodies of the two women were found on the Katsura River. One, the wet nurse, held the little head. The other, the lady attendant, held the little headless body. However pitiful, it was the duty of a wet nurse to follow her master to the world beyond. The act of the lady attendant, however, was extraordinary.

---

[1] A sort of earlier gembuku.

[2] Court ladies did not show their bare feet at this time, although there may have been a custom of offering prayers barefoot at shrines or temples. The translator suggests that these ladies went barefoot to degrade themselves before Yoshitsune when begging for their master's head.

CHAPTER XVII

KOSHIGOE

A ccompanied by Yoshitsune, Munemori set out from the capital for Kamakura at dawn on the seventh day. As he passed the first station, at Awataguchi, the Imperial Palace was receding beyond the clouds. When he saw a well at the Osaka Checkpoint, he composed this poem in tears:

> When I see this well
> At the Osaka Checkpoint
> As I leave Kyoto,
> I wonder—will I return
> To reflect on this again?

All the way down to Kamakura, Munemori looked so wretched that Yoshitsune, sympathetically, sought for words to cheer him: "Let me do my best to plead with my brother, Yoritomo, for your life. I do not think that he will demand your head if I offer in exchange for it my rewards from successful battles. You may set your mind at rest."

"I wish I could be spared," replied Munemori. "Then I would be glad to accept banishment, even to Ezo[1] or Chishima."[2] His words were cowardly for one who had once taken command of the entire force of the Heike.

Days went by. Yoshitsune finally arrived at the west gate of Kamakura on the twenty-fourth day of the fifth month.

Prior to Yoshitsune's arrival, however, Kagetoki had told Yoritomo a slanderous tale about Yoshitsune: "The people throughout the land are now under my lord's control. There is, however, one who stands in your way—your younger brother, Yoshitsune. He seems to be your last enemy. During the war, for instance, Yoshitsune claimed, 'If I had not attacked Ichi-no-tani from the rear over the mountain, the east and west gates of the stronghold would not have fallen into our hands. All the captives, as well as the heads of the fallen enemies, must be inspected by no one but me, Yoshitsune. For what reason do we have to send them to my brother, Noriyori, for his inspection? Go and bring back Shigehira! If Noriyori refuses to give him to us, I will go and get him!'

"It was thus apparent that Yoshitsune and Noriyori were ready to battle each other at any moment. At that time Shigehira was in my charge. To avoid strife, however, I handed him over to Sanehira who was under the command of Yoshitsune. This is how Yoshitsune's anger was appeased."

Yoritomo believed Kagetoki's story. He armed himself and gave orders to his men: "Yoshitsune is arriving here today. Arm yourselves and watch him!"

At this command, the lords of both large and small domains gathered around Yoritomo's mansion. The mass soon swelled to several thousand horsemen. Kane-araizawa[3] was arranged as a temporary checkpoint. Here Munemori and his son Kiyomune were handed over to Yoritomo's men, and Yoshitsune was forced to withdraw to Koshigoe.[4] Safeguarded by seven or eight ranks of armed soldiers, Yoritomo exclaimed: "Since Yoshitsune is a man of such dexterity, he might try to penetrate this heavy guard even by crawling beneath the tatami mats. But, I, Yoritomo, shall never give him a chance!"

Yoshitsune was grieved by Yoritomo's cold rebuff. "Ever since I destroyed Yoshinaka last spring, I have not placed my duty second even to my honor as a warrior. From Ichi-no-tani to Dan-no-ura I fought and destroyed the entire force of the Heike at the risk of my life. What is more, I safely recovered the casket of the sacred mirror and captured the commander-in-chief of the Heike and his son. Inasmuch as I have brought them to Yoritomo, why can I not be granted a private audience with him? I expected to be appointed commander-in-chief of one of the western districts. I was convinced that Yoritomo would rely on my service in one of these posts. I cannot understand why I am now shunned, after having been allowed to govern only the small province of Iyo. What heartless treatment this is! Was it Yoshinaka or Yoshitsune who restored peace to this country?

"Yoritomo is my older brother, begotten by the same father only a few years before me. Who can say that I am inferior to him in ruling the country? I might forget the belittling I have had to endure, except for this one refusal. That I am not allowed to see Yoritomo—and am thus driven away—is a perplexing matter of great regret for me. I do not know what to say, because there is nothing for which I must apologize to him."

Yoshitsune was helpless, and yet he tried to vindicate himself by writing to Yoritomo a series of letters pledging his loyalty before the gods and the Buddhas. Yoritomo, however, disregarded the letters, for he still believed the slanderous tale of Kagetoki. Finally Yoshitsune, in tears, wrote to the chief registrar, Hiromoto: "I, Minamoto no Yoshitsune, hereby submit a petition to Your Excellency, the chief registrar. I was once chosen to represent Lord Yoritomo and received an edict of the cloistered emperor to destroy the emperor's enemies. I have fulfilled my duty. I cleansed the shame of our previous defeats by crushing the Heike. No one can deny that I should be properly rewarded for my services. But I am now bathing in a pond of tears because of a slanderous tale told by the wicked Kagetoki. Lord Yoritomo dares not interrogate the slanderer nor allow me to enter Kamakura. Thus I cannot vindicate myself. Days have passed in vain. If I cannot see Lord Yoritomo after my long absence from Kamakura, I will have no choice but to renounce our brotherly ties of blood and bone.

"Has this separation been predetermined by karma? Or is it retribution for an offense to the Buddha committed in a former life? Alas! Should the departed spirit of my father no longer appear in this world, who else would listen to this grief of mine? Who will have pity on me? I know it is foolish to complain of my fate, but I must express what I truly think.

"Shortly after I received soul and body from my parents, my father, the captain of the Imperial Stables of the Left, was executed. My mother held me in her arms and fled to Uda County in Yamato Province. Since then I have not been at rest. Though my worthless life was sustained, I was long forbidden entry into the capital. I was obliged to live far from Kyoto. At times I had to move from one place to another to hide myself from the eyes of the Heike. I worked as a servant for peasants.

"Despite these hardships, however, my vow to the gods was suddenly fulfilled. To test myself before going to the capital, I fought with Yoshinaka and defeated him. Then, to overthrow the Heike, I whipped and spurred swift stallions over the craggy and steep mountains. I pushed into the raging sea. I feared neither ruin on land nor that at the bottom of the sea. I took a set of armor and helmet for my bed without complaint. I suffered any hardship. I had no other wish but to avenge my father.

"My appointment as captain of the fifth court rank was one of the greatest honors ever given to the house of the Genji. Despite this promotion, my grief is now deep. I can appeal to none but the gods and the Buddhas! I offered my fervent prayers to them and then wrote several petitions to Lord Yoritomo on the backs of large amulets issued by the great shrines, hoping to vindicate myself. But all have gone unanswered. I have been given no pardon.

"There is no one but you to whom I can turn for aid. I throw myself upon your great mercy. I pray you to find the opportunity to convey word of my innocence to Lord Yoritomo and entreat him for my pardon. If I am pardoned, his house will acquire merit and all his descendants will flourish. Thus will my sadness vanish, and I shall be content throughout my life. My true wish beggars both pen and paper.

"Yoshitsune respectfully addresses you. The fifth day of the sixth month of the second year of Genryaku. Minamoto no Yoshi-tsune."

---

[1] The old name for Hokkaido.
[2] The old name for the Kurile Islands.
[3] Present-day Shichiri-ga-hama, west of Kamakura.
[4] Located at the western end of Shichiri-ga-hama.

CHAPTER XVIII

THE EXECUTION OF MUNEMORI

Munemori was brought before Yoritomo. He was given a seat in a room separated by a courtyard from the room in which Yoritomo was seated. Yoritomo, after looking at Munemori from behind a bamboo curtain, greeted him through Yoshikazu, saying: "I have no particular enmity toward the people of the Heike. Ike no Zenni pleaded with your father, the late Priest-Premier, for my life, and I would not be alive today had he not pardoned me. It was indeed his great favor that lightened my sentence to exile and that has enabled me to live some twenty years more. Your house, however, was dishonored by being declared an enemy of the throne, and an edict was issued by the cloistered emperor to overthrow your house. As I was born in the land of the Imperial Law, I am obliged to obey its command. I am powerless. Thus it is that I have the honor of your presence here. I am indeed pleased to see you."

When Yoshikazu brought this message to him, Munemori bowed obeisantly in an attempt to ingratiate himself with Yoritomo. This was a cowardly act! Around him sat a number of the lords of large and small domains, some from the capital and some who had once served the Heike. Most of these men were sickened by his unlordly act and whispered to one another: "Does he think that his life will be spared if he humbles himself before a messenger? He should have taken his own life while still in the west. No wonder he was taken alive and has been brought down to Kamakura, only to expose himself in such a contemptible manner."

Some lords, however, shed tears of pity, saying: "A fierce tiger deep in the mountain is a terror to all beasts. But when it is in a cage, it will wag its tail, begging for food. However violent a general may be, when all is lost, his courage will disappear. Munemori is now a tiger in a cage."

Meanwhile, the repeated petitions of Yoshitsune were ignored by Yoritomo, who was still under the influence of Kagetoki's slander. Instead there came an order for Yoshitsune to set out for the capital immediately. On the ninth day of the sixth month, Yoshitsune left Kamakura. Again he rode with Munemori and his son. Pitiably, Munemori hoped that his life would be prolonged. Even a day or two delay of his execution meant much to him. At every station, however, he feared that he would be put to death. In such a state of apprehension he rode on from station to station, from province to province. When he arrived at Utsumi in Owari Province, where Yoshitsune's father, Yoshitomo, had been put to death, he thought his time had come. But when he was allowed to pass on, he was relieved, still hoping that he would be permitted to live after all. Thus he buoyed himself with vain expectations.

His son, however, did not share this hope. "We cannot escape the death penalty," Kiyomune thought. "It is simply that in such hot weather they cannot carry rotting heads all the way to the capital. I am certain that they will behead us when we near the capital."

He said nothing of this to his father, for he knew that Munemori would despair. In his heart, however, he silently chanted "Hail Amida Buddha."

Days passed in this manner until they arrived at the station of Shinohara in Ōmi Province, which lay within a few days journey from the capital. Yoshitsune was a compassionate man. From this station, he sent for a priest of Mount Ohara named Tangō, hoping that he might enlighten Munemori and his son before their execution. Until then father and son had been kept together, but on this day at Shinohara they were separated.

"Finally, today, we will be beheaded!" sighed Munemori, his heart sinking deeper into despair. When the priest, Tangō, appeared before him, Munemori inquired: "Where is Kiyomune? I want to walk with him arm in arm on the shaded road. Though our heads will fall separately, I wish our bodies to lie on the same mattress. Why do they part us while we are still alive? For seventeen years we have not been separated even for a single day or a single hour. It was only because I wished to be with him constantly that I did not throw myself to the bottom of the sea and dared to set my shame adrift in this world."

Tangō was moved to tears, but he hardened himself, thinking

that his weakness would never be able to lead Munemori to Buddhahood at the moment of his death. He wiped away his tears and
said in a normal tone: "You must not think about your son. If you
see him executed before your eyes, you will feel more miserable.
Since you were born into this world, you have prospered and
flourished beyond all others. You are one of a few very rare persons
in our history. You became a relative of the imperial family on the
maternal side and rose to the high position of chief minister. There
is nothing more for you to attain in this world. It is because of the
karma of a former life that you must meet your end like this. Do not
blame either the world or men. King Bonten leads a tranquil life
at his palace. But remember that even a pleasant life like his is also
evanescent. How much more so should your life be in this world,
where everything is transient as a flash of lightning or a drop of
dew!

"They say that the residents of Tōri Heaven[1] can live for a
hundred million years. Even so, it is nothing but a dream when
that many years have passed. The thirty-nine years of your life
are no more than the twinkling of an eye.

"Who has ever tasted the medicine of eternal youth ardently
sought by Emperor Shi-huang in the Ch'in dynasty and Emperor
Wu in Han? Who has ever been able to prolong his days like Tung-
fang Shuo or Si-wang Mu? Great was the glory of Emperor Shi-
huang in Ch'in, but he was unable to escape being buried in his
tomb on Mount Li. Life was so dear to Emperor Wu in Han, but
he too met his end only to decay under the moss of Tu-ling.

"State Councilor Oe Asatsuna says in one of his poems, 'All
lives are destined to die. Sakyamuni could not escape cremation in
sandalwood. Pain comes when pleasure is at its height. Even the
angels are not exempt from the Five Signs of Decay.'

"The Buddha says in the *Sutra for Meditating on the Teachings of
Fugen Bodhisattva*,[2] 'The mind is void in itself. There is no substance
either in sin or wealth, for it is caused by the mind, which is pri-
marily void. When you view the mind, you will find nothing. All
laws have no permanent life in the Law.' Thus, if we regard both
good and evil as void, we are truly in accord with the mind of the
Buddha.

"Amida Buddha spent five kalpas in his meditation on how to
save sentient beings, and after overcoming many difficulties, he was

[708]

at last able to make the great vow. How foolish we will be if we continue to spend myriad ages bound to a revolving wheel of birth and death and come out of a mountain of treasures with empty hands! Do not bother yourself with earthly trifles, but concentrate on attaining Buddhahood!"

After preaching thus, Tangō urged him to chant "Hail Amida Buddha." Munemori believed that this saintly priest would not fail to guide him to Buddhahood. Ridding himself of all vain thoughts, he joined his palms and began to chant "Hail Amida Buddha" in a loud voice. Then a soldier, Kinnaga, drew his sword and moved behind Munemori to his left side to cut off his head. His sword was about to swing down when Munemori suddenly stopped chanting and inquired: "Is Kiyomune already dead?"

At this moment Kinnaga stepped forward. Then Munemori's head fell on the mattress in front of him. The saintly priest and the rough warriors were all moved to tears, saddened to see the end of the overlord of the Heike. How much sadder Kinnaga must have been, for he was formerly an hereditary retainer of the Heike and had attended Tomomori. People jeered at him, saying: "We know we must flatter those who are in power to make a better living. But what a cruel man he is to cut off the head of a man who is related by blood to his former master!"

Kiyomune was also advised to chant "Hail Amida Buddha." Touchingly concerned for his father, he asked: "How did my father meet his end?"

"He met a lordly end!" replied Tangō. "So I pray you to set your mind at rest."

"Then I have no more concern with this fleeting world," exclaimed Kiyomune. "Cut off my head at once!"

This time the execution was carried out by a swordsman named Chikatsune. Yoshitsune had his retainers carry the heads of the father and son, and he hurried on to the capital. As for their corpses, he allowed Kinnaga to bury them in the same grave. Munemori's fatherly affection had been so profound that Kinnaga had entreated Yoshitsune for this privilege.

On the twenty-third day of the month, the heads of Munemori and his son were brought into the capital. The officials of the Police Commissioners Division came out to the banks of the Kamo River on Sanjō to receive them, and they then paraded the heads through the main street and hung them on a sandalwood tree that stood to the left of the prison gate.

In a distant land there may be an example of the head of a courtier above the third court rank being paraded through the streets. In our land, however, there was no precedent. We remember that even Nobuyori, in the Heiji era, proud and violent though he was, was not shamed like this after his execution. The Heike were the first to be treated in this dishonorable manner. While still alive, when they were brought back from the western provinces, they were paraded east on Rokujō; and again, after death, when they were brought back from the eastern provinces, they were paraded west on Sanjō. Which dishonor was more intolerable?

[1] Located atop Mount Sumeru.

[2] Skt. *Samantabhadra-bodhisattva-dhyānacargādharma-sūtra*. This sutra teaches the proper form of meditation and how to repent the evils resulting from the actions of the six senses.

CHAPTER XIX

THE EXECUTION OF SHIGEHIRA

Shigehira, who had been placed in the charge of Munemochi in Izu Province the previous year, was now repeatedly demanded by the monks of the south capital. Yoritomo at last decided to send him to Nara. He was escorted by Yorikane, the grandson of the late priest of the third court rank, Yorimasa. Since they had not been instructed to pass through the capital on their way to Nara, they turned off at Ōtsu to take the Daigo Road through Yamashina.

Just off the Daigo Road was a hamlet called Hino. It was here that the wife of Shigehira was living in seclusion with her sister. She was a daughter of Vice-Councilor Korezane and had later been adopted by Councilor Kunitsuna. And she had served Emperor Antoku as wet nurse. After Shigehira had been captured at Ichi-no-tani, she had remained with the emperor and jumped into the sea at Dan-no-ura. She was dragged from the water by the Genji and sent back to the capital. She then took shelter at Hino with her elder sister, who had formerly waited upon Emperor Rokujō. When she heard that her husband was still alive, in prison, she trembled like a drop of dew on a leaf. She longed to see him face to face just once more. Nothing was left for her but to spend her days in vain weeping and wailing.

"You have been so kind to me that I hate to make such a request," Shigehira said to the soldiers escorting him, "but I would like you to do me one last favor. Since I have no child of my own, I have no regret at leaving this world. And yet I hear that the wife to whom I have long been married is now living at Hino. I wish that I might be allowed to see her but once more to ask her to pray for my afterlife."

These warriors were made of neither wood nor flint, so, in tears, they sympathized with him and gave him immediate permission, saying: "There could be nothing wrong with your seeing her."

Shigehira was greatly pleased and sent a messenger to the house where his wife was rumored to be: "Is this the house in which Shigehira's lady is living? Shigehira, who is on his way to Nara, wishes to see her now out in the garden."

These words had hardly been spoken when the lady ran out from behind a silk screen. Before her appeared not an apparition but her husband, leaning on the veranda, thin and suntanned and clad in navy blue robes and hat. Drawing herself to the bamboo curtain, she cried: "Is it a dream or phantom? Come in!"

Tears rushed down his cheeks, and his voice was choked. His lady wept bitterly. Then Shigehira moved to the curtain and thrust himself halfway into her chamber.

"In the spring of last year I was to be killed at Ichi-no-tani. It was because of my crime of burning down the temples of Nara that I was taken alive, paraded through the streets of the capital, and sent to Kamakura. I am now on my way to Nara to be handed over to the monks for execution. How I have longed to see you once more! Since I have been able to see you, I can die without a bit of regret. I wish I could take the tonsure and give you my hair as a memento, but I am not allowed to do so."

Shigehira took a lock of hair from his forehead, pulled it down to his mouth, bit it off, and handed it to her, saying: "Keep this in memory of me."

Now the lady was more sorrowful than if she had not seen him. She said in tears: "It was my intention to drown myself like Kozai-shō. But when I heard that you were still alive, I clung to the faint hope of seeing you once more. Indeed, I wished to see you again unchanged! I have dwelt in misery. It is only in hope of seeing you that I have remained alive, but this is to be our last meeting in this world!"

Tears rushed down their faces as they spoke of things dear to them.

"Your robe is terribly shrunken. Change into these new ones that I have made for you." She took out a lined short-sleeved kimono and a white hunting suit for him.

When Shigehira had put them on, he said: "Keep this old robe and look at it from time to time in memory of me."

"I will, I will!" replied the lady. "But I pray you, write a memorial for today so that I may treasure it till the end of my life."

When she brought an ink stone to him, he took up a brush and, in tears, composed the following poem:

> Crying ceaselessly,
> You have made these robes for me
> To be worn but once.
> In memory of your tears
> I shall never take them off.

The lady replied with this poem:

> How foolish of me
> To make these new robes for you
> In expectation.
> This change of robes means nothing.
> It is but our last farewell.

"If the bonds of husband and wife are predetermined in a former life," said Shigehira, "we shall be reborn together in the world beyond. Pray that we will be seated on the same lotus in paradise. It is getting late now. Nara is still far off. I must not keep the guards waiting any longer."

Shigehira was about to leave her, but she clung to his sleeve and held him back, crying: "Please stay a little longer! Why must you leave so soon?"

"I pray you to understand what I feel in my heart," replied Shigehira. "It is the realization that men are not made to live forever. Let me see you again in the next world."

Shigehira turned to walk away. But knowing that he would never see her again in this world, he could hardly resist the temptation of turning back. He resolved to show no weakness and went on his way. His lady crouched by the bamboo curtain and cried for him. Her wail was heard far beyond the gate. With his heart almost too heavy to bear, Shigehira could not lift his hand to whip his horse. His eyes brimmed with tears; he could see nothing before him. He regretted that he had been able to see her only for such a heart-rending farewell. His wife started to run after him, but seeing that her attempt would be to no avail, she fell prostrate, her face buried in the sleeves of her robe.

No sooner had the monks of the south capital taken possession of Shigehira than they held a council to determine what should be done with him. "Lord Shigehira," they declared, "is the worst kind of criminal, who deserves three thousand and five varieties of punishment.[1] He must go through all of them until he repents of the malignant karma that caused his evil deeds. Since he is an enemy of the Buddha and his Law, he must first be paraded around the walls of Tōdai-ji and Kōfuku-ji. Then we will decide how to execute him—to behead him with a saw or to bury him except for his head and then cut it off."

"That is what we priests should not do, for the Buddha does not permit violence," said one of the elder priests. "We must hand him over to the militia for execution. Let us then demand that he be beheaded on the bank of the Kizu River."

This opinion prevailed, and Shigehira was delivered to the militia. When he was taken to the bank of the Kizu River, a great mass of people, including a few thousand monks, were assembled to watch the execution.

Now there was a certain warrior who had formerly waited upon Shigehira, a man named Tomotoki. At that time he was in attendance upon the daughter of Emperor Toba. Hoping to see how his former master would depart from the world, he hurried to attend the execution. Arriving at the bank, he pushed through the crowd to reach his master's side and cried out in tears: "Here am I, Tomotoki. I have come to see how you will meet your end!"

"Your loyalty," replied Shigehira, "is highly commendable! Before I die, I wish to worship the Buddha. My offense is so grave that, begging his pardon and adoring his great benevolence, I wish to die before his image. Can it be arranged?"

"It is quite a simple matter, my lord!"

With this reply, Tomotoki turned to the guards for negotiation. He then went off to a nearby hamlet and brought back an image of Amida Buddha. After setting it on the sand of the riverbed, Tomotoki drew a cord from the sleeve of his hunting suit, fastened one end of it to the hand of the Buddha, and gave the other to Shigehira. Holding it firmly, Shigehira made a low obeisance to the Buddha and said: "I have heard that Devadatta[2] committed the Three Cardinal Crimes and burned eight thousand sutras. Sakyamuni, however, had foretold that Devadatta would be made a Nyorai in the world beyond. Solely because of this prediction, his great offense was pardoned and his evil karma was changed to enable him to enter the way to salvation. Indeed, it was not my intention but foolish weakness that made me follow the ordinary rules of the world and commit crimes. How can a mortal such as I take it upon himself so lightly to disobey the emperor's command? At the same time how can a mortal such as I refuse a father's will? I can disobey neither the emperor nor my father. May the Buddha be witness of right and wrong! A swift retribution has fallen upon me. My doom is nearing. Thousands and thousands of repentances will avail me no longer. I understand that the Buddha resides in a world of mercy and extends to us many paths to salvation. I believe that the Buddha can change an evil karma to a good one, for this is what the Tendai sect teaches us. It is said that one utterance of 'Hail Amida Buddha' will wash away a thousand sins and crimes. I pray that my evil karma will be changed to a good one. Now let me chant my last 'Hail Amida Buddha' so that I may be reborn in the Pure Land Paradise."

Thus invoking Amida ten times, he stretched out his neck and the blow fell upon it. Though his crime was grave, his eagerness to repent moved all the spectators to tears. His head was then fixed by a nail on the great gate of Hannya-ji. This was done because it was there that he took command of the army that burned down the temples of Nara during the battle in the Jishō era.

When the news of Shigehira's death reached his wife, she thought that the executioners would not take his corpse with them. In order to perform a Buddhist rite for him, she sent a palanquin for the corpse. As she had thought, it had been abandoned near the river, and so it was put in the palanquin and brought back to Hino. How sad she was when she received her husband's remains in such a form!

The next day the corpse decomposed rapidly in the hot weather. Unable to keep it by her side any longer, she took it to a nearby temple called Hōkai-ji. Though she called many priests, most of them hesitated to chant sutras for Shigehira because of his offense to the Buddha's Law. At the earnest request of his wife, they finally agreed to perform the rite. The head was recovered through the good offices of a priest, the so-called Shunjō-bō of Daibutsu, who obtained permission from the monks and sent it to Hino. Thus it was that the head and body were cremated together. Shigehira's bones were sent to Mount Kōya, while his tomb was built at Hino. His wife took the tonsure and thereafter spent her days in constant prayer for his better lot in the world beyond.

¹ According to old Chinese law, there were three thousand and five varieties of punishment that could be employed.

² A cousin of the Buddha. Originally a follower, he later disagreed with the Buddha and attempted to destroy him.

BOOK TWELVE

"... Rokudai would be finally deprived of the last *dewdrop* of his life."
—Book 12, Chapter VII, page 742

CHAPTER I

A GREAT EARTHQUAKE

Since the entire force of the Heike had been destroyed, peace was restored to the western provinces. Now all the provincial governors and landlords could regulate the affairs of their domains from central offices in the capital, and officials and peasants alike could set their minds at ease.

However, on the ninth day of the seventh month, at the hour of the horse [noon], a great earthquake shook the capital for several minutes. Near the capital the six temples of Shirakawa were destroyed. The upper six stories of the nine-story pagoda of Hosshō-ji crashed to the ground. Seventeen ken of the Thirty-Three-Ken Hall at Tokujōju-in crumbled. The Imperial Palace, shrines and temples, as well as the homes of commoners were demolished. The roar of their crumbling was like thunder; dust rose up like clouds of smoke. The sky darkened; not a shaft of sunlight could be seen. Both young and old—men with office or without—were lost in fear. Provinces both near and far were affected by the disaster. The earth was split asunder, and water gushed forth. Rocks were cracked and tumbled down into the valleys. Mountains crumbled and filled rivers. The sea surged, and the shores were flooded. Boats wallowed on the waves. Horses lost their foothold on the ground. Had there been a high tidal wave, men would have been unable to climb the hills for shelter. Had there been a fire, only a great river would have been able to prevent its spread.

Humans were powerless; all were fearful and trembling. How could they flee—like birds in the sky? How could they escape—riding on clouds like dragons? Countless numbers were buried alive in the capital. Of the four elements, water, fire, and air had always been the causes of disaster; earth alone had never before brought harm to men. Now the people shut themselves up in their houses behind sliding screens of wood and paper. When the sky roared and the earth shook, they thought they would soon perish. They wailed in terror and chanted "Hail Amida Buddha." Men of seventy or eighty—they too were upset; for even they whose ends were imminent had never expected that the world would come to an end so suddenly.

The day of the earthquake the cloistered emperor was at Imagumano. Upon seeing so many deaths and injuries there, he abandoned his worship at the shrine and hurried back to Rokuharadono. How terrified were the nobles and courtiers of his train as they turned back to the palace! Finding the palace demolished, they set up a tent in the south court and placed the cloistered emperor within it.

The reigning emperor entered his palanquin and took refuge at the edge of the pond. The empress and princes were taken out of the razed palace and carried to safer places in palanquins and carriages. Panic struck again when the chief of the astrologers informed the nobles that another great quake could be expected between the hour of the boar and the hour of the mouse [10–12 P.M.] that night.

Of old, during the reign of Emperor Montoku, on the eighth day of the third month of the third year of the Saikō era [856], there was a great earthquake. At that time the head of the Buddha at Tōdai-ji was broken off, and it fell to the ground. On another occasion when tremors shook the earth, on the fifth day of the fourth month of the second year of the Tengyō era [939], a large tent, five jō high, was built in front of the Jōnei-den hall, and the emperor was taken into it. Since these events happened in ancient days, we cannot particularize them. But in a degenerate age such as this, there was no one who could have foretold the extent of the disastrous earthquake. However, it was recalled that Emperor Antoku, who had mastered the Buddha's Ten Precepts, had recently been obliged to leave the capital only to be drowned at the bottom of the sea; and his ministers and courtiers had been captured only to be brought back to the capital for punishment—first paraded in the streets and then beheaded and their heads hung on the prison gate. The intellectuals lamented that the earthquake had been caused by the evil spirits of these dead. Dreadful is the revenge of an evil spirit!

CHAPTER II

CONCERNING THE DYER

O n the twenty-second day of the eighth month of the second year of Genryaku, Mongaku, a priest of the Jingo-ji temple at Takao, set out for Kamakura. Around his neck hung a small box, which contained the skull of Yoritomo's father, the late captain of the Imperial Stables of the Left, Yoshitomo. Around the neck of one of his disciples hung another box, which contained the skull of Masakiyo, one of Yoshitomo's retainers.

Now the skull that Mongaku brought to Yoritomo in the fourth year of Jishō [1180] was not the true skull of Yoshitomo. Mongaku pretended it was authentic, for he wished to incite Yoritomo to raise the standard of revolt against the Heike. When Yoritomo saw the skull wrapped in white linen, he believed it to be the skull of his father. Indeed, buoyed by Mongaku's deception, Yoritomo succeeded in holding the entire country in his sway.

The true skull of Yoshitomo involves the following story. A certain dyer, to whom Yoshitomo had given a special favor, saw the head of his master hung on the prison gate with no one to perform Buddhist rites for the departed soul. The dyer thought that Yoritomo, though in exile, might someday rise again in the world and search for the head of his father. So he begged the head from the superintendent of the Police Commissioners Division and concealed it deep in the inner temple of Engaku-ji on Higashiyama. Later, when Mongaku learned of the skull's whereabouts, he decided to deliver it to Kamakura, accompanied by the dyer.

When Yoritomo heard that Mongaku was arriving at Kamakura, he went out to the Katase River to meet him. There Yoritomo changed into mourning robes, and he returned, weeping, with Mongaku to his mansion. At his mansion Yoritomo had Mongaku stand on the main veranda, while he himself stood in the courtyard below to receive the head of his father. All the lords of large and small domains who were witness to the scene wet their sleeves with tears.

Yoritomo cut into a craggy hill, and there built a temple so that prayers could be offered to the spirit of his father. He called this temple Shōjōju-in.[1] When the court heard that Yoritomo had built a temple to commemorate his father, the secretary of the Left, Kanetada, was dispatched as an imperial envoy to Kamakura to honor Yoshitomo with the title of state minister of the senior grade of the second court rank. Now that Yoritomo had established his fame as a great warrior, not only his house but also the spirit of his departed father were thus highly honored.

[1] Located at Mount Amida, Yukinoshita, Kamakura. Yoritomo and his wife, Masako, were also buried there.

CHAPTER III

THE EXILE OF TOKITADA

O_{n the twenty-third day of the}
ninth month of the year, Yoritomo sent a letter to the court, requesting that all the Heike who were still imprisoned be sent into exile
to distant provinces. Thus it was that the court decided Councilor
Tokitada should be banished to Noto;[1] the chief of the Imperial
Household, Nobumoto, to Sado;[2] Lieutenant General Tokizane,
to Aki; the secretary of the War Planning Division, Masaakira, to
Oki;[3] the priest of the second court rank, Senshin, to Awa; the
superintendent of Hosshō-ji, Nōen, to Bingo; and Vice-Councilor
Chūkai, to Musashi. With their hearts full of sadness, they all set
out on their journeys, some upon the western sea, some through
the mists of the eastern provinces. They knew neither where they
were heading nor when they would return.

Of these exiles, Tokitada was allowed to visit the former imperial consort, Kenreimon-In, at Yoshida[4] to bid her farewell.
"My crime is so severe that I am to be sent in exile to a far-off
province," Tokitada said in tears. "I wish I could remain near you
in the capital so that I might take care of you. When I think of your
uncertain future my heart aches. Leaving you behind in such great
anxiety makes my departure even more painful."

"Indeed," replied Kenreimon-In, "you are the only one who is
still alive to remind me of my past glory. When you are gone, to
whom can I turn. Whom can I rely on?" She wept bitterly.

Now Tokitada was the son of the minister of the Left, Tokinobu,
and the grandson of the governor of Dewa Province, Tomonobu.
He was the elder brother of the late Empress Kenshunmon-In and
the uncle of the late Emperor Takakura on the emperor's maternal
side. Tokitada secured public support and earned luxury and splendor. Since he was also the younger brother-in-law of the late Priest-
Premier Kiyomori the conferments of rank and title were at his

disposal. Tokitada advanced in rank so rapidly that while still young, he rose to be councilor of the senior grade of the second court rank. He was so influential that he held the powerful position of superintendent of the Police Commissioners Division three times.

When he was superintendent, he arrested vagrants, thieves, and robbers, and without any interrogation, cut off their right arms at the elbow and banished them to far provinces. Thus it was that he was nicknamed the "Wicked Superintendent." Again, when Hana-kata was sent as an envoy of the cloistered emperor to the Heike at Yashima to demand the return of Emperor Antoku and the Three Sacred Treasures, it was Tokitada who had the characters *nami* and *kata* branded on Hanakata's face. Because of his close relationship, that of brother-in-law to the cloistered emperor, some had expected His Majesty to grant him a private audience or to extend aid in lightening his punishment. In reality, however, because of his insult to the envoy Hanakata, Tokitada had earned the enmity of the cloistered emperor, who eventually closed his heart to him. Yoshitsune, as his son-in-law, did his best to save Tokitada from banishment, but it was to no avail.

At the time of Tokitada's exile, his son, Tokiie, was sixteen years old and living with his uncle, Tokimitsu. Fortunately he escaped banishment. The day before his father's departure from the capital, Tokiie went with his mother to visit him. They clung to the sleeves of Tokitada's robe in despair at being separated from him.

"Do not make this parting so wretched!" said Tokitada. "Even without it—someday, somehow—we would be separated by death."

Though his words were controlled, Tokitada must have repressed great sorrow in the depths of his heart. He was already getting on in years, yet he was to bid farewell to his beloved wife and son and to set out from the capital, which he knew so well.

At last his journey to the northern provinces had to begin. He looked back longingly at the Imperial Palace as he headed for a far-off region that he knew only by name. He went on—passing Shiga, Karasaki, and the bay of Mano. On the lakeshore at Katada, Tokitada composed this poem:

Tears rush down my face,
For I shall never return

To the capital.
The fishnet of Katada
Traps neither water nor tears.

Not long before, he had been on board a boat drifting from battle to battle upon the waves of the western sea. Now after parting from his beloved wife and children, he was on a journey to the northern provinces only to be buried under the snow. It seemed as though his sorrows were piling up as high as the clouds over the capital.

[1] Present-day Ishikawa Prefecture, it is a peninsula jutting into the Japan Sea.

[2] With Noto it was one of the seven provinces of Hokuroku-dō. A large island on the west coast of Japan, Sado is part of present-day Niigata Prefecture.

[3] One of the eight provinces of San-in-dō, it comprised the Oki Islands, which now belong to Shimane Prefecture.

[4] Located at present-day Sakyō-ku, Kyoto.

CHAPTER IV

THE EXECUTION OF TOSA-BŌ

hus, as the tale tells us, among the warriors in attendance upon Yoshitsune, ten lords of large domains had been dispatched to Kyoto by Yoritomo. Having an inkling of Yoritomo's distrust in Yoshitsune, they feared to be with Yoshitsune and returned to Kamakura.

Yoritomo and Yoshitsune were brothers by the same father. After they had sworn a special allegiance to each other, like father and son, Yoshitsune destroyed Yoshinaka. Since Yoshinaka's defeat in the first month of the previous year, Yoshitsune had fought many battles and had finally overthrown the Heike in the spring. It was Yoshitsune alone who had restored peace to the whole country.

For this contribution, he should have been honored with some extraordinary reward. Instead, without reason, he was suspected of treachery. All the people, even the emperor, wondered why Yoshitsune was so discredited. But they learned that this misfortune was due to the slanderous tales told repeatedly by Kagetoki, who bore a deep-seated grudge against Yoshitsune. Kagetoki's antipathy arose from Yoshitsune's ridicule of his suggestion to place oars at the bows of the boats sailing from Watanabe in Settsu Province to Yashima. Yoritomo, convinced of Yoshitsune's treachery, said to himself: "If I send a great army, Yoshitsune will certainly destroy the bridges at Uji and Seta. This would bring confusion to the capital, and I do not think it would achieve anything."

So after long meditation, Yoritomo summoned the priest Tosa-bō and said: "I command you to go up to the capital! Pretend to make a number of pilgrimages but strike off the head of Yoshitsune!"

Tosa-bō solemnly received this command, and without even returning to his temple to prepare for the journey, he set out. On the twenty-ninth day of the ninth month, he arrived at the capital. However, he did not immediately pay a visit to Yoshitsune. The day after his arrival, when Yoshitsune learned that Tosa-bō had come into the capital, he sent Musashi-bō Benkei to fetch him. Before long Tosa-bō was brought into the presence of Yoshitsune, who inquired of him: "Tosa-bō, have you brought a letter from Lord Yoritomo?"

"As there was no matter of great importance," replied Tosa-bō, "Lord Yoritomo did not write a letter to Your Excellency but ordered me to convey these words to you, 'Since you are now in the capital, everything is secure. Peace in the capital depends upon you, so keep a strict guard.'"

"Is that truly what he said?" retorted Yoshitsune. "I know you have been sent here to assassinate me. Yoritomo must have said to you that if he sent a great army, I would destroy the bridges at Uji and Seta, and that the confusion this would cause in the capital would achieve nothing. Then he commanded you to come up to the capital on the pretense of making a number of pilgrimages and behead me. Now answer me! Did he not order you to do so?"

Tosa-bō showed great astonishment, saying: "That will not happen! I have come up to the capital for no reason but to make a pilgrimage to Kumano to fulfill a vow."

"Then tell me what you think of this," said Yoshitsune. "Owing to Kagetoki's slander, I was not allowed to enter Kamakura. Lord Yoritomo did not wish to see me but drove me away."

"This matter is no concern of mine," replied Tosa-bō. "I have no enmity at all toward your lordship! Shall I write a statement of my innocence in pledge to the gods?"

"Do whatever you wish! But I know Lord Yoritomo will not change his mind." So saying, Yoshitsune grew increasingly angry with Tosa-bō.

In order to calm Yoshitsune's wrath, Tosa-bō wrote seven oaths at once. Some of them he burned and, mixing their ashes with water, swallowed them. Some he deposited in the altar of a shrine. After making these proofs of innocence, he was finally released. As soon as he returned to his lodging, he gathered the guards stationed in the capital under orders from Yoritomo. Tosa-bō decided to attack Yoshitsune that night.

At that time there was a young lady named Shizuka, a daughter of a white-suit dancer, Iso no Zenji. To Shizuka Yoshitsune gave his true love. She returned his love and remained constantly at his side. Now she said: "The streets are full of soldiers. Why are they assembled without your command? This is truly the vicious plan of that priest who swore his innocence to my lord today. I advise you to send someone to reconnoiter."

Yoshitsune sent two soldiers as spies, but they did not return. Upon learning of their disappearance, he said: "For this mission, a girl may be better than a boy."

Yoshitsune then sent one of his lowly maids, who after a while came back with this report: "I saw our two spies lying dead by the gate of Tosa-bō's lodging and many saddled horses standing neck to neck ready for a fight. Behind a great tent were a number of soldiers in full armor with bows and swords. They did not look as though they were setting out on a pilgrimage."

Upon hearing her report, Yoshitsune leaped to his feet. Shizuka seized Yoshitsune's armor and flung it over his shoulders. Even before all the cords of the armor were tied, Yoshitsune snatched up his sword and raced out to the middle gate where his horse stood saddled. Springing onto it, he shouted: "Open the gate!"

Thus he was waiting for his enemy's attack when Tosa-bō at the head of forty or fifty horsemen in full armor galloped to the gate and screamed a war cry. Standing high in the stirrups, Yoshitsune shouted in a thunderous voice: "In battle, either by night or by day, you can find no one superior to me, Yoshitsune, among all the warriors of Japan!"

Yoshitsune charged alone into the enemy. In fear of being kicked, they divided their ranks to let him gallop through.

Before long Eda no Genzō, Kumai Tarō, and Musashi-bō Benkei rushed to their master's side and joined the battle. Then the rest of Yoshitsune's retainers came rushing from all directions, and soon they numbered sixty or seventy. Tosa-bō attempted a reckless assault against Yoshitsune, but he saw most of his men overrun. Few survived.

Tosa-bō himself narrowly escaped and hid deep in the mountains of Kurama. Since Kurama was the place where Yoshitsune had spent his younger days, people there still favored him. Therefore Tosa-bō was soon captured and brought under arrest to Yoshitsune.

Now Tosa-bō was dragged into the courtyard of Yoshitsune's mansion. He was wearing a dark blue battle robe and a hood over his head. Yoshitsune first laughed a great laugh and then roared at him: "Tosa-bō! Your false oath deserves punishment. Do you not think so?"

Tosa-bō, undaunted, laughed and replied in a loud voice: "As I swore falsely to the gods, they now will have their way with me!"

"That you regard your own life less than your loyalty to Lord Yoritomo is to be highly commended!" Yoshitsune exclaimed. "If you wish to live any longer, I will allow you to go back to Kamakura."

"That is a favor I cannot accept," replied Tosa-bō. "You say that you will spare my life if I express a wish to live longer, do you not? But, inasmuch as Lord Yoritomo chose me for this mission, placing his full trust in me and saying that I was the only one who would be able to do away with you, my life has been decided by him. How can I ask for its return now that my mission has resulted in failure? If you wish to do me a favor, please cut off my head at once!"

Thus it was that he was taken out to the Kamo River beach at Rokujō and beheaded there. Everyone admired his bravery and loyalty.

CHAPTER V

YOSHITSUNE ABANDONS THE CAPITAL

Now there was a lowly servant of Yoritomo, a man named Shinzaburō. Yoritomo had given him to Yoshitsune, saying: "He is only a servant but a fellow of keen mind. So I ask you to use him."

Shinzaburō, however, had been ordered to keep an eye on Yoshitsune and to report back to Yoritomo. No sooner had Shinzaburō seen Tosa-bō beheaded than he went galloping back to Kamakura to report to Yoritomo. Hearing his account, Yoritomo at once ordered his brother Noriyori to set out for the capital to kill Yoshitsune. Noriyori declined this order many times, but Yoritomo was so persistent that he could no longer refuse. Clad in full armor, he presented himself before Yoritomo to bid him farewell. Yoritomo said: "You had better be careful not to behave like Yoshitsune."

To Noriyori this was a terrible warning, for he sensed that he would be the next victim after Yoshitsune had been executed. He was so disturbed that he took off his armor and remained at Kamakura. In order to convince Yoritomo of his innocence, he wrote ten oaths of his loyalty every day and read them aloud in the courtyard every evening. He did this for a hundred days and sent a thousand such oaths to Yoritomo. But this was to no avail, as Noriyori was eventually put to death by Yoritomo.

Later, when it was reported that Yoritomo was going to send an army under the command of Tokimasa up to the capital, Yoshitsune decided to flee to Kyushu. Koreyoshi was the great military power in Kyushu, and Yoshitsune wished to turn to him for protection. It was Koreyoshi who, some time before, had permitted none of the Heike to stay in Kyushu and evicted them at the point of his sword. Before he left to seek refuge Yoshitsune sent a message to Koreyoshi, asking: "Can I count on your support?"

"If you wish to depend upon my support," replied Koreyoshi,

"I have a request for you. Among your retainers there is a certain Takanao who has been my enemy for a long time. In exchange for his life, I will be glad to be of assistance."

At this request, Yoshitsune immediately handed Takanao over to him. Koreyoshi beheaded him on the bank of the Kamo River at Rokujō. Koreyoshi thus agreed to support Yoshitsune and to serve him faithfully.

On the second day of the eleventh month of the year, Yoshitsune went to visit the cloistered emperor and presented a petition through the finance minister, Lord Yasutsune, who said: "I, Yoshitsune, have been loyal to Your Majesty. The many contributions that I have made to Your Majesty are clear evidence. However, owing to the slanderous tale told by his retainer, Yoritomo has decided to destroy me. So I wish to retire for a while to Kyushu. I beg Your Majesty to issue an edict that will allow me to make a peaceful retreat."

Upon hearing Yoshitsune's petition, the cloistered emperor summoned all the courtiers and demanded their opinions, saying: "If Yoritomo were to hear that I have issued an edict in favor of Yoshitsune, how would he feel?"

"If Yoshitsune remains," said the courtiers, "we shall have a great army from the eastern provinces breaking into the capital. Apparently there will be no end to violence and confusion here. If he retreats for a while to a far land, there will be no fear of this happening, Your Majesty."

Thus it was that the cloistered emperor summoned Koreyoshi and issued an edict ordering Koreyoshi and all the clans in Kyushu— Usuki, Hetsugi, and Matsuura—to support Yoshitsune. On the next day, the third, at the hour of the hare [6 A.M.], Yoshitsune rode away from the capital without incident at the head of some five hundred horsemen.

Now in the province of Settsu there was one of the Genji named Yorimoto. When he heard that Yoshitsune had left the capital, he exclaimed: "If I let Yoshitsune pass by my gate without shooting an arrow at him, Yoritomo will censure me in the days to come."

So saying, he rode out in pursuit of Yoshitsune, and soon caught up with him at Kawazu. There Yorimoto, with only sixty horsemen, made an assault against Yoshitsune. Since Yoshitsune had five hundred horsemen, they easily surrounded the enemy and counterattacked fiercely, determined to let none escape. Many of Yorimoto's men were killed; when Yorimoto's horse was shot in the belly, he withdrew. Yoshitsune cut off the heads of the fallen enemy warriors and hung them on trees. By offering them to the god of war, he celebrated a victory at the start of his journey.

With a great shout of triumph, Yoshitsune boarded a boat at the beach at Daimotsu to sail down to Kyushu. During the journey, however, the west wind blew so violently that his boat was driven back to the shore at Sumiyoshi. He was obliged to go deep into the mountains of Yoshino to hide. He was then attacked by the monks of Yoshino, and so he fled to Nara. There, again, attacked by the monks of Nara, he returned to the capital and eventually sought refuge in Mutsu province.

Yoshitsune had taken with him ten ladies. But when the boat was driven ashore, he had to abandon them at Sumiyoshi. On the sands of the beach, under the pine trees, they fell prostrate. With their hakamas in disorder and their faces covered with the long sleeves of their robes, they wept in despair. Seeing their misery, the priests of Sumiyoshi Shrine were moved to compassion. They put the women into litters and sent them back to the capital.

The boats that Yoshinori, Yukiie, and Koreyoshi had boarded were cast onto beaches and islands. None of Yoshitsune's men knew what had happened to the others. The impetuous wind that rose suddenly from the west was said to have been caused by the angry spirits of the Heike.

On the seventh day of the eleventh month of the year, Tokimasa arrived in the capital at the head of sixty thousand horsemen. Now, on behalf of Yoritomo, he demanded an edict from the cloistered emperor that would grant him the right to destroy Yoshitsune, Yukiie, and Yoshinori. The edict was issued. Only five days before, at Yoshitsune's request, an edict had been issued in opposition to Yoritomo. Now, at Yoritomo's request, an edict was issued in his favor to destroy Yoshitsune. In this way fortunes changed so precipitously—favor in the morning and banishment in the evening—that the whole world seemed to be in a lamentable state of uncertainty.

CHAPTER VI

COUNCILOR TSUNEFUSA

Now Yoritomo was appointed commander-in-chief of the entire land of Japan. He sent a request to the court that he should be granted the right to levy tax on every part of the country to supply rations for his soldiers. It is written in the *Muryōgi Sutra*[1] that one who destroys an enemy of the throne shall be entitled to receive half of the country. In our land, however, there has been no precedent of this kind. Thus it was that the cloistered emperor heaved a great sigh and exclaimed: "Yoritomo's demand is excessive!"

But when the courtiers gathered in council, they concluded: "Lord Yoritomo's demand is not unreasonable."

So the cloistered emperor could do nothing and granted Yoritomo his demand. Yoritomo lost no time in placing his retainers in all provinces and manors to oversee the government officials. Thus it was that none would be able to stand against Yoritomo or hide themselves from his guards.

Yoritomo had quite a number of adherents among the courtiers. However, in making his request to the cloistered emperor, he placed his whole trust in Councilor Tsunefusa. It was said that this councilor was a man of uncompromising character. There were many courtiers who had formerly been on good terms with the Heike. But when the Genji ascended, these courtiers tried to ingratiate themselves with Yoritomo by sending letters and messengers. Lord Tsunefusa did nothing of the kind. At the time of the Heike's dominance, when the cloistered emperor was confined at the North Palace of Toba, it was this councilor and Lord Nagakata who were appointed superintendents of the palace of the abdicated emperor.

Tsunefusa was the son of Lord Mitsufusa. When he was only twelve years old, his father passed away. Even so, Tsunefusa was able to rise rapidly in rank and office. After his distinguished services in the important offices of archivist of the fifth court rank, aide to the chief of the guards of the Imperial Gate, and executive officer of the Grand Ministry, he continued to advance from one to the next, eventually reaching the position of councilor. He had outstripped many others, never having been passed over in their favor.

People try to conceal their evil deeds, but they cannot do so successfully, as their misgivings show through in the end. So innately good was Tsunefusa that he did not have to deceive others. What a blessed man he was!

¹ Skt. *Amitārtha-sūtra.*

CHAPTER VII

ROKUDAI, THE LAST OF THE HEIKE

Now Tokimasa, a retainer of Yoritomo in the capital, proclaimed: "Anyone who can give me information on the whereabouts of the offspring of the Heike shall receive any reward he wishes."

The people of the capital, familiar with every corner of the city, were so eager to gain rewards that they began to search. As a result many children of the Heike were discovered. Driven by excessive greed, people seized even the children of the lowest servants, particularly if they were handsome and of fair complexion, saying: "This is the heir of a lord of the Heike."

When fathers and mothers pleaded, weeping, for their children, they would tell the Genji that the wet nurses had lied that these were Heike children. If the child discovered was very young he would be thrown into the water or buried alive. If he was older he would be strangled or stabbed. The grief and lamentation of mothers and wet nurses numbed both mind and tongue. Tokimasa was moved, for he too had children. When he saw the mass slaughter, his heart sank, for he had committed himself to the evil ways of the world.

Among the children of the Heike was Rokudai, the heir of Lieutenant General of the Third Court Rank Koremori. Rokudai stood in the pure line of the Heike and was now quite grown-up, so Tokimasa had sent many men in all directions to search for him. After their vain search, Tokimasa was about to set out from the capital for Kamakura when a woman came to Rokuhara and said: "To the west, at a place called Shōbudani, north of the mountain temple of Daikaku-ji, before which lies Henjō-ji, the wife and children of Koremori are in hiding."

Upon hearing this, Tokimasa immediately sent a man to spy on Shōbudani. He found a temple in which many women and children had carefully hidden themselves. When he peeped through a chink in the fence, he saw a very handsome boy running out after a white puppy and a woman who seemed to be his wet nurse rushing after him to draw him back. The woman said to the boy: "How terrible it would be if anyone should see you!"

"This must be the heir of Koremori!" exclaimed the spy and he hurried back and reported to Tokimasa what he had seen and heard. The next day Tokimasa himself went to Shōbudani and instructed his men to surround the temple. Then he sent one of his men into the temple with this message: "I have heard that Rokudai, the son of Lieutenant General of the Third Court Rank Koremori is residing here. The representative of Lord Yoritomo, a man named Tokimasa, is now here to see him. Please bring Rokudai out at once."

When Rokudai's mother heard this, she lost her senses and knew not what to do. Saitō-go and Saitō-roku, Rokudai's two faithful retainers, tried to find some way to flee with him. But when they saw the soldiers surrounding the temple on all sides, they had to concede that the end had come for their master. The wet nurse fell to the floor before Rokudai and wept bitterly. While in hiding, they had scarcely dared to breathe. But now, with no more fear of being overheard, Rokudai's mother and attendants raised their voices in despairing wails. Their cries pierced even the heart of Tokimasa. So he sent another messenger, to say: "Since the world is not yet stable, I am afraid someone might do violence to the prince of the Heike. I have simply come to fetch him to a safer place. You have nothing to fear. Let him come out at once!"

Upon hearing Tokimasa's message, Rokudai said to his mother: "Since there is no way out of this dilemma let me go without delay. Otherwise the soldiers will break in and see our wretched state. Even if I go, I will soon ask for their permission to come back. So please do not cry anymore."

His mother finally gave in to the miserable fate of having to part with her son. Still weeping, she smoothed his hair and dressed him anew. He was about to leave her when she took out a beautiful little rosary of ebony and handed it to him, saying: "Take this with you and be sure to repeat 'Hail Amida Buddha' so that you will be able to find paradise."

"I am leaving you now," replied Rokudai as he took the rosary. "I wish I could go where my father is."

When his younger sister, a girl of ten, heard this, she ran out after him and cried, "Let me go with you to visit my father," but she was intercepted by the wet nurse.

Although Rokudai was then only twelve years old, he looked more grown-up than boys of fourteen or fifteen. He was handsome and elegant. He tried not to show his weakness to the enemy, but tears rushed down his cheeks as he climbed into a palanquin. The palanquin was then surrounded by soldiers. When it moved off, Saitō-go and Saitō-roku walked on either side. Seeing them, Tokimasa had two of his men dismount to give them horses, but they declined the offer and walked barefoot all the way from Daikaku-ji to Rokuhara.

Rokudai's mother and wet nurse looked up to heaven and then fell wailing on the ground. After a while his mother said to the wet nurse: "They say that the children of the Heike have been routed out and put to death in various ways. They have been drowned, or buried, or strangled, or stabbed. I wonder how they will deal with my son. Since he looks rather grown-up, I think they will cut off his head. I know many mothers who have put their children into the care of wet nurses and go to visit them only from time to time. Even for these mothers, the parting would be a wrench. How much more so should it be for me, for since he was born, I have always kept him by my side. My husband and I thought that we were given this child by the gods as a most precious gift, which no one else could deserve, and we have brought him up with utmost care, watching over him morning and evening.

"Especially since my husband has gone, it has been my sole consolation to have my son and daughter on my right and left. Now one of them has been taken away. What shall I do from now on? For three years my heart has been tense both day and night with the apprehension of this terrible fate. But I never expected that it would befall me so suddenly. Though I have long worshiped the Kannon of the Hase Temple, my trust in her mercy seems to be of no avail. Perhaps at this very moment they are beheading my son."

She could do nothing but continue her weeping. Her heart beat faster as the night wore on, and she could not sleep at all. She said to the wet nurse, who was also awake: "A while ago I fell into a doze for a moment. In a dream I saw Rokudai riding toward me on a white horse. He came and sat by my side, saying, 'I missed you so much that I begged Tokimasa for a short leave to see you.' He was weeping and looked terribly sad. At this point I awoke and found myself searching around me in vain. To be with him even in a dream would please me. But how short is a dream and how miserable is this awakening!'"

While relating her dream, she wept; so did the wet nurse.

The night watchman announced the arrival of dawn as Saitō-roku returned to Daikaku-ji. At the frantic inquiry of his mistress, he handed her a letter from Rokudai, saying: "So far he is all right. Here is a letter to you, my mistress."

She opened it and read: "My heart aches when I imagine how deeply you are worried about me. Thus far I have been safe. But I miss you and everybody at home."

It was written in a manly style. Without a word, the lady put it into the folds of her robe and threw herself on the floor. She remained, weeping violently, for some time. Then Saitō-roku said: "I hate to be away from my master's side even for a moment. I must hurry back to see how he is."

So, in tears, the lady wrote a reply and handed it to him. Accepting the note, he departed.

The wet nurse had been so fretful over the uncertain fate of her master that she had run out of the house and walked about aimlessly. As she wandered, weeping desperately, she came across someone who told her: "Deeper in these mountains is a temple called Takao. In this temple lives a saintly priest named Mongaku, who has great influence over Lord Yoritomo. I understand that he is looking for a son of a nobleman to make his disciple."

Encouraged, the wet nurse did not return to the temple, but made her way straight to Takao. There she begged to see Mongaku, and she said to him: "My young master, a boy of twelve, whom I have nursed since I took him out of the womb of his mother, was carried away by the soldiers yesterday. Could Your Reverence beg for his life and bring him up to be your disciple?"

With these words, she fell before the priest and wept violently. Moved to compassion, Mongaku asked her who the boy was.

"He is the son of Lord Koremori of the Heike," replied the wet nurse. "I am indeed his nurse. I think someone must have informed the Genji of the whereabouts of my young master. Otherwise, the soldiers would not have come and taken him away."

Mongaku asked her: "Can you tell me the name of the warrior who took him away?"

"He declared himself to be Tokimasa," replied the wet nurse.

"Well, I will go and see him."

Mongaku had barely finished speaking when he turned and ran toward the capital. Though she could not place her complete trust in Mongaku, the wet nurse felt somewhat relieved and hurried back to Daikaku-ji. When she returned to the house, her mistress said: "I thought you had gone out somewhere to drown yourself. I can understand how you feel, for I also wished to throw myself in a river or abyss."

After these words the lady asked where she had been. In reply the wet nurse told her all that had taken place and all that the priest had said.

"Ah, this priest might be able to beg for his life and bring him back. Oh, I wish I could see Rokudai again!" In tears of joy, she joined her palms, expressing her deep gratitude to Mongaku.

Now, at Rokuhara, Mongaku met with Tokimasa and asked him about Rokudai.

"It is by the order of Lord Yoritomo," replied Tokimasa, "that quite a number of the offspring of the Heike who are still alive in the capital must be rounded up and put to death. Chief among them is Rokudai, the son of Lord Koremori from the womb of the daughter of Lord Narichika. He is the last of the pure line of the Heike, and furthermore he is nearing adulthood.

"It was the special order of Lord Yoritomo to find him by any means and do away with him. I was able to find most of the offspring of the Heike, though younger in age, except this prince. After my vain search, I was about to set out for Kamakura, when the day before yesterday I unexpectedly received information about him. So yesterday I went to fetch him here. But since it is a pity to execute such a good-looking boy, I am keeping him here unharmed."

"Now let me have a look at him," said Mongaku, and he went in and saw Rokudai. That day Rokudai was dressed in a double-woven battle robe and held the ebony rosary in his hand. He was beautiful in the richness of his hair and in the nobility of his bearing. He looked somewhat weary because of his lack of sleep the previous night, and yet he hardly looked like a creature of this world. To the eyes of Mongaku, Rokudai was indeed an awesome sight. When the boy turned his eyes to the priest, tears could be seen. For some reason or other, Rokudai was weeping. Mongaku too moistened the sleeves of his black robe with tears. He found it difficult to believe that such a lovely boy would ever grow up to be a warrior and kill many men. Even if by some chance Rokudai were to become a warrior and stand in the way of the Genji, Mongaku could hardly endure the thought of his being beheaded.

Now, turning to Tokimasa, he said: "I feel related to Rokudai by karma. I am filled with pity for him. I pray you to postpone this execution twenty more days. Let me go down to Kamakura and obtain a pardon for him from Lord Yoritomo. I would like to keep Rokudai in my care. It was I, Mongaku, who made a great contribution to Lord Yoritomo in establishing his present position. Though I was an exile as well, I came up to the capital to procure an imperial edict for him. One night during the journey up to the capital, I was nearly washed away and drowned in the rapids of the Fuji River. Again, when I was attacked by robbers on Mount Takaichi, I made a narrow escape by begging them for my life. It was after these hardships that I was able to go on to Fukuhara and finally receive the edict through the courtesy of Lord Mitsu-yoshi. In recognition of this service, Lord Yotitomo promised that he would accept whatever request I might make of him through-out his life. Even after procuring the edict for Yoritomo, I have rendered to him many services. Since you used to sit by the side of Lord Yoritomo and saw how devoted I was to him, I do not think I have to mention each and every service I rendered. Pro-mises must be placed before life. Lord Yoritomo would never forget his promise, unless he has become arrogant, indulging in his present extraordinary position of commander-in-chief of Japan."

It was still morning when Mongaku set out from the capital for Kamakura. When Saitō-go and Saitō-roku heard of Mongaku's efforts to save the life of their young master, they felt as though he were a living Buddha and joined their palms in their deep grati-tude. In tears of joy, they hurried back to Daikaku-ji to deliver the news of Mongaku's departure for Kamakura to plead for Roku-dai's life. How pleased his mother was when she heard it. Rokudai's life was now in Yoritomo's hands. Rokudai's mother and wet nurse were afraid that Yoritomo's decision would be unfavorable. But inasmuch as Mongaku set out for Kamakura with firm conviction to save Rokudai, and his life was to be prolonged for at least twenty more days, they felt some relief from their apprehension. Now they believed that their earnest prayer had been accepted by the Kannon of the Hase Temple and that the unexpected support of Mongaku had been a sign of the Kannon's profound mercy.

The twenty days passed as in a dream, but Mongaku did not come back. "How can this be?" said Rokudai's mother and wet nurse, and they were again driven into a great sorrow.

Now Tokimasa busily began to prepare for his return trip to Kamakura, saying to himself: "The number of the days that I agreed to wait for Mongaku's return have passed. Since I am not a permanent resident of the capital, I can no longer stay here. I must go now."

Tokimasa's preparations for his journey terrified Saitō-go and Saitō-roku. But they could do nothing for their master, for Mongaku had not come back nor sent any message to the capital. Thus it was that they returned to Daikaku-ji and, in tears, reported to the two ladies: "The saintly priest has not yet returned. Tomorrow at dawn, Tokimasa will set off for Kamakura."

At this news, the ladies' hearts sank.

"Find a reliable old man," said Rokudai's mother, "who might be kind enough to stay with Rokudai until Tokimasa meets the priest Mongaku on his return journey. What a tragedy it would be if Mongaku came back with a pardon after Rokudai has already been put to death! Tell me what are they going to do with Rokudai? Are they going to kill him soon?"

"They might behead him at dawn tomorrow," replied one of the two servants. "I am quite certain of this, for some of Tokimasa's retainers at his residence look terribly sad, so they must be expecting an end to my master's life. In sympathy, they are weeping and chanting 'Hail Amida Buddha.'"

"Now tell me how he looks," asked Rokudai's mother.

"When someone is near him, he tries to brace himself," replied the retainer. "But when no one is near him, he presses his sleeves to his face and weeps."

"That is the way Rokudai is," said his mother. "He is still young, but already he has the heart of a man. I can imagine how sad Rokudai must be if he understands that it might be his last evening in this world! He said he would come to me if there were a little time. More than twenty days have passed thus far, but it has been impossible for us to visit each other. Now I have no hope of seeing him again! What are you going to do?"

"We will be by our master's side," replied the retainers, "to see how he meets his end. If he is put to death, we will take his bones with us to Mount Kōya, take the tonsure, and pray for his afterlife. This is what we are determined to do."

"Now I pray you to return to Rokudai at once," said the lady. "He must be wretched without your attendance."

Weeping bitterly, Saitō-go and Saitō-roku departed.

Now, at dawn on the sixteenth day of the twelfth month of the year, Tokimasa, taking Rokudai with him, set out from the capital. Saitō-go and Saitō-roku, in tears, went with their master. Again Tokimasa offered them the horses of his soldiers, but they refused to mount, saying: "Since this is our last escort for our master, we wish to suffer the tortures of hell."

Tears rushed down their faces as they walked barefoot. Rokudai had parted from his mother and wet nurse, and now, leaving the capital behind in the clouds, he was on a long journey to the eastern provinces. If one of the warriors quickened his pace, his heart sank, fearing that the warrior was coming to cut off his head. And if one of them tried to speak to him, he was frightened, thinking that his end was being announced at last. The procession moved on. Rokudai thought he would be killed at Shinomiya. He was so absorbed in the contemplation of death that he did not realize the procession had already passed the Osaka Checkpoint and was approaching the lakeshore of Ōtsu. Dusk fell near Awazu. The first day of his journey was over. Station after station, province after province, the procession kept moving until it came to the province of Suruga, where there was a rumor that Rokudai would be finally deprived of the last dewdrop of his life.

Now at a place called Sembon-no-Matsubara all the warriors dismounted from their horses. The palanquin was set down, and Rokudai was ordered to get out. Tokimasa's retainers spread a deerskin on the ground and placed Rokudai upon it. Tokimasa then stepped forward and said to Rokudai: "I have brought you this far simply because I expected to meet the priest Mongaku on his way back from Kamakura. You can see how kind I have been to you, but I can no longer continue this treatment. If I were to take you beyond Mount Ashigara I do not know what the Lord Yoritomo would say. If I execute you here, I shall be able to make a false report to him, saying that I did away with you in the province of Ōmi. Since your sad fate in the continuum of the Heike deeds was decided in a former life, you cannot escape, no matter who might plead for your life."

Rokudai made no reply but summoned Saitō-go and Saitō-roku and said: "After I die go back to the capital. But do not tell my mother and wet nurse that I have been beheaded on my way to Kamakura. I know they will find out after all, but if they are informed of the truth, their grief will be so great that I will be hindered from salvation after death. So tell them that you accompanied me as far as Kamakura."

At their master's words, the two retainers sank into such deep sorrow that they could not speak. After a while, however, Saitō-go suppressed his tears and said: "After your execution we might be unable to return alive to the capital."

Now Rokudai, knowing that his last moment had come, turned to the west, joined his palms, and, chanting "Hail Amida Buddha," stretched out his neck. Chikatoshi, who had been chosen as executioner, seized his sword and moved around behind Rokudai from the right. He was about to deliver the blow when his sight darkened and his heart sank, so he could not strike.

"I cannot do this," he exclaimed in dismay, throwing down his weapon. "I pray you to choose someone else."

The warriors began to discuss who should take his place when a priest in a black robe, a messenger from Mongaku, came galloping up on a cream-colored horse. Arriving at the place of execution, he sprang from his horse, and after catching his breath, exclaimed: "Lord Yoritomo has pardoned the young lord of the Heike. His order is written here!" With these words, he took out a letter and handed it to Tokimasa.

Opening the letter, Tokimasa read: "To Tokimasa: I understand that you arrested the son of Lord Koremori, lieutenant general of the third court rank. He is now pardoned at the request of the priest Mongaku from Takao. Do not doubt, but put him into the care of Mongaku. Yoritomo."

[743]

Tokimasa read it two or three times and cried out: "Wonderful! Wonderful!"

With great excitement, he canceled the execution. Saitō-go and Saitō-roku as well as the warriors of Tokimasa shed tears of joy.

CHAPTER VIII

THE KANNON'S MERCY UPON
ROKUDAI

After a while Mongaku appeared. He seemed overjoyed with the success of his petition to Yoritomo.

"At first," Mongaku said to Tokimasa, "Yoritomo declined my request, saying, 'Lord Koremori, the father of this young lord, was my first enemy at the time I raised my banner in battle. The son will not be pardoned, no matter who pleads for his life.' So I reproached him, saying, 'If your lordship makes me feel sad, how can you expect to receive favor and support from the Buddha?' But he replied to my petition with a blunt 'No,' and went out hunting on the plain of Nasu. Determined to persuade him, I followed him to the hunting ground, where I finally obtained his pardon. You must have been anxious at such a delay in my return!"

"When our agreed deferment for twenty days expired," replied Tokimasa, "I was obliged to conclude that Lord Yoritomo would not spare him. Even so, I have brought him with me this far. Though I was about to behead him here, I was able to give him a thread of hope."

Tokimasa then provided Saitō-go and Saitō-roku with saddled horses and said: "I wish I could go with you some distance. But since I have many important matters that I must hasten to report to Lord Yoritomo, I must take leave of you here. Farewell!" With these words, he resumed his journey to the east. He was indeed a warrior of gentle heart.

Mongaku hurried with the young lord and retainers up to the capital, traveling both day and night. When they arrived at Atsuta in Owari Province, the year had already come to an end. It was the evening of the fifth of the New Year days when they arrived at the capital. At the crossroads of Nijō and Inokuma was a house in which Mongaku had occasionally stayed. Here Rokudai was taken for a short rest. Thus it was that they arrived at Daikaku-ji at

[745]

midnight. They knocked at the gate, but no one came out; nor was there any sound from within. Only the little white puppy that Rokudai had kept came running out, through a chink in the clay wall, wagging its tail in joy at seeing its master again. "Where is my mother?" Rokudai asked his dog pathetically.

Saitō-go and Saitō-roku climbed over the clay wall and opened the gate from within. Rokudai went into the temple but found no trace of his mother. The fireplace was cold. It seemed that no one had been there recently. Rokudai wept, saying: "It was only to see my mother and sister and wet nurse once more that I have managed to sustain this worthless life, clinging to the faint hope of living longer. What has happened to them?"

When dawn came, they inquired of a man who lived in a nearby village. He replied: "They said they were going to Nara to worship Daibutsu[1] at the end of the year. But I hear they are staying at the Hase Temple during the New Year days to offer prayers to the Kannon. Of late I have seen no one going in or out of that house."

Saitō-go hurried to Hase and informed his mistress of the return of Rokudai. When they heard this news, Rokudai's mother and wet nurse could hardly believe their ears and cried out: "Are we dreaming?"

Without a moment's delay, they started back for Daikaku-ji. In this way, mother and son were able to see each other once more. Streams of tears prevented them from speaking their words of joy. After a while Rokudai's mother advised him to take the tonsure immediately. But Mongaku felt so much pity for Rokudai that he would not shave his head. Soon afterward Mongaku received Rokudai at Takao, and it is said that he built a little cell for his mother also, so that she would be able to seclude herself from the world. Great is the mercy of the Kannon, who succors both sinners and innocents alike. It is indeed a wonderful blessing.

Some time before, when Tokimasa was on his return journey to Kamakura with Rokudai, he met a messenger from Yoritomo at the station at Kagami. In reply to Tokimasa's questioning, the messenger said: "I hear that Yukiie and Yoshinori have been in alliance with Yoshitsune. It is the order of Lord Yoritomo that you should destroy them."

"I am now escorting an important captive to Kamakura, so I myself cannot go in search of them." So saying, Tokimasa decided to send his nephew Tokisada in his place. At that time Tokisada happened to be in the same procession to see off his uncle. Thus it was that Tokimasa summoned Tokisada and issued an order to him: "Turn back at once. Find Yukiie and Yoshinori and destroy them."

Tokisada hurried back to the capital and began an immediate search. It happened that a certain monk who was interrogated by Tokisada said: "I have no idea of where Yukiie is, but there is a monk who does know his whereabouts."

Thus informed, Tokisada went out and arrested the monk.

"What are you doing? Why am I under arrest?" asked the monk.

"Because I have heard," replied Tokisada, "that you know of Yukiie's whereabouts."

"If so," complained the monk, "you can simply say, 'Tell me where Yukiie is,' instead of arresting me like this without any reason. I have heard that he is now at Tennō-ji."[2]

"Then, guide us there!" So saying, Tokisada set out for Tennō-ji at the head of some thirty horsemen, including his four retainers.

At Tennō-ji Yukiie had two lodgings—one at the house of a musician named Kaneharu and the other at the house of Shinroku and Shinshichi. At that time Yukiie was staying with Kaneharu. When he saw a number of men in armor breaking in, he fled from the rear of the house. Kaneharu had two daughters, both of whom were Yukiie's concubines, and so they were arrested and interrogated. In reply, however, the elder said, "Ask my sister," and the younger said, "Ask my sister." Since Yukiie had fled suddenly, neither of them had been told where he would seek refuge. Tokisada, however, took the women with him when he returned to the capital.

Meanwhile, Yukiie had headed for Kumano, accompanied by only one of his retainers. Since this retainer suffered from a foot ailment, Yukiie was obliged to stay for a while at the village of Yagi[3] in Izumi. The owner of the house in which they took shelter knew Yukiie was a fugitive, so he ran by night to the capital and reported Yukiie's whereabouts to Tokisada. Upon learning that Yukiie was in Izumi, Tokisada said to himself: "The soldiers sent out to Tennō-ji have not yet returned. Whom shall I send to Izumi?"

He then summoned one of his retainers named Muneharu and

inquired: "The monk from Mount Hiei who built your house—is he still at your place?"

"Yes, my master, he is," replied Muneharu.

"Then," exclaimed Tokisada, "send for him!"

When the monk came into his presence, Tokisada commanded: "Yukiie is hiding at Yagi in Izumi. Attack him and receive your reward from Lord Yoritomo."

"Certainly, Your Excellency!" replied the monk. "Now may I have some of your soldiers with me in this action?"

At this request, Tokisada turned to Muneharu and said: "Only you, Muneharu, can go with him. We lack soldiers now."

Tokisada then ordered fifteen retainers and ox tenders to accompany Muneharu and the monk, Hitachi-bō Shōmei. Upon arriving at Izumi, Shōmei ran into the house where Yukiie was supposed to be staying but Yukiie was nowhere to be seen. Shōmei then broke the wooden floors and looked inside a small storeroom. Yukiie was not to be found. After searching in vain, Shōmei went out and stood on the road, looking around. When he caught sight of a woman who seemed to be a farmer's wife, he called her and inquired: "Is there any place near here where some traveling strangers are now staying? If you do not tell me the truth, you shall die."

"At the house where you broke in," replied the woman, "two well-dressed travelers stayed until last night. This morning, however, they left and moved into that large house over there."

That day Shōmei wore armor laced with black leather cords and carried a great curved sword. Running into the house, he saw a man, about fifty years of age, wearing headgear and dressed in a dark blue battle robe. Beside him were Chinese cups and bowls, and he was pouring saké into a cup held by a man sitting near him. At Shōmei's sudden intrusion, he ducked and fled. As Shōmei turned to pursue him, the other man exclaimed: "Hey there! He is not Yukiie. Yukiie is here!"

Shōmei wheeled around and confronted Yukiie, who was dressed in a white short-sleeved kimono and wide hakama and holding a short gold-studded sword in his left hand and a great curved sword in his right. Shōmei cried out: "Throw away your swords!"

At this demand, Yukiie burst into great laughter. Shōmei then stepped forward and aimed a mighty blow at Yukiie; Yukiie caught it on his sword. Again and again Shōmei made assaults. The fight continued in this way for two hours. Then Yukiie stepped back to take shelter in a small storeroom. Shōmei cried after Yukiie: "Come out! Have you no warrior's spirit left?"

"You are right," replied Yukiie. "I must come out."

Again Yukiie sprang from the storeroom and fought. Shōmei threw away his sword to grapple with him, and they fell together to the floor. They were struggling, rolling on the floor, when Muneharu dashed toward them. Hastily, instead of drawing his sword, Muneharu picked up a stone and hit Yukiie on the forehead. At this attack, Yukiie burst into laughter and said: "You are a worthless soldier. You do not know the proper manners in a fight. Attack the enemy with your sword—do not make mistakes."

Once Shōmei had Yukiie pinned to the floor, he ordered Muneharu to bind Yukiie's feet. But Muneharu was so upset that he bound them up with those of Shōmei. Later Yukiie was properly bound and seated on the floor. Yukiie then said: "Bring me some water."

At this request, they brought him some dried rice[4] in water. He drank only the water. Then Shōmei ate the rice.

"Are you a monk from Mount Hiei?" asked Yukiie.

"I am," replied Shōmei.

"What is your name?"

"I am Hitachi-bō Shōmei, a resident of the north hollow in the West Precinct."

"Was it you who once came to me offering some services?" inquired Yukiie.

"Yes, it was I."

"Tell me," asked Yukiie, "who was it, Yoritomo or Tokisada who sent you here?"

"It was Lord Yoritomo," replied Shōmei. "Did you really intend to destroy him?"

"Since I have been taken alive," replied Yukiie, "it is all the same whether or not you believe I intended to raise a rebellion against him. I know I shall be put to death in any case. That suits Yoritomo. Now tell me how you like my strength and skill in a fight?"

"Up on the mountain," replied Shōmei, "I fought many men of great strength. At times I felt like fighting three of them at once. But I have never before met as tough an opponent as you. Now what do you think of my strength and skill?"

[749]

"I cannot criticize you after I have been defeated," replied Yukiie.

When they examined the swords used in the fight, they saw that the blade of Yukiie's sword had not been scratched at all but that of Shōmei's had been nicked in forty-two places. Soon afterward, a horse was brought from a nearby station, and Yukiie, still bound, was put on its back. Shōmei and Yukiie started back to the capital. That night they stopped at the house of the head prostitute at Eguchi.[5] From this place they sent an urgent messenger to the capital. The next day, at the hour of the horse [noon], they met Tokisada at Akai[6] on the bank of the Yodo River. Tokisada led some one hundred horsemen with banners flying above their heads. Tokisada said to Shōmei: "It is the edict of the cloistered emperor that we must not bring Yukiie alive into the capital. It is also the command of Lord Yoritomo. So cut off his head at once! Then make your way to Kamakura and visit Lord Yoritomo. You will receive a reward from him."

This order was carried out, and Yukiie was executed at Akai.

Now it was rumored that Yoshinori had been in hiding deep in the mountains of Daigo. An army was sent there, but the search was in vain. Then another rumor had it that he had fled to Iga Province. This time one of Tokisada's retainers, Heiroku, set out for Iga at the head of an army. Heiroku finally found Yoshinori at the mountain temple of Sendo,[7] where Heiroku's army attacked him. When Yoshinori, dressed in two short-sleeved kimonos and a wide hakama, knew that his end had come, he cut open his belly and died. Heiroku cut off Yoshinori's head and took it back to the capital. When he showed it to Tokisada, Tokisada commanded: "Take it to Kamakura at once. Present it to Lord Yoritomo for his inspection and receive your reward from him."

Thus it was that Shōmei and Heiroku went down to Kamakura with the heads of Yukiie and Yoshinori. But when they took out the heads before Lord Yoritomo for his inspection, Yoritomo rewarded them only with these words: "You are to be highly commended!"

Shōmei was then ordered to be exiled to Kasai, and so he lamented: "I have come down to Kamakura, expecting to receive a reward from Lord Yoritomo. Now I receive no reward. In addition to this injustice, I am to be exiled. What an absurdity this is! If only I had known, I would not have fought at the risk of my life!"

His complaint was to no avail; Shōmei was exiled. Two years later, however, he was summoned back to Kamakura and was received by Yoritomo, who said: "You must understand that he who has destroyed a commanding general is forsaken by the gods and the Buddhas. This is why I punished you."

This time, however, as a reward, Shōmei received the stewardship of two villages—Tada-no-shō[8] in Tajima Province and Hamuro[9] in Settsu Province.

As for Heiroku, because he had formerly been a retainer of the Heike, he had been deprived of his stewardship of the village of Hattori. He was now reinstated in this stewardship.

---

[1] The great statue of Buddha at Tōdai-ji, which had been burned down and not yet reconstructed. The narration contradicts historical circumstances.

[2] The shortened name of Shitennō-ji, located at Tennō-ji-ku in the present-day city of Osaka.

[3] Located on the outskirts of present-day Kishiwada, Osaka Prefecture.

[4] *Hoshii*. Rice dried in the sun after cooking, it was often carried by travelers.

[5] The present-day ward of Higashi-Yodogawa, Osaka.

[6] The present-day town of Yodo, Kuze-gun, Kyoto.

[7] The present-day village of Ōyamada, Ayama-gun, Mie Prefecture.

[8] Located in the present-day town of Hidaka, Hyogo Prefecture.

[9] Located in the present-day city of Takatsuki, Osaka.

CHAPTER IX

THE EXECUTION OF ROKUDAI

Thus, as the tale tells us, Rokudai grew to be fifteen years old. He was an exceedingly handsome young man. His mother said: "If only the world were ruled by the Heike as before, Rokudai would be captain of the Imperial Guard by now." Though she spoke the truth, it was impertinent of her to speak of such matters so openly.

Yoritomo, at Kamakura, had long felt hostility toward Rokudai. In his letters to Mongaku he mentioned Rokudai repeatedly, and in one of them he inquired: "How is the son of the Lord Koremori faring? Years ago Your Reverence prophesied my future. Now tell me if you see in his face any possibility for destroying an enemy of the emperor or washing away an old shame of defeat."

In reply, however, Mongaku wrote: "Rokudai is a spineless coward. . . . Please set your mind at rest."

These words did not satisfy Yoritomo, so he wrote to Mongaku: "Your Reverence has a habit of giving support to anyone if he raises a rebellion. But as long as I stay alive in this world, no one shall attempt to destroy my family. I do not know what Rokudai will do after I die."

These words were dreadful. When Rokudai's mother heard of them, she was terrified and urged her son to take the tonsure. She thought Rokudai had no choice but to do so to sustain his life. Thus in the spring of the fifth year of the Bunji era [1189], at the age of sixteen, Rokudai had his beautiful hair cut off. Wearing a robe, a hakama of a subdued color, and carrying a traveling box on his back, he took leave of his mother and Mongaku, and set out on a pilgrimage. Attired in similar clothing, Saitō-go and Saitō-roku accompanied him. Rokudai first went to Mount Kōya and visited the priest Tokiyori, who had helped his father to attain Buddhahood. From him he heard in detail how his father had become a monk and how he had died.

"Kumano is an important place for me, both for learning about Buddhahood and retracing my father's steps." So saying, Rokudai went on to Kumano.

In front of the Hama Shrine he looked across at the island of Yamanari, near which his father had drowned himself. He wished to row a boat to the island, but as the wind blew from the wrong direction and the waves rose high, he was obliged to give up the idea. He stood gazing at the offing, questioning the white foaming waves in whose waters his father had drowned. Rokudai felt affection for the sand of the shore, as though there he might find the bones of his father. All the while his sleeves were wet with tears, as wet as those of fishermen soaked with the splashes of the waves. He spent all that night on the beach, chanting "Hail Amida Buddha," and, with his fingers, drawing the image of the Buddha in the sand. When dawn came, he summoned a priest and asked him to chant a sutra for the consolation of his father's soul. He felt as though the image of the Buddha in the sand and the chanting of the sutra on the beach would reach his father in the world beyond. Having endless talks with his father in his heart, Rokudai made his return journey.

Now Tadafusa, a son of Lord Shigemori, had not been found since he had fled from the battle at Yashima. This was because he had fled to Kii Province, and turning for aid to a native of that province named Muneshige, Tadafusa had confined himself at Muneshige's castle. Upon hearing that he was alive in Kii Province, the warriors of the Heike who had survived the battle at Dan-no-Ura rallied to Tadafusa. Among them were the former generals Moritsugi, Tadamitsu, and Kagekiyo. Several hundred soldiers of the Heike in the provinces of Iga and Ise vied with each other to be by Tadafusa's side.

Upon orders from Yoritomo, the Superintendent of the Kumano Shrine, Tanzō, attacked Muneshige's castle. There were eight battles during a period of three months. The soldiers within the castle fought recklessly, risking their lives. After a great number of Tanzō's soldiers had been killed or evicted in each battle, Tanzō sent a message to Yoritomo: "We attacked Muneshige's castle eight times. However, the soldiers within the castle fought so desperately that my soldiers were always defeated. I am no longer confident of defeating the enemy. I would like to be reinforced by the soldiers of two or three other provinces."

To this, Lord Yoritomo replied: "That would cause a great loss to the national wealth and great confusion to the people. I do not think that the soldiers within the castle are loyal retainers of the Heike. They must be pirates and mountain robbers. Close the gates and let no one pass in or out of the castle."

Tanzō faithfully followed Yoritomo's command. As Yoritomo had expected, the castle was completely isolated. Again Yoritomo contrived a plan and spread this rumor: "I intend to spare the sons of Lord Shigemori. This is because I owe my life to him. Indeed, it was he who, as a messenger of Ike no Zenni, presented a petition to his father Kiyomori to lighten my sentence to exile."

When Tadafusa heard of the rumor, he slipped out of the castle and surrendered himself to the officials of Rokuhara. Then he was taken to Kamakura. Upon seeing him, Yoritomo said: "I pray you go back to the capital. I have a certain quiet place in mind for your residence. It is my intention to offer it to you."

With these words he betrayed Tadafusa, for he sent an assassin to follow him. It was near the Seta Bridge that Tadafusa was killed.

In addition to his six legitimate sons, Lord Shigemori had another son named Munezane. At the age of three he was adopted by the minister of the Left Tsunemune. Thus he became a member of a family that lived by the pen instead of the sword. Though no one came from Kamakura to look for him, his foster father, fearing Yoritomo's hostility, drove him from his house. Munezane was then eighteen years of age.

Having no place to settle down, he went to visit Shunjō-bō of Daibutsu and said: "I am Munezane, the youngest son of Shigemori. At the age of three I was adopted by the minister of the Left, Tsunemune. Becoming a member of an entirely different family from the Heike, I gave up the sword and devoted myself to the pen. I am eighteen years old now. Though I had nothing rebellious in mind to make me suspected by Lord Yoritomo, I was evicted from the house of my foster father who feared the censure of Yoritomo. I pray Your Reverence to accept me as your disciple." He then cut off his topknot, adding: "If Your Reverence also fears the trouble

I might cause, please report me to Kamakura. Since I was born of an evil karma, I shall endeavor to go any place you recommend."

Shunjō-bō was so profoundly impressed that he performed the ceremony for Munezane's priesthood and put him in the oil storehouse at Tōdai-ji. After a while Shunjō-bō reported Munezane's presence at Tōdai-ji to Kamakura. When Yoritomo heard of this, he exclaimed: "Whatever Your Reverence may plead for Munezane you must first let him come down to Kamakura. I will decide what to do with him only after I see him."

Shunjō-bō could do no more and sent Munezane down to Kamakura. From the day that he set out from Nara, Munezane ate nothing and drank nothing. He refused even to gargle hot or cold water. Thus it was that at a place called Sekimoto, among the mountains of Ashigara, he finally starved to death. He had been aware of his inescapable fate. This was how he had decided to make a silent protest against the world.

Thus, as the tale tells us, on the seventh day of the eleventh month of the first year of the Kenkyū era [1190], Lord Yoritomo came up to the capital. On the ninth day of the month he was appointed councilor of the senior grade of the second court rank. On the eleventh day of the month he was given another title, general of the Right. But soon afterward he resigned from the posts of councilor and general of the Right. On the fourth day of the twelfth month he started back to Kamakura.

It was the thirteenth day of the third month of the third year of the Kenkyū era [1192] that the cloistered emperor passed away. He was sixty-six years old. That night the bell that he had rung during rituals of the Shingon sect ceased to toll. At dawn his voice was no longer heard chanting the *Lotus Sutra*.

It was decided that the ceremony for the reconstruction of the Daibutsu-den should be held on the thirteenth day of the third month of the sixth year of the era. Again, in the second month of that year, Lord Yoritomo came up to the capital. On the twelfth day of the month, while paying a visit to the Daibutsu-den to offer prayers, he summoned Kagetoki and said: "I noticed a dangerous looking man behind a group of monks at the south side of the west gate of Tōdai-ji. Arrest him and bring him here!"

At this command, Kagetoki departed and soon returned to Yoritomo with the suspect. He was a man whose beard was shaved but whose topknot remained uncut. Yoritomo interrogated him: "Who are you?"

"Since my fate is sealed," replied the man, "I no longer dare to make any evasive reply. I am a retainer of the Heike named Iesuke."

"Now tell me what has made you come here."

"I have come here hoping to kill you, given the opportunity."

"Your attempt to revenge your master," exclaimed Yoritomo, "is highly commendable!"

When Yoritomo came back to the capital after the ceremony, he had his men execute Iesuke on the bank of the Kamo River at Rokujō.

The offspring of the Heike had all been arrested or killed since the winter of the first year of the Bunji era [1185]. It seemed that none of them except those who had been still in the wombs of the Heike ladies had survived. Even so, there remained alive, in hiding, the youngest son of Tomomori, a boy named Tomotada. When the Heike abandoned the capital, he was three years old.

At that time a warrior of Kii Province named Tamenori began taking care of him. They wandered from place to place, seeking shelter, until they found security at the village of Ōta in Bingo Province. However, when Tomotada grew up to celebrate his coming of age, he came under the suspicion of the overseer of the village. Thus it was that he came back to the capital and took shelter at Ichi-no-Hashi,[1] which once had been the palace of Fujiwara no Tadahira. This was also a place that Tomotada's grandfather Kiyomori had designated as a stronghold; in preparation for attack, it had been fortified with double moats and bamboo groves on all sides. Now Tomotada had sharpened stakes set up for reinforcement. In the daytime no voice nor noise was heard there. But at night many cultured men gathered and amused themselves by composing poems and playing the biwa and flute.

At that time there was a warrior of the Genji named Mototsuna. His father was Motokiyo, who had waited upon Yoshiyasu, a brother-in-law of Yoritomo. He was notorious for exercising his excessive influence upon people. One day Mototsuna heard that there was a certain outlaw at Ichi-no-Hashi. Thus it was that at the hour of the dragon [8 A.M.], on the seventh day of the tenth month of the seventh year of the Kenkyū era [1196], Mototsuna led a hundred and forty or fifty horsemen to attack Ichi-no-Hashi. The battle raged. Some thirty men inside the stronghold fought with all their might, letting fly a shower of arrows from behind the bamboo groves. Many men and horses of the opposing side were shot to death. The invaders seemed to have no chance of winning over the few within.

When the Heike resistance was reported to the capital, a great number of Genji warriors, more than a thousand, rushed to Ichi-no-Hashi. They destroyed all the small houses near the stronghold and filled the moats with their remains. Now with a great shout, they made an onslaught into the stronghold. The men within dashed out brandishing their swords. Some fought to the death and others killed themselves. Severely wounded, the sixteen-year-old Tomotada put an end to himself. His foster father, Tamenori, held him on his knees and wept. After chanting "Hail Amida Buddha" ten times, he cut his belly open. His two sons, Tarō and Jirō, fought to the death.

The stronghold was set afire. The warriors of the Genji vied with each other to get the heads of the fallen enemy. They came out with heads skewered on the ends of their swords or sickle-bladed halberds and hurried back toward the mansion of Yoshiyasu. Yoshiyasu came out in a carriage to meet them at Ichijō and inspected the heads there. Among the warriors of the Genji, there were some who were able to tell the head of Tamenori from the others, but none of them was able to identify that of Tomotada. Since his mother was in attendance upon Princess Hachijō, she was summoned to Ichijō to identify it.

When she saw the head of her son, she wept bitterly and said: "He was three years old when I left him and accompanied my husband, Tomomori, to the western provinces. Since then, I have not heard of him. Uncertain of his whereabouts, I have had no way of finding out whether he was alive or dead. This is truly the head of my son, for it resembles my late husband, Tomomori, in many respects. Yes, this must be. . . ." This was indeed how the head of Tomotada was identified.

Now one of the warriors of the Heike, a man named Moritsugi, had fled to Kehi in Tajima Province, where he was married to a daughter of Dōkō. Dōkō, who was head of the most influential family in Kehi, did not know of Moritsugi's career as a Heike warrior. At night Moritsugi used to ride his father-in-law's horse, and his outstanding mastery in the saddle was soon well known among the villagers. Takakiyo, the overseer of the village, became more and more suspicious of him. Though nobody knew how, Yoritomo happened to know of Moritsugi's whereabouts, and he sent an order to Kehi, which stated: "Takakiyo: I hear that a former warrior of the Heike named Moritsugi is living there in Tajima Province. Bring him to me under arrest!"

Dōkō was a father-in-law of Takakiyo as well, so they met and discussed how to arrest Moritsugi. They decided to attack him in the bathhouse. When he was bathing, they sent six men of great strength to attack him, but they were all overcome. As they tried to get up, they were kicked to the floor again. Moritsugi's body was wet and slippery, so they found no way to hold him. Thirty more men joined the struggle. Mighty though he was, Moritsugi finally fell in the unequal fight. They struck him with the backs of their swords and the shafts of their halberds. He was bound tight and sent down to Kamakura.

Yoritomo had him sit before him and interrogated him.

Finally he said to Moritsugi: "You are a warrior who served the Heike for many years. Now tell me why you did not share their fate at Dan-no-ura."

"The Heike were defeated so quickly that I lost the chance to put an end to myself," replied Moritsugi. "Since then, I have been looking forward to the opportunity to kill you. It is only the hope of killing you that has kept me alive, sharpening the blade of my sword and the heads of my arrows. I know my time is drawing near. There is nothing more I want to say."

"You are to be highly commended!" exclaimed Yoritomo. "Now if you wish to come over to my side, I shall spare your life. What do you think?"

"A brave warrior does not serve two masters. If you confide in a warrior like me, you will regret it in the days to come. Behead me at once."

Thus it was that Moritsugi was taken to the beach of Yui, where he was finally executed. All the warriors of the Genji admired his bravery.

At that time Go-Toba was on the throne. This emperor, however, did nothing but amuse himself with songs and dances. Therefore all affairs of state were administered at the whim of his wet nurse, Noriko. This caused great distress among the people.

Of old, when the King of Wu in China favored retainers skilled in swordsmanship, many farmers were wounded while practicing, and when the King of Ch'u showed a particular interest in girls with small waists, many court ladies, trying hard to reduce their weight, starved to death. It is a matter of course that the people of lower rank imitate the people of higher rank in their mode of life.

People who understood the situation were deeply concerned about the emperor's neglect of administrative duty. The one who was most critical of Emperor Go-Toba was the priest Mongaku. He was a man of impetuous character, so eager to meddle in state affairs that he was soon involved in a plot. At that time there was a prince, second in succession to the throne, who did not neglect learning and put proper principles first. Mongaku wished this prince to be enthroned. However, he could take no step in this direction while Yoritomo was still alive and in power. Then, on the thirteenth day of the first month of the tenth year of the Ken-kyū era [1199], Yoritomo died. Mongaku was about to raise a revolt when his attempt was discovered. His residence at Nijō Inokuma was raided by the officials of the Police Commissioners Division. Mongaku was arrested. He was already more than eighty at the time. Despite his old age, the punishment was severe. He was sent in exile to the province of Oki.

When he set out on the journey, he exclaimed: "Damnable wooden-ball-loving youth[2]—what a fool he is! What does he mean by banishing an old man like me, even though I am condemned as the emperor's enemy, to a far province—as far as Oki? He should not do this to an old man who himself does not know how many more days he may live. Does he know of his own fate? Someday he will be banished to the very province where I am now going into exile."

These words were indeed terrible, because some time afterward —when war broke out during the Shōkyū era and Emperor Go-Toba was defeated by the Hōjō clan—the emperor met the fate of being exiled to the province of Oki, though many other provinces could have been chosen for his exile. Mongaku had spoken the truth! It is said that the priest's evil spirit raged about in the province of Oki, and from time to time he appeared to haunt Go-Toba.

Rokudai, who had been made a monk and given the name Sani no Zenji, led a secluded life at Takao, where he devoted himself entirely to Buddhist rites.

"He is the son of Koremori and the disciple of Mongaku," said Yoritomo.[3] "Though he changed his appearance by adopting the tonsure, he can never shave his rebellious heart."

By the order of the lord of Kamakura, the captain of the Police Commissioners Division, Sukekane, arrested Rokudai and took him to the eastern provinces. It was on the bank of the Tagoshi River that Rokudai was finally beheaded by a native of Suruga Province, a warrior named Yasutsuna. His life had been spared from the age of twelve to that of thirty through the mercy of the Kannon of the Hase Temple.

With the death of Rokudai perished the Heike—for evermore.

[1] Located in present-day Fushimi, Kyoto.
[2] This is a reference to a court game similar to croquet.
[3] This narration is a flashback to the time previous to Yoritomo's death.

EPILOGUE

EPILOGUE

"Hearing . . . [Kenreimon-In's] *prayer* . . . [they] knew her last moment had come
. . . ."
—Epilogue, Chapter V, page 781

CHAPTER I

THE FORMER EMPRESS TAKES THE TONSURE

Kenreimon-In had left the capital for Yoshida in the foothills of Higashi-yama. She was to make her home in a run-down hut owned by Kyōe, a priest of Nara. Clusters of vines crept over the rotting roof. Weeds grew tall and thick in the garden. The bamboo curtains crumbled. The bedchamber was exposed to wind and rain. Flowers flourished each spring, but no one came back to admire them. Moonbeams stole in night after night, but no one awoke to appreciate them.

In days past the former empress had sat on a jeweled dais within brocade drapes. Now, separated from her family, she had come to this. She must have been as sad as a fish on dry land or a bird deprived of its nest. Her hardship was so severe that even her abode on the waves of the western sea was remembered with a fondness that developed into a painful yearning. Her thoughts floated in the clouds far above the azure waves, then sank deep into despair. As she stood, bathed in moonlight, near the reed-thatched hut, tears rushed down her cheeks and dampened the garden moss.

On the first day of the fifth month of the first year of Bunji (1185), Kenreimon-In took the tonsure. It is said that the priest who performed the ceremony for her was Inzei, a priest with a cell at Ashō at Chōraku-ji.[1] As a token of her gratitude to the Buddha, she presented to Inzei a robe that had belonged to her son, the late emperor. It was the robe that he had worn until just before plunging into the deep; his own odor mixed with his perfume still remained upon it. She had brought the robe with her all the way from the western provinces, for she had wished to keep it as a remembrance of her son. She had never thought of letting it go, but now, as she had nothing else to offer to the Buddha, she brought out the robe in tears, hoping that this offering might cause the Buddha to bless her son in the world beyond. Inzei could not utter even a single word of gratitude when he received it, for he was weeping bitterly; the sleeves of his black robe were soaked with tears as he retired from her presence. It is said that the former emperor's robe was later made into a hanging, and placed before the main image of the Buddha at Chōraku-ji.

Kenreimon-In had received imperial edicts that made her one of Emperor Takakura's consorts at the age of fifteen and empress at the age of sixteen. She was always by the emperor's side. By day she assisted him in his administrative duties; by night she accepted his love. At the age of twenty-two she bore him a son who was made crown prince. When he was enthroned, she received the title empress dowager and took the name Kenreimon-In. Because she was the daughter of the Priest-Premier and because she was the mother of the emperor, she was greatly revered. Now, at the age of twenty-nine, she was still beautiful, as beautiful as peach or apricot blossoms. Her elegant form was like a lotus flower. But what was the use of keeping her raven locks, as lustrous as jade?

At last she renounced this fleeting world and became a nun. Even after entering the Buddha's Way, she found it difficult to assuage her deep grief. All the horrible scenes—her son, the emperor, her mother, Nii-dono, her companions sinking in the waves—could not be swept from her eyes. Brooding over these past miseries, she regretted that the fragile dewdrop of her life had not fallen from the leaf.

The nights of the fifth month are short, but to Kenreimon-In they were endless. Her tears poured forth unremittingly. She remained always awake, for if she did not sleep, she could not dream of her miseries. A dim candle light cast her shadow upon the wall; melancholy was the sound of the rain tapping at the latticed windows. Her life seemed more pitiful than that of Emperor Hsüan-tsung's consorts, who had been confined at the Shang-yang Palace in ancient China.[2]

A mandarin-orange tree grew close by the eaves of the hut. Perhaps it had been planted by a former resident who remembered his past with the aid of its sweet scent. Now it was in full bloom. As the fragrance wafted into her hut and the note of a cuckoo was heard now and again, Kenreimon-In recalled an ancient poem and wrote it on the lid of her ink-stone case:

Sweet scent of orange.
A cuckoo sings his praises—
A song of the past.
Where are those whom I have loved?
Wither have they departed?

Other court ladies had not been as resolute as Nii-dono and Kozaishō, who had thrown themselves into the waves. Most were captured by the rough warriors of the Genji and were brought back to their old homes in the capital. These ladies, both young and old, became nuns to live in seclusion in deep valleys or among mountain rocks. Their former homes had vanished in smoke. The ruins, covered with tufts of grass, were left unvisited by those who had once been frequent callers. They compared themselves to the legendery traveler who spent half a year in the enchanted house of a mountain nymph and upon coming home, found not his sons but descendants of the seventh generation.

The hut and its hillside garden were severely damaged by the great earthquake in the seventh month. Though her little shack had become almost unlivable, the former empress had nowhere else to go. The imperial guards were no longer sent to her gate. The untrimmed hedges were heavy with dew. The humming of insects foretold the arrival of autumn. As the nights grew longer, her sleeplessness grew more unbearable. The poignancy of autumnal decline deepened her sorrow.

In this fleeting world the hearts of men also change. Those once close to Kenreimon-In no longer came to visit. Few remained loyal to her.

[1] A branch temple of Enryaku-ji, it was located on Higashi-yama to the southeast of Maruyama. Inzei lived in one of the cells of a temple called Ashō-bō.

[2] Emperor Hsüan-tsung of the T'ang dynasty fell in love with Yang Kuei-fei so blindly that, in order to avoid her jealousy, he confined the other beautiful court ladies in the Shang-yang Palace.

CHAPTER II

THE FORMER EMPRESS GOES TO ŌHARA

The wives of Councilor Takafusa[1] and Lord Nobutaka[2] secretly visited the hut of Kenreimon-In from time to time to bring her aid. "I never imagined," Kenreimon-In said in tears, "that I should have to depend on the support of my sisters." At these words, the ladies in attendance upon her wet their sleeves with tears.

The hut where the former empress had settled was too near the capital for her to escape the curious eyes of passers-by. She sought to find a mountain hideaway far from the public gaze. Although her life seemed as transient as a dewdrop before the wind, she wished to pass her days in quiet solitude until that drop should evaporate in the breeze. But she had no one to whom she could turn for assistance.

One day, however, a certain lady-in-waiting came to visit her at Yoshida. "To the north, deep in Ōhara, there is a quiet place called Jakkō-in," reported her visitor.

"A mountain hamlet is lonesome, but there I shall be able to seclude myself better," Kenreimon-In replied.

A palanquin was sent by the wife of Councilor Takafusa. At the end of the ninth month of the first year of Bunji [1185], the former empress moved to Jakkō-in. As she went along a path leading deep into the mountains, the veil of early evening began to fall. The trees were tinged with color; leaves whirled in a blast that swept down from the mountain. The curfews of mountain temples echoed through the valleys and mingled with the hum of insects and the occasional faint cries of a fawn. Clouds gathered; a soft shower dampened the sleeves of her robe as she passed through the thick grass. Each new sensation deepened her misery. Drifting homeless from shore to shore had not caused such pain.

Upon arriving at Jakkō-in, she found herself among rocks covered with a velvety green carpet of moss. She felt at one with the frost-laden bush in the garden and the withered chrysanthemums on the hedge; she would share their fate. She knew this would be her last home.

Entering the temple of Jakkō-in, she knelt before the main image of the Buddha and offered a prayer: "I pray thee to save the departed spirit of my son so that he may attain perfect Buddhahood and lead all the departed spirits of the Heike to salvation." As she prayed, the image of her son, Emperor Antoku, filled her mind. She would never be able to forget him.

A small hut, just one jō square, was built for her near the temple. She had two rooms made—one for her bed, and the other for an image of the Buddha. In this tiny cell, day in and day out, she offered prayers to the Buddha.

One evening during the tenth month, she heard footsteps falling on the oak leaves in the garden.

"Who comes?" inquired Kenreimon-In, turning to her attendant, Dainagon-no-suke.[3] "Go see who it is. If it is an unwelcome caller, I shall hide."

When Dainagaon-no-suke went out, she found that it had only been a deer passing by. Kenreimon-In urged her to tell who the visitor was. Dainagon-no-suke, suppressing her tears, replied with a poem:

> What visitor dares
> Tread this rocky mountain path
> To see my lady?
> It was only a young stag
> That rustled the fallen oak leaves.

Kenreimon-In was so impressed she wrote it on a paper panel in her window.

As dreary as life seemed to her, the former empress discovered some simple pleasures. She trimmed a stand of trees by the eaves of her hut to look like the Seven Jeweled Trees[4] of Paradise. A pool in a rocky hollow became for her the Lake of Eight Virtues.[5]

Transient were the spring flowers, easily swept away by the breeze. Vagrant was the autumn moon, shaded by the fleeting clouds.

In former times, at the Imperial Palace, she had spent her days playing among flowers. Their graceful scent had risen through the breeze to her dwelling place. Viewing the hazy moon had inspired many poems. Her palace had been all gold and jewels. Gorgeous brocade had been spread over her bed. Now she lived among thatch and brushwood.

[1,2] Daughters of Kiyomori and younger sisters of Kenreimon-In.

[3] The wife of Shigehira.

[4] According to the *Amida Sutra* (Skt. *Sukhāvatī-vyūha*), the trees of paradise, standing in seven rows, have gold roots, copper-gilt trunks, white-gold branches, agate twigs, coral leaves, moonstone blossoms, and pearl fruit.

[5] According to the *Amida Sutra*, there is a pond in paradise, the water of which has eight virtues—purity, coolness, sweetness, softness, luster, peace, medicinal properties, and power of growth.

CHAPTER III

THE CLOISTERED EMPEROR
VISITS ŌHARA

Thus, as the tale tells us, in the spring of the second year of Bunji [1186], the cloistered emperor decided to visit Kenreimon-In at her secluded hut in Ōhara. However, it was so windy and cold—the snow remained on the mountaintops and the icicles hung in the valleys—that he was unable to visit her.

Spring had passed, summer had begun, and the festival of the Kamo Shrine was already over when the cloistered emperor finally set out by night for Ōhara. Though this was an informal trip, he was accompanied by six nobles, eight courtiers, and some palace guards. The procession took the Kurama Road. The cloistered emperor stopped at Fudaraku-ji[1], which had been built by Kiyohara no Fukayabu,[2] and at the ruins where Grand Empress Dowager Ono[3] had lived in retirement as a nun. There the cloistered emperor got down from his carriage and entered a palanquin. He followed the road that led to Jakkō-in. The white clouds over the distant mountains reminded him of cherry blossoms whirling in the wind. Spring lingered in the remaining flowers upon the fresh green boughs. It was past the twentieth day of the fourth month, so the summer grass had grown tall and thick.

As the procession moved through the grass, His Majesty was gripped by a sense of complete solitude. He had never seen such a desolate place.

At the western end of Ōhara stood a small temple of but simple architecture. This was Jakkō-in. The pond and the grove of trees in front of the temple evoked a sense of the past. Indeed, it called to mind a poem:

> The roof tiles all lie broken.
> The mist hangs thick as incense smoke.
> The doors have fallen from their hinges.
> Moonbeams are eternal lamps.

Young grass grew thickly in the garden. Shoots of willow hung in tufts. Water plants afloat on the pond looked like a brocade spread. Deep purple waves of wisteria mingled with the green of the pine trees on the small island. The late-blooming cherry blossoms were a more splendid sight than that of the early blossoms; yellow roses were in full array on the bank. Through the clouds the call of a cuckoo was heard, as though its notes were saluting the imperial procession. Soothing was the sound of water falling from the clefts of time-worn rocks. The green of the hedges overgrown with ivy was striking against a background of craggy hills. The beauty of the scene would defy the brush of a painter. Truly impressed, the cloistered emperor composed this poem:

> The cherry blossoms
> Have blown from the trees
> That stand on the bank.
> They are once again blooming
> Upon the ripples of the pond.

When the cloistered emperor turned his eyes toward the hut of Kenreimon-In, he saw eaves over which ivy and morning-glory crept. Nearby yellow day lilies mingled with hare's-foot fern.

In ancient China there were two disciples of Confucius, who spent simple lives in poverty. At the house of Yen-yüan, the drinking gourd had often been empty, and the grass had grown wild; at the house of Yüan-hsien, the doors had been soaked with rain, and the goosefoot had grown thick.

As humble as these houses in ancient China was the hut of Kenreimon-In, for the cedar bark of the roof gaped here and there, allowing the autumn rain, the frost, and the dew to vie with the moonbeams in gaining entrance. Behind the hut was a mountain, and before it was a field. The leaves of the bamboo in the small thicket rustled in the wind. As one who had renounced the world, Kenreimon-In was obliged to suffer a great number of hardships, as many as the joints of a bamboo. She seldom received tidings from the capital. Only the cry of a monkey as it sprang from tree to tree and the sound of a wood-cutter's ax in the mountain could be heard through the dense ivy-covered shrubs surrounding the hut. The approach of visitors went unnoticed.

"Is anyone there?" "Is anyone in?" cried the cloistered emperor into the doorway of the hut. There was no answer. After a while an old emaciated nun stepped out.

"Where is the former empress?" His Majesty inquired.

"She is out now. She is on the mountain over there picking flowers for the Buddha's shrine."

"Is there no one who can do service of this kind for her?" asked His Majesty, "Though she had renounced the world, it is indeed a pity that she must look after her own tasks."

"Though she had mastered the Five Cardinal Virtues and the Buddha's Ten Precepts in a former life," replied the nun, "it has been her fate to suffer in this world. Why should she mind the austerities of the flesh? The *Yinkuo Sutra*[4] says, 'If you wish to know the cause in a former life, you must look at the effect in the present life. If you wish to know the effect in a future life, you must look at the cause in the present life.' She is enlightened to the cause and effect of both past and future lives, so she is now free from worldly grief, desirous only of having a happier fate in the world beyond the grave. Sakyamuni, as a young prince of nineteen, left his castle, Gayā, and found his dwelling place at the foot of Mount Daṇḍaka.[5] He covered himself with the leaves of trees, climbed the mountains to provide himself with firewood, and descended the valleys to get water. As a reward, he finally attained Buddhahood."

The cloistered emperor was unable to tell whether the rags that the nun wore were silk or cotton. He thought it strange that one in such a humble life could still uphold her belief in the Buddha's Way, and so he asked who she was.

For some time she could not utter a word in reply, as she was choked with tears. Now, suppressing her tears, she answered: "Though I am hesitant to tell you, I am a daughter of the late priest Shinzei. In the old days I used to wait upon Your Majesty as a wet nurse. I am Awa-no-Naishi. At that time you were kind to me. Now you do not even recognize me. Ah, I have lost the charms of my youth. Indeed, it makes me miserable to admit that I am already bent under the weight of years." She pressed her sleeves to her face and wept bitterly.

"You are truly Awa-no-Naishi!" exclaimed the cloistered emperor. "What a shame it is that I have forgotten you! I feel as though I were dreaming."

Tears filled his eyes. The nobles and courtiers in attendance upon him were also moved to tears and said to each other: "Indeed, we could sense her greatness!"

When the cloistered emperor looked around, he saw that tufts of dew-laden grass had crept over the bamboo lattice. The rice fields were so flooded that there was not even a dry patch for a snipe to alight upon.

At last the cloistered emperor entered the hut. When he opened the paper sliding door, he saw in one of the rooms the images of three bodhisattvas, Amida, Kannon, and Seishi. In the hand of Amida, who stood in the middle, was a cord of five colors.[6] on the left was a picture of Fugen Bosatsu; on the right was that of the renowned Chinese priest, Zendō.[7] Next to it hung a portrait of the late Emperor Antoku. Eight volumes of the *Lotus Sutra* and nine books of the teachings of Zendō lay near the altar. Instead of the fragrance of orchid and musk, which had filled the imperial rooms, the smoke of incense rose before the holy images.

Seeing these things in Kenreimon-In's humble hermitage, the cloistered emperor remembered the story of Yuima,[8] who had invoked thirty-two thousand Buddhas from the Ten Quarters into his one-jō-square hut. On the paper sliding doors of Kenreimon-In's hut were pasted excerpts from various sutras written on small square pieces of paper. Among them was a poem composed by priest Ōe no Sadamoto on Mount Ch'ing-liang in China:

> The celestial melody of the pan pipe is heard
> From the lonely cloud above,
> and the bodhisattvas come gliding down
> To meet me and lead me to paradise.

Next to this was a poem that seemed to have been composed by Kenreimon-In:

> Did I ever dream
> That I would behold the moon
> Here on the mountain—
> The moon that I used to view
> In the sky o'er the palace?

On the opposite side of the little hut, the cloistered emperor saw what appeared to be Kenreimon-In's bedchamber. On a bamboo rack hung her hempen robes and paper bedquilts. Gone were the days when she lived among countless beautiful robes of twill, sheer silk, brocade, and embroidery from the finest looms. Tears rushed down the cheeks of the cloistered emperor.

In the distance he saw two nuns making their way down a steep grade. His Majesty inquired of Awa-no-Naishi who they were.

"The one carrying a basket of mountain azaleas on her arm," replied the old nun, "is Kenreimon-In, and the other carrying the bundle of firewood and edible bracken is Dainagon-no-suke, the daughter of Lord Korezane. She was adopted by Councilor Kunitsuna, and it was she who served the late Emperor Antoku as a wet nurse."

Before she could finish her reply, she was choked with tears. The cloistered emperor too wept. When Kenreimon-In noticed her imperial visitor, she hesitated to approach him, saying to herself: "Although I am now a nun, I am ashamed to show my humble looks to His Majesty. I wish I could vanish."

The sleeves of her robe were always wet, for night after night she drew water from a nearby stream to offer to the Buddha. This morning they were soaked through, for she had climbed the dew-covered mountain. Now she could neither turn back to the mountain nor step forward into her hut. She was standing transfixed when Awa-no-Naishi came to her side and took the basket from her.

[1] Established in 940, it was located on the present site of Shizuhara, Sakyo-ku, Kyoto.

[2] The great grandfather of Sei-Shonagon, the authoress of *The Pillow Book*.

[3] The wife of Emperor Go-Reizei. It is said that she became a nun and spent a secluded life at the foot of Ebumi-yama near Shizuhara.

[4] Literally "Cause-Effect Sutra." It teaches the balance of cause and effect, i.e., a good cause has a good effect, and a bad cause a bad effect.

[5] Located in Gandhāra, North India.

[6] A cord of five colored threads: blue, yellow, red, white, and black. A worshiper of Amida Buddha believed that if he held one end of this cord when uttering his dying prayers, and extended the other end to the image of Amida, he would be led to the Pure Land Paradise.

[7] Known in Chinese as Shan-tao (A.D. 613–681), he was a pioneer of Chinese Pure Land teachings.

[8] A wealthy man mentioned in the *Vima Lakīrti-nirdésa Sutra*.

CHAPTER IV

THE PASSAGE THROUGH THE
SIX REALMS

"Anyone who has renounced the world," said Awa-no-Naishi, "would be dressed in a robe as humble as yours. What is wrong with looking as you do? I pray you to come and greet His Majesty so that he may soon be on his way."

Kenreimon-In finally gave in to her entreaties and entered the hut.

"I have taxed heart and soul invoking Amida Buddha," said Kenreimon-In, so that he might throw his light upon my window and lead me to paradise. I have looked forward, with growing fervor, to receiving him at the door of my hut so that he might carry me off to paradise. This is all that I have sought. Your Majesty's visit, however, is one that I had not expected at all."

"Even those who live for eighty thousand years in the highest heaven are destined to decay," replied the cloistered emperor. "The residents of the Six Realms cannot escape the Five Signs of Decay. The wonderous banquets at the Palace of Correct Views and the flowery festivities at the high pavilion of Mahabrahman[1]—all these pleasures too were as fleeting as empty dreams of dreams and empty delusions of delusions. All is vanity, as evanescent as the eternal turning of the Wheel. Sad are the Five Signs of Decay for celestial beings! How much more so should it be for us, the sentient beings of this world! I suppose, your old acquaintances come to see you from time to time, even to a terrible place like this. When you talk with them you must renew old memories of your glorious days."

"No, Your Majesty, they never come to see me here," replied Kenreimon-In, "And no one but my two sisters sends me tidings. In days past, however, I never thought that I would need their assistance."

As she spoke, she wept bitterly. The nuns in attendance upon her wet their sleeves with tears.

[774]

Suppressing her sorrow, Kenreimon-In continued: "Though I am now obliged to suffer great hardships, they are nothing but momentary torture in this world. I believe it will turn out to be a blessing for me in the world beyond, where I hope I shall be able to attain Buddhahood. I feel happy already, thinking of my next life, in which I shall be allowed to join the disciples of Sakyamuni and escape the tortures of the Five Limitations and the Woman's Three Duties.[2] With my firm belief in the original vows of Amida Buddha, I strive to purify my six senses so that I shall be reborn in paradise. I pray for the better lot of our entire family. My faith is unswervingly placed upon a visit from Amida Buddha. And yet there is one hindrance to my salvation—the memory of my son, Emperor Antoku. Though I try to forget him, I cannot. Indeed, nothing is more uncontrollable than parental affection. This is why I pray constantly for his Buddhahood in the world beyond. This too, I believe, accords with the teaching of the Buddha, for the affection for my dead son could at least be a motive for my enligtenment."

"Although our country is small, its islands scattered like grains of millet," said the cloistered emperor, "you became the mother of the emperor, who held the place of supreme honor as a result of his a mastery of the Buddha's Ten Precepts in his former life. You were able to possess whatever you wished. Above all, you were born in an age when the Buddha's Law prevailed throughout the land. Inasmuch as you desire to practice the Buddha's Way, you will no doubt be reborn in paradise. Everything is evanescent in this world, but when I see you in your present condition, I cannot but feel pain in my heart."

In reply to these words of consolation, Kenreimon-In continued: "Born the daughter of the overlord of the Heike, Priest-Premier Kiyomori, I became the mother of the emperor and held heaven and earth in my palm. On the occasion of state ceremonies—the New Year celebration, the ceremonies of changing clothes in summer and winter, and the Year End ceremonies—I was surrounded by nobles and courtiers as well as the emperor's councilors and ministers. I felt like one waited upon by eighty thousand attendants in the Six Realms or the Four Dhyāna Heavens.[3]

"I used to live in the Seiryō-den behind jeweled curtains. In spring I had the pleasure of seeing cherry blossoms in full bloom

in the Imperial Garden of the Left. On hot days I refreshed myself by drawing water from a spring. In autumn I never had to endure loneliness when viewing the moon above the clouds. On cold
nights I warmed myself in layers of kimonos. The one thing left
for me to desire was the secret of longevity or elixir of immortality.
I prayed to the gods only for eternal youth. Night and day there was
nothing but merriment and entertainment, so it seemed as though
no one, even in paradise, could surpass my happiness.

"In early autumn of the second year of Juei (1183), however,
when Yoshinaka threatened the capital, the entire family of the
Heike fled to the western provincess. We saw our homes burning
beyond the clouds. Drifting along the shores of Suma and Akashi,
which I had known only by name in times past, I felt terribly sad.
As our boat rolled on by day, the sleeves of my kimono were wet
with salt spray. At the cry of the sea plovers on the sand bar by
night, I reflected upon my sad fate and wept. Despite the majestic
scenery from shore to shore, from island to island, my heart ached
for the capital. Completely forsaken, I have no one to turn to now.

My distress is like the Five Signs of Decay. I have suffered all
that one is supposed to suffer—the sorrow of parting from my loved
ones and the pain of hating others in battle.

"Ah, how wretched I was when the Heike were evicted from
Dazaifu in Kyushu by Koreyoshi. Although the mountains and
fields lay vast before our eyes, there seemed to be no place where
we could hope to take shelter. Late in the autumn of that year, I
viewed the moon over the waves, the same moon that I had viewed
before above the palace. And then, in the tenth month, Lieutenant
General Kiyotsune drowned himself, saying, 'At the approach of the
Genji we were obliged to flee from the capital. Driven out of Kyushu by Koreyoshi, we are now like a school of fish in a net. How
can we escape? There is no chance of living any longer.' This was
but the beginning of our sad demise. As we spent day and night on
board boats drifting upon the waves, no tribute was brought from
the provinces to use in preparation of meals for the emperor.
Often when we wished to prepare food, we had no water with
which to do so; though we were adrift upon the vast sea, we were
unable to drink its salt water. Our suffering was indeed like that
in the world of hungry spirits.

"Then, after we had won battles at Muro-yama and Mizushima,

[776]

our men seemed to come alive again. But it was only a short period of time before many men of the Heike were again lost in the fight at Ichi-no-tani. After that battle, even the civil officials threw away their ceremonial robes and always wore armor in preparation for a fight. The din of battle was heard day and night; our men looked like Asura in a constant fight against Taishaku.[4]

"After our fortress at Ichi-no-tani had been destroyed, parents lost their sons and wives lost their husbands. At the sight of a fishing boat on the offing, we were aghast, taking it for an enemy boat. Even a flock of white herons far-off in the pine trees terrified us, as if they were the banners of the Genji.

"Finally, when the battle at Dan-no-ura was at its height, my mother, Nii-dono, saw that doom marked our destiny, and so she said, 'I believe our last hour has come. One out of a thousand of our men may be able to survive this fight. If any of our distant relations are left alive, they cannot be counted on to pray for our afterlife. From of old it has been a rule that warriors spare the lives of women, so you must at all costs stay alive to pray for the departed spirit of your son, the emperor. I ask you also to pray for my better lot in the world beyond.'

"I was listening to those words as in a dream when, all of a sudden, a strong wind began to blow and billowing clouds came hovering over us. This ill omen deprived us of all hope. Forsaken by heaven, we could do nothing.

"It was at this moment that Nii-dono admitted the Heike had been conquered. She held the emperor in her arms and came out to the gunwale of the imperial vessel. The emperor was upset. With a puzzled expression on his face, he asked, 'Where are you going to take me?' Nii-dono turned her eyes brimming with tears to her grandson and replied, 'Your Majesty does not know what this is all about! Since you mastered the Buddha's Ten Precepts in a former life, you were blessed with the supreme place of honor in this world. But the days of your glory are over, and now an evil karma is about to carry you off to the world beyond. I pray you to first turn to the east to bid farewell to the Sun Goddess of the Great Ise Shrine, and then to the west to repeat 'Hail Amida Buddha,' so that Amida Buddha will welcome you to the Pure Land Paradise in the west. The islands of our small country, scattered like grains of millet, are poisoned by troubles. Now let me take you to the Pure Land Para-

[777]

dise.' The emperor was then dressed in an outer robe of parrot green silk and had his hair bound up at the sides. Tears rushed down his cheeks as he joined his little palms. He first turned to the east to bid farewell to the Sun Goddess and then to the west to chant 'Hail Amida Buddha.' Nii-dono held him in her arms again and jumped overboard. His image at that moment struck the very center of my soul, clutching my heart in a fit of grief. No matter how I try to forget, I cannot. As hard as I try not to think of it, the image is ever before my eyes. Among those who remained alive there arose so great and horrible a cry that it seemed to exceed the shrieks of all criminals in the fires of hell.

"After I had been taken alive by the warriors and was on my way back to the capital along the shore of Akashi in Harima Province, I had a dream. In this dream I saw a palace, much more gorgeous, than my former one, in which sat my son, the emperor, with all the nobles and courtiers of the Heike in full array. This was a sight that I had not seen since leaving the capital, so I cried out, asking where the palace might be. Then a nun, presumably Nii-dono, replied, 'This is the sea palace of the Dragon King.' 'What a magnificent palace!' I cried again and asked, 'Is this then a region where there is no more sorrow?' 'You will find it in the *Dragon Animal Sutra*,'[5] replied the nun. 'Never neglect to pray for our happiness in the next world.' As she spoke these words, I awoke. Since that time I have done all within my power to chant sutras and offer prayers for the better fortune of my son in the world beyond. I believe that all I have seen and undergone corresponds to the passage through the Six Realms."

"In China," replied the cloistered emperor, "Hsüan-tsang witnessed the Six Realms before he attained enlightenment. In Japan Nichizō[6] was allowed to gaze upon them through the power of Zaō Gongen.[7] That you have been privileged to see them with mortal eyes is rare indeed."

[1] Bonten.

[2] Confucianism teaches women: to obey their fathers before marriage; to obey their husbands when married; and to obey their sons after the deaths of their husbands.

[3] Entrance to these four heavens depends upon one's devotion through meditation to the Buddha. The first heaven is a liberation of the senses, taste and smell. The second heaven is a liberation of all remaining senses. The third heaven is a liberation of the state of consciousness. The fourth heaven is a state of total bliss.

4 Asura has many beautiful women but no food, while Taishaku has an abundance of food but no women. Thus they are constantly fighting with each other.

5 This sutra cannot be found in any source.

6 A renowned priest who took the tonsure on Mount Kimbu in Yoshino.

7 The main image of the Buddha at the Zaō-dō on Mount Kimbu.

CHAPTER V

THE DEATH OF KENREIMON-IN

A s the evening sun was about
to go down behind the mountain, the bell of Jakkō-in temple began
to toll. Day was done. The cloistered emperor was reluctant to
leave, but holding back his tears, he set out on his return journey.
Kenreimon-In wept bitterly as thought of her past possessed her.
She stood watching the imperial procession until she could see it
no more. Back in her hut, she offered a prayer to the main image
of the Buddha: "I pray thee to save the departed spirit of my son
so that he may attain perfect Buddhahood and lead the departed
spirits of all the Heike to salvation as well."

In times past she had turned to the east and offered her prayers to
the Sun Goddess of the Great Ise Shrine and to the great bodhisattva
Hachiman. But now she turned to the west and joined her palms,
praying: "May all the departed spirits of the past attain Buddhahood
in paradise!" On the paper sliding door of her bedchamber she
wrote these poems:

> What has become of me?
> I cannot but long to see
> How nobles fare in court.
> Luxuries I abandoned
> Weigh upon my heart again.

> Irretrievably
> Gone are the days of glory—
> My dream has vanished!
> Surely the day will soon come
> When I leave this brushwood hut.

It is said that Lord Jittei, who waited upon the cloistered emperor
that day, wrote the following poem on one of the posts of her hut:

[780]

You were my bright moon.
How I admired your luster
When you were at court.
You are shining no longer
Deep in the mountain village.

Kenreimon-In was meditating, in tears, upon the past and the future when she heard the voice of a cuckoo and penned this verse:

There you are—cuckoo!
Let me sing your song with you—
Let me share your tears.
My days are passed in weeping
Like you—lamenting my fate.

The men of the Heike who had been taken alive at Dan-no-ura were paraded through the streets of the capital and then beheaded. Some were separated from their wives and exiled to distant provinces. Only Lord Yorimori was allowed to remain in the capital. For the ladies of the Heike, who numbered more than forty, there was no punishment at all. To sustain themselves, some turned to their relatives and others to their acquaintances. They could find no peace, whether they lived behind jeweled curtains or brushwood doors. Couples who had shared pillows were separated by mountains and seas. Parents and children were wrenched from one another. Their vain hopes of reunion were boundless.

Their suffering was in retribution for the evil deeds of Kiyomori, the leader of their clan. He had held in his palm both heaven and earth; but to the throne above he paid no respect, and to the people below he paid no heed. He had put many men to death and had exiled many others at his whim, ignoring the mood of the people. None of his descendants could escape retribution for his crimes.

The months and years passed. At length Kenreimon-In became seriously ill. Holding a cord of five colors that extended to the image of Amida Buddha, she chanted: "Hail to the savior of the world, Amida Buddha in paradise—I pray thee to lead me to thy land." Hearing her prayer, Dainagon-no-suke and Awa-no-Naishi knew that her last moment had come, and so they sat by her side, wailing inconsolably. As her praying voice became weaker and weaker, purple clouds floated over the mountains to the west. An ambrosial fragrance wafted down, and celestial music filled the room. In the middle of the second month of the second year of the Kenkyū Era [1191], Kenreimon-In passed away.

Dainagon-no-suke and Awa-no-Naishi had served her faithfully since she became the empress. The anguish of parting from her was unbearable. Now they were completely alone, there was no one they could turn to. Each succeeding year after her death, they persevered through great sorrow and hardship and performed memorial services for their departed empress. They followed the examples set by the daughter of the Dragon King[1] and Lady Idaike,[2] who achieved Buddhahood, and so it is said that, in the end, Dainagon-no-suke and Awa-no-Naishi were able to attain Nirvana.

[1] At the age of eight she was awakened to Buddhahood by Sakyamuni's speech.

[2] Skt. Vaidehi. The wife of King Bimbisāra, she attained Buddhahood after listening to the preachings of Sakyamuni.

APPENDIX

CHRONOLOGICAL TABLE

Dates and events in the table are based on descriptions in *The Tale of the Heike*. Dates in parentheses are those corrected by historians. Asterisks indicate bissextile months.

Era	Year	Month	Day	Events	Book	Chap.
Tenshō	1 [1131]	3	13	Tadamori's first attendance at court.	1	2
(Chōshō	1 [1132])					
Nimpyō	3 [1153]	1	15	Tadamori (58) dies.	1	3
Hōgen	1 [1156]	7	2	The cloistered emperor Toba (54) dies.	1	7
		7	10–29	Hōgen Insurrection.	1	3
Heiji	1 [1159]	12	9–26	Heiji Insurrection.	1	3
Eiman	1 [1165]	6	25	Rokujō is made crown prince.	1	8
		7	27 (28)	The abdicated emperor Nijō (23) dies.	1	8
Nin-an	2 [1167]	2	11	Kiyomori is appointed premier.	1	3
	3 [1168]	11 (2)	11	Kiyomori enters the priesthood.	1	4
		3	20	Takakura (8) succeeds Rokujō	1	9
Kaō	2 [1170]	10	16	Motofusa's clash with Sukemori.	1	11
Shōan	2 [1172]	2	10	Kiyomori's daughter Tokuko (16) becomes Takakura's consort.	1	5
	3 [1173]	5	16	Mongaku is exiled to Izu.	5	9
Angen	2 [1176]	summer		The fight at Ugawa.	1	13
	3 [1177]	1	24	Shigemori becomes minister of the Left.	1	5
				Munemori becomes minister of the Right.	1	12
				Go-Shirakawa and Narichika plan to overthrow the Heike.	1	12
		4	13	The monks of Mount Hiei appeal to the court to punish Morotaka.	1	14
		4	28	The great fire in Kyoto.	1	16
Jishō	1 [1177]	5	21	The exile of the chief priest Mei-un of the Tendai sect.	2	1
		5	29	Yukitsuna reports Narichika's plot to overthrow the Heike to Kiyomori.	2	3

Era	Year	Month	Day	Events	Book	Chap.
		6	1	Kiyomori arrests Narichika and other plotters.	2	3
		6	22	Shunkan, Naritsune, and Yasuyori are exiled to Kikai-ga-shima.	2	10
		8 (7	19 9)	Narichika is killed in Bizen.	2	10
		12	27	Jittei is appointed general of the Left.	2	11
	2 [1178]	9 (1	4 20)	The monks of Mount Hiei oppose Go-Shirakawa's plan to hold the Kanjō ceremony at Mii-dera.	2	12
		7	(3)	Naritsune and Yasuyori granted amnesty.	3	1
		11	12	Tokuko gives birth to Antoku.	3	3
	3 [1179]	3		Ariō travels to Kikai-ga-shima to visit Shunkan.	3	8
		5	12	A wind of ill-omen blows	3	10
	(4 [1180]	4	29)	throughout Kyoto.		
	3 [1179]	6	2	The capital is moved from Kyoto to Fukuhara.	5	1
		8 (7	1 29)	Shigemori (42) dies.	3	11
		11	14	Kiyomori, leading his forces, comes back from Fukuhara to Kyoto.	3	15
		11	20	Kiyomori confines Go-Shirakawa to the North Palace of Toba.	3	18
	4 [1180]	2	21	Takakura abdicates.	4	1
		4		Yorimasa advises Prince Mochihito to lead a rebellion against the Heike.	4	3
		4	22	The coronation ceremony for Antoku (3) is held.	4	2
		5	15	Prince Mochihito's plot is discovered.	4	5
		5	18	Prince Mochihito takes refuge at Mii-dera.	4	6
		5	23 (26)	Prince Mochihito and Yorimasa and his soldiers, are attacked and killed by the Heike army at Uji.	4	11
		6	2	Go-Shirakawa, Takakura and Antoku leave Kyoto for Fukuhara.	5	1
		7	14	Yoritomo orders his clansmen	5	10

Era	Year	Month	Day	Events	Book	Chap.
		(6	24)	in the eastern provinces to rally against the Heike.		
		8	17	Yoritomo attacks and kills Kanetaka.	5	4
		9	7	Yoshinaka rebels against the Heike in Shinano Province.	6	5
		9	20 (29)	The Heike forces set out for the eastern provinces to fight Yoritomo	5	11
		(10	6	Yoritomo establishes his headquarters at Kamakura.)		
		10	20	The Heike and the Genji meet on the banks of the Fuji River; the Heike flee without a fight.	5	11
		11	26	The capital is moved back to Kyoto.	5	13
		12	28	The burning of the temples at Nara.	5	14
	5 [1181]	1	14	Takakura (21) dies.	6	1
		1	15 (14)	Michinobu attacks and kills Saijaku.	6	5
		*2	4	Kiyomori (64) dies.	6	7
			(7	Kiyomori's villa at West-Hachijō burns down.)		
		3	16, 17 (10)	The Heike forces commanded by Shigehira and Koremori defeat Yukiie's forces at Sunomata.	6	10
Yōwa	1 [1181]	12 (11	24 25)	Tokuko receives the title of Kenreimon-In.	6	12
	2 [1182]	9	9	Yoshinaka wins the battle at Yokotagawara.	6	12
Juei	1 [1182]			(The entire country suffers a severe famine.)		
	2 [1183]	3		Yoritomo tries to destroy Yoshinaka. Yoshinaka sends his son Yoshitaka as a hostage to Yoritomo for reconciliation.	7	1
		4	27	The Heike attack the Genji at Hiuchi.	7	4
		5	11	Yoshinaka wins the battle at Kurikara.	7	6
		5 (6	21 1)	Yoshinaka and Yukiie win the battle at Shinohara.	7	7
		7	8	Munemori asks the monks of Mount Hiei to support the Heike.	7	12

[785]

Era	Year	Month	Day	Events	Book	Chap.
		7	22	Yoshinaka advances to Kyoto. Yukiie approaches the capital through Yamato Province.	7	13
		7	24	Go-Shirakawa secretly leaves for Mount Hiei.	7	13
		7	25	With Antoku and the Three Sacred Treasures, the Heike flee from the capital to the western provinces.	7	13
		7	27	Go-Shirakawa returns to the capital.	8	1
		8	10	Yoshinaka is appointed chief of the Imperial Stables of the Left and governor of Echigo Province.	8	1
		8	20	Go-Toba is enthroned without the imperial regalia.	8	2
		8	17 (26)	The Heike arrive at Dazaifu, Kyushu.	8	2
		10	12	Yoshinaka destroys Kaneyasu in Bitchū Province.	8	8
		10		The Heike escape from Kyushu to Yashima, Shikoku.	8	4
		*10	1	Yoshikiyo fights Shigehira at Mizushima and is defeated.	8	7
		11	19	Yoshinaka burns down Go-Shirakawa's palace.	8	11
		11	29	Yukiie is defeated by Norimori and Shigehira at Muroyama.	8	9
	3 [1184]	1	20	Yoshitsune wins the battle at Uji. Yoshinaka is killed at the battle at Awazu.	9	1–4
		1	29	Noriyori and Yoshitsune set out from Kyoto for the western provinces to confront the Heike forces.	9	3–4
		2	7	Yoshitsune's armies attack Ichi-no-tani and kill Tadanori, Tomoakira, Atsumori, and Michimori; Shigehira is captured.	9	7–18
		2	14	Michimori's wife, Kozaishō, drowns herself.	9	19
		2		Go-Shirakawa orders Shigehira to write a letter to the Heike demanding the return of the imperial regalia.	10	2
		3	10	Shigehira is sent to Kamakura.	10	6

Era	Year	Month	Day	Events	Book	Chap.
		3	28	Yoritomo receives Shigehira at Kamakura.	10	7
		3	28	Koremori drowns himself.	10	12
Genryaku	1 [1184]	5 (5	16 8)	Yoritomo entertains Yorimori at Kamakura.	10	13
		8	6	Yoshitsune is appointed chief of the Police Commissioners Division.	10	14
		8	8	Noriyori leaves Kamakura for the western provinces to destroy the Heike forces.	10	14
		9 (2)	12	Noriyori sets out from the capital for western provinces.	10	14
	2 [1185]	1 (10)	6	Yoshitsune sets out from the capital for the western provinces to destroy the Heike.	11	1
		2	16–19	Yoshitsune attacks the Heike at Yashima and drives them out to the Inland Sea.	11	3
		3	24	Yoshitsune defeats the Heike forces at Dan-no-ura.	11	7–10
		4	28	Kenreimon-In moves to Yoshida.	Ep.	1
		5	7	Yoshitsune leaves the capital for Kamakura.	11	16–8
		5 (15)	23	Yoshitsune is not allowed to enter Kamakura.	11	17
		5	20	Tokitada is exiled to Noto Province.	12	3
		6	9	Yoshitsune sets out on a return journey to Kyoto.	11	18
		6	21	Munemori and Kiyotsune are executed at Shinohara and Noji.	11	18
		6	23	Shigehira is executed at Nara.	11	19
		7	9	Great earthquakes in the capital and the neighboring provinces.	12	1
Bunji	1 [1185]	10	17	Tosa-bō is defeated by Yoshitsune and flees to Kurama.	12	4
		11	3	Yoshitsune and Yukiie leave for Kyushu to reorganize their armies and lead a rebellion against Yoritomo.	12	5
		(11	29	The court approves of Yoritomo's establishment of the military government at Kamakura.		
		12	17	Rokudai is arrested.	12	7

APPENDIX

Era	Year	Month	Day	Events	Book	Chap.
	2 [1186]	1	5	Mongaku returns to Kyoto.	12	7
		4		Go-Shirakawa visits Kenrei-mon-In at Ōhara.	Ep.	3
		5	20	Yukiie is arrested and executed.	12	7
	5 [1189]	(*4	30	Yoshitsune kills himself at Koromogawara.)		
Kenkyū	1 [1190]	11	7	Yoritomo travels to Kyoto.	12	9
		12	14	Yoritomo returns to Kamakura.	12	9
	2 [1191]	2		Kenreimon-In dies.	Ep.	5
	3 [1192]	3	13	Go-Shirakawa (66) dies.	12	9
		7	12	Yoritomo is appointed commander-in-chief of the forces to fight the barbarians.	12	9
	6 [1195]	3	4	Yoritomo revisits Kyoto.	12	9
	9 [1198]	2	5	Rokudai is executed at Kamakura.	12	9
	10 [1199]	1	13	Yoritomo (53) dies at Kamakura.	12	9
		3	19	Mongaku is exiled to Oki.	12	9
Shōkyū	3 [1221]	7	13	Go-Toba is exiled to Oki.	12	9

[788]

STYLES OF DRESS

Warrior

helmet

arrows

short sword

Sickle-bladed
halberd

sword

fan

armor

bow

shin guard

fur shoe

Foot Soldier

Woman's kimono

Court lady's costume

Warrior-Monk

hood

priest's robe

sword

body-armor

rosary

Warrior's
ceremonial
costume

Hitatare

Hunting
suit

Ceremonial robe
of
civil official

Naoshi

MAPS

CENTRAL AND WESTERN JAPAN

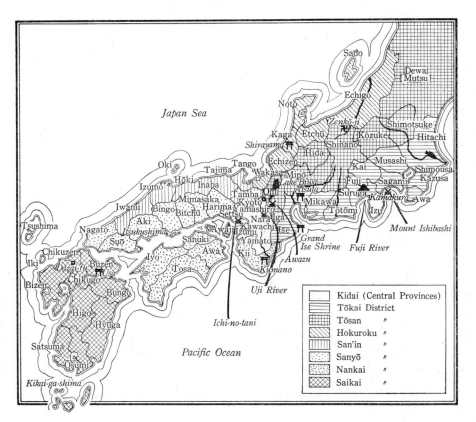

KYOTO AND ENVIRONS

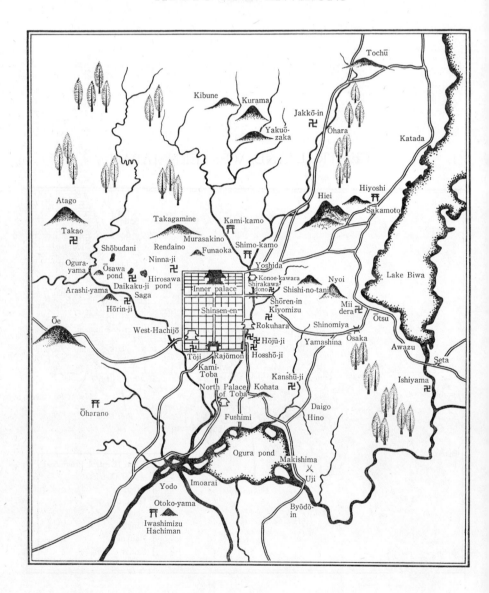

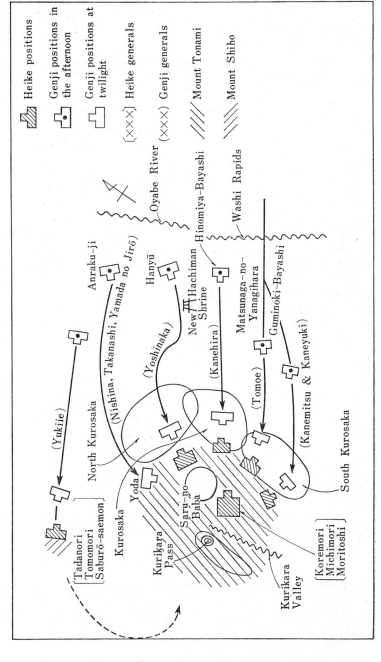

THE BATTLE AT HIUCHI

THE BATTLE OF DAN-NO-URA

The First Half of the Battle
12 : 00 A.M.—2 : 30 P.M.

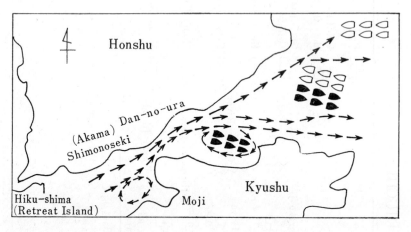

The Second Half of the Battle
2 : 30 P.M.—4 : 00 P.M.

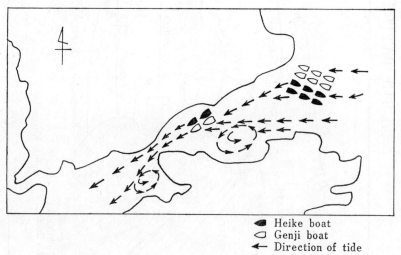

◖ Heike boat
◁ Genji boat
← Direction of tide

Many historical records say that the naval battle at Dan-no-ura began at the hour of
the horse (12 : 00 A.M.) on the twenty-fourth day of the third month of the second
year of Genryaku (1185). The tide was running from the open sea to the inland
sea to the advantage of the Heike. Yoshitsune knew that the direction of the tide
would change after 2 : 30 P.M., so he believed his fleet would be able to take advantage of this if his soldiers could fight a defensive battle till 2 : 30 P.M.

BIBLIOGRAPHY

Most of the materials listed here are in Japanese; however, books or articles marked with an asterisk are available in English.

Versions of the *Heike Monogatari*

*Sadler, A. L. "The Heike Monogatari," *Transactions of the Asiatic Society of Japan* 46 (1918): 1–278 and 49 (1921): 1–354.

Sasaki Hachiro. *Heike monogatari hyōkō* (Lectures on the *Heike monogatari*). Tokyo: Meiji, 1963, 1964.

Takagi Ichinosuke *et al.*, eds. *Heike monogatari, jō, ge.* [*Nihon koten bungaku taikei* (Complete Japanese Classics Series) 32, 33]. Tokyo: Iwanami, 1959; 1960.

Tomikura Tokujirō. *Heike monogatari zen-chūshaku* (The *Heike monogatari* with Notes and Comments). 4 vols. Tokyo: Kadokawa, 1966–1968.

Yamada Yoshio. *Heike monogatari.* Tokyo: Hōbunkan, 1933.

Heike Monogatari References

Atsumi Kaoru. *Heike monogatari no kisoteki kenkyū* (Basic Studies on the *Heike monogatari*). Tokyo: Sanseido, 1962.

Goto Tanji. *Senki monogatari no kenkyū* (Studies on War Chronicles), rev. ed. Kyoto: Daigakudo, 1972.

Ishimoda Sho. *Heike monogatari.* Tokyo: Iwanami, 1957.

Mizuhara Hajime. *Heike monogatari no keisei* (Formation of the *Heike monogatari*). Tokyo: Katochudokan, 1971.

Mushakoji Minoru. *Heike monogatari to biwa hōshi* (The *Heike monogatari* and Biwa Hōshi). Tokyo: Awaji, 1957.

Nagazumi Yasuaki. *Chūsei bungaku no tenbō* (A View of Medieval Literature). Tokyo: University of Tokyo, 1956.

Sasaki Hachiro. *Heike monogatari no kenkyū* (Studies on the *Heike monogatari*). 3 vols. Tokyo: Waseda University, 1948–1951.

Takahashi Teiichi. *Heike monogatari shohon no kenkyū* (Studies on Various Texts of the *Heike monogatari*). Tokyo: Fuzanbo, 1943.

Tani Hiroshi. *Heike monogatari.* Kyoto: San'ichi, 1957.

Yamashita Hiroaki. *Gunki monogatari to katariomono no bungei* (War Chronicles and Oral Traditions). Tokyo: Hanawa, 1972.

Historical Background

*Hall, J. W. *Japan : From Prehistory to Modern Times.* Tokyo: Charles E. Tuttle, 1971.

Ienaga Saburo *et al.*, eds. *Nihon rekishi* (Japanese History), Vol. 5:1. Tokyo: Iwanami, 1971.

*Morris, Ivan. "The World of the Shining Prince—Court Life in Ancient Japan." Harmondsworth: Penguin, 1969.

Murai Yasuhiko. *Heike monogatari no sekai* ('The World of the *Heike monogatari*). Tokyo: Tokuma, 1973.

*Reischauer, E. O. and Fairbank, J. K. "East Asia: The Great Tradition." Boston: Houghton Mifflin, 1962.

*Sansom, G. B. "Japan: A Short Cultural History," rev. ed. Tokyo: Charles E. Tuttle, 1973.

Uwayokote Masataka. *Heike monogatari no kyokō to shinjitsu* (Fiction and Facts in the *Heike monogatari*). Tokyo: Kodansha, 1973.

Articles

*Butler, K. D. "The Textual Evolution of the *Heike monogatari*," *Harvard Journal of Asiatic Studies*, Vol. 26, Harvard-Yenching Institute, 1966.

*Butler, K. D. "The *Heike monogatari* and the Japanese Warrior Ethic," *ibid.*, Vol. 29, 1969.

Kobayashi Hideo. "*Heike monogatari*," *Kobayashi Hideo shū* (A Collection of the Essays of Kobayashi Hideo). Tokyo: Chikuma Shobo, 1944.

Umehara Takeshi. "*Ashura no sekai—Heike monogatari*" (The World of Asura—the *Heike monogatari*), *Jigoku no shisō* (Thoughts Based on the Buddhist View of Hell)," rev. ed. Tokyo: Chūokoronsha, 1973.

Dictionaries

*Hayashima Kyosho *et al.*, eds. "Japanese-English Buddhist Dictionary." Tokyo: Daitō, 1965.

*Papinot. "Historical and Geographical Dictionary of Japan." New York: Frederick Unger, 1968.

Takayanagi Mitsutoshi and Takeuchi Rizo, eds. *Nihonshi jiten* (Dictionary of Japanese History). Tokyo: Kadokawa, 1966.

Tsuji Zennosuke, ed. *Nihon bunkashi nempyō, jō* (A Chronological Table of the Cultural History of Japan). Tokyo: Shunjusha, 1956.

INDEX